THE SECRET
DIARY OF
LIZZIE BENNET

THE SECRET DIARY OF LIZZIE BENNET

Bernie Su and Kate Rorick

SIMON &
SCHUSTER

London · New York · Sydney · Toronto · New Delhi

A CBS COMPANY

First published in Great Britain in 2014 by Simon and Schuster UK Ltd
A CBS COMPANY

First published in the USA in 2014 by Touchstone, a division of Simon & Schuster Inc.

1 3 5 7 9 10 8 6 4 2

Simon & Schuster UK Ltd
1st Floor,
222 Gray's Inn Road
London
WC1X 8HB

Simon & Schuster Australia, Sydney
Simon & Schuster India, New Delhi

A CIP catalogue record for this book
is available from the British Library.

PB ISBN: 978-1-4711-2322-1
eBook ISBN: 978-1-4711-2323-8

This book is a work of fiction. Names, characters,
places and incidents are either the product of the author's imagination
or are used fictitiously. Any resemblance to actual people living or dead,
events or locales is entirely coincidental.

Printed and bound by CPI Group (UK) Ltd, Croydon, CR0 4YY

www.simonandschuster.co.uk
www.simonandschuster.com.au

To the fans,
and everyone who ever loved a Lizzie and a Darcy.

THE SECRET DIARY OF LIZZIE BENNET

SATURDAY, APRIL 7TH

"It is a truth universally acknowledged that a single man in possession of a good fortune must be in want of a wife."

My mom gave me that quote on a T-shirt.

That's really where I got the idea. Well, that and the previous four years of undergrad and two years of grad school, studying Mass Communications with a focus on New Media. Now, almost in my last year of graduate school, in between trying to figure out how I am going to turn my forthcoming degree into a profession and manage to have a life while paying off my mountain of student loans, my mother gave me a T-shirt which, to her mind, will solve all of my (read: her) worries.

Worse yet, she tried to make me wear it. To school.

Curious how my mother would *make* a 24-year-old who has been dressing herself for technically decades wear a certain article of clothing? Then you don't know my mother. Or her underhanded nature. I'd managed to keep the shirt buried in a drawer since Christmas, but then there was a hostile laundry takeover. That's all I'll say.

Luckily, I managed to avoid this sartorial horror by keeping my gym bag in my study cubicle, letting me change from my offensive yet clean shirt into an inoffensive yet smelly oversized tee. It was really a rock/hard place situation.

The only person who saw me in the offending T-shirt with this random quote (by the way, I have no idea who said this phrase, but whoever did, I hope they were being sarcastic) was my cubicle mate and fellow grad student Charlotte Lu.

"Hostile laundry takeover?" she asked knowingly.

Did I mention that we are also best friends?

I didn't think anything of the shirt until later in the day, when Charlotte and I were leading the Communications 101 discussion group. Somehow conversation turned from cross promotion on social media platforms and their relative efficacy to how to reach different generations via mass communications.

As discussion continued, Charlotte said the following:

"Well, the difficulty with reaching different generations via *any* platform has always been within the message itself."

"Er . . . care to elaborate?" I said, hoping she had something up her sleeve to steer the discussion back to the curriculum.

"Well, take that T-shirt your mom gave you, for example." I was very glad at this point that I was not wearing the shirt, as it would have invited thirty 18-year-old freshmen to stare at my boobs. After paraphrasing its message for the class, she continued. "Your mother—and consequently, many of her generation—have an entirely different mindset about what your future should be. And therefore communication with them is hindered by more than just the platform—it's the message itself."

In other words, my plan for my future happiness involves a lot of hard work and ingenuity; Mom's plan for my future happiness includes my marrying a rich guy. And apparently, every rich single guy out there is just *dying* to take on the job.

Later, I was talking to Dr. Gardiner, and I mentioned the T-shirt to her and what Charlotte had said in class. Dr. Gardiner laughed, and thought it was a deep well of conflict.

Yes, a "deep well of conflict" is an excellent way to describe interactions with my mother.

"Perhaps exploring whether disparate messages and platforms can coexist, in the same way disparate people exist in the same house, should be part of your end-of-term project," Dr. Gardiner mused.

Ah, yes. The dreaded end-of-term project for Dr. Gardiner's

Hyper-Mediation in New Media class. It was meant to be a large multimedia project, and I'd been having trouble coming up with an idea. On top of that, Dr. Gardiner was also my faculty advisor— meaning she'd been prodding me for weeks to *also* define what my thesis would be, and what I'd spend all of next year on.

One overwhelmingly large project at a time, I'd begged her. And I went home to ponder the possibilities of the shorter but sooner end-of-term project.

While at home, I listened to my mother harass my long-suffering father because someone bought the big house in Nether-field (a new McMansion community, with the biggest house on the hill taking the name of the whole development as its own) and that someone is supposedly male, rich, and single.

And my mom has called dibs.

Not for herself, of course, but for me or for my sisters, Lydia and Jane. Any one of us would do; she's not particular. Really, depending on his net worth, she'd probably be willing to do a two-for-one type deal. Or three.

That made my mind up. The fact that my mother had so little concept as to who her daughters were and what society we currently live in that she was ready to doll us up and trot us out like debutantes at our first ball for a stranger just because he was rich . . . The fact that she was so desperate to meet this stranger that she was nagging my father—on those occasions he's home from the office earlier than dark—to go pay a call on the new neighbors like he's the local welcoming committee . . . The fact that she has absolutely no clue what it is I do or what I'm studying, just telling people that I "like to talk . . . maybe she'll end up on morning television!" . . .

Well . . . perhaps there *is* a way to show the world the disparate "messages" I've been forced to listen to for far too long. And use a new media platform to do it.

So, that's what I decided to do for Dr. Gardiner's class. I will attempt to explain my mother and my life to the world at large. Via New Media.

After some discussions with Charlotte, I've come up with a few rules and stylistic choices that I think will work.

It seems obvious, but I've decided to do a video blog. Me, talking to the camera. It's straightforward. I don't feel like I will be capable of capturing the moments of veracity necessary for a documentary, given that I have no money to pay a crew and I have to spend half my time in class, anyway. I'm a fan of the Vlogbrothers and other videos of this style, so it can't be too hard to produce, right?

Of course, consistency is key. We decided to post videos to YouTube twice a week, Mondays and Thursdays, without exception. Even when I have nothing to talk about, these videos will go up. Part of the project is mining the "deep well" and becoming a consistent content creator.

"But what *will* I talk about?" I asked Charlotte, as we broke down the idea.

"You've never been short of things to say," Char reminded me.

"But just me on camera for five minutes?" I said. "Nothing happening? I could recount things that happened, but that's boring, too."

"Well, make it *not* boring," Charlotte said. "When you're recounting events—reenact them. With costumes."

"Costumes?" I asked. Dr. Gardiner had been going over this theory in her class this past week. "You mean, dress up like my mom and dad talking about the rich single guy who moved into Netherfield?"

"Why not?"

Why not indeed? So—I've stolen Dad's bathrobe and an old church hat of Mom's, and I'm brushing off my Southern accent to impersonate my mother. Any pertinent interactions that have occurred previous to my filming will be reenacted in this way with what I'm calling Costume Theater.

I'll try to present interactions as fairly as possible, but I know I will also be presenting them from my point of view. However, I will not allow the coloring that comes from my perspective to affect the veracity of the content.

In other words, I'm not making stuff up. Everything I put online will have actually happened. We're here to tell the truth, after all.

Obviously, I'll also need to present documentation for the project. A record of my impressions of the act of making a long-form vlog and how the platform services the message. And a venting of my occasional frustration. I guess the fact that I've been keeping a diary my entire life will finally result in more than carpal tunnel syndrome!

That's really it. I'm sure I'll have more rules as I go along, but for now, it's time to see if I can make a video. The school has loaned me a camera, I have digital storage chips lined up on my desk, and Charlotte has been roped into—er, I mean, *volunteered* to assist me with filming and editing.

So, here we go—let's make a vlog!

"What do you think?" I asked Charlotte, as I leaned over her shoulder watching the playback on her computer.

Even though this is my project for Dr. Gardiner's class, I am making use of my best friend. Specifically, her editing software and her talent with it. (There's a reason that she's the go-to aide for all the underclassmen in the edit bays at school. She knows her stuff.)

"I think it's good," she answered. "For the thousandth time. So, let's do this."

Her finger hovered over the "upload" button.

"Wait!" I blurted out. "I still think I'm wearing too much makeup. And what about—"

Charlotte gave me the side eye. "Do you want to reshoot the whole thing?"

"God, no." Filming the first video—which clocked in at three minutes, twenty seconds—was so much harder than I'd anticipated. Figuring out what to say, writing the intro, scrounging for costumes, writing the bit where I dressed up as my mom and strong-armed Charlotte into playing my dad . . . add that to the four hundred times I tripped over my own tongue and we had to reshoot something I said, and a three-minute video took about five hours to make.

"So we'll pull back on the makeup on the next one." Char turned an impatient glare on me. "But right now, it's Monday morning, the day you told Dr. Gardiner you were going to upload your first video, and we have class in thirty minutes. I'm pressing this button."

"But—"

"Lizzie, part of having a vlog is actually *putting it out there*."

I know. I mean, I *know* communication is an exchange, and for it to actually occur there has to be a beginning. But Char was about to put my entire life—my room, my parents, my sisters, my bad makeup—on display. With the click of a mouse. It was a little nerve-wracking.

But Charlotte was, as usual, right. We couldn't just hang out in my room all day, tweaking. Sometimes, you have to actually put it out there. So I took a deep breath and gave Charlotte a quick nod. And a few seconds later, my video was online.

"So, you ready to go?" Char said, closing up her computer.

And that was it.

It's very strange. I knew that there wouldn't be comments yet, but all I wanted to do was stare at the screen, waiting for something to happen on the Internet. I don't have really high expectations. I'd be shocked if anyone outside of my graduate studies program watched it. But when you put your life up for public consumption, you can't help but worry over the response.

However, the best thing I could do in that moment was go to class and be forced to be offline and not thinking about it for a couple of hours. So I started to pack up my bag.

"OMG YOU ACTUALLY DID IT THIS IS GOING TO BE SO AWESOME!"

Exactly three minutes and twenty seconds after posting, my little sister Lydia ran from her room across the hall and burst through my door, tackling me. (And yes, this dialogue is verbatim. I forget nothing.)

"I love it so much—especially the part with me in it—it's going to be so awesome!"

"You said that already." I groaned under her weight. "What's going to be so awesome?"

"Your video blog—*duh*! Seriously, it might actually make you a fraction less lame. Especially if you keep having me in them."

"Lydia—how did you know it had posted?"

"Because, *duh*, I have an alert set on my phone for when you post something." Lydia looked at us both as if we were stupid. Which, in this instance, I suppose we kind of were.

Of course Lydia would be the first person to see the video. She was the first person to find out about them (other than Charlotte), by barging into my room while I was shooting to tell us that the elusive stranger who bought the house in Netherfield is young and single and named Bing Lee. Which I could care less about, but Lydia shoved herself into my project and onto camera.

That's really the perfect encapsulation of Lydia. She's a photogenic, hyperactive steamroller. And as the baby of the family, she always gets her way.

"Mom is going to *fuh-reak* when she finds out. Also, you should totes lay off the makeup counter, sis—or at least leave it to people who have been outside of a library and know what looks good on, like, humans."

"Uh, about Mom," I said, trying to get my sister's attention away from her phone, where she was I can only assume emailing or texting or tweeting someone about my slight overuse of the lip liner. "I would rather not tell them. Mom and Dad, I mean."

"Oh, really?" Lydia got this look on her face, one I know all too well. "What's in it for me?"

"Lydia, we have to get going if you want me to drop you off at school before I go to work . . . Oh, hi, Charlotte, it's so good to see you!"

And now my older sister, Jane, entered. Really, my tiny bedroom was too small for this many people.

"Hi, Jane," Charlotte replied. "How's it going?"

"Good!" Jane smiled brightly. "I love Mondays, don't you? You get to see everyone back at the office and share what you did that weekend. How was your weekend?"

"Well," Charlotte said, "I was here, helping Lizzie . . ."

There is not a kinder, more solicitous soul than my sister Jane. She knows very well what Charlotte was doing this weekend. She spent most of it in this very room. But Jane was still going to be polite and genuinely interested in what Charlotte would say.

I figure her extreme niceness evolved naturally over the past twenty-six years as a defense mechanism for her beauty. You may want to hate Jane because she's so pretty, but it's really hard when she's baked you cookies and made you tea.

Case in point: When I was in junior high, I decided to despise Jane for being a beautiful, sophisticated high-schooler and Lydia for being happy, carefree, and generally getting whatever she wanted. (What can I say? I was going through an awkward phase— as one does—and I was very tired of being the middle child.) My annoyance with Jane lasted all of about six hours, ending when we got home from school and she taught me how to side-braid my hair.

My annoyance with Lydia is ongoing.

"That's right, you were doing the video!" Jane said. "Lydia showed it to me. Lizzie, it's fantastic, very funny."

"Really?" I said. "You think I looked okay? My makeup?"

Jane blinked at me twice. "Hmm." Well, that answered *that* question. "You know, you should wear that maroon blouse next time—it really makes your skin glow."

Jane works for a design house in what passes for our little downtown. They do a lot of different aspects of styling—interiors, furnishing, etc.—but Jane works in their fashion department. She is the only person I know who can take a thrift shop housedress and turn it into something that could conceivably be worn to an awards show. So if there is anyone's fashion opinion I trust, it's hers. But . . .

"I would, but there's something wrong with the buttons— there's gappage."

"Oh, I can fix that." Jane waved away any arguments. She went into my drawer and found the blouse. As she did, she turned to Lydia.

"You ready? I should be able to get you to Art History class if I speed."

Jane doesn't speed.

"Ugh, Art History is so lame—the lecturer just drones and laser-points at the peen on old statues. Total perv."

"I was just telling Lydia," I interrupted, bringing us back to something a bit more pertinent than genitalia on old statues, "that I don't think it would be a good idea if we were to tell Mom and Dad about my videos. The project is about portraying my home life through new media, and I can't really do that if . . . Besides, it's only going to last a few weeks, anyway." I can feel my teeth grate at the glint in Lydia's eye. "Please?"

"And again I ask," Lydia smirked, "what's in it for me?"

This forced me to pull out the big-sister guns.

"Oh, I don't know," I mused. "Maybe I'll refrain from telling Dad about that box of fake IDs under your bed."

We stared down. Lydia is only twenty. This fact is not well known to the local bartender community.

"Fine," she relented. "Mom and Dad would spoil the fun, anyway."

"Great!" Charlotte said brightly. "Now can we go to school and/or work?"

As we shuffled out of my room, Jane spoke low to me. "Lizzie, are you sure about Mom and Dad? If they find out . . ."

"Please," I said, with an approving glance at Charlotte. "Do you know how many hours of video get uploaded to YouTube every minute? Nobody is ever going to watch these."

"Ha!" Lydia laughed. "Don't be so sure, nerdy older sister. *I'm* in your video, and I'm *destined* for fame."

Saturday, April 14th

Home from morning office hours with Dr. Gardiner, and I feel a little better. I'd been nervous after the second video went up. (That one only took four hours to make, so . . . progress!) We've gotten some views—a couple thousand, actually. Which isn't Charlie Bit My Finger levels by any means, but I'm still kind of shocked that a couple thousand people have had this tiny glimpse into my life. And seemingly came back for another.

The people on the Internet must be really bored.

And so far, most of the feedback has been positive. But I've been a little nervous about how I portray my family. Specifically my mom and dad.

"Are you being honest about how they interact with you?" Dr. Gardiner asked.

"Yes, but . . ."

"But what?"

And that's the question. Ever since Jane expressed concern about it, it's been on my mind. Am I being too harsh? Especially considering my parents don't know about the videos. I don't need their consent to portray them, only their consent if they appear on camera, which is NOT going to happen. Still, they're my parents. My frustrations with them are probably pretty normal. Until one airs them for the entire world to see. Then the magnifying lens of public opinion warps everything.

But Dr. Gardiner reminded me that honesty in the portrayal of my life is all I can do—and actually, is the point of the whole project. So I left her office feeling a little more confident, and came home to what was apparently the World Ending (™ my mother).

"Your father is the reason none of you girls will ever get married!" My mom was in the kitchen, wailing this latest revelation to Jane, who took it with her usual grace while helping her prepare lunch.

"He won't even go introduce himself to the new neighbor!"

Oh, yes. The new neighbor. This current World Ending has been going on for about a week now—I had almost blissfully forgotten about it, what with school and my videos. But Mom is obsessed with meeting Bing Lee and getting one of her daughters in front of him. So you would think she would just go up and introduce herself . . . but no. That's not how Mom operates.

Perhaps it's because she knows she might be a tad overwhelming to the uninitiated?

Could she be that self-aware?

"We're not exactly neighbors, Mom," I tried. The house in question is at least twenty minutes away, on the other side of town. The nice side. The McMansion side.

"Which is why I can't provide the introductions!" my mother said between splotchy sobs. "If they were nearby I could just walk over with a welcome plate of cold meats and cheeses. But I need your father to do it, and he will not oblige me! I am bereft!"

Occasionally, my mom thinks it's the nineteenth century. And that she's Scarlett O'Hara.

I could only roll my eyes and back away slowly, because from the look on my mom's face, anything else would just be instigation. So I wandered over to my other parent.

"Hey, Dad, thanks for being the reason I'll never get married," I said from the doorway to the den.

"You're welcome, Lizzie. Anything I can do to help," he answered from behind the newspaper.

"You could just go introduce yourself to this Bing Lee and end Mom's torture, you know." Another wail erupted from the kitchen. "And ours. Conversely, we could time travel to the twenty-first century and we girls could introduce ourselves. Oh, look at that!" I glanced at my watch. "We're already here!"

"Now, are you going to spoil all my fun?" There is a glint in his eye. It's a glint similar to Lydia's when there is mischief to be had.

Now as silly as this whole thing was, if Dad was anti introducing himself, he would have flat-out said so, and my mom would have started scheming up a new way to get Bing Lee in one of her daughters' (read: her) grasp. But from the fact that it's played out this long, combined with that little glint, and what appeared to be a smirk, I knew something was up.

"Dad . . . is it possible that you have *already* met Bing Lee?"

He shrugged.

"*Dad . . .*"

"All right," my father sighed. "It is possible that I was at the club the other day, and it is possible that young Mr. Bing Lee happened to be there signing up for a new membership. It's also possible that I took the opportunity to introduce myself and mention that I have three daughters around his age."

My eyes went wide. "You did not. You sold us out, packaged us off just like Mom wants?"

"I didn't package you off—trust that I have a hair more tact than your mother," he said with a grin.

"What were you doing at the club?" My parents have a weekly bridge night at the club, but it's on Mondays.

"Canceling our membership," my father replied. "Now that you all are grown and no longer taking tennis lessons, we hardly use it."

Right. Except for bridge on Mondays. So, that's not weird.

"Well . . . what's he like? Bing?" I asked. Hey, he'd been the topic of discussion in my house for a week now; I'm allowed to be a little curious.

"You can find out for yourself next weekend—he'll be at Ellen Gibson's wedding. Apparently he went to school with her fiancé."

Right. Ellen Gibson's fiancé went to Harvard. Therefore, Bing Lee went to Harvard. When my mother found this out, Bing Lee went from a major catch to the mythical unicorn/phoenix/centaur she'd always hoped would wander into her daughters' lives.

"Okay," I said, sitting down next to my father. "How much longer are you planning on keeping this from Mom?"

"Not much longer. I thought I might spring it on her at the wedding."

"Dad, I know you like winding up Mom, but do you also enjoy post-apocalyptic nuclear hellscapes? Because that's what the house will be if you don't tell her. Soon."

"I have no idea what half that sentence means, but I take your point." My dad lifted himself out of his chair with a sigh.

"And if your father doesn't care enough about you to introduce himself to Bing Lee, chances are we won't meet him until he marries Charlotte Lu!" my mother ranted, while simultaneously crushing pecans with a mallet. Cooking de-stresses her. We eat well in this house.

"I'm sorry to hear it," Dad said. "If I had known that I'd be ruining Charlotte's future happiness, I would not have introduced myself to Bing Lee the other day."

As my mother shrieked and squealed and pressed my father for more information, I couldn't help but watch my parents do this dance—Dad winding up Mom, Mom getting flustered, then happy—that they've been doing probably since they met. It made me smile.

And I realized Dr. Gardiner is right.

This is my family. If I can't be honest about them, then I'm not being honest about myself. This is my life, warts and all. And that's what I'm putting out there.

Tuesday, April 17th

My mother has reached a whole new level of crazy.

You'd think that with the news that we'd meet Bing Lee at the wedding this weekend, she would be satisfied. But no, now the rumor is that he's bringing guests to the Gibson wedding, so he must have a girlfriend. Or multiple girlfriends. She's freaking out about it. Again, my mother has reached a whole new level of crazy.

I was driving to the library (side note: Thank God for these free mornings on Tuesdays. I don't know when I would document or brainstorm ideas for the vlog otherwise. The end of the semester is coming up fast and my workload shows it.) and I saw my mom making the turn into the Netherfield development. And it struck me: She's doing drive-bys. Trying to catch a glimpse of the elusive man himself and whoever he has with him and find out if it's possible to wrest him from that person's clutches.

She doesn't even know this guy! He could be nice, sure. But he could also be terrible . . . an aimless drug addict, or worse yet, an East Coast elitist with a crippling downhill skiing addiction. Yet she has already claimed him as her future son-in-law. And that's what worries me most. I had been vacillating between being sorry for Bing Lee and being sorry for us Bennet girls, but the fact that Mom is more than willing to hook one of us up with him without even having had a conversation with him means that she's not thinking about what might make us happy. Only about what might make *her* happy, and one of us possibly secure.

Either way, Bing Lee had better fasten his seat belt for the wedding this weekend. He doesn't know it yet, but it's going to be a bumpy ride.

"Oh, my God. Lizzie, did you see this?" Charlotte burst into our cubicles at school. I was working on a paper for Advanced Theories of Media Criticism. At least, I should've been. What I was really doing was iChatting with Lydia, who'd been swimming in the Mom crazysauce, speculating about Bing Lee's guests. Although speculation seemed pointless. Lydia had already done her usual snooping and found out that his guests were only his sister and some dude named Darcy. Which—if it's his first name—sounds like a Judy Blume heroine, but I digress.

Charlotte was shushed by the other grad students, but, for once, didn't care.

"See what?"

"Your *numbers.*" She leaned over my shoulder and pulled up the Internet.

On the screen was my YouTube channel. And she pointed at my views. Which had suddenly gone up to 60,000. Per video.

"Oh, my God!" Now it was my turn to be shushed.

"Oh, shut up," Charlotte said to the shushers. "Something is actually happening here."

"I didn't think it would work," I said.

"What wouldn't work?"

"I . . . I emailed a few people. And tweeted. Vloggers. And asked if they would check it out." I had been secretly hoping that they would check it out and love it so much that they would recommend it to their viewers, but I really didn't think it would work. It was a shot in the dark.

Oh, my God.

"Who did you approach?" Char asked, but her fingers were

already flying, searching my email and my Twitter feed. "Hank Green?!" she squealed. Then . . . "*Felicia Day* tweeted about your videos?"

"I didn't think it would work," I repeated dumbly.

"Lizzie, you're a hit! You have a legitimate audience now!"

"I have a legitimate audience," I said. "And they're going to want more videos." My stomach turned. "*Good* videos. Oh God, what if I don't have anything to say anymore? What if I have nothing to talk about?"

Char smirked at me. "I've known you since birth, Lizzie. You've never had nothing to say."

"But . . . I'm pretty boring."

This is sadly true. Lydia isn't totally wrong about me. I'm fairly nerdy. I read books and write term papers. I'm (annoyingly) perpetually single. I may have a point of view to express, but still . . . it's not the stuff compelling content is made of.

"How do I keep people's interest five, ten videos from now?"

"You're overthinking it," Charlotte said, which is her version of soothing. "Don't worry about five, ten videos from now, worry about the next one. And with the Gibson wedding tomorrow, you should have something at least halfway interesting to say on Monday."

I took deep breaths. Any IChat convo with Lydia or advanced theory of media criticism was forgotten. Charlotte was right. I just have to focus on the next one. And if I know my mother, at least the Gibson wedding will yield something interesting to talk about.

SUNDAY, APRIL 22ND

It's about 2 a.m., and if I were smart I'd be asleep right now. Check that—if I had a best friend who wasn't wasted and pocket-dialing me, I'd be asleep right now. But I just received a call from Charlotte that went something like this:

(*garbled noise*) . . . "Either I'm drunk, or this party just came down with a bad case of Fellini." . . . (*more garbled noise*) . . . "Why is my phone lit up?" (BEEP)

To be fair, I wasn't asleep yet anyway, since we just got home from the Gibson wedding about an hour ago. My mom is currently in a state of glee (or slumber. Gleeful slumber). Because, according to her joyous monologue on the way home, all of her pain and plotting were worthwhile as Mr. Bing Lee, admittedly good-looking wealthy type and recent homeowner, has now met and been smitten by one of her daughters.

Specifically, Jane.

I, however, am in a state of unbridled annoyance, because of one single person.

Specifically, William Darcy.

But I'm getting ahead of myself.

The wedding ceremony was lovely. Outdoors, in the afternoon. Why live in a sleepy coastal central California town if not to take advantage of the weather for your nuptials? Our longtime friend Ellen pledged to love, honor, and cover her new husband on her work's health insurance plan for as long as they both shall live, while Ellen's mother sniffled her way through the ceremony—her sniffles only slightly softer than my mother's wails. (Note: Ellen Gibson was in the same class as Jane since first grade; her mother and ours cut up orange slices for soccer practice together. Mom can barely hold her head up in front of Mrs. Gibson now, as her daughters remain tragically unwed.)

Of course, during the entire ceremony, my mother was craning her neck across the aisle to better stare at Bing Lee and his companions. Luckily, he didn't notice, but his overly tall, stuck-up friend certainly did. He frowned at us from beneath this ridiculously hipster newsboy cap. Although I can't even be sure it was a frown now. From what I saw of him that evening, his face just stays that way.

Regardless, the newlyweds kissed, the recessional played, and it was time to party! But before we could even get to the car to drive to the lovely restaurant overlooking the town that was hosting the reception, Mom had pulled Jane and Lydia (okay, I went along, too) into Bing's path and got herself the introduction she'd been yearning for.

"You must be Mr. Lee! Or is it Mr. Bing? I know some countries put the last name first but I never know which!"

Yes. That actually happened.

Luckily, the gentleman in question just smiled, introduced himself, and shook my mother's hand. Then, he turned his eyes to Jane.

And they never left.

"Hi, I'm Bing."

"I'm Jane," she said. "It's so nice to meet you."

"It's nice to meet you, too."

And then, they just stood there. Basically holding hands. Until someone behind Bing cleared his throat.

Someone in a newsboy cap. And a bow tie. (The bow tie I can forgive, but seriously, who wears a newsboy cap to a wedding?)

"This is my sister, Caroline, and my friend William Darcy."

"Hi . . ." Caroline Lee said in a slow but polite drawl. While their friend Darcy might be a little on the hipster side, Caroline was a little on the my-hair-is-perfectly-shiny-and-don't-you-like-my-

Prada-sunglasses side. But at least she had the decency to say "hi."

"Bing, the driver will be blocked in if we don't get going soon," said Darcy.

Charming.

"Right," Bing replied, this prompting him to finally drop Jane's hand and notice the rest of us. "I guess we'll see you all at the reception?"

My mother could not get to the reception venue fast enough. She made my dad weave through all the traffic, run two stop signs, and almost cause an accident just so she could get to the card table first and fidget things around so Jane was sitting only a table away from Bing and Co.

Meanwhile, I was happy to sit next to Charlotte.

"I saw your mom finally managed to corner the elusive Bing Lee after the ceremony," she said, between bites of crab puffs.

I will say that the Gibsons really know how to throw a party. It was a beautiful room, with chandeliers, old-Hollywood table markers, a jazz trio near the dance floor, and some insanely delicious food, as evidenced by Char's devotion to the crab puffs.

My eyes immediately went to the table where Bing sat. Or rather, where he leaned over to the next table, talking to Jane. She blushed and smiled.

"And it looks like he picked out his favorite Bennet already," Charlotte observed. "Jane has thoroughly charmed him."

"Jane thoroughly charms everyone," I replied.

"Yeah, but maybe she's charmed, too, this time."

I continued watching. There was a lot of blushing and smiling and nodding going on between those two. But . . . "My sister is not going to fall immediately for a guy my *mother* picked out for her. She's too smart for that."

But Charlotte just shrugged and took another sip of her vodka tonic. "I'll bet you drinks that she spends the whole evening talking to him."

"It's an open bar," I noted. One at which Lydia had already parked herself.

"Hence how we can afford the bet. Every hour that she spends with him, you have to fetch me a drink. Every hour they spend apart, I fetch you one."

"Deal."

Just then, Darcy leaned over and said something to Bing, which brought his attention away from Jane and made Bing's smile slide off his face. Like he had been admonished.

"At least Jane caught the eye of someone with manners," I grumbled, "and not his friend. What's his deal, anyway?"

"Who—William Darcy?" Charlotte asked. "According to my mom, he's an old school friend of Bing's. Apparently he inherited and runs some entertainment company, headquartered in San Francisco."

"Oh, yeah, that bastion of entertainment, San Francisco." (I have a dry wit.) "And by 'runs' I assume you mean he flips through the quarterly reports in between daiquiris on the beach."

"He's a little pale to be a beach bum." (Charlotte's wit may be even dryer than mine.) "And a bit too serious to be a trust-funder. Also, you should consider yourself lucky that your mother is not actively targeting him, too. The Darcys are worth twice as much as the Lees."

I eyed Charlotte. "Why do you know this?"

"Mrs. Lu wouldn't mind my marrying rich, either." Charlotte took a final sip of her drink and held out the empty glass to me. "Oh, look, Bing is talking to Jane again. Why don't you go and preemptively get me another vodka tonic?"

Charlotte was proved right about Bing and Jane. They spent the whole evening talking to each other. And when they weren't talking, they were dancing.

But she was wrong about something else. My mother *was* going to actively target William Darcy. I saw the moment it happened.

She was sitting with Mrs. Lu, gabbing away, her eyes on Bing and Jane. Then I saw her *pump her fists* in triumph. Mrs. Lu, not to be outdone, leaned over and whispered something in my mom's ear. My mother's eyes immediately zipped to where William Darcy was standing against a wall, frowning (of course) and typing on his phone.

Then her eyes zipped toward me.

That was when I decided to hide. I found a nice spot on a far wall, with some decent shadowing. With any luck my mother would not be able to find me and instead target her matchmaking onto Lydia, who was currently grinding against two different guys on the dance floor.

Of course, I don't have any luck.

I was pretty happy by my wall. I watched Jane and Bing dance. I watched my mom try to talk to Darcy and get a literal cold shoulder. And then . . . I watched my steely-eyed mother march over and whisper something in the bride and groom's ears.

"All right, everyone!" Mrs. Gibson called out. "Time for the bouquet toss!"

Oh, dear God.

This is every unattached person's least favorite part of any wedding. Might as well herd all us single folk into a pen to be gawked at like an exhibit at a zoo: Look! Unmatched pairs, in the wild!

But I could feel my mother's eyes staring daggers at me. I would be disowned if I didn't participate.

I found Charlotte in the crowd of reluctant young ladies. We shared a shrug of sympathy.

Jane came up next to me. "Hi! Isn't this such a wonderful wedding?" She glowed. If infatuation were radioactive, she would be Marie Curie. "I'm so happy. For Ellen and Stuart," she clarified.

"Aw, Ellen and Stuart are so super cute together, it's gross!"

Lydia said from my other side. "But Stu has the *hottest* friends—which one do you think I should sneak out to the car with?"

Lydia finger-waved to the two inebriated bros she'd been dancing with.

Since there was only a 50 percent chance she was joking, I opened my mouth to say something that would hopefully cajole my younger sister into not banging some random dude in the car we all had to ride home in, when out of the corner of my eye I saw a bouquet of peonies headed right for my face.

Holding up my hands was a natural defensive reaction.

So there I was, bouquet in hand and a bunch of relieved single women around me clapping. I noticed my mother in the crowd beyond. She was giving the bride two thumbs up.

Next up: the guys. One guess as to which self-inflicted social pariah stood as far away as possible from the crowd but still got the garter slingshot into his chest.

William Darcy.

We locked eyes. He looked grim. To be fair, I'm sure I did, too.

As the music started up and the dance floor cleared for this most terrible of traditions, I was actually feeling a little sorry for William Darcy. He was clearly not comfortable. He didn't dance well—just sort of swayed in time to the music, and kept me at arm's length like a seventh grader, his chin going back into his face like a turtle trying to hide. (I'm not a professional dancer by any means, but I enjoy a good turn across the floor with someone fun, and I regularly kick Lydia's butt in Just Dance.) He also did his best to avoid my eyes. Maybe he was just a little socially awkward. After all, Bing seemed fun and outgoing, and Darcy is Bing's friend, so there has to be something more to him, right?

Wrong.

I tried a little conversation to break the silence.

"This is a pretty incredible party, don't you think?"

"If you say so."

Wow. Okay.

"Well, it's what passes for incredible in our little town. How do you like it here so far?"

"I don't, especially."

Wow. Way to be open and accepting of my hometown there, fancypants.

"Do you . . ." I searched for something, anything. ". . . like to dance?"

"Not if I can help it."

"Do you like anything?" I couldn't help but say.

That got him to look at me. He was shocked, but hey, at least it was some response.

"Look, I'm trying here," I said, "but that was basically my entire small-talk repertoire. So, you could either lob the ball back in my court, or we could sway here in silence for the remaining two minutes of this song." I waited. "Your choice."

He said nothing.

And I don't know why. How hard is it to ask someone what kind of movies she likes, or what she studies in school? Basic chitchat stuff? Apparently for Darcy, lowering himself to converse with a townie-dwelling occasional dancer who appreciates all the hard work that Ellen and Mrs. Gibson put into a wedding like this was too degrading a concept.

So he just pulled his chin back farther and let the song end.

"Thank you," he said, after stopping abruptly when the music faded.

No, Darcy, thank *you* for putting that dance out of its misery.

We separated. Luckily, the band struck up another song, and the rest of the partygoers filtered back onto the floor, masking any embarrassment. And I have to admit, it *was* kind of embarrassing. For him to not even pretend politeness? Way to make me feel like an unworthy troll.

But I found Charlotte by my lovely shadowed spot on the wall, and she had a way of making me feel better about the whole thing—by laughing about it.

"That was the most awkward dance ever," she said. "Worse than your wedding dance with Ricky Collins in second grade."

"True. Ricky at least had been enthusiastic. Although he did have to get a cootie shot before touching me."

Charlotte laughed so hard, she got dizzy. "Whoa . . ." She closed her eyes. "Room spinning."

"Yeah, I think you're done with the vodka tonics for now. Although you won the bet, hands down. No contest."

"Yup. Can't wait to be invited to Jane and Bing's wedding." She smirked. Then turned green.

"Let's get some air, okay?" I said. I didn't tell her this, but the idea of Jane marrying Bing at my mother's urging made me want to turn green, too.

Outside, Charlotte took some deep, easy breaths. The green faded from her face. We were about to go back in, when I heard two familiar voices from around the corner.

"Can we go home, please?" Darcy said.

"Come on, it wasn't that bad. Could you try to enjoy yourself? A little?" Bing replied.

"In a town that wouldn't know a Barney's from a JCPenney? I don't see how."

"Well, you could try dancing again."

"Because it went so well the last time."

"It wasn't that bad." There was silence, and I imagine a sardonic look exchanged between friends that mirrored the sardonic look exchanged between Charlotte and me.

"Listen, you're having fun," Darcy said. "You have somehow managed to find the only pretty girl in this town. Go back in and keep dancing with Jane Bennet. I'll go home and send the driver back for you."

"Come on, don't do that," Bing said. "Stay a little while. I want to introduce you to Jane. Properly. You'll like her. She's . . . I've never met anyone like her."

I had to give Bing props for that. Whether or not he's good enough for Jane, he's got good taste.

"I've never met anyone that smiles that much."

There's that Darcy charm. Finding fault with *smiling*.

"And you know what," Bing continued, ignoring his friend's attitude, "her sister Lizzie is pretty nice, too. I bet if you asked her to dance again, she'd say yes. Give you a do-over?"

Before I could even wonder if I actually *would* give him a do-over, I could feel icy derision coming off Darcy in waves, curving around the corner to my hiding spot and leaving me cold.

"Lizzie Bennet is . . . fine, I suppose. Decent enough. But why should I bother dancing with her when no one else is?"

My jaw dropped silently. So did Charlotte's. I mean, seriously. Who the hell does this guy think he is? I didn't really hear what was said next because of the rage flooding my ears, but Bing must have worked some magic on Darcy (or more likely had some dirt on him) and got him back inside the party.

"Wow," Charlotte said.

"And to think, I was beginning to feel I had been too harsh on him."

"Well, at least you have an out with your mom. All you have to do is relay that little conversation to her and she'll never bug you about marrying into the Darcy fortune again."

And that was basically the Gibson wedding. Charlotte was pretty tipsy the rest of the night, but held it together. I left her in good hands with her mother, her little sister Maria, and a tall glass of ice water. Lydia danced too much, and didn't alternate water with her hard liquor and ended up vomiting in the bushes outside (very near where Charlotte almost did), and that was about the time the Bennet family decided to go home. Mom tried to persuade Jane to stay with Bing and have him give her a ride home (*in his limo*), but Jane was pretty tired by that point, too.

Tired, but smiling. A lot.

My mother crowed the whole way home about watching Jane and Bing dance together. Calling it the happiest day of her life. Which sums up my mother for you.

Charlotte was right, though. My mom was willing and able to dislike Darcy. She had found him pretty rude when she'd tried to speak with him before the Most Awkward Dance Ever (™ Charlotte Lu). I gave her a truncated version of our conversation while dancing, or lack thereof. I kept what I'd overheard outside to myself. Mom might be a little hyper-focused on marriage, but she's also a mama bear. Don't mess with her cubs. And under no circumstances insult them.

Charlotte was right about something else, too. At least I have plenty to vlog about when we record tomorrow. Although, considering the number of vodka tonics I fetched her (and the slurring pocket-dial), I may have to do this one without my bestie. She's going to need to sleep her victory off.

* * *

P.S. Before I went to bed, I was idly checking my phone. Bing and Jane have followed each other on Twitter. Jane only follows family and fashion on Twitter.

I know my sister. And I don't know how to feel about this.

TUESDAY, APRIL 24TH

I'm feeling a little . . . bad today. It's hard to put my finger on it, but there's just an overwhelming sense of unease.

This is what happens when Charlotte goes out of town.

She called me yesterday after the latest video posted and asked me to cover for her at discussion group this week—there was a family emergency she had to deal with. As the world's best bestie, I am taking on all her grad student responsibilities (thankfully I still have my Tuesday morning study period), while doing all the filming for the videos by myself.

On the plus side, the last video I posted had the most views yet—likely a combination of the fact that I mercilessly teased Jane about how she met Bing at the wedding and the fact that I accidentally showed a close-up of my boobs (thanks again for being hung over, Charlotte).

And I think that is why I have been feeling bad of late. Not about my boobs, but about Jane, and the merciless teasing. She's just been so . . . happy. And yes, Jane is normally quite happy. But this is different—at least it is to me, since I know her so well. There's an inner glow, a quickness to blush. Humming under her breath.

Am I wrong in thinking this is a little quick? She *just* met Bing. Less than three days ago. There is way too much we don't know about him for Jane to be thinking of him this much.

But don't tell my mom that. She's got them married off already. And while Jane would usually have the presence of mind to gently stop Mom's imagination from speeding like a runaway freight train, this time she's just . . . going along with it.

Take this morning. Jane was running late for work, a job she LOVES, but didn't blink when Mom stopped her from heading out the door and asked her if she knew what Bing's favorite food was.

"No. We haven't talked about food," Jane said. And by the look on her face, I could tell she was wondering if she should know what kind of food he likes.

"Well, let me know when you do," my mother said. "I want to practice recipes before he comes over for dinner."

"Whoa—Bing's coming over for dinner?" I asked.

"Well, no—not yet," my mother conceded. Then she gave Jane a coy, teasing look. "But sooner or later he'll be eating here. Dinner. Breakfast. Thanksgiving."

All I wanted to do was slap my forehead and beg my mother to pull up on the reins, but Jane just gave a little laugh, and shook her head, before waving good-bye on her way out the door.

I remind you, Jane and Bing met three days ago. All they have done since is text a little. And my mother is ready to welcome him into the family.

I wonder what Jane is thinking. Is she being biased by Mom? Mom, who is so eager to love a rich potential son-in-law that she's blind to all his faults (whatever they may be) and pushing her daughter into a currently nonexistent relationship?

It makes me wonder what would happen if we were not forced to live at home.

"Forced" is perhaps too strong a word, but circumstances certainly require it. Jane doesn't make enough money at her entry-level job to take her student loans out of deferment, let alone pay rent and utilities somewhere. She's lucky she makes enough to keep her junker of a car running.

And I moved back when, after four years of living on my own for undergrad, I got accepted to the grad school with the best communications program . . . within driving distance of my parents' house (luckily, my car is less of a junker—I bought it off of Dad when I went away to college with three years' worth of summer job money). Considering the student loans I had already amassed, I traded in my independence for some small relief.

I have another year left before I have to start paying off the stellar education my penchant for studying and learning bought me, and the prospect of it scares me to bits.

Since Lydia only goes to community college, her expenses are admittedly less, but she still doesn't have any money coming in—just money going out. (She also doesn't have a car, and has to share with Mom and beg rides off of everyone else.) In some parts of the world, we would have been left to our own devices the second we turned legal, so it's actually really good of our parents to let us continue to live at home.

But if we didn't? If we were able to be as adult in reality as we are in age . . . maybe Jane wouldn't be taking the prospect of Bing so seriously. Maybe she'd be able to keep it casual with him, without the constant reminder of our mother's expectations. Without the pressure cooker of five adults living on top of one another with only one bathroom, and being unavoidably mixed up in each other's business at all times.

Sometimes it feels like a prison. But it's the prison I know.

Hence the merciless teasing of Jane in my last video. (I can be passive-aggressive at times. I do get some things from my mother.) I really should apologize. I really should try to be more open-minded about Bing. Jane knows what she feels, right?

But then again, Jane is a lot stronger than she looks. When I teased her about Bing, she started teasing me about Darcy, and now that's all the commenters want me to talk about. They think I "met" someone at the wedding. Someone that my mother may one day invite over for dinner, breakfast, and Thanskgiving.

Ha ha, no. Sorry, viewers. I'll simply have to tell them about what he said to Bing about me, and put his prickishness front and center. That will get them off the scent. And no, I'm not at all worried about impugning the character of a douchebag on the Internet. After all, I'm just going to say what actually happened.

SATURDAY, APRIL 28TH

Comment from *****: Lizzie your impression of Darcy is hilarious!
   More please!
Comment from *****: Darcy can't be that bad. Come on. Really?
Comment from *****: More Darcy! Hahahaha!

Jeez, more Darcy? That's all they want? Me to talk about a wedding that took place a week ago now? I have other things going on in my life, you know. I have school, and finals coming up, and . . . okay, I guess just more school—but that's important to me! Darcy is most certainly *not* important to me.

PIE CHART: THINGS THAT ARE IMPORTANT TO ME

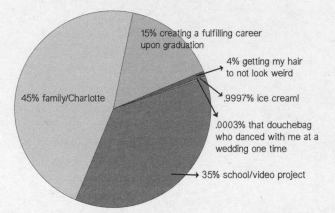

Honestly, I would rather just forget him. Hope and pray that our paths cross as little as possible while he visits Bing and not at all thereafter. But then I think about my audience—the semi-large one (and growing!) that I weirdly have now. Do I make it clear to them just how awful he was? After all, I still haven't detailed the Most Awkward Dance Ever (™ Charlotte Lu, but I'm stealing it) on air yet. Surcly, that would make them realize how awful he is. Or is that just feeding the beast? And is feeding the beast something I want to do?

Ugh, I wish Charlotte were here. She would help.

. . . Fine. You want more Darcy, people? You get him.

TUESDAY, MAY 1ST

I got my Charlotte back! I picked her up at the bus stop today. She'd been in Fresno (glorious Fresno!) for the past week.

"Why Fresno?" I asked the second she got into my car, hugging her. "Why did you abandon me in my hour of need?"

"You mean why did I abandon you in your hour of needing someone to help you film videos to go take care of my aunt who landed in the hospital?"

"Well, when you put it like that . . ."

Charlotte's had a close relationship with her aunt ever since she was little, and they ended up bonding on a family trip to China when Char was eight. Her aunt even helps pay for Charlotte's school, which is good because her family is in even worse straits than mine.

"How's Aunt Vivi doing, anyway?"

"She's better," Char said. "The timing couldn't have been much worse, though."

"What do you mean?"

She waved her hand dismissively. "Just that missing school with finals looming is not ideal, that's all. How much make-up stuff do I have to do, anyway?"

I fill her in on the papers and other assignments that got handed out in her absence. I took over our discussion group, so luckily she doesn't have the annoying busywork of grading freshman essays.

I feel like something is going on with Charlotte that she's not telling me. But if Charlotte doesn't want to talk about something, it doesn't get discussed. Seriously, when she got her first kiss in ninth grade, she didn't tell me. And it wasn't because she thought I'd be jealous—I'd gotten my first kiss the year before in a harrowing game of spin the bottle and lorded it over her, as one is wont to do. She just didn't think it warranted a conversation. So she decided to not talk about it.

Thus, I've decided that Char was not off visiting her aunt—an aunt who, by the way, knows how much school means to Charlotte. Heck, said aunt is helping to pay for it. There is no way she would condone the removal from her studies for a week. No, I've decided Charlotte was having a torrid holiday with a tall, dark, and handsome stranger. That's my headcanon, at least.

But when Char doesn't want to talk about stuff, she just turns the conversation to another topic. Which she did then, with supreme skill, before I could ask her anything cropping up in my suspicious mind.

"So how's Darcy?"

I nearly swerved off the road. "What?"

"Darcy. You know, the guy you've made the last three videos about."

"I have not," I protested, but it was admittedly weak.

"Uh-huh. Why are you spending so much time talking about a guy who you met once, at a wedding, ten days ago?"

My bestie sure knows how to cut to the core of the . . . everything.

"I . . . The comments . . ." I tried. "It's all everyone wants me to talk about!"

"They're *your* videos, Lizzie. If you don't want to talk about him, don't."

"But audience expectation . . ."

"You can't just give them candy, Lizzie. You have to control your content. Take back the videos—talk about what you want to talk about." Char looked at me, peering over the top of her sunglasses. "Now, if you *wanted* to talk about Darcy . . ."

"I most vehemently do *not*." Except maybe one more time. Just to clarify that I don't want to talk about him, of course.

"Fine."

We then let the radio take over. The best thing about a best friend is that there isn't always this burning need to fill the silence. Instead we can just sit together in the car and sing along to the radio, neither of us caring how off-key we are.

And it was on the incredibly high, unsingable part of "Defying Gravity" (there's nothing wrong with a deep love of show tunes) that we happened to pull up to a stoplight right in front of Jane's work. They have a pretty, quaint storefront on our town's pretty, quaint downtown main street. (Every time I walk by, I want to make over my bedroom with embroidered throw pillows and my closet with fashion-forward silhouettes.) Jane, as the lowest man on the totem pole, does a lot of driving to go fetch samples of fabrics and shots of espresso. Which it seems she had just done, because we saw her pulling bags of material out of the trunk of her car.

Or rather, one Mr. Bing Lee was pulling the bags out of the car, eager to help. Behind him stood a sour-faced Darcy and Caroline, at a distance. Caroline had shopping bags in hand. Bing held up a fabric-laden hand to his friends, indicating they should wait, and followed my sister into the store.

I watched them in the rearview until I couldn't watch them anymore. Or rather, until the light turned green and the Ford Fiesta behind me honked and made me drive.

"He probably just ran into her on the sidewalk," Charlotte said.

"Probably," I agreed. What else is a rich guy summering in a new town supposed to do but wander the stretch of street between the yogurt shop and the independent movie theater that happens to include my sister's place of work? "Or he could be stalking her."

"Yes, because you always stalk someone with your sister and friend in tow."

Well, yeah, but . . . fine. Point to Charlotte.

"It's was awfully nice of him to help her carry all that stuff in," she continued.

"Or it'll undermine the way her superiors at work perceive her, if she can't even carry in a couple of shopping bags by herself."

Charlotte just stared at me, straight-faced. "Grasping at straws does not become you, Lizzie Bennet."

The thing is, I don't think I'm grasping at straws. Or, more accurately, I *should* be grasping at straws. If there is a single straw that ends up being questionable about Bing, I need to find it—because my mother sure won't. And Jane . . . Jane thinks the best of everyone. She's going to think especially best of a guy she happens to like.

Of course, the obvious question to ask is what is a guy like Bing doing in a hamlet like ours? Shouldn't he be in the big city, moving and shaking with the people who will be coming to him for nose jobs once he's out of med school?

Maybe he's looking for a more idyllic life?

Maybe he's running from a deep, dark family secret?

Oh, maybe he's committed a crime and is on the lam! (Although, who brings his sister and douchebag best bud on the lam?)

But seriously, what prompts an otherwise seemingly normal single guy in his twenties to up and buy a house in the middle of nowhere?

Someone has to play devil's advocate. And that someone might as well be me right now. And yes, so far, Bing seems okay. But how okay can a guy be when he's best friends with a guy like Darcy?

SATURDAY, MAY 5TH

If there were one benefit to having my sister in the opening steps of the love dance with a rich guy, you would think it would be that my mother would be satisfied by it. That she would allow herself to sit back and sigh with a deep contentedness and raise a mint julep to the fruits of her machinations.

But no.

All it means is that she has more time to focus her zeal on her remaining daughters.

Take dinner last night.

"Do you think Bing has friends at that medical school of his?" my mom asked as she spooned out a serving of lasagna that probably took her nine hours to prepare.

"I would imagine so," my father said, not looking up from his plate. "Most young people enjoy interaction with other young people with similar interests, I'm told."

"Perhaps Jane can convince him to have some of them visit this summer," my mom mused. Jane is currently out to dinner with said Mr. Lee, and my mother's imagination is in overdrive because of it. "Better ones than that disagreeable William Darcy," she continued. She still hadn't forgiven him for the way he was rude to her at the wedding (and me, if she had known about it). I consider it one of life's small blessings.

My mom left her last sentence hanging in midair. I locked eyes with Lydia across the table. Neither of us wanted to be the one to take the bait. My father knew better than to do so, too. But then again, when had my mother ever needed conversational prompting?

"He could make it a party. It would be wonderful if you girls could meet some nice young men. Before it's too late."

"Too late?" Lydia snorted. "Mom, I'm, like, *twenty.*" I kick her under the table. It's just the sort of opening our mother is angling for.

"There have been studies done, Lydia. Oh, yes! Studies." She said that last word reverently, as if the information she was about to impart would be life-changing. "They say that by the time you graduate college, you have more than likely already met your life mate."

"Well, it was certainly true of you, my dear," my father said, between mouthfuls of lasagna.

"And I still have a couple of years." Lydia smirked. "You're screwed, though," she said to me.

I wisely kept silent.

"When I was your age, Lizzie, I was already pregnant with Jane. Time is ticking. Did you know there is a higher chance of getting killed by a terrorist than a woman getting married after thirty?" my mother continued, enjoying having the table in her thrall.

"Did you know your data is specious and you're citing an article that is thirty years old, which has been disproven a dozen times since then?" I couldn't help it. Sometimes, the research monster in me comes out.

But my mother just clucked her tongue.

"I never did understand your humor, Lizzie."

"Well, if my choice is death by terrorist or hasty marriage to someone I already know in the hopes of staving off singlehood, I choose Option C."

"Option C?"

"Yes. Where I have a successful career, a healthy disposable income, and a close group of single friends with whom I can travel the world."

"You would deny me grandchildren?" My mother's voice quavered, hinting at the threat of tears. Which I think they taught her how to do in Southern Lady School.

"Oh, no!" I grin at my dad, who is trying to hold his own smile in. "Once I'm established in my career, have paid back my loans . . . there's always artificial insemination."

I fully expected my mother to explode. But instead, she just took a deep, steadying breath and continued spooning out lasagna.

"You may not even have Option C, Lizzie." Her voice became hushed, as if she were telling a horror story around a campfire. "You know your Aunt Martha started menopause when she was *forty*."

The thing is, my mother believes deeply every false fact she spouted at dinner. She is legitimately worried that I will end up a spinster, at the age of twenty-four. It keeps her up at night.

As divorced from reality as she is, I don't want to be the reason my mother can't sleep.

So I spent my Saturday morning at the library, researching data and statistics about modern marriage — and it turns out that no, at twenty-four, I am not statistically likely to die sad and alone. In fact, the chances that I will have a more substantial relationship and stable children go up if I marry later.

I came home today ready to present these facts to my mother, in the hopes they would assuage her feelings and maybe, you know, get her to back off the marriage train just a smidge. But before I could approach her, Lydia blocked me from entering the kitchen.

"Um, hey, Lizzie. Whatcha doing?"

"I was going to go talk to Mom."

"Uh-huh, cool . . . Wanna go to the mall?"

"No, not really." Lydia was literally standing in the kitchen doorway, impeding my path.

"Well, I do. Drive me, okay?"

Then I heard a sob. Not a short, swallowed thing, either. A long, mournful wail. The wail of the severely disappointed.

"What's going on?" I asked as I tried to peer around her.

"Nothing!" Lydia said brightly. "If you drive me to the mall, I'll go with you to that boring British movie you want to see. Come on, let's go! Now!"

"Mom?" I called out. "What's wrong?"

"No, Lizzie, don't go in there! Trust me!" Lydia tried to pull me back. When I just shot her a look, she crossed her arms over her chest. "Fine, don't say I didn't try to warn you. The mall would have been better."

I dropped my bag on the floor. I found my mom in tears, sitting at the kitchen table. "Mom, did something happen?"

I knelt beside her, and she clasped my hand.

"Oh, Lizzie, it's the most horrid thing." She took a deep breath. "Cindy Collins from across the street . . . she's spending the summer in Florida with her new boyfriend."

"Okaaay . . ." I said. My mom and Mrs. Collins were friendly, but they weren't exceptionally close.

"She came over to ask"—*sniffle*—"to ask us to water her plants until her son Ricky comes to town."

"Okaaay . . ." I tried again. Charlotte and I had gone to grade school with Ricky Collins. His parents had gotten divorced when we were in middle school, and they decided to have Ricky live full time with his dad, since Mr. Collins moved to a better school district. We only saw Ricky for a couple of weeks in the summers after that. But he had been memorable, if only because he was so annoying.

"But it might be a little while before Ricky gets here because she said he's starting a business . . . and he's *just gotten engaged!*"

Oh. Oh, dear.

"If Cindy Collins's dickheaded son can find someone, that's one less person for you!" (I flinched when she said "dickheaded."

I didn't know she even had that in her vocabulary. But desperate times call for lapsed standards, I guess.) Then, my mother pressed a handkerchief to her mouth in horror. "That's just one step closer to Option C! Oh, Lizzie . . . Where did I go wrong?"

As I pressed my fingers to my temples, and promised to fetch Mom (and myself) some aspirin, I could hear the screech of tires on the driveway out front.

And I realized my car would be blocking any other car in, so who could have possibly pulled out? My eyes flew to my bag on the floor—the contents spilled out, my keys notably not among them.

Lydia had stolen my car and taken off to the mall. And as my mother gave another mournful wail, I could only wish I had gone with her.

TUESDAY, MAY 8TH

As much as my mother's wailing has continued on (and no, my carefully researched statistics didn't assuage her fears), I have come to the conclusion that I am fine with my life choices. In fact, I'm great with them. I *much* prefer to have my mind on my studies and not guys. Honestly, Option C doesn't strike fear into my heart the way it does my mother's. And Lydia's. Working hard at something I love, having great friends, and seeing the world? That sounds like the brass ring.

Sure, I'm in debilitating debt. And sure, I won't be able to afford to own a shoe box, let alone a place to live until I'm . . . ever. But then again, who *isn't* in debilitating debt right now? We worked hard to get this debt-ridden, and we'll work equally hard to get out of it.

Charlotte is a perfect example. Even with her aunt helping her, she is in even more debt than I am, because I had a partial undergrad scholarship. But I just ran into her outside the registrar's office, getting things set up for the summer.

"You're doing *what*?"

"I'm going to be working on campus for the summer semester. The editing lab, and the administrative offices. I just set it up."

"But what about your thesis?" Yes, my school runs on a trimester schedule—but our grad program doesn't offer the courses we need during the summer. So, we are told that the break between the second and third years of grad school is the best time to dig in and do as much work on your thesis project as possible, before the hecticness of school returns

"It won't be so bad—I'll just be making sure a bunch of Editing

101 kids don't destroy the computers, and I'll have access to the editing suites and be able to work on my projects there."

I must have looked obviously dubious.

"Work study really helps me defray my expenses at school. And if I save up enough, maybe I'll be able to devote more time to work in the fall."

Again, I got the impression that Char wasn't telling me everything, but she wasn't about to.

"Well, I have huge plans for the summer. Just so you know," I said.

"That so?"

"Oh, yes. Aside from my thesis, I've taken on a couple of high school students for tutoring in English. So, I'm finally going to stake my claim to the comfy chair at the library. The one at the big table, so I can spread all my papers out. Stay there all day."

"Wow. You really know how to live large."

I shrugged, cocky. "That's just how I roll."

Yeah, I'm happy with my life choices. Studying what I love, and great friends. What more could anyone possibly want?

Saturday, May 12th

Okay, I have to admit that maybe . . . *just maybe* . . . I'd been a little bit judgmental about a certain young man who is spending this summer in our quaint little town. What with the rampant speculation about his being on the lam, hiding out in a McMansion, or at the very least questioning why on earth he'd decide to move here.

I'm just lucky that my sister is a big enough person to not hold it against me.

Yes, ladies and gentlemen (of my imagination, because seriously, who would be reading this?), I might have been a little too harsh on Bing Lee.

It all started with flowers. After their date last week, Bing sent Jane flowers at work to let her know he was thinking of her. First of all, points to him for not sending them to the house, where my mom would jump all over them, read the card, and then likely get it framed. Secondly, he'd been on Jane's Pinterest apparently, because he knew her favorite flower.

But the flowers did come with a card, one that also bore an invitation to a dinner party. For Jane and for me. My mother, being my mother, figured that the mythical medical school friends must have come into town, and to better her chances for all of her offspring, decided to try and wedge Lydia in (as well as herself, for some reason).

But Bing handled it like a champ.

He thanked my mom for dropping off Jane and me at the door, and sent Mom and Lydia away by promising to come over for dinner sometime next week.

My mother was satisfied, having finally gotten the promised

chance to feed Bing Lee. Lydia, for her part, seemed fine with it. She wasn't enthusiastic about a "sit-down-take-a-sip-of-wine-and-spit-it-out type thing, anyway."

It was a gorgeous party. And Netherfield is a really gorgeous house. I have a feeling that Caroline did a lot of shopping and hiring of painters to get it to look like more than just a young bachelor lived there. Bing was also the perfect host—kind to everyone, happy to see them, and going out of his way to make people feel comfortable.

"Hey, Lizzie," Bing said to me when we entered. "I'm glad you could come."

"I'm glad you invited me."

"Well, I knew Jane would be more comfortable with other people around . . . you especially."

"Bing, did you throw an entire dinner party just to make Jane comfortable?" I asked, things clicking to place in my head.

"Well . . ." He blushed. "I want to get to know everyone else, too."

"Wow," I said. "That's some dedication to your courtship."

Bing looked uncomfortable (in a manful way), so I decided to cut him some slack and change the subject. But can I help it if I changed the subject to something I wanted to know?

"So what made you decide to move here, anyway?" I asked. "Buying a house is a big decision."

He shrugged. "I told my parents it was an investment property." Which I guess is a rich-person term for *I have a half dozen houses and flit between them*, but Bing continued. "But really, I came up here for Stuart's bachelor party, and I just . . . fell in love with the place. The town. The people."

It was no surprise to me that his eyes were following Jane as she greeted Caroline across the room.

"Anyway, I just thought being here would be nice."

And it was. It was really nice. *He* was really nice. After I freed him from my inquisition (skills honed from my mom), Bing spent the entire evening next to Jane. But not in a cloying, stalkery way. In an *I'm truly interested in you and your opinions* way. He asked her what she thought of the house. Asked her for her professional design opinion. I can't imagine that went over well with Caroline, but she didn't say anything, just smiled at Jane and enthusiastically agreed with whatever she said.

Charlotte was there, too (for Jane's comfort, but I was happy about it myself), along with a couple other people we knew from school, some from Jane's office, and a few others we'd met at the wedding.

"Bing Lee makes friends easily, it seems," Charlotte said to me.

"Yeah," I mused, all the while keeping my eyes on Jane and Bing. The look on his face spoke volumes. "He really likes her, doesn't he?"

"Yup," Charlotte agreed. "So . . ."

"So maybe I was a little hard on him."

"Aw, you admitted your mistake." Char grinned at me. "I've never seen that before."

I swatted her arm for that, making her spill a little of her drink. Which, thankfully, was just water. She told me she's decidedly off vodka tonics for a bit.

"Yes, this is that rare occasion where external factors were perhaps influencing my first impression of someone."

"Translation: you were wrong."

"I am capable of changing my mind, when it's warranted." I let my eyes find Jane and Bing again, across the room. "And I was wrong about Bing. Which is good, because Jane really likes him."

"Really?" Charlotte asked. "How do you know?"

"Because she told me," I replied. "And besides, just look at her."

At that moment, Bing whispered something in Jane's ear and she laughed. Then she turned away to address something Caroline said, trying to pay as much attention to other people as she did Bing.

"Then maybe she should show it more," Charlotte said, frowning.

"She shows it plenty," I replied. "She's at this party, isn't she? She's sitting next to him at dinner."

"Jane would have sat next to anyone who requested it of her."

"You think that?" I asked. "Why, just because she's nice?"

"Exactly! She's nice. And she's nice to everyone. If she really likes Bing, she should show him a little bit more favor than she would a random stranger, is all I'm saying."

Actually, I'm fine with the way Jane was acting. As much as I've changed my mind about Bing tonight, I am happy that she is remaining her usual composed self, at least publicly. Playing it cool means it won't go too fast, and Jane can keep some boundaries—and keep some of herself. Maybe this will turn into something real. I just don't want her to fall so hard (with our mother's encouragement) that she forgets who she is, and what's really important.

The rest of the evening went well. Bing had apparently wanted to grill burgers on his back patio, but Caroline made him hire caterers for the evening, which I can't fault because it resulted in the best crostini (which I would never admit to my mother) I've ever had. Charlotte ended up talking to a guy (!) for forty minutes, debating whether or not the French New Wave was overhyped. (Charlotte's take: it was.) And there was even some dancing, of the mildly embarrassing, "Hey, you guys remember the electric slide?" variety. All in all, it was a pretty great evening. In fact, the only burr in its side was that perpetually sour-faced buzz kill known as William Darcy. But hey, we expected that, didn't we?

Darcy spent most of the evening hanging back in the corner of the room, watching the merriment with disdain. Caroline would occasionally go over to him, and they would exchange presumably snarky banter. More than once I discovered his eyes following me, but he would look away the second I caught him. I could only imagine that he was recalling the horror of our dance.

I will give him this: at least with Darcy you know for certain whether he likes you. Or in my case, whether he does not. Unlike Jane and Bing, there is absolutely no guesswork involved.

Tuesday, May 15th

Comment from *****: Lizzie, if you can change your mind about Bing, what about Darcy? Or Lydia? Jeez, judgmental much?

I've been getting comments like this lately on my videos. And I know you're not supposed to read the comments, or feed the trolls, or whatever—but the fact of the matter is, comments are how I communicate with the viewers, so I have to.

Let me just say, the vast majority of the feedback I have received has been great. As a woman putting herself out there on YouTube, the fact of the matter is I expected far more "Show us your tits!!!!!!!" and "she ugly ho" comments than I have received. (The debate about gender norms in new media as filtered through anonymity would fill up this entire journal, so we won't go there.) So, the negative comments I do get I tend to take pretty seriously— as constructive criticism. However . . .

"It's not a negative comment," Dr. Gardiner told me when I cornered her at lunch yesterday.

"It's not?"

"No—it is questioning your presentation and your world-view . . . which is exactly the kind of back and forth you want in an open communication," Dr. Gardiner said. "In fact, what you're doing with your video project is really quite exciting—I have not seen a community form around a voice like yours in a long time. But you do have to address the concerns of your community."

Which has gotten me wondering about what comes next. It's just an idea right now, and I don't want to overthink it, but what if my videos could be something bigger than just my end-of-term project?

But Dr. Gardiner makes a solid point. To have a true dialogue with the world (which is the whole point of this video project), I have to think wider than my narrow viewpoint.

The thing is, though, I don't think I'm being overly judgmental. I think I'm being pretty true to life. But how to make this clear to the faceless masses on the interwebs? If they won't take my word for it, whose word would they take?

SATURDAY, MAY 19TH

I didn't make it to the library this morning. I was on my way out the door when my mother pulled up in the driveway, honking like a madwoman and effectively blocking me in.

"Oh, good, Lizzie, you're still here! You can help me with the groceries!"

In the trunk of my mother's car was the *entire* grocery store. She had bought out every department.

"I'm headed to the library, Mom. Can't Jane or Lydia . . ." I tried, but my effort was weak.

"Jane had to work at the design center this morning, and Lydia is still asleep. She was up studying too late last night." My mother clucked her tongue.

Let's be clear: Lydia was not up late studying. She was up late watching cat videos online. She's obsessed with cats lately. I could hear her across the hall as I was trying to sleep.

"Today is too important for the library," my mother said, handing stuffed bags of produce to me. "We have to make the very best impression, and that means cooking everything perfectly. You've just been elected my helper. Come on!"

If my hands weren't laden down with what was a ridiculous four pounds of lamb, I would have smacked my forehead. Of course. Tonight is the night that Bing and Caroline Lee are coming over for dinner. Tonight is the night my mother goes full-on crazy.

And I've been "elected," as my mother put it, to be the one who keeps her from that fate.

"What is all this?" Dad asked, emerging from his den with the newspaper in hand.

"It's dinner." I heaved the bags onto the kitchen table and went back out for more.

As I passed, I heard my dad say, "For who?"

"The Lees."

"There are only two of them, correct? We didn't invite all the Lees in the world, did we?"

"Oh, honey." My mom simply laughed, waving off my father's objections.

"How much did you buy?"

"I wanted a variety. Jane has told me so little about what they like—"

"How much?"

The tone in my dad's voice shocked me. He never gets angry. He rarely ever gets above bemused. I quickly got the last of the bags out of the trunk of the car and came back into the house.

"I told you, Marilyn, we can't just go spending—"

"And I told you, honey. It's for a special occasion—"

"They can't all be special occasions! We cannot keep on like this!"

Mom and Dad didn't notice me at all standing in the hallway. They were too involved in their conversation. And there was no way I was going in there at that moment, so I just slid into the den, waiting it out.

It shouldn't have taken more than a few moments, I figured. And I don't think I had any perishables in my bags.

It's really weird being an adult child and listening to parents fight. Especially when your parents never fought much in the first place. Or at least, they didn't in front of us. Part of me wants to crawl up into a ball, regress to the age of seven and hide, pretend that it wasn't happening. But another part of me is too smart, too curious, to not want to know what the problem is.

And I suppose that curiosity is what led me to my dad's desk. And to glance at his calendar. Mostly it was normal—business meetings, bridge night at the club (now crossed out). But there was an entry for next week, written like it was the most normal thing in the world: *2 p.m. Bank—Mortgage Refinance.*

Now, that could be something normal, right? I don't know a lot about mortgages, but they get refinanced all the time because of changing interest rates and things like that . . . I think. But adding this entry onto the fact that they cancelled their club member-ship . . . and now Dad and Mom are having conversations about how much she spends . . . it seems like things are starting to pile on top of each other.

Dad's office laid off about 30 percent of their workforce a few years ago. He managed to keep his middle-management position, thank God, but had to take a bit of a pay cut. Of course, at the time they reasoned everything would be fine because Jane would be on her own soon enough, and I was about to graduate undergrad, so they wouldn't have me to worry about, either. Instead, Jane and I are still both at home. And Dad and Mom are having hushed conversations in the kitchen about how four pounds of lamb is too expensive.

But then I heard my mom laugh again, a little trill that told me their brief disagreement was over.

"Lizzie? Where are the rest of the bags?" she called out, after I heard my dad move down the hall and close the bathroom door. (If Dad's not in his den, he's in the bathroom. He told us a long time ago that it's a man thing.)

I plastered a smile on my face as I came out of the den, carrying the rest of the groceries. I couldn't think about the money issue any more. At least not today. Because my mother was strapping on her apron and beginning to flutter all over the kitchen, and it wasn't even ten in the morning yet.

I figured if I could just focus on getting Mom through the dinner, everything else could wait.

"Now Lizzie, do you think I have time to learn how to make sushi? It's not as if I have to cook anything, right?"

Tonight is going to be a doozy.

Sunday, May 20th

3 a.m. I can't sleep. Not because I'm wide awake, but because there is literally no room. Lydia is hogging all corners of my not-exactly-spacious double bed. Oh, and when Lydia drinks, she becomes a thrasher in her sleep. Seriously, I was about to try and climb in next to her, when she kicked wildly and gifted me with a healthy bruise on my shin.

Suffice to say, the evening did not proceed even remotely as planned. Oh, Bing and Caroline came over for dinner. Bing brought a bottle of wine, which was a lovely gesture. (But by the way my mom fawned over it, you would think such a thing was rare and exquisite, and that we didn't live within driving distance of the entire Central California wine valley region.) And yes, Mom cooked food. And she only asked Bing and Caroline once if they minded that she didn't use soy sauce. But sometime around the appetizers, things started to go awry.

We were all sitting in the formal living room—which is really just Dad's den, but Mom forced him to hide all his papers and desk stuff and move the "good" couch from the regular living room in there. Then she made him feng shui the entire space. (Another aside: I know formal living rooms are a relic from when people "paid calls" on each other and sat sipping tea, but when did we stop having formal living rooms? The eighties?)

Mom had also demanded that her daughters dress appropriately. For my mother, "appropriately" means something akin to a debutante ball. I wouldn't be surprised if she had lace parasols in a closet somewhere, ready to be pulled out at a moment's notice. Luckily, Jane got home from her work in time to bring some fashion expertise and sanity to the situation, and we all looked normal, if a little dressy.

"You look amazing," Bing said to Jane, as he sat next to her. "Is that new?"

"Oh, my, is it from Marc Jacobs's fall collection? You have samples at your store?" Caroline fawned, reaching forward to touch the skirt.

"No, actually—this is a vintage dress I altered," Jane replied.

While that made Bing light up with admiration, I couldn't help but notice that Caroline dropped the material instantly.

"My Jane can make a ball gown out of sack cloth, if she puts her mind to it," my mom said, sitting on the arm of my dad's chair. "She is so talented. And smart. If only that job of hers appreciated her skills. To be honest with you, I think her employers are using the economy as an excuse to keep her pay low. Why, with a little more money, imagine what Jane could do—start her own clothing line, move out on her own. Of course, you don't need to imagine, Bing, you *know*."

"Erm," my father interjected, picking up the bottle Bing had brought. "Shall we try this wine?"

Whatever conversation my dad had with my mom earlier, it must have been extreme to have unsettled her like this. Because my mother would never—*never*—talk about money in front of new acquaintances. Especially ones she wanted to impress.

It's also possible that she'd been taking nips of some cooking sherry in the kitchen. Sometimes the cooking itself isn't enough to de-stress her.

But Bing didn't seem to notice anything untoward, launching into a polite conversation about the wine with my father, how they had picked it up at a local winery, and venturing that perhaps he and Jane could go there sometime, make a day of it.

From there, we repaired to the dining room (we only have the real one, thank goodness), where Mom served everyone an . . . international array of cuisine. The evening was still going okay at this point, which was when Lydia decided to make herself known.

I can only guess that she was pretty bored and no one was paying much attention to her.

"So, um, Bing," she started, scooting her chair closer to his. As I was Mom's assistant in the kitchen, I had to be near the kitchen door, and thus was not able to position myself to block Bing's non-Jane side from familial intrusion. "You're, like, a med student, right?"

"Yes," Bing smiled, a little cautious. After all, he'd been thoroughly questioned already about his medical studies at UCLA, his choice of specialty, and the weird growth on my dad's big toe.

"Do you, like, examine people yet?"

"Not yet—I still have another year to go before we see patients on our own."

"Then, how do you, like, practice? Do you—oh, my God—play Doctor with your fellow med students? You'd have to, like, look at their privates and stuff. That would be so crazy. You'd have to see them *naked*." Lydia's eyes went wide. "And I just got the *best* idea of how to pick up guys." She turned back to Bing. "Do you have a stethoscope? Can I borrow it?"

"Actually—"

"OMG, can you imagine the number of guys I can get to take their shirt off, just by saying I need to listen to their heartbeat? Good way to find out if they are too hairy to take home first, am I right? Caroline, you *must* have tried it before. No? Bing, please can I borrow your stethoscope? Please? *Pleaaase?*"

"Lydia," I warned, kicking her under the table.

"What?" Lydia answered with a responding kick. "What did I say?"

That's Lydia for you. She has no idea when she's gone too far for fancy-dinner conversation. Or for regular conversation. Even my mother, who usually indulges Lydia's enthusiasms (after all, boy-crazy is only one step removed from marriage-crazy), had turned a mottled shade of pink.

Swiftly, I tried to adjust Lydia's line of questioning to something more palatable. "So, Bing, when do you head back to school?"

"Oh. Um . . ."

"My grad program is on a trimester schedule," I continued. "When we get off in June, I actually don't have to go back until October."

"And sometime in the middle of September, Lizzie will start to go stir-crazy without lectures to attend and papers to write," Jane finished for me, giving me a smile from across the table.

"Usually, it's August," I replied.

"Well, I have some time," Bing answered. When Caroline cleared her throat, he continued. "Until I have to go back to school, that is. And I'm lucky that my sister could take time from her own work to help get me settled."

Caroline smiled graciously at him. "And decorate! Which is really why I came—Bing's idea of furnishing is an armchair and TV. Besides, who wouldn't like to paint on a blank canvas?" she said to Jane, who giggled.

"And does Darcy like to decorate, too?" I asked. I couldn't help it.

"No, decorating's not really his thing." Bing laughed. "He's just hanging out with me. He doesn't love telecommuting, but he can still pop up to San Francisco when he needs to."

Yeah, I highly doubt that. More likely, he inherited his business, and it's run by people who actually know what they're doing so he can take weeks off at a time to "just hang" with his buddies.

"But whatever are you going to do about that gorgeous house of yours?" Mom interjected. She fanned herself lightly, the picture of Southern fragility. She was stuck on the idea of Bing going back to school—i.e., leaving without her having secured him for Jane. "It's not meant to be a summer house. It's meant to be a family home, with children and dogs, and . . ."

"My brother's a very busy young man," Caroline jumped in, saving us all from Mom dropping her widest hints. "But don't worry, if there's anyone who can handle the rigors of being a medical student and then a doctor along with the joys of homeownership, it's my brother."

"You know, there's an excellent medical program right here . . ." my mom tried again, but thankfully she was stopped this time by someone with a little more force.

"Well, my dear, I believe it is time for dessert!" my dad said, rising from the table. "She's been putting together something special for tonight—she wouldn't even let me see what it was." He smiled at the guests.

"Oh, yes! You all stay right here—I'll be back in a moment!" Mom said brightly, bringing attention back to where she (read: we) were comfortable having it: the food. It was admittedly delicious (which is standard for my mom; she really knows how to cook), but in a terrifyingly overelaborate way (which is not standard, and you will see the terror it invokes in a moment).

My mom trotted off to the kitchen, and after refusing assistance from her appointed helper (me) came back with a wheelie cart.

And a blowtorch.

"Bananas flambé!" she cried. "Girls, this is how I snared your father."

My dad looked a little taken aback, but he played along. "Yes, she was training to be a table-side dessert chef at a restaurant when we met." There was a brief pause. "Thirty years ago."

"And I remember exactly how it goes—don't you worry, honey." My mother smiled, and turned on the blowtorch.

I think you can guess what happened next.

I doubt we will ever get the smell of burned bananas out of the dining room drapes.

Once we'd put out the tablecloth—Dad fetching the fire extinguisher and Bing smothering the flames with a casserole pot lid;

I like to think they bonded during this small crisis—Mom looked ready to break down in tears.

My dad only had to shoot me one look for the appointed helper to spring into action.

"Jane, I have a thought," I said. "Why don't we go out and grab a drink?"

"Oh, yes!" she said gratefully. "The night is still young."

"That sounds like a great idea," Bing approved, with visible relief. "Carter's Bar?"

"I'll text Charlotte, have her meet us." We would need reinforcements to get over the trauma of dinner.

"And I'll tweet Darcy," Caroline added, her fingers already flying on her phone. Which I had actually seen her do a couple of times during dinner. Great—that meant chances were Darcy was informed of the Great Bennet Dinner Debacle already (™ the Universe).

I had been trying to do a video update during this dinner, running up and down the stairs to film short snippets in my room as the meal spiraled out of control. (Considering the number of times I excused myself to "use the bathroom," I can only imagine that Bing and Caroline now think I have an incontinence issue.) I wanted to see if immediacy added to the energy of my posts (boy, did it!), but I had to abandon the story half told to go to Carter's.

Where the second half of the evening was, if you can believe it, even more interesting than the first.

And once again, Lydia played her part.

At first things were going well. The addition of Charlotte and the atmosphere of Carter's helped to normalize everyone. Also, alcohol.

Darcy, of course, kept to himself. Even when he was sitting at the table with us. His mouth shut and his chin pushed back in a look of complete condemnation of anything, you know, *fun*.

Saturday night and the bar was packed, so of course Lydia would run into someone she knew.

"Oh, my God, guys, this is Ben from school! Ben, my sisters Lizzie and Jane." Lydia dragged a nice-looking guy over to our table. "Hi—my name's David, actu—" he said, extending his hand to me. But before he could finish, Lydia cut him off.

"Bing! Ben and I were just talking and we decided that it would be *so awesome* of you if you threw a party. Like an end-of-semester thing. Your house is perfect, and Ben's band could play."

"But, I don't have a—"

"Whatever, I would be the cutest groupie you ever saw." Lydia gave David-not-Ben a once-over. "It's too bad I didn't bring my stethoscope with me," she sighed, her words beginning to slur. "So, what do you think, Bing?"

Bing was a couple of beers in at this point, and I didn't blame him for it. After all, he'd survived dinner with my mom, and he had a driver. But this made his eagerness to please susceptible to those who always had an angle. Like Lydia. "You know what, a party sounds like a great idea, Lydia. Thank you for sush—suggesting it." Then he turned his smile back to Jane. "Would you like to come to a party at my house?"

She smiled back at him, and they were lost in their own little world.

"Yes!" Lydia fist-pumped, taking this drunken agreement as the full-on promise she would inevitably force it to be. Of that I have no doubt. Then her eyes hit on something on the far side of the bar. "No way! When did Carter's get Whac-A-Mole? Come on, Ben! Let's play!"

"It's David—" But Lydia didn't seem to care, as she dragged him off toward the game.

I turned around. In my rush to get us here and out of the house, I hadn't noticed that Carter's had really spruced up the joint. There was new felt on the pool table, and yes, a Whac-A-Mole game, and . . .

"Oh, Lizzie," Charlotte said, eyes wide. "Is that Just Dance?"

I am a sucker for Just Dance.

"Oh, my God." I grinned. "Char, play with me."

"Hell no. Not in public."

"Oh, come on!"

"If you want to embarrass yourself, go right ahead. I'm fine right here."

Embarrass myself? As if. I *rule* at Just Dance.

"If you like, I'll—" Darcy cleared his throat, but I didn't catch the rest because I was digging in my purse for quarters.

"That's fine," I said, pulling out three bucks in quarters, my emergency parking-meter money. "I'll just play against the computer. And kill it. Like I always do."

just dance:

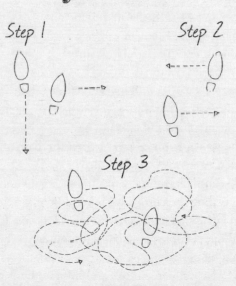

Step 1

Step 2

Step 3

I didn't kill it.

In my defense, the computer on Carter's game must be different from the computer on the home game, because it started doing some beyond-crazy steps. Did I accidentally hit the setting for cephalopod? However, I had a good time, and by the time I got off the machine I was laughing, and Charlotte, Jane, and Bing cheered me when I finished.

But Darcy? No, Darcy had removed himself to the wall. The dark shadows that are his natural habitat. He was talking to Caroline. Charlotte walked by and she immediately shut up, so I know they were talking about me and my spectacular failure. So I looked Darcy dead in the eye, just to let him know that I knew he was talking about me.

And what did he do?

He started texting. Fake texting.

As well he should, the little snob. (Okay, the tall snob.)

I rejoined the table after that, and after laughing at my Just Dance prowess, I told Charlotte what I did to Darcy.

"Uh, that's not what they were talking about," she said.

"Then what was it?" I asked.

"Well, they were talking about you, but not in the way you think."

"What way *were* they talking about me, then?" Could they have been discussing something worse than my dancing? Was my bra strap showing or did my skirt flip up?

Charlotte was about to answer, when the bartender, the aptly named Carter, came over to our table.

"Hey," he said, glowering. "You need to get your sister out of here, or I'm calling the cops. This is a public place."

Jane and I whipped our heads around, searching for Lydia. She was by the Whac-A-Mole game, all right, but what she was whacking wasn't a mole.

Her shirt was pretty much off, and her hand was down David-not-Ben's pants. They seemed to have forgotten the existence of other people.

Jane and I were on our feet, immediately sober.

"Hey, Lydia, we have to go home now," I said, and then turned to her partner in crime. "Sorry, David." Who, for his part, at least seemed sheepish about his state, and the encroaching reality that yes, he was on second base in a crowded bar against a Whac-A-Mole machine.

"No," she whined.

"Lydia . . ." I tried, but she pushed me away.

"No!" she yelled, belligerent. "I wanna keep playing the game!"

"Well, you're out of quarters, honey," Jane said in her nicest voice. "There are more in the car."

Lydia blinked at Jane. "Can Ben come to the car, too?"

The noncommittal noise Jane made was enough to have Lydia willingly go with her sisters. We said our good-byes to Bing and the others quickly and got Lydia into the car. I was the designated driver, and I even dropped David-not-Ben off at his place on the way. Luckily, by that point, Lydia was asleep and could not protest the loss of her gaming partner.

This is what worries me the most about Lydia. She isn't a thoughtless person. She can actually be really sweet. But she is careless. And mostly, she's careless about herself. She's home right now and asleep in my bed, thank God, but what if we hadn't been there to take care of her? What if she'd been out on her own, met up with David, and ended up getting arrested, like Carter threatened? Or ended up in David's car, and he drove her home drunk? Or they ended up together somewhere, and she passed out, like she did in the car on the way home—only this time, Jane and I weren't there?

Anything could have happened to her. Yes, women should be able to go out and have fun without fear of consequences the way men do—but that's not the reality. There are a lot of unenlightened douchebags out there. And my biggest fear is that Lydia is going to fall prey to one of them.

But right now, I'm tired, and Lydia seems to be in the non-thrashing part of her REM cycle, so I'm going to hold my baby sister and try to get some sleep.

I am in term paper/studying hell, and this is the time that Charlotte decides to annoy me about annoying things. Namely, Darcy.

"I'm telling you, he would have played Just Dance with you."

"I'm only *decent enough*," I said. "Why would he play Just Dance with me?"

"I don't know. Maybe he doesn't think you're *decent enough* anymore."

"No, after my performance, one has to assume he thinks I'm worse."

Charlotte shot me her patented "you're-an-idiot" look. Which is awfully close to her normal face, but after years of study I can tell the difference.

"You didn't hear what he said to Caroline," Charlotte said. "I did. He was saying that you actually looked really pretty when you were dancing. Especially your eyes. That you have 'fine eyes.'"

"And by that he meant my eyes are just fine. Passable," I countered. "Again, decent enough."

Charlotte just rolled her eyes this time. "Or he was trying to give you a compliment. He might just be, oh, I don't know . . . shy?"

This wasn't the first time Charlotte had tried to convince me Darcy is anything other than the boorish snob I know he is. Ever since that night at Carter's, she's been on a mission. But that's Charlotte—always looking for a narrative where there isn't one. And it was nice to see her in a good mood. More often than not these days, she's all about schoolwork. And Charlotte is normally very practical, but that practicality is starting to feel very . . . cynical.

Again, I think she isn't telling me something, and it's starting to itch at the back of my mind.

"Shy is unassuming. Meek," I replied, keeping on subject. "Darcy is not meek. He makes his opinion very well known."

"Apparently not."

"Char, stop it, okay?" I couldn't help it. "I can't joke with you right now about this stuff. I have four term papers due this week, my write-up on the videos for Dr. Gardiner's class, three exams to take, and then sixty essays to grade. Not to mention finals are in a few short weeks. I can't even think about what I'm going to do for a video this week, let alone play along with your wild Darcy theories."

"Fine." Char threw up her hands. "I'm sorry. I know this week isn't fun. It's not fun for me, either."

"Yes, but you already turned in all your projects at least. All that extra editing-lab time. Kiss-ass."

She smirked back. "Fair enough. How can I help?"

"Do you have a time-turner?"

"If I did, I wouldn't give it to you. It'd be my secret." Charlotte laughed. "But seriously, what if I do a video this week? I can take that off your shoulders at least."

I couldn't help but feel relieved. "Would you? That would be so great. But I know you don't like being the main one on camera."

"I can handle it once." She shrugged. "Besides, I'll get Jane to help me."

"What will you talk about?"

"Something with narrative cohesion. Probably Bing. Or something similar."

Char smiled at me, and I smiled back, grateful. I don't know what I'd do without my bestie. She always has my back.

Friday, June 1st

There is something in the air around town today. The hyped-up heartbeat of anticipation. The bitter taste of adrenaline filling your mouth. The faint but distinctive smell of chlorine.

The . . . abdominal muscles on display.

"Woo-hoo! It's Swim Week!" Lydia screamed as she climbed into my car.

Oh, no. Not now. Not this.

Our sleepy little central California town is noted for two things: its Brady Bunch–era suburban architecture and the fact that sometime in the seventies, an Olympic swimmer was from here. Not a famous one or anything—I think he might have come in fourth (just shy of a medal!) in the 200-meter breaststroke. But he (or she? I can't remember) dedicated all his post-Olympics money to building a state-of-the-art swimming program and facility right here in town.

It was a huge economic disaster, but it did leave us with a honking big pool. The builders also got some state funding for it—which is why for one week, once a year, our hamlet gets invaded by collegiate swim teams from all across the state for the Speedo-and-shaved-chest bacchanalia/competition known as Swim Week.

"Aren't you excited? It's going to be awesome! All those hot guys . . ." Lydia looked over the top of her sunglasses at me.

"Not really. I have a lot of work to do before the end of the semester."

"You know, I've found that my schoolwork gets a lot easier if I party a little bit beforehand. A little beer makes my papers *way* better." She nodded at me, all innocence.

"I haven't found that to be the case."

"Ugh, we need to get you out of the house. You are in danger of becoming criminally boring. You, me, Carter's, every ranked freestyle swimmer in the state . . ."

"Yeah, well, I don't think you're going to Carter's anytime soon."

Seriously. The last Carter's incident was two weeks ago. I still haven't emotionally recovered. But Lydia is a bouncing ball of energy, ready to go go GO!

"You can't stop me."

"No, but your car privileges are still suspended." Hence my picking her up from school today. "And I certainly don't have to drive you."

"And whose fault is that?" Lydia pouted.

I could barely contain my sarcasm. "*Yours.*"

Contrary to what Lydia likes to believe, neither Jane nor I mentioned to our mother what happened at Carter's last time. But this is a small town. Word got around. And for once, my mother showed some sense and tried to rein Lydia in by taking the car away from her.

All it really means is that now Jane, Mom, or I chauffeur Lydia everywhere, but hey—Mom made an effort!

"You all think I'm still a little kid." Lydia shook her head. "Well, I'm not. And you and I are going to go out and try to catch some man-meat at Carter's during Swim Week. You'll see."

"Uh-huh. You keep telling yourself that."

I can tell you one thing. Between my workload and my post-traumatic stress from last time, the one place I most definitely will NOT be going is Carter's.

Tuesday, June 5th

We went to Carter's.

In my defense, it was really the best option. Lydia was going to go, anyway—her car privileges got miraculously reinstated when she mentioned Swim Week to Mom, who wouldn't mind an athletic aquatic son-in-law—and at least this way, I could keep an eye on her.

And it turned out to be not too bad. Heck, it might even have proved . . . interesting.

As you will note, we even got home at a reasonable hour (11 p.m.! No chance of turning into a pumpkin!). The usual coterie of beer-slogging swim jocks were of course in attendance—and Lydia was in heaven. And to give her credit, she was nowhere near as crazy as last time and stayed far away from the Whac-A-Mole machine.

But wading through their drunken bro-ness might actually have been worth it, because—dare I say it?—there was possibly a diamond amidst the rough.

We had been at the bar for about half an hour (Carter the bartender had already spotted me, and we had a wordless conversation along the lines of *"You gonna keep an eye on your sister? Okay. You have my permission to be here."*) when the guy who had wedged his way by me to the bar knocked my arm and caused me to spill my drink all over the bar stool I was just about to occupy.

"Whoa, hey!" came this voice from my other side. "Dude. Not cool."

But my assailant had disappeared into the crowd. I turned to find myself staring up at this . . . *perfect* chin. Chiseled. A slight dimple. Looking up, this perfect chin was attached to a sculpted face, with amazing blue eyes. (Looking down, this perfect chin was attached to a gorgeous neck and amazing shoulders, and the flattest stomach I've seen in real life. And it was *inches* from me. But I digress.)

"Sorry about that," he said.

"Why?" I asked. "It's not your fault."

"Still, on behalf of guys in general . . ." He smiled at me. Oh, my God, that smile. "Can I buy you a replacement?"

I looked down at my now near-empty glass. "Oh, you don't have to."

"Trust me, guys in general have a lot to make up for." He nodded to the bartender, and, using some kind of magic considering how crowded that place was, I had a new drink in hand in less than a minute.

"And your chair," he tsked, noticing the puddle of liquid occupying the indentation of my seat. "Hold on a sec."

He leaned over, grabbed a handful of paper towels, and sponged the seat down. Then, after wiping away the majority of the liquid, he put his jacket down over the seat.

"*Voilà*," he said with a flourish.

"Wow," I replied as he handed me into my chair. "You literally put your jacket over a puddle for me."

"I'll let you in on a secret." He leaned forward, whispering. "Most swimmer-owned apparel is waterproof."

"Still, I don't think anyone has put clothing—waterproof or not—over puddles since Elizabethan times."

"Well, Elizabeth is my girl." He grinned at me. "I take all of my social cues from the dudes that surrounded her."

"That works out in my favor—since my name is Elizabeth."

"Is it really?"

"Lizzie." I held out my hand for him to shake. And he raised it to his lips.

Oh, yes, that actually happened.

"George Wickham. Pleasure to meet you, Lizzie. May I join you—or is this seat reserved for someone?"

"Not reserved. I'm just here with my sister tonight."

I pointed to where Lydia was surrounded by a number of swimmers. She waved when she saw me, and seeing George, gave me an only mildly embarrassing thumbs-up.

"I can see the family resemblance," George replied. "Although I can tell you are the more discerning of the two."

"Why, because I'm not surrounded by twenty guys?"

"No, because you're with me."

I laughed. "No, you don't think too highly of yourself."

"Eh, I just think lowly of everyone else. At least when they're drunk, and bump into beautiful girls and spill their drinks."

I had to admit, this George Wickham had game.

"So I take it you are among the competitors who are gracing this fair town for a week?" I asked.

He winced. "Do I really look like I'm a college kid? Oh, man—that's tragic. I'm capable of growing a full beard, you know. It takes three weeks, but still . . ."

I laughed—I couldn't help it. Self-deprecation is one of the more charming aspects of the incredibly handsome.

"No, I'm a conditioning coach—brought on when swimmers have technique issues," George replied.

"So you're a teacher."

"Kind of. A traveling, seasonal one. Although I'd love to stay in one place for a little while, so if you need any help with your freestyle or butterfly, just let me know."

"Sadly, no, I'm not taking any swimming classes this semester."

"A student!" He leaned into the table. "I knew you had the look of academia about you. So, what do you study, peach?"

And maybe it had something to do with the fact that Jane has been so gooey-eyed-happy with Bing lately, and that she, too, sees no reason that I should be "perpetually single," as Lydia likes to call it, but I found myself enjoying my conversation with George Wickham. There was no pressure. And no reason not to enjoy it.

We talked about my studies for a little while, and I told him all about my video project. My hopes for post-school life. He told me all about being a swim coach, shaping young athletes—and, while growing up in San Francisco, that time he saw a walrus on a boat tour around Alcatraz Island.

"But the walrus didn't seem to notice he was out of place," he said.

"Oh, really?"

"Well, he'd spent his whole life behind bars already."

I snorted into my drink. But in a classy way. "Wow. That is perhaps the worst joke I have ever heard."

"No, I can think of way worse jokes."

"Oh, no—don't strain yourself."

"Well, give me your number," he leaned forward and played with a bit of my hair, "in case I think of a worse one later."

Really, how can anyone refuse the promise of future bad jokes?

After the exchange of numbers, it was pretty much time to go home. (I. Have. Classes.) Lydia was extracted from the bar with minimal whining, and George walked us to our car.

"Are you sure you're okay to drive?" he asked.

"Yes," I replied. My sole drink had been finished off over an hour before—which shows you how long George and I had been talking. "But thanks."

"Then—awesome to meet you, Lizzie Bennet."

I'm pretty sure at this point I was rendered speechless by his charm.

"And awesome to meet you, too, G-Dubs!" Lydia called after his retreating form, only a little tipsy. "Wow. A hottie *and* he didn't hit on me tonight but kept his eyes on you. Lizzie Bennet, you may have broken your perpetually single streak." She gasped and squealed, grabbing my arm in glee. "Can I be the one to tell Mom that the artificially inseminated Option C is off the table?"

* * *

I had put my diary away and was climbing into bed when my phone lit up with a new text.

> Just wanted to make sure you and your sister got home okay. — GW

I couldn't stop grinning as I typed back:

> We did. Thank you for the escort to the car.

Two seconds later, my phone flashed again.

> Anything for you, peach.

My heart picked up to double time. Anticipation made my toes wiggle.

Well played, George Wickham. Well played.

SUNDAY, JUNE 10TH

Lest one think that with the advent of swimmers to our potential pool of husbands my mother had forgotten all about the sweet budding relationship of Jane and Bing, think again.

They have been out at least half a dozen times now—in company as well as by themselves—and they are endlessly sweet around each other. Considerate. Jane has already started doing that thing where activities are reserved for Bing-time. (Not *those* activities. Although Lydia speculates wildly about it.) But there has been more than one occasion where I'll mention the idea of going somewhere, and Jane has replied, "Oh, Bing mentioned that he liked that place." If I ask Jane to see a certain movie, she replies, "I already told Bing I'd see it with him."

They are dating. It may not be officially listed as such on social media sites, it may not be the rollicking mad descent into love the books make it out to be, but it is progressing in its own tentative way.

But things are not progressing fast enough for my mother.

I spent all day yesterday dealing with her Convoluted Plan to have Jane stranded and naked at Bing's, thus resulting in (one assumes) a torrid afternoon of premarital passion, followed by a shotgun wedding.

This Convoluted Plan involved:

- Me traveling to the grocery store with Mom at four in the morning to purchase via coupon green beans packed in cranberry sauce. And gelatin.
- Mom making use of a cake mold.
- Mom trying to convince Jane it was a good idea to wear a white dress, carry the gelatin mold to Bing's, and get soaked

by a predicted-yet-currently-unseen rain shower, which would lead to the aforementioned torridness.

- Dad and Mom arguing about a second mortgage in the den, while I snuck into the kitchen and stole the cranberry gelatin mold on its decorative plate.
- Me nearly throwing up from having to eat the whole thing, green beans and all, thus foiling Mom's plan.

I'm sure there will come a day that I will laugh over this. But it's not today.

Why can't Mom just let things happen on their own? Why must she push and rush and force a skewed view of what's important on us all?

Case in point: This past week, all my mother has done is ask me whether I've heard from "that nice swimmer you met with your sister." (Yes, Lydia did rush home and tell Mom about the possible destruction of Option C, right before chugging a Red Bull and passing out on the living room couch for twelve hours after a sugar crash.) Not the fact that I have some of the biggest finals of my life looming. Not inquiring what I'm going to do for my thesis, and about the inkling of a plan I have for it.

(George and I have texted a bit back and forth, but as the team he's currently coaching had to flee town after Swim Week, I have not seen him. But he does hope to be back sometime this summer, having picked up some private coaching clients at the swim center.)

I know I should be used to my mother by now. I know I should be able to just sigh and shake my head at her antics. I know she loves us. But there could be real consequences. What if her pushing actually causes Bing and Jane to break it off? What if she pushes us all so far she alienates her daughters into a lifetime of chain smoking and resentment?

My latest theory is that all of her hysteria about Bing and Jane is fear-induced. And not fear that we won't ever get married and provide her with grandchildren to manipulate, but fear about bigger things, things that can't be solved by a convoluted plan.

After all, Mom no longer goes to bridge club. Instead she joined an online coupon club, and has begun insisting we bargain shop at a time when no one we know is likely to see us. (Note to self: Mom seems to have become more proficient at the Internet. Find way to block her search engines from finding the videos.)

And then there's that fight I overheard yesterday about a second mortgage on the house. I guess the meeting with the bank that I saw on Dad's calendar didn't go very well. Mom and Dad are all smiles in front of us, but their stress manifests in different ways.

Dad trims back his bonsai trees too far.

Mom tries to pair off her daughters.

Maybe it's because she wants to see something progressing in a positive direction. And I don't blame her for that. But if Dad and Mom have started having fights about money, it's only going to get worse before it gets better.

And the nerves-inducing thing for me is—I included all of this in my next video. Mom's insanity, the convoluted plan, and the issues about money. I filmed it yesterday; it goes up tomorrow.

I've never talked about my family's financial issues online before. And honestly, I haven't been this nervous about posting something since the first video. Is it too real? People like the fluff— Lydia's zaniness, the Bing and Jane romance, the Darcy bashing. But if I'm being honest . . . this is what's going on in my life right now. This is what creeps into my brain before I fall asleep, when I should be worried about finals and term papers and when George Wickham will come back to town.

So this is what I have to talk about.

No more pencils! No more books! No more teachers' looks of approval and validation for a job well done!

At least, not until the fall.

Finals are done, and I can breathe a sigh of relief for a few days at least. But not too long . . . because I have a thesis to start work on!

Although, it turns out, I've already begun it.

"Dr. Gardiner!" I cornered my professor outside her offices, just as she was closing up for the day—and possibly the rest of summer.

"Lizzie," she replied. "Great paper on your experiences with your videos and audience interaction. Really top-notch work."

"That's sort of what I wanted to talk to you about. I want to continue my video project—but as my thesis."

Dr. Gardiner lifted an eyebrow. I hope one day, when I am ushered into the realms of higher academia, I will be taught the secrets of the supercilious eyebrow.

"What would your focus be?"

"I'll cover all aspects of the project: the production and distribution models, what works and what doesn't in terms of engaging an audience and communicating a message, the process of branding, as well as the character and psychological impact of talking about personal issues in an increasingly popular public forum."

Dr. Gardiner seemed to think about it for a second. "Your videos do have momentum, but more importantly, they have message. Especially your most recent one, where you were honest about your family's financial straits. That had resonance, and depth."

I could feel myself flushing. First, out of relief knowing I made the right decision to put that last video online, then with the creeping realization that Dr. Gardiner was watching my videos—long after I turned in my paper on my end-of-term project.

"You might want to also consider going to VidCon," she mentioned. "To gain other vloggers' perspectives for data."

"Charlotte and I are talking about it—we really want to go." VidCon is a huge convention about web video, and it would be an incredible opportunity to meet people in this new industry—and luckily, it's in California, only a couple of hours' drive away.

"Okay. I'll sign off on the thesis topic," Dr. Gardiner declared.

I'll admit, I squeed.

"But—" She held up a hand, halting my glee. "I want to give you a warning. You'll be letting strangers into your life, your world, for almost a full year. And your videos have gotten more popular than I think any of us expected."

At this point I've posted twenty videos and I have over 100,000 views each. That's two million views. And we've even made a little money, what with YouTube advertising. Not a lot—but maybe enough to buy some VidCon tickets?

So yeah, I'd say we exceeded expectations.

"You need to be mindful of what you put out there, and how it's affecting the people you involve," Dr. Gardiner continued. "Your sisters, Charlotte Lu . . . even the people you talk about but we don't see. You're not dealing in theoreticals anymore. These are real people. There will be consequences—some good, some not so good—for having their lives exposed via your lens."

"But you just said that when I talked about something real— my family's money problems—it gave the videos depth and resonance."

"True. You still need to be honest. But you also have to figure out how far the contract you have with your audience extends." She smiled at me. "It's a fine line to walk, and it's one you're going to have to figure out."

I thanked Dr. Gardiner, and wished her a happy summer before I left.

On my drive home, I thought about what Dr. Gardiner had said. And she's right. What I do and say on the videos has affected me, and the people around me. For people like Jane and Lydia, it means some notoriety—but I would never put anything involving them on the videos that they didn't want seen. And Lydia especially doesn't seem to mind the notoriety. In fact, she's thriving on it. She has gotten so many Twitter followers since I started these videos. Hell, since the video that she posted ON HER OWN this morning with Charlotte (and you'd better believe I'm gonna have a talk with both of them about that later) even Lydia's new cat, Kitty, is getting a record number of Twitter followers.

It's a little surreal.

For myself, it's startling to realize that my professor has been continuing to watch my videos and will know everything about my life in the upcoming year. Everything. As well as all my classmates—it's sobering to walk into a classroom and realize everyone there has seen you in your pajamas because you wore them on camera. And there are a lot of faceless other people who know my business, too. That's part of having a message people engage with.

But those faceless people have been so supportive. The feedback, the commentary, has been immensely gratifying. It's like being told that yes, maybe I am cut out for this industry. Maybe my voice does matter in the grand scheme of things.

I have a lot of ambitions and dreams for what I want to do with my life: I want to be able to effect change. To make at least my small corner of the world better in some way. To inspire and be inspired. (I would also like to find a way to get paid for it.) It may seem silly and grandiose, and not at all the practical thinking that my generation is told we need to overcome our lack of job opportunities and our belief in our specialness. But it's how I think. And every time people online contact me and say they like my videos and it makes them feel not alone, I feel kind of like I'm doing it.

So, I *do* have a contract with my audience, and well-meaning warnings aside, I do have to honor it.

I have to be as real and open as possible with them. And hopefully, they'll continue to watch.

TUESDAY, JUNE 19TH

One of the more enjoyable aspects of being on summer vacation is my lack of schedule. Oh, trust me, I'm still doing a lot of work, but I'm not beholden to a rigid class structure. Instead, my only parameters for when I get work done are the hours the library is open. Thus I can indulge in the occasional sleeping in, linger over a cup of coffee in the morning . . . and I can get the mail.

I *love* getting the mail. It's a personal quirk. It's so much more satisfying than checking my email in-box, because I have to wait. The postman has to bring messages to me. Could it be a missive from a friend or relative? A check that will solve all my problems?

No. Usually it's just bills and catalogues—but I have hope for a real piece of mail in my lifetime!

And today I was rewarded for my efforts, because today came a letter . . . on pressed paper. With a Netherfield return address.

"Lydia," I said, upon quietly entering her room. All right, perhaps I barged in and forced her out of bed. "Is this what I think it is?"

Blearily, she took the envelope from me. When she read the return address, she smirked and ripped it open.

"Lydia!"

"What? It's addressed to the Bennet Sisters. I'm a Bennet sister, too." She scanned the card. "Formal invitation, very nice. This is gonna be swank."

"I can't believe that you got Bing to actually throw a party, for no reason other than you asked him to."

"Hey, there are benefits to extracting promises from people when they're buzzed, and then stalking their street until they get home and you can casually run into them and demand they fulfill said promises."

It's hard to argue with that logic.

"Still—let's not tell Mom," I said. "For a little while at least. The less time she knows about the party, the less time she has to scheme."

She shrugged, handing the card back to me and then springing out of bed like a chipmunk on a sugar high. "Whatever. Oh! But I get to tell Jane!" She turned contemplative. "I wonder what I'll have Jane wear?"

"What you'll *have* Jane wear?" I asked. "She's pretty good at picking out her own clothes."

"For like, work, and looking classy or whatever. At this party . . . Jane is gonna step up her sexy game."

"She is?"

"Once *I* get through with her." Lydia winked and was out the door. I could hear her humming dubstep under her breath on her way to the bathroom.

I'm not worried about Jane's wardrobe. She is far better at controlling/indulging Lydia than the rest of us—even our parents. She'll wear only what she wants to. But I have to admit, I am sort of dreading the party.

Jane and Bing are rolling along merrily, but that can be a little . . . exclusive. They can be in their own little bubble. And I'm sure that the party will be great, but with George Wickham out of town, it's not like there is anyone that I'm looking forward to seeing. Add to that, I don't know what I'll have to contribute to any conversation. Let's face it, Bing—while great and open—and his friends attract a certain type of person. The rich and driven kind. Who's likely to be at this party? Not just locals like me. Med school friends, maybe. Prep school and Harvard chums. Wealthy family friends. Caroline's elite crowd. Darcy.

What do you talk about at a party when school's out for summer, and you have no job and an uncertain future? It's a recipe for awkward.

But awkward or not, when an invitation arrives on embossed card stock, you can't ignore it. I'm enough of my mother's daughter to know that.

We're going to VidCon! Charlotte made it happen. Somehow she contacted them, pointed them to our videos and views, and they sent us tickets!

But it's not just us going. They also sent Jane a ticket—and Lydia, too.

Jane's happy to go—she's happy to meet people who like the videos, and she's going to meet with her work's LA-based flagship branch, just to see the place and come face-to-face with some of the people she talks on the phone with all day long.

Lydia is also happy to meet people who like the videos . . . and to see if she can get said people to buy her drinks during the convention.

I'm not speaking on a panel or anything (what would I talk about, anyway? How to leverage your mother's insanity for tens of dollars and the occasional gif-set?), but I'm going to try to learn as much as I can (half of the programming is for people who want to make videos, not just watch them) and hopefully meet some cool people.

"We should bring some business-type clothes, too," Charlotte said, raiding my closet and pulling out my sole suit jacket. "We need to be presentable."

"Presentable? We're not street urchins."

"This is not only an opportunity to learn—it's going to be an opportunity to network. There will be dozens of new media companies there. And in another year we are going to be looking for jobs. Probably at these very same new media companies." She pulled out a jean jacket I haven't worn since seventh grade. "What about this?"

"No. Jane would kill me."

"Oh? Jane's survived your mother with enough strength left over to kill you?"

"Barely." I snorted.

Bing's party went off without a hitch. And it was actually more pleasant than I expected. I shouldn't have worried—of course Bing's friends are as nice as Bing himself (with a certain notable exception), and nobody wants to talk about their real lives, anyway; we'd much rather talk about music and art and the latest Internet meme. So, obviously my bout of nervousness was just a momentary lapse into hereditary drama.

The *real* drama was the fact that Jane didn't come home with us. She didn't come home until the next morning.

And Mom was *livid*.

Not because Jane didn't come home until morning—but because Jane came home at all.

What did she expect? That a date that lasts until dawn is an unequivocal proposal of marriage? I'm half shocked that Mom didn't have Jane's belongings already packed up and in the trunk to take over to Netherfield.

But when Jane came home, after being told that she was neither engaged, pregnant, nor cohabitating, Mom just tightened her lips and went into the kitchen, unwilling to look at or even talk to her daughter. She just changed the subject by vaguely commenting that the cabinetry was looking outdated.

What Mom didn't seem to notice is that Jane came home . . . different.

She was lighter, somehow. Glowing. And no, it wasn't a glow that comes from sex. Because according to her she didn't have sex:

> Stayed up all night with Bing.
> Just talked. It was so perfect.
> Having breakfast with him.
> Talk later.

But it was more like all the little steps that she had been taking with Bing—the tentative getting-to-know-you, getting-to-like-you dance—had led up to this. She was no longer slowly falling. It had happened. She was there.

I could hear Jane through our shared bedroom wall. She was on the phone with Bing, telling him about what she was packing for VidCon. She was laughing, her voice itself smiling. Whatever happened that night deepened everything. For Jane, at least. One assumes for Bing, too.

Oh, my God. I think I witnessed my sister fall in love.

Strangely, I can't help but feel a little . . . sad. I don't know why, though. Jane's in love! Jane's happy! That's a fantastic thing! But it also means change is coming. Jane doesn't belong to just us anymore.

But I couldn't be sad at that moment. Because I was picking out panels I wanted to attend from the VidCon schedule on my laptop, and Charlotte was picking a truly hideous peacock-blue pantsuit my mother got me upon college graduation out of my closet. (Because every proper young lady needs a peacock-blue pantsuit for "interviews, dear. We want you to look your best for those—especially if the interviewer is a handsome, successful man.")

"No!" I said, horrified. "Not unless you want potential networking opportunities to think I time-traveled here from the seventies."

"Hey—as long as potential networking opportunities remember you." Charlotte grinned, throwing the pantsuit on the pile.

"You're as bad as my mother."

"I can live with that."

I laughed. See? It's hard to be sad when this time tomorrow . . . we'll be at VidCon!

SATURDAY, JUNE 30TH

Vidcon was Amazing! And yes, that capital "A" is intentional.

I learned so much. I met people—people!—who watch my videos. I saw Driftless Pony Club perform and laughed my ass off while Hannah Hart spoke.

I MET HANK GREEN.

And it wasn't all just fun and games and fangirling over You-Tube vloggers and buying awesome not-ironic-therefore-ironic T-shirts from the exhibit hall. As per Charlotte, we did actually "attend some educational panels and participate in networking events." The industry panels were all about how to grow and sustain an audience—how to best use the tools available to us (seems like everyone is working on a shoestring on the Internet) and how to market most effectively. We learned about the future of storytelling from Loose-Fishery, the biggest transmedia company around, and saw another talk about multi communication platforms from a designer at an app company called Pemberley Digital. And I know to the layperson (aka Lydia, who camped out in the hallway and set up her own mini autograph-signing station until the event organizers told her to stop) it seems boring, but I was deeply intrigued. And Charlotte? Charlotte was *fascinated*.

Aside from the awesome weirdness of meeting people who watch my videos in real life—and *like* them—we met several people who run their own companies, who were enthusiastic about talking to us about what we were doing and how we did it. We collected business cards out the wazoo. ("Wazoo" is the technical term.) Charlotte even arranged for us to take a tour of the You-Tube offices in Los Angeles on the way back home.

I am so, so lucky to be a part of this ridiculously weird and wonderful community.

But not every encounter was full of enthusiasm and learning experiences. There was one particular out-of-the-blue moment that was not wonderful—just plain weird.

After all, it's not every day your second-grade husband comes up to you while you're filming and demands that you call him "Mr. Collins."

That's right, Ricky Collins, the spastic kid who played the Wizard of Floss in our elementary school play about hygiene and managed to fall off the stage, has decided to become a web video content creator. Oh, and he tricked someone into giving him money for it. Although, from what I could gather, he doesn't know much about web video—but it's okay, he likely has "people" for that. People who call him Mr. Collins.

Also, he seems to have developed a fondness for multisyllabic words. I guess that's what comes from losing the school spelling bee at an impressionable age to the ever-impressive Charlotte Lu. And he was rather overdressed for the conference. Web video is more of a blazer-over-jeans-and-graphic-T-shirt crowd, not a Men's-Wearhouse-oversized-suit type place. (Although there's a man who would appreciate a peacock-blue pantsuit on a woman. Too bad he's engaged.)

I was so taken aback by him, I sort of brushed him off. Charlotte says I should have been nicer. More open and politically conscientious. After all, he's a man with investors and a company in our field. But it's kind of hard when the annoying kid who grew up down the street from you is tumbling into your videos and demanding that you address him like he's lord of the manor.

But enough about Ricky Collins. I doubt our paths are destined to cross much in the future. That's what Facebook was invented for—to keep people you don't care to remember at a polite distance.

For now, we are headed home . . . except we don't have a home to go to.

Not kidding.

When Jane got back from her perfect night with Bing and Mom "decided" that the kitchen cabinets were out of date, she was apparently inspired to have the entire kitchen redone. She justifies it by saying it will raise the value of the house—which makes me nervous that my parents really are thinking about selling the house—but I know her reasoning is deeper. More twisted and devious.

She is using this remodel to kick us all out . . . and cleverly deduced that upon hearing our predicament, Bing would offer Jane a place to stay.

So for the next two weeks, Bing and Jane will be cohabitating, ostensibly to save her the double commute from cousin Mary's house an hour south. But we all know the real motive. And I'm happy to do my little part to thwart it.

What Mom didn't count on is that when Jane asked, Bing was happy to extend me an invitation to stay at Netherfield as well.

So, instead of being squished up in Mary and Aunt Martha's two bedroom bungalow with my parents, Lydia, and her cat, I will be enjoying my own en-suite bathroom while playing chaperone to the lovebirds.

I can't wait to see Mom's face when we tell her.

But now, instead of going home and relaxing after these crazy, exhausting, oh-my-God-I-haven't-walked-that-much-in-years past few days, we get to go home and spend the next week moving everything out of the kitchen and packing up the house.

Thank goodness we already filmed next week's videos here at VidCon.

. . . Oh, no. How am I going to film my videos when I'm a guest at Netherfield?

MONDAY, JULY 9TH

Oh, my God. Jane just prevented a heart attack—I thought I had lost you! My diary! My precious. I thought that somehow in all the packing (and seriously, the way Mom made us pack up the house, you would think we were going on a six-month safari, not spending two weeks inconveniencing friends and relatives within driving distance of our home), my darling diary got lost in the shuffle. I was certain that my poor little book, with all its secrets, had been accidentally left behind and was going to land in the hands of one of the construction workers who would read and then ridicule me privately forever. Or worse—it *had* gotten packed, and ended up in the wrong hands here.

When we arrived at Netherfield on Saturday (although the work on our house wouldn't start until today, Mom wanted us—read: Jane—to have the time to get "settled in" at our home-away-from-home), Bing, Darcy, and Caroline met us at the door.

"Hi," Jane said to Bing, smiling.

"Hi," Bing said to Jane, smiling right back. This could have gone on for hours had someone not judiciously cleared her throat.

"Er, we're so glad you're here," Bing said, coming out of his love haze. "Let me show you guys to your rooms. Oh, you can leave your bags—they'll be taken care of."

"Oh—no, we couldn't . . ." But everyone was already moving inside without me.

I didn't think at the time about my diary, possibly stuffed in a suitcase. I only marveled at the idea that somewhere, hidden in the background of this echo-y McMansion, there was someone whose job it was going to be to carry and unpack our things, like we were visiting aristocrats to Buckingham Palace. So really, I was thinking about how embarrassing it was that I had basically thrown my laundry basket into my bag and I was going to have to ask this no-named someone to not do my laundry, but instead let me do it myself. And then have that person show me where the laundry room was.

Netherfield is gorgeous; I'm sure I don't need to elaborate. We spent the morning by the pool, enjoying a late Saturday brunch buffet and the company of Bing. Caroline was very polite and welcoming, too. Darcy was . . . there.

When Jane and I were finally led back to our *own private wing* of the house (technically not specifically built with us in mind, but instead the generic guest wing, but come on!), it was to find that our stuff had indeed been unpacked and my laundry had indeed been taken away to be cleaned (talk about a hostile laundry takeover—I surrendered before I knew there had been a war). But going through my other things, I knew something else was missing. And then I realized it was my diary.

Panic set in. I've never really been without my journal, my means to express my most private feelings and keep safe. My videos—that's something put out there for public consumption. That has a filter. My journal is everything else.

My brain briefly went to the construction worker, and I snuck back to the house this morning to see if I could find it—but the house was a disaster, and I couldn't even get in the door without a hard hat, what with all the things being torn out and moved in.

It was while I was at the library this morning researching that I remembered the nameless, faceless someone that unpacked our bags. And then I thought about my darling diary, somewhere in the bowels of Netherfield, making its way back to the wrong bedroom . . . landing in Bing's hands . . . or landing in *Darcy's*.

I didn't get much work done after that.

So I came back to Netherfield and started tearing my room apart. This is where Jane saved me.

"What are you doing?" she asked, coming to the door, looking flushed and lovely after a hard day at the office ("flushed" is really as disheveled/tired/cranky as Jane Bennet ever gets).

"I can't find my diary," I said. "I know I packed it. At least I think I did."

"You did. Or rather, you gave it to me to pack, remember?"

My head came up. "I did?"

"You did." She smiled, and beckoned for me to follow her to her room. "You needed more room for your camera and stuff in your own bag, so I took your books in mine."

Ah, yes, my camera equipment. School lent it to me for the summer. But in case anyone here ever happens to see it (read: Bing or Darcy), Charlotte and I came up with a cover story—I'm going to say that I'm sending video letters to Charlotte, as an experiment for one of our communications classes. Because that's totally a thing that schools give credit for these days.

Jane went to the little desk in her room and picked up a shoulder bag, and rifled through. "Including one red Moleskine journal."

And now, you are in my hands, and I feel normal again.

Can you imagine if someone had read it? It's hard enough trying to be private here—for such a large house it feels awfully crowded. Mostly since Bing is being so polite and welcoming and trying to make us feel at home that you can't help but *not* feel at home. But if someone had found my diary, and read all my deepest thoughts and feelings about my family? About my future? It would be like exposing a wound.

I mean, I'm still reeling from the implications of Caroline knowing about my videos.

Yes. That's the big news.

I was making a video yesterday, and she came in and totally called me out on my "Letter to Charlotte" ruse. Apparently, unlike anyone else in this house, Caroline knows how to use Google, and she found the videos a while ago and has been watching.

The good:

1. She hasn't told Bing about them. (Thank God.)
2. She hasn't told Darcy about them. (THANK GOD.)
3. She wasn't weirded out by the Bing/Jane-heavy focus and speculation the videos have taken thus far.

The not so good:

1. I don't know if there is a downside to this. Caroline, who could have been very angry and rightfully so, was remarkably cool about the whole thing. She came on camera, wanting to be in the video—even going along with my opinions about Darcy. She told me that "even though he's my friend, sometimes you just want to shake him."
2. However, I am a little uneasy. After all, this is the first time someone who's been talked about on the videos has known about the videos. And I'm not exactly known for my niceness. But then again, neither is Caroline. And she took it in stride.
3. And I guess that's what's bothering me most about this. Caroline has always seemed rather stuck-up to me, in a "fake-smile" kind of way. But she's been great about having us stay with them, and she's totally fine with my project. Could it be I misjudged her the same way that I misjudged Bing? (Next, you'll be telling me that I misjudged Darcy, too—which, no. That one I see clear as day.)

Maybe I did misjudge Caroline. But that can only be a good thing, because my initial opinion wasn't very nice. And it's actually a little bit of a relief to have Caroline know. It'll make the two weeks we are here at Netherfield a lot more comfortable.

Friday, July 13th

So, this is life at Netherfield:

I get up early, because sleep has never been better on 3,000-thread-count Egyptian cotton sheets.

I go down to the breakfast room (yes, it has its own room) to find a buffet already arranged with piping-hot coffee (and lattes!) and every iteration of egg and bacon known and yet to be discovered.

I am not-so-secretly glad to be the first one down, because it means I might be able to slip out of the house to the library without having to go through the rigmarole of being asked how I slept four different times by four different people. Plus, I like to read the news on my phone while enjoying a mocha latte. I am the twenty-first-century version of my father.

I am only seventeen seconds into my news reading of the morning when my solitude is interrupted by Netherfield's other early riser, who apparently has been in the house gym, judging by his for once not overly fussy attire—Darcy.

If he is startled to see me, he doesn't show it. In an effort toward good manners, and an acknowledgment of our forced cohabitation, I greet him.

"Good morning," I say.

"Good morning," he replies. After an awkward moment, he continues. "Did you sleep well?"

"Very much so," I reply. "And yourself?"

"Yes." He nods. Then, after another moment of staring, as if he can't comprehend that I have the gall to exist, he grabs a cup of coffee and leaves the room.

I read a bit about world news and then about celebrities and their Twitter habits, finishing my latte. I then grab my bag and head out to the library, just missing the sleepy yet bright-eyed happiness of Jane and Bing greeting each other in the breakfast room.

Study. Tutor. Study.

I come home to an already prepared evening of entertainment, be it a movie in their private theater, a five-star meal prepared by their personal chef, or a beta test of the next generation of a video game that won't be out for another year. (I don't know how Darcy got that. Or why. Caroline says it must be for work, but to my mind, Darcy doesn't do much but work on spreadsheets on his computer while the rest of us are having a relative amount of fun. Which means I was wrong about him being a trust-funder with no responsibilities, when really, he's a stuffy, boring workaholic with no personality.)

I go to bed. On a new set of Egyptian cotton sheets, because God forbid I sleep on the same set two nights in a row.

Try not to notice when Bing sneaks into my sister's bedroom in the middle of the night, and you can hear her giggling.

Repeat five times, so far.

I don't mean to complain—after all, this is WAY better than living with Mom, Dad, and Lydia at Aunt Martha and cousin Mary's—but I'm definitely the third wheel on the Bing and Jane Shack Up tour. Caroline and Darcy are extra wheels, too, but they at least were here already. They had squatter's rights.

So I escape as much as I can. Most of the time to the library, either to tutor or work on documenting my videos for my thesis (again, I am glad for my prolific writing habits—this journal will very much come in handy). But I've been kind of lonely, because unfortunately Charlotte's summer of double shifts in the edit bays and admin offices has already begun, and she's working harder than ever. In fact, this afternoon was the first time she managed to get away long enough for us to catch up over coffee.

"Oh, my God, I miss you!" I cried, upon seeing my dear Charlotte enter the café. I hugged my bestie to me, unwilling to let go.

"I missed you, too," Charlotte gasped. "But now I miss breathing."

I let her go.

"So how are you?" I asked. "Tell me everything."

It's strange, but Charlotte and I have never had to fill each other in on our lives before. Even though we hadn't seen each other in a week, we've still been texting and tweeting, and she's been editing my videos. But that's not the same as talking about things in person, or more likely, experiencing them together in real time.

She told me all about work and her little sister (who's been losing it over the latest *Doctor Who* news and makes me wish my little sister were a bit more like Maria—how do you solve a problem like Lydia?), and I filled her in on Netherfield.

"Everything's fine. Bing is great—"

"Of course."

"And even Caroline is being really nice."

"Uh-huh," Charlotte said, unable to hide her inherent skepticism. "If you say so."

"Hey, you saw Monday's video." She'd edited it, after all.

"True. And she was very understanding about the videos."

"Then what's the problem?"

"I don't know." Charlotte shrugged. "I just think Caroline always has a reason for doing things. Including being nice."

"Well, maybe her reason is that Jane and Bing are getting serious," I offered, giving Caroline the benefit of the doubt that I, admittedly hadn't given her before. "And she wants him to be happy. You should see the way they are together—Jane has the tiniest cold and Bing just wants to wrap her up in cashmere and feed her soup until she gets better."

"Oh, I did see," Charlotte replied. "After all, you caught them on camera."

I had. The video I posted yesterday included one Mr. Bing Lee. Jane was filming an actual video letter to Charlotte—and not just using that as an excuse in case someone interrupted. Lo and behold, Bing Lee did interrupt! They were unbearably cute together, on camera, for about three minutes.

So, unbeknownst to both of them, I posted it.

"And Bing really doesn't know?" Charlotte asked.

"No clue," I said, grinning. But Charlotte's face was a bit more studious. "Well, how could I not?" I justified. "We've been talking about Bing on the videos for so long . . . In the comments everyone kept asking to see him!" And oddly, they also had a fascination with seeing Darcy. Although that will never happen.

"I don't fault you for it," Charlotte said eventually. "It *was* too good to deny. The response was awesome, so ethical lines be damned!"

Wait, what?

"Ethical lines?" I asked.

"About showing someone on your videos who has no idea they exist. Or that his love life is fodder for thousands."

Huh. I didn't really think of it like that. I just thought that Bing and Jane together were too cute to pass up.

And then I began to get that feeling in the pit of my stomach. The one that crops up when perhaps you've done something wrong and only now realized it. Like you cut someone off while driving but didn't see him. Or you egregiously violated someone's privacy.

"So, are we ordering?" Charlotte asked. "I have twenty minutes before my next edit bay shift and I need to caffeinate."

As Charlotte flagged down a barista, I couldn't stop one single phrase from rolling over and over in my head. *Oh, crap—what have I done?*

I cannot wait to get out of here. Not that I don't like it here—it's impossible to dislike any place that has poolside margaritas nightly and a masseuse visit biweekly. But Jane and I have been here almost two weeks now, and I jump every time my phone dings, thinking that it's going to be my parents letting us know that the house is done and it's time to come home.

My antsy-ness to leave is not predicated on my ethical quandary of putting Bing's adorableness online, thankfully. Caroline actually made me feel a lot better about it, because she says he knew the camera was on, thanks to the "sending Char video letters" ruse, and that if he was okay with Charlotte seeing the video, it was already meant for semi-public consumption.

Plus, Bing seems to be fairly blissfully oblivious to most non-Jane things, anyway.

I'm still a little wary, but I also have to think about my audience, and the honesty of my video project. And if nothing else, it'll make an interesting point for analysis in my thesis.

And I'm not antsy because I miss my family. How can I possibly miss my family when Mom calls me every day asking for updates on Jane and Bing (right, like I'm going to tell her about running into Jane coming out of Bing's room in her PJs yesterday morning) and Lydia's making videos of her own?

That's right. Lydia is making videos. What kind of monster have I created?

Actually, they're not too bad. I've watched a couple. They're . . . cute. I guess. Lydia seems to be mostly torturing cousin Mary, exploiting the Internet's love of cats, and being her hyper,

Adderall-fueled self. It's fun, but silly. Like glittery vaudeville. Not exactly substantive.

No, my antsy-ness can rest squarely where it usually does, on the scarf-clad shoulders of one William Darcy.

But now, it has reached new levels.

Because last night, Darcy introduced us to his List.

We had all gathered in the "family room" as per usual, but had sort of split off into doing our own things. Bing and Caroline were trying to teach Jane to play Apples to Apples, but she never wanted to insult anyone by possibly not choosing their card, so it mostly devolved into fits of laughter.

"This game needs more players." Caroline sighed. "Darcy?"

But Darcy just tucked his chin back farther and kept his eyes on his computer. As previously mentioned, Darcy is not one to take part in anything involving fun, so he had drifted away back to his spreadsheets and his artfully arranged hipster scarf.

Yes, he was wearing a scarf. In July. In California. Inside.

"Lizzie?" Caroline turned to me. "Why don't you join us? Oh, but you don't like games like this, do you? You more into video games?"

"I like games of all sorts," I said, and held up my book. "But unfortunately, I have to get through this."

"*Anna Karenina?*" Jane said. "Lizzie, you've read that book a dozen times."

"I know, but I have a tutoring student, so I need to brush up for her."

I think the biggest indication that we live in an extremely competitive culture is that the students who seek out tutoring are often not looking to catch up, but instead are looking for an edge over everyone else. Such is the case with most of the kids I tutor. The aforementioned student is actually going into AP Lit in the fall, and in our school district, AP Lit means Tolstoy. So instead of spending her summer at the beach and having a social life, she's spending it in the library with me, trying to be first in her class.

"They're reading Tolstoy in high school now." Bing shook his head. "Man, everyone has to be so accomplished these days. It must be exhausting."

I find myself smiling, thinking of my student. "Girls especially."

"Oh, girls will always have a leg up on guys when it comes to having their act together." Bing held up his hands. "You'll get no argument from me."

"I don't know that many women who have their act together," Caroline argued. "Really, we're few and far between."

"What are you talking about?" Bing argued. "Every woman I've met around here has it together. Darcy—back me up."

Darcy's head didn't even come up from his computer. "I'm afraid I have to side with Caroline on this one."

Caroline preened. "See, I told you."

"Come on. The women around here have grace and style," Bing said. He did glance at Jane then, and I watched her blush. "They're funny, and kind, and can balance a checkbook. What more do you want?"

"And that's the problem. The bar is set too low. Some women are considered together if they know how to tip a waiter and go to the gym twice a week. I doubt there are half a dozen women I know who actually have their lives together," Darcy said.

I can feel my blood starting to boil just remembering him saying that.

"Then you must have a very strong opinion of what constitutes someone who is together."

He looked at me directly then.

"I do."

"Oh," Caroline said, not noticing the stare-off between us. "Like what, Darcy?"

And then he proceeded to reel off his List.

"Someone who is together is someone who is fiscally responsible . . . and interested in arts and culture beyond the standard Hollywood movies or pop music. Someone who is physically fit, and takes care of herself. And also takes care of others by being courteous, and has a charitable nature.

"But she should be selective of who she spends her time with. Education is important, so she should at least have or be pursuing an advanced college degree, and fluency in more than one language is so important in this day and age. As is being up to date on current affairs, and I'm not talking about who did what on whatever reality show seems to have gripped the nation at the moment. That is not a talent anyone need pursue." He paused, seeming to consider a moment. "Oh, and she should be well read, especially in the classics."

I don't know which was more amazing—the fact that Darcy said that many words to me at once, or the fact that he obviously meant it.

You hear about guys who have prerequisites. You read articles about them putting those requirements up on their online dating profile and then being shocked when they get no dates . . . and you laugh and laugh at their boy rage. But I've never actually met a guy who has such a list. Or at least, I've never met someone willing to admit it.

"You said that you know six women that fit these standards?" I asked bluntly.

"I said I doubt I know as many as six."

"I can't imagine you know any."

"I do!" Caroline piped up. "There's Gigi, Darcy's sister—"

"There is no woman in the world who meets every requirement on that list. In fact," my eyes fell to my book, "the only one I can think of is Anna Karenina. And she's fictional."

"Anna Karenina?" Darcy asked, skeptical.

"Tolstoy wrote the perfect woman. Elegant, refined, socially savvy. She was, in fact, *your* perfect woman. Until she dared to be herself."

"And that didn't go so well for her, did it?"

I felt the corners of my mouth tighten. "No. But I like to think that women don't live and die by what people think of them anymore."

Before Darcy could respond, Caroline broke in, her voice overbright.

"Ugh, this is so boring. Bing, deal out another round—or better yet, who wants a cocktail? I have a great organic juice Daquiri recipe!"

Darcy seemed happy to go back to his computer, and I was happy to drop the subject. But that didn't mean I got any reading done.

I couldn't help running the list over in my head. Trying to imagine the person that would pass muster. It sure isn't me. Honestly, I think I hit three—maybe—out of all eleven requirements.

I am pursuing an advanced degree, and I do read a lot. When it comes to languages, I'm passably fluent in HTML. But everything else . . .

Jane's the charitable, courteous one. I have too short a temper, am too quick to bring the snark.

As for exercise, I haven't played tennis in years.

My student loan situation speaks to my fiscal responsibility.

While not a fan of most reality TV, *Top Chef* rules.

And you know what? I occasionally like going to see the latest cheesy blockbuster with a big bucket of popcorn. So sue me!

Darcy's list is preposterous. Unachievable by human standards—male or female. Though apparently he was raised to expect no less than Wonder Woman as his potential life mate.

But the scary thing is he'll probably end up with a reasonable facsimile. There is a bubble of delusional privilege that people like Darcy live in, so he's likely to find someone who wants the status he has to offer so much, she'll bend herself into a pretzel trying to hit every check box on his List.

That's what his money will buy him. Someone perfect, but empty.

All last night did was solidify my opinion of Darcy, and make me glad that our two weeks of house-guesting will be up any minute.

I cannot wait to get out of here.

Saturday, July 21st

We're still here.

The remodel has been extended. According to Mom, and every single home repair show I've ever watched, this is normal. It always takes longer than the time quoted by the contractor.

But I can't help but be frustrated by the fact that we are *still here*. We still have to wear a bra under our pajamas when we leave our rooms. We still are not allowed to pour ourselves a bowl of raisin bran for breakfast on the way out the door, lest the chef think we don't prefer his morning quinoa-and-cranberries mix. And we are still forced into group activities, to foster . . . I don't know. A higher tolerance for a certain douchebag?

Don't get me wrong, Bing and Caroline have been great, but there is only so long a person can be on her absolute best behavior without psychosis setting in.

I've resolved to spend as little time as possible at Netherfield, and for the past two days, I certainly managed it. I have my comfy chair in the library for thesis work and tutoring students. I roped Charlotte into yet another twenty minutes of coffee and catch-up. And I even went to the movies by myself, enjoying a vat of popcorn and gratuitous explosions (followed by a British costume-drama palate cleanser).

But weekends are harder. I do occasionally need a day to recharge my brain. Plus, Jane has weekends off, and she wants me to join in with everyone at Netherfield—and it's hard to say no to her.

But of course, on weekends, Darcy doesn't have anyplace to go, either.

Today, we enjoyed a nice, lazy afternoon. I was in the family room helping Jane put together a care package for Lydia. Everyone was there. Caroline was idly reading her iPad, while Bing was ostensibly trying to find a college football game on TV, but really he was too invested in seeing what Jane was putting in the care package to channel-surf. I had been put in charge of curling ribbon. Jane knows my visual/craft talents are limited, and that I'm best left to basic manual labor.

how to curl ribbon:

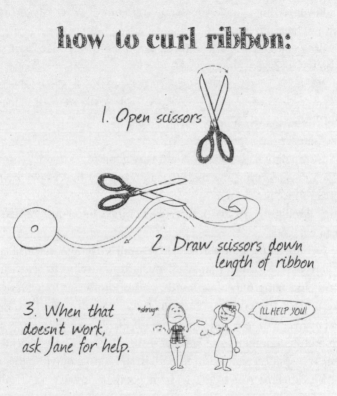

1. Open scissors

2. Draw scissors down length of ribbon

3. When that doesn't work, ask Jane for help.

shrug

I'LL HELP YOU!

Darcy of course was in the farthest possible corner of the room, click-clacking away on his laptop, as per usual.

"That is a lot of glittery unicorn stickers," Bing said, seeing the piles of sticker books going into the care package.

"Yes, but I couldn't resist. They are all so Lydia." Jane wrinkled her nose as she put them in the box, along with a few lipsticks and a bell toy for Kitty. "I miss my little sister."

I met Jane's eyes. I do, too, I suppose. There has been a certain amount of boy-crazy hyperactivity and chaos missing from my life the past couple of weeks.

"Speaking of little sisters," Caroline jumped up, carrying her iPad over to Bing, "have you seen Gigi's new Twitter background? I know she did it herself."

Bing glanced at it and showed it to Jane. "Very nice," she said. "She has a good eye for colors."

"Good eye?" Caroline scoffed. "Gigi Darcy is *soooo* talented." She marched over to Darcy, on the far side of the room, and leaned over his keyboard and typed in the URL.

"See? I'm in *raptures* over it."

Darcy sighed. "I've seen it. It's very good."

"Are you writing an email to Gigi? Tell her that I love the new background. It's so cute!"

"I'll tell her to call you. I'm sure I couldn't do your enthusiasm justice."

I'm still a little clueless about Caroline's friendship with Darcy. When she's with him, she's all over him—trying to get him to come and hang out, play games, compliment her hair (which is like a black silk curtain—how do I get my hair to do that?). But when she's with me, and especially on the videos, she's more than happy to encourage my Darcy-bashing. It's as if she won't let me keep my opinion about him to myself; she wants everyone to know.

Maybe she's just trying to be a good hostess to her brother's friend? And expressing her frustration with him when she's with me?

But at that moment, she was draped on his chair's arm, trying to get him to engage with the group. Which he seemed bound and determined to not do.

"That sister of yours is going to do something amazing." Caroline gasped. "Like . . . oh! Maybe she'll create her own handbag line! You should suggest that to her."

"I don't know if my sister has much interest in handbags. I think that suggestion might be better coming from you."

He went back to typing.

"You are so dedicated to your business. I can't seem to focus when I'm out of the office."

"Good thing you don't have my job, then."

More typing.

"Good Lord, you type fast!" Caroline remarked.

"On the contrary. I type slow, comparatively."

"Oh?" she smiled at him. "Comparative to what?"

"People who don't think about what they say. They just send it off in a rush."

Bing barked out a laugh. "Don't get offended, Caroline. That one was directed at me. Darcy keeps sending me back my own emails with my typos fixed. Put the laptop away, man. No one else is working. It's weird."

"That was why I was working in my room, until you insisted I come down here. The only strange thing is you thought it wouldn't be weird," Darcy said.

"I thought you could use a break."

"You thought wrong." Darcy went back to his computer for a moment; then his head came up again. "And as for your typos—you're going to be a doctor, Bing. Being clear is important."

"It's true." Bing smiled, and winked at Jane. "There aren't that many letters difference between 'Advair' and 'Advil.'"

Jane giggled. And I have to admit, I did, too. Whatever criticism Darcy whips out, it just rolls off of Bing.

But Darcy remained stern. "It's not just that. You could be less . . . effusive."

"It's true." Caroline sighed. "My brother has always said whatever he's thinking at the moment, no filter whatsoever."

"And I don't consider it a bad thing," Bing replied.

"Neither do I," Jane added sweetly.

"Of course you don't, Bing—you consider it a mark of pride," Darcy chided. "Every typo and illegible autocorrect is a badge of honor. It means you are thinking so fast you can't be bothered with circumspection. And such a lack of circumspection opens you up to being used."

Used. He didn't have to look at us as he said it, but I knew he was talking about me and Jane, *using* Bing while our house is being remodeled. It was all I could do to not growl under my breath.

"So basically, what you're saying is that Bing is too open and too nice?" Caroline raised an eyebrow.

"That's not possible." Jane squeezed Bing's hand, but she shrunk back a little. This argument was getting a little too combative for her, even though Bing was still smiling.

"There is one person in this room studying communications," Darcy said abruptly. "Perhaps we can ask her which is better." He kept his eyes on his computer. But he had stopped typing.

Everyone else was looking at me. I swallowed. Then I gave my honest opinion. "I think that, of the two, being an open person is certainly better."

Darcy looked up at me. I met him stare for stare.

"Too much restraint in communication is just as bad as none at all. If you're too careful, you can never really say what you mean. Or, mean what you say."

"Thank you, Lizzie," Bing said. "And what I mean to say right now is that I think we should check out that winery we saw on our carpool the other day. Now that Jane's cold is gone we all can go. What do you think?"

Jane smiled at him, much more comfortable with the change

of subject. Caroline was in wholehearted agreement on the winery plan, going on about driving with the convertible top down and plotting what to have the chef make for a picnic. Meanwhile, Darcy held my gaze for another long second, until he returned to his keyboard.

TUESDAY, JULY 24TH

Almost through week three at Casa de Lee, aka Netherfield, and things have only gotten weirder.

Earlier tonight, Caroline asked me to take a turn about the room.

She's gotten this new fitness band that buzzes when she's been sitting for too long. It's supposed to encourage movement and health. Although why Caroline decided to suddenly get physically fit now is beyond me—she's already a macrobiotic goddess.

Anyway, I came into the sitting room (or is it the living room? I remember Bing calling it something else but I don't know what. So many rooms!), and Darcy and Caroline were there. Darcy was on his computer—let's not be shocked—while Caroline was talking to him.

" . . . said open is better, so she obviously wouldn't mind. Your house would be overrun with in-laws," Caroline was saying to a tight-lipped, computer-focused Darcy.

"What are you guys talking about?"

"Oh, Lizzie! Come join us!" Caroline cried, jumping up and waving me over to them.

"Are Jane and Bing not back yet?" I asked. Bing had taken to "giving a ride" to work with Jane in the morning and evening. Except, Bing didn't have a work to go to, so basically, he was driving Jane around. Which gave them some much-needed alone time, and often, they would take the long way home, meandering down country roads and driving to the coast to watch the sunset. I'm going to assume that's not a euphemism, because it's Jane. She really likes a good sunset.

I came and sat beside Caroline.

"So, Lizzie . . ." she said.

"So . . . Caroline."

"How was your day?"

"Good," I replied, dodging a hair flip from her. She seemed to be oddly postured, like she was trying to show herself off to advantage. "I . . . am through *Anna Karenina* with my student. On to *War and Peace*." I was also really pleased with myself because I had finished laying out my rough outline for the framework of my thesis. Although I don't talk much about my thesis in front of anyone here, since there is the chance I would then have to explain it. Which means I would have to tell them about my videos, and that would not end well.

"Good for you, and good for your student!"

"Thanks," I said. "Well, I should go read." Again. Some more.

"Don't let our presence send you away," Darcy droned from behind his computer. "If you wanted to read in here, we would not bother you."

"Right!" Caroline agreed immediately. "Darcy has work to do; so do I. It'll be like a . . . study session."

And with that enticing invitation, I sat down on the couch and proceeded to read.

Darcy returned to typing and ignoring everything else.

Caroline, however, did not settle into her work as easily as we did. Whatever her work may be, I doubt it involved Twitter, which is what I saw on her screen when I glanced over her shoulder.

"Oh, my God, Darcy, you have to see this ugly baby picture our friend posted."

Darcy didn't look up.

Caroline blew out a sigh, meeting my eye with a frustrated smile. I guess Darcy had been getting to her all day.

"Isn't this so much fun?" she asked no one in particular, breaking into the silence again. "I can't imagine a better way to spend my afternoon in this town."

I smiled at her, trying to commiserate, but pretty soon I fell back to reading, the only sound in the room being the clickety-clack of Darcy's keys. (He types with some serious force. He must go through keyboards by the dozen.) Until, of course, Caroline's wristband buzzed.

"Oh!" she said, popping up. "Time to walk!"

She proceeded to walk the length and breadth of the room, in a big, wide circle. It was a little strange, but people have done stranger for physical fitness.

"Lizzie!" Caroline came over to me. "Join me! Come on, it feels good to move after sitting for so long. Let's take a turn about the room."

A slightly odd request, but then again, no one wants to look silly alone. So I figured what the hell, and joined her in another circle of the room.

"I knew it," she whispered to me. "I knew that if we both started walking around, Darcy would have to stop being so rude and look up from his 'duties.'"

I stole a glance at Darcy. Yes, for the first time that evening, he'd brought his eyes up from his computer, and was watching us. In fact, he'd even closed his computer.

"Would you like to join us, Darcy?" Caroline asked sweetly as she passed him.

"No, thank you."

"Why not? It's good for you."

"Because I can see through your deceptive motives, Caroline."

"Deceptive motives?" she gasped. "Me? Lizzie, what is he talking about?"

"I'm sure I don't know," I replied, trying to stay out of it.

"The two of you are either together to banter about secrets, or you know the aimless strolling about the room shows your figures." He laced his fingers over his closed laptop. "If the first, I should be in your way. If the second . . . the view from here will do."

Okay, wait . . . did Darcy just say he was ogling us? I didn't know if I should be insulted, complimented, or shocked . . . I decided to go with shocked. Shocked that he'd closed his computer. Shocked that he said something slightly risqué. Shocked that he was looking at me as he said it.

Apparently I wasn't the only one who was shocked, because Caroline's jaw dropped and she squeaked. "Darcy! How can you say that?!"

"I'm just being honest. Saying what I mean."

Well, I could say what I mean, too.

"It's fairly pompous of you to think that we would display ourselves for your benefit."

"Seriously!" Caroline agreed. (Even though she had sort of admitted to me that had actually been the point.) "We should punish you for that."

I really wish I had just laughed at him. Seriously, his arrogance was so comical, having someone tease him might take him down a peg and make him more bearable. However, that's not what I did.

"Let's not," I said quickly, trying to pull Caroline away. "After all, it would just . . . feed his vanity and pride."

"Do you mean to imply vanity and pride are weaknesses?" Darcy cocked his head to one side, his mouth turning back down into his characteristic frown.

"I'm just being honest."

He seemed to think a moment. "Vanity, while a weakness, is not one of mine."

I opted against pointing out his affinity for the trendy hipster aesthetic typified by newsboy hats and indoor scarves.

"But pride is," I said, giving up the ruse of walking in a circle and standing directly in front of him.

"Pride isn't a weakness. Pride is earned."

"Earned?" I crossed my arms over my chest, not believing what I was hearing.

"One is legitimately allowed to be prideful in his hard work and success."

"And disdainful of those who refuse to meet the same standard?"

He shrugged. "I am more than willing to give people the benefit of the doubt in the beginning, but yes—if they lose my good opinion, it's gone. Lost forever."

"So you're perfect. And have no faults," I said sarcastically. "Except for that darn short temper, which goes with the stuck-upness and pride. So at least you have a matching set."

"I never said anything like that. For someone who prefers openness to restraint in communication, you seem to willfully misunderstand everything I'm saying."

"You can't *willfully* misunderstand. A misunderstanding by its very nature lacks intention—"

"Bing! Jane!" Caroline cried, hearing the front door with her bat-like sonar. "Just in time—we're starving!"

And with that, Caroline grabbed my arm and hustled me out of the room to meet Jane and Bing in the foyer.

"Oh, my God—I can't wait to see your video on this encounter," Caroline gleefully whispered to me, once we were out of the room. But I wasn't really feeling it.

Maybe we've been here too long, maybe my frustration with Darcy has reached a point to which I can either incinerate with rage or let it go, but honestly, that little skirmish was nothing out of the ordinary for him. I know he's a pompous windbag. I know he and I do not get along. These are accepted facts.

Why harp on it further?

Saturday, July 28th

This is getting ridiculous. Having to stay here. But Mom says the contractors keep finding other things that have to be addressed, pushing back the finish date. She sounds pretty upset about it, actually. So instead of being in my own room, comfortable and happy, I get to play the game of Another Saturday, Another Darcy Run-in.

Today's run-in occurred in the rec room. (Not to be confused with the lounge, family room, sitting room, living room, movie theater, or conservatory.) I needed a big-screen TV. As part of my thesis work I want to compare and contrast my videos with those of other vloggers, so I needed to watch some online media on a big screen in order to be able to analyze it properly.

I would have co-opted the TV in the lounge, but Jane and Bing were in there. They would have absolutely welcomed me in, but I didn't want to disturb them. They looked so happy together. A fashion show of some kind was on the screen, Jane had her legs over Bing's lap, and they were giggling over a private joke told at a volume only they could hear.

Bing looked like he was in a bubble of bliss. And Jane . . . Jane looked like she was at home. Like this is where she's meant to be.

I wasn't about to interrupt that scene, so I headed to the rec room, where I found Darcy kneeling by the entertainment console.

"Oh, I'm sorry," I said, and turned to go.

"No, it's fine. I'm done." He stood up. I stayed where I was. There was the obligatory awkward standoff. Finally he broke it by clearing his throat. "Did you need something?"

"Just the television," I said. When he didn't move or, you know, do anything, I explained. "I need to stream something from my computer to the screen. Thesis stuff."

He nodded. "I can help you with that."

"No, that's all right, I can manage—" But before I could say more, he had gotten the hookup for the computer (my computer being too old and feeble to do wireless streaming) and attached it to the correct TV import.

Then he handed it to me.

"Thanks," I mumbled. I plugged in the computer and queued up an innocuous music video, just to make sure the connection was going to work. I was not going to play any video that was even thesis-adjacent in front of him. It could too easily lead to questions about the thesis subject and . . . yeah. Don't want my videos known. (Luckily, most of my videos and related files were not on this laptop, but on a separate hard drive. I know how to keep my business private.)

I hit play. Cheerful pop music filled the room.

"Does it look and sound okay?" he asked.

I nodded. He shuffled his feet and cleared his throat.

"Hey . . . since you're kind of into audiovisual stuff, how do you like these speakers? They have a 270-degree delivery system, providing true stereoscopic sound." His voice became overly boastful. Like he was about to offer proof that he was the be-all and end-all. "I put them in myself."

I tried not to roll my eyes. "The sound quality? Mediocre at best." Which it was. Although that may have had more to do with the fact that I was playing an online video than with the speakers, but whatever little thing I can do to take him down a peg is worthwhile in my book.

"Oh, yeah. Yes." He nodded, unwilling to be criticized. "Have you ever heard a gramophone? It has a really interesting sound. I actually prefer its authenticity and rustic feel to big speakers like these . . . It's more personal."

"If you say so," was all I could manage. I couldn't understand why he was still standing there, watching British boy-band members sing their one hit song to well-lit and overly emotional teenage girls on the screen.

"This song is . . . catchy. I hear it's popular. Good for dancing."

Well, what was I supposed to say to that? So I just nodded and continued watching.

"You like this kind of music, right? That's what Caroline said. Not that we talk about you, but . . ." He blew out a breath, unable to comment any further on what he obviously thought was an atrocity of acoustics. "It's, uh, dance music."

When I didn't answer him, he repeated himself, at a slightly louder volume. "I said, this music — it's really good for dancing. Yes?"

"Oh, I heard you the first time," I said. "But I can't decide how to answer. Either you want me to admit that I enjoy this music, so you can make fun of me for liking it and liking dancing, or you want to see if you can get me to reject something I like so as to not raise your ire."

"That . . . was not my intention."

"Oh, come on. I know you're only saying this so you can make fun of my tastes. I'd rather not give you the pleasure, so go ahead and hate me, anyway. If you dare."

Darcy put his hands in his pockets and looked away. And then he spoke so softly, I didn't think I heard him properly.

"I wouldn't dare hate you."

A throat cleared behind us.

"Hey, Lizzie," Jane said from the doorway, her hand entwined with Bing's. "We just came to see if you wanted to use the TV in the lounge."

"Jane," I hissed, closing my laptop and walking over to her. "How long have you been standing there?"

"Long enough." Bing grinned at me, and Jane gave a conspiratorial eyebrow raise.

Really, between the Jane and Bing super-team and the scheduled Darcy run-ins, I can't wait to go home.

Please, please soon.

MONDAY, JULY 30TH

Apropos of nothing, Jane is acting a little strange. While she's been so happy here at Netherfield (yes, we're still here. Dear God, it will never end. We'll have to move in . . . which means Mom's Convoluted Plan has paid off, and I can never let that happen. It would only encourage her.), she's suddenly a little . . . withdrawn. I only noticed because I am well versed in the Many Moods of Jane Bennet (™ Charlotte), but a big sign was when she asked Bing to let her drive herself to work this morning. The evening sunset drive was cancelled, and he was mopey all day.

I tried to talk to her about it tonight, but she just said she was getting a little homesick. Which certainly didn't seem to be the case even yesterday.

Even though I normally enjoy a good mystery, I think I should give Jane her space with this one. God knows, she could be telling the truth. After all, we all have our breaking points. And it's a testament to Jane's good nature that she lasted so long.

WEDNESDAY, AUGUST 1ST

We are home! We snuck back in! This morning, Jane did a drive-by of the house and ran into the contractor, who told her we could have moved back in a WEEK ago. So Jane and I hightailed it out of Netherfield and back to our newly redone house.

Which looks an awful lot like our previously un-redone house. Seriously, not even the kitchen cabinets, which apparently offended Mom to the point where she engaged upon this scheme, have been changed.

We didn't tell Mom or Dad or Lydia that we were coming home until we called them from the house line, a couple of hours after settling in. Which was a fun conversation.

"LIZZIE, WHAT ON GOD'S GREEN EARTH ARE YOU DOING IN THAT HOUSE?" My mother's voice had reached a pitch only dogs and daughters were capable of hearing.

"We live here, Mom, or have you forgotten?"

"That . . . that house is not finished! It's dangerous for you to be there! You and Jane should just go back to Bing's right now! Tell them you were wrong and the house isn't ready yet—"

"Well, that's going to be difficult, seeing as how we already unpacked."

"Lizzie! You! It's! I . . . !" Mom's sentences devolved into a series of high-pitched squeaks, until I could hear some shuffling, and suddenly Dad was on the line.

"Well, Lizzie, I take it the house is fine?" Dad asked.

"Yup, except for an empty fridge, everything is normal," I replied. "But Jane and I are ordering pizza for dinner."

"Excellent. Pineapple on mine. We'll see you in a few hours."

Before he hung up, I could hear the keening wail of my mother's despair beginning.

"How did it go?" Jane asked as she came out of the bathroom.

"Dad wants pineapple on his pizza. Just be glad we're not Lydia and forced to be in the car with Mom on the drive home." I looked up. Jane was smiling, but she had a watery look in her eyes.

"Jane?" I asked, concerned. "Have you been crying?"

"No," she assured me, waving any wetness away from her eyes. "I'm . . . I'm just glad to be home. Aren't you?"

Considering that if I'd had to take another evening of Darcy staring daggers at me I was going to do something violent, and this way I get to avoid criminal charges? Yes. I am very glad to be home.

But that wasn't the reason for Jane's puffy eyes, nor her sniffles. And when she leaned her head back against the bathroom door, I for once decided to call her on it.

"Jane . . ." I said, approaching with care. "What is it? What's wrong?"

"Nothing's wrong, Lizzie," she replied. "I'm just . . . I'm so relieved."

"About what?"

"I finally got my period."

WEDNESDAY, AUGUST 1ST—AGAIN

It's late at night and the house has finally settled. *I* have finally settled. Because I finally got the chance to talk to Jane.

Of course I wanted to question her immediately after that WHOA statement she made. But unfortunately, she made it right before a knock on the door. Charlotte had seen our cars in the driveway and had pulled a U-turn to see if we were home. And I could have handled it if it were just Charlotte, but she'd had her little sister Maria in tow, who pigeonholed me into a conversation about the latest season of *Doctor Who*. Then the pizza came. Then Mom, Dad, and Lydia came.

Mom of course was not happy to find us in residence, pizza in hand, upon her return, but she also knew the jig was up, and thus gave in to us living in our own house again with only the expected amount of disappointment.

Little did she know.

Then we had to put the house back together. (Half of the kitchen stuff was in our bedrooms. I have no need to be awoken tomorrow morning by my mother searching for her waffle iron.) So after catching up with the family, finding out what kind of havoc Lydia got up to while away—apparently those stickers Jane sent her came in handy—manual labor, and our own unpacking, everyone was saying their good nights by the time I finally got Jane alone again.

"It's no big deal, Lizzie," Jane whispered, smushed up between pillows on her bed.

"Excuse me, I think it *is* a big deal—or it very easily could have been," I replied—and not in a whisper, causing Jane to shush me.

"Sorry."

"Just so you know, we were always careful," Jane said.

"I would never think that you wouldn't be," I said. Bing's a med student. Of course he's going to insist on being safe. And Jane is Jane. She's too considerate of herself and others to get swept up in condomless passion.

"But I was expecting my period on Sunday, and when it didn't come, I got a little worried."

A little worried. Worried enough that on Monday she decided to drive herself to work, leaving Bing out in the proverbial cold. Worried enough that this morning, she took a detour to the house, to see if we had to stay at Netherfield any longer.

"But it doesn't matter now," she continued. "Because it turns out there's nothing to worry about."

"What would you have done?" I asked after a moment. "If . . ."

Jane looked to her window. "I'm very happy I don't have to think about that."

"What did Bing say?" I said. "Did he try to pressure you or—"

"No. Of course not." She chewed on her lip. "I didn't tell him."

I blinked in surprise. "Are you going to?"

"I don't think so . . . I don't think he could process it right now." Before I could ask what she meant by that, she shrugged it off. "Besides, there's nothing to tell. I was a little worried for seventy-two—no, forty-eight hours. That's all."

But Bing had noticed the worry. He'd asked me about it. I'd written it off as Jane's good nature with having to be a houseguest finally wearing thin, but it turns out I was just projecting my own feelings of overstaying our welcome onto her. I should have known it would have taken much more than that to unsettle unflappable Jane.

"I understand," I said. "I would have been freaked out, too. That's definitely not what I want out of life—to be single and knocked up and living with Mom."

Jane smiled. But then she shook her head. "That's not what freaked me out, Lizzie. I mean, that's not what I want out of life, either. At least, not right now. Maybe in a couple of years . . ." She let the thought trail away, before shaking it off. "Right now, I want to work, and see places and meet interesting people. But what scared me the most is that . . . if it *was* going to happen, I'd want it to happen with Bing."

"You would?"

"Yeah." She smiled wide, admitting her deepest secret to me. "He's so . . . he just fits. Does that make sense?"

I nodded, since I was pretty much unable to speak.

"So, if it did happen, it would be scary and change *everything*, but it would also be okay, because it would be the two of us going through it together." She sniffled a little, her eyes going watery again. "I didn't realize it could happen so fast. This . . . feeling. And that scared me a little."

Wow. Jane's in love. All the looks, all the speculation I'd gleefully been engaging in, were nothing compared to this confession. She's in love with Bing. Not even forty-eight hours of worry could temper that. In fact, it made it grow.

I had no response (which is highly weird for me), so I simply leaned forward and hugged my sister.

"I hope this isn't a pity hug," she said into my shoulder.

"No, this is a happy hug," I replied. "I'm happy about your feelings for Bing, and really happy your forty-eight hours of worry are over."

She chuckled. "Me, too."

We stayed like that for a while, finally breaking apart when her phone buzzed.

"It's Bing," she said, glancing at her phone. "He probably just wants to say good night."

I didn't ask her again if she was going to tell him. Jane had already made up her mind about that.

"I'll leave you alone, then," I said, standing up from the bed. "Good night."

"Good night, Lizzie." She smiled. "But, can you do me a favor?"

"Anything," I replied, my hand on the doorknob.

"Don't . . . don't tell anyone about this," she said, the phone still buzzing in her hand.

"Of course not!" I replied. If I told Mom, she would freak out and start planning the wedding. Lydia would tell everyone under the sun. I'm not sure I could even trust Charlotte with this one, and I trust her with everything.

And forget about mentioning it in my videos. The world doesn't get to have every piece of the Bennet sisters. Some things are too personal, too important, for mass consumption.

"Just . . . pretend it never happened," she said. "Because, as it turns out, it didn't."

I nodded. As I closed the door behind me, I could hear Jane's voice soften with love as she answered her phone. "Hi, Bing . . . I miss you, too . . ."

MONDAY, AUGUST 6TH

Home for a few days now, and we have settled back into some kind of normalcy. Charlotte and I have spent all weekend together—I'd never really thought about it before, but our friendship is really reliant upon the fact that we live down the street from each other and can hang out at odd hours because of it. No more speed coffee dates. No more catching up on webcam. We just pop over to each other's houses, second children in each of our families.

I can't imagine what would happen if either of us ever moved away from each other. Which is all the scarier because it could happen relatively soon. We are setting our schedules for our last year of grad school—course registration is next week. One more year, and then . . . the real world.

But right now, I'm just glad to be back in *my* real world.

Lydia, of course, is still Lydia—bubbling over from her adventures with Mary and prodding Jane for details of the month with Bing. Jane is handling it well, the forty-eight hours of worry quickly fading away while the previous twenty-eight days of wonderful remain strong in her mind. For me, however, the glowy feeling of missing my little sister and appreciating her energy wore off after the first couple of days, and now I'm back to being more or less perplexed by Lydia and shaking my head ruefully at her antics.

Mom is back to her normal self—humming, cooking, asking passive-aggressive questions about her daughters' love lives. Which can only mean one thing: that she is currently thinking up her next Convoluted Plan. And I'm pretty sure it involves me.

And Ricky Collins.

Yes, my second-grade betrothed and recent annoying run-in at

VidCon turned up on our doorstep on Saturday. He's in town to help pack up his mother's house—she's decided she likes Florida and it's the perfect place to retire. Since she left my parents with the keys to her house, to help keep an eye on the place, it makes logical sense that he would stop by first thing.

It makes less logical sense that my mother would pull him to her bosom and invite him to dinner. But when presented with a young man of marriageable age—fiancée or not—she is not about to let him out of her sight.

And of course, she seated him right next to me.

"Well, the two of you have sooooo much in common," Mom said as she served up her famous shepherd's pie. "You're studying communications . . . something, and Ricky—oh, I'm so sorry, Mr. Collins has a company that does communications . . ." She giggled like a schoolgirl. "Surely the two of you will find just *oodles* to talk about."

It is at times like this that I appreciate my father. Because my father has tact, and the discretion to know when to use it.

And when not to.

"So, I understand we are to congratulate you on your recent engagement, Mr.—er, Ricky," Dad said, earning a look from my mother, and a noticeably small portion of shepherd's pie.

"Oh, yes! Thank you, Mr. Bennet! I am supremely gratified that my darling fiancée has agreed to become my permanent life partner," Ricky said so gleefully that little flecks of mashed potato ended up in his George Lucas beard. (The definition of a George Lucas beard being a beard grown to indicate a maturity that one's boyish features or a naïve aspect might otherwise belie. See also: lack of chin.)

"That's so sweet." Jane smiled. "How did you meet?"

"We met among the electrical synapses of the World Wide Web! It was an incredibly exciting and educational experience for me, and I like to think for us both. It allowed us the leisure of getting to know one another on an intimate level without the societal pressures of personal interactivity."

So, he met his fiancée online. Not too weird in this day and age, and given that Ricky Collins can be a lot to take in person, it actually made a lot of sense. Until . . .

"I like to think that upon the august occasion when we finally stand before each other, we will have made such strides in our personal connection that there is little we need say to each other."

"Wait . . ." Lydia piped up. "You mean, you haven't, like, *met* each other yet? For real?"

Ricky bristled. "I like to think that the meeting of our harmonious minds via the Internet is, as you say, 'for real,' but if you are asking if we have met in person, the answer is no."

"OMG," Lydia giggled under her breath, reaching for her phone. "I have to tell everyone I know."

I swatted her hand away and forced her to calm down. "I'm sure there is a perfectly logical reason for . . . not having met." Although I couldn't think of one at the moment. Seriously, how can you know if you want to spend the rest of your life with someone if you haven't even been in the same room together?

But Ricky brightened, and turned his cheerful smile on me. "Indeed there is, Miss Bennet! My betrothed and I unfortunately live some distance apart—I wading into the waters of the Silicon Valley–adjacent suburbs, and my fiancée in the wild and wooly northern plains of Winnipeg, Manitoba! Add to that the hard work and dedication I have been required to outlay in the growing of my titular company, Collins & Collins, and finding the time to travel to each other has been more of a challenge than previously expected."

See what I mean about him being a little overwhelming in person?

"There, Lydia," I said, trying to be kind. "Perfectly—"

"And as my primary investor, the estimable Catherine De

Bourgh, has always said, 'the work must come first!'—especially as I am spending her money to do it."

"Catherine De Bourgh!" my mother exclaimed, passing. "Just her name makes her sound like someone important . . . How lucky for you she took an interest in your company."

"Lucky, indeed!" Ricky replied. "She is the most helpful of all venture capitalists! She has advised me invaluably on all aspects of my business—who to hire, what to produce, where to lease office space. I find her to be the most glorious of mentors."

"Er, yes," my father said, clearing his throat. "And what is it that your company does? Collins & Collins, was it?"

"Yes, the small stipend bequeathed to me by my father upon my matriculation is what I used to initially fund the company, thus I thought it a fitting tribute to name the venture after him."

"But what does it *do?*"

"Oh! We make audiovisual content meant to be primarily consumed via streaming methods. Or at least, we will."

"Will?" I asked. "You haven't begun yet?"

"Sadly, I have not the staff nor infrastructure in place, but I hope to soon. We will begin by producing instructional videos of basic yet perplexing household tasks for corporate partners producing said household goods. Then, with time, we will venture into the lucrative world of reality television! While it may be lowbrow, as Catherine De Bourgh says, 'catering to the lowest common denominator is an essential part of any money-making venture'!"

So. He makes—or will make—lame corporate "how-to" videos with aspirations for reality TV. One can only assume, given his venture capitalist's apparent love of the lowest common denominator, that their titles will be akin to *Fat People on Skinny Island* or *Extreme Hoarding Bridezillas*. But far from being put off by these revelations, my mother just leaned in and put her hand over Ricky's, a consummate gesture of affection (or, a gesture of "I'm not letting you go").

"Such ambition! Starting your own company, making money . . . and making audiovisuals! Why, I cannot comprehend the creativity of young people these days. Can you, Lizzie?"

"Well, of course Miss Lizzie Bennet can," Ricky replied before I could. "After all, she is well versed in the field of online video."

"Is she?" my mom asked, visibly confused. I felt a tingle go up my spine. "Well, I know she's getting her degree and all that . . ."

"Yes, of course her degree. But there is also the project she and Miss Lu are endeavoring to—"

"Ricky!" I exclaimed. "I mean, um, Mr. Collins. That's, um . . . that's boring. So, tell me—"

"I beg to disagree, Miss Bennet! Why, you are—"

"God, Ricky," Lydia jumped in. "No one wants to hear about that *paper* Lizzie's been writing all summer. Trust me, if Lizzie says it's boring, it's WAY boring. But you know what's *not* boring? Going to Carter's! We haven't been in ages!"

"Carter's? If I recall correctly, isn't that an establishment that serves alcoholic beverages?" Ricky looked aghast. "And are you not underage?"

"Oh, um, they don't serve me," Lydia said, with a sly look to our parents. "I just play the video games."

"Still, as my VC Catherine De Bourgh says, 'today's youth must be vigilant if they are not to become brain-dead sucking upon the teat of every stimulant and pleasure they can find.'"

As Ricky droned on, mostly about Catherine De Bourgh, a little about his fiancée, and thankfully never touching on my videos again, I shot a look to my mother. She looked as if she was down, but not out of this particular fight.

However, I could only shake my head and sigh. Sorry, Mom. But Ricky is engaged, and even if he weren't, he's a bit too enraptured by his shady online video company and imperious benefactor to take much notice of me.

Better luck next time.

Friday, August 10th

Mom is not the type to give up that easily, it seems.

So what if Ricky's engaged? So what if he's a polysyllabic idiot? He's here, he's technically single, and she has the one thing he can't say no to.

Food.

When in doubt, Mom breaks out the recipe box.

Thankfully, she's skipped the salmon and lamb, sparing my father a finance-induced aneurysm. But she can do amazing things with plain old meat and potatoes. So far, we've had shepherd's pie, apple and cheddar meat pasties, spaghetti with homemade meatballs, and a more successful reprisal of the bananas flambé (Lydia told me she'd been practicing at Aunt Martha's). If Mom had any objection to having been limited to the cheaper end of the meal spectrum, she hasn't said anything.

And Ricky, poor soul that he is, has joyfully taken the bait. He's been our guest at dinner every night this week. Mom's rationale is that he's just down the street, and he must be so tired after working on packing up his mother's house all day that he requires sustenance. And that's fine, and likely fair . . . if I had ever *seen* Ricky doing any hard labor. Mostly, when I drive by his mom's house on the way to the library, I have spied him sitting in a lounge chair outside, talking on his phone, while young men in logoed moving company shirts and weight belts do all the heavy lifting. (Let's be thankful Lydia hasn't felt the need to wander down that way, else she'd disrupt their work entirely.) Forget hard work; I've never even seen Ricky out of his ill-fitting suit.

And he's always coming by the house, with the seeming specific intention of talking to me. Butting into my life—hell, barging into my bedroom! Which I do not get. Not the basic manners thing, although I don't get that, either, but his constant hovering. Charlotte says that we should be nicer, and maybe try to learn a little bit from him—of all the people we met with at VidCon, Ricky is the only one who's here. And I didn't even contact him afterward, like I did everyone else I collected business cards from. He just . . . showed up.

However, I don't know what it is I would learn from Ricky . . . After all, he's never made a web video as far as I can tell. He decided on working in online content because he considers the market largely untapped—not because he has any great love or understanding of it. Hence, his desire to create corporate videos and bad reality TV.

Maybe, however, it's the reverse. Maybe he wants to learn about web video from me—after all, he knows about my videos. Thankfully, with Lydia's intervention and a discreet after-dinner conversation, we managed to clue Ricky in to not mentioning the videos in front of my parents anymore, but now . . . now he sort of thinks he's in on this great secret.

First Caroline, now Ricky Collins. The oddest people have discovered my videos. I don't really know how to feel about it, except that Ricky never seemed to notice that I (and my mother) called him a dickhead on them. Which, is good, I suppose.

I just wish I could figure out what he wanted from me. From us. Other than a bunch of fancy meals my mom labors over for hours and then forces us to sit through multiple courses of with painfully polite conversation. Mostly from Ricky, and mostly about Catherine De Bourgh.

I would like to figure this out before Mom gets desperate, decides to up her game, and goes back to bankrupting the family with her elaborate meals. I did spy another mortgage meeting in my dad's day planner (yes, I've taken to snooping through my dad's desk, what's your point?) and with that and the remodel, it makes me worried that such a time is coming sooner than I think.

Monday, August 13th

My phone lit up like a Christmas tree this morning. Kitty was
sleeping on my chest and stared at me angrily when I moved her.
If Kitty was here, it must have meant that Lydia had gotten up
very early that morning, to catch the bus to community college
for class registration. Lydia had lost car privileges again and been
forced onto public transit ever since she got bored and decided
to teach herself papier-mâché and left her life-size replica of her
old pony Mr. Wuffles in the backseat of her/Mom's car, wherein
it melted.

Mom was not happy.

Neither was Kitty when I pushed her off my chest to reach for
my phone.

You're probably still asleep, but I
couldn't wait to tell you I'll be swinging
back through your area — hopefully
soon! — GW

My heart started going a little faster. It had been a while since
I'd heard from George Wickham. His job rolled out of town and
he got caught up in other things, as did I. Truth be told, I hadn't
thought that much about him . . . except for the occasional day-
dream about his surprisingly charming shoulders. But now . . . he
was texting me again. Interesting.

> You're ignoring me now, aren't you? Is it because I make bad walrus jokes? — GW

I couldn't stop the smile from spreading across my face. I typed back:

> No, it's because you have to give a girl time to collect herself in the morning. :)

(I put the smiley face on just in case. But then I worried I should have gone with the winky face.)

> I DID catch you in bed, didn't I? Wow, I didn't take you for the lazy type. My preconceived notions are challenged.

> It's 8 in the morning. And you're awake. *My* preconceived notions are challenged.

> Morning is the best pool time. No one stares at me in my Speedo. I can just swim, and not worry about being objectified.

And now, I was picturing him in a Speedo. How did it get so hot in my room?

> I feel your pain.

> Oh, really? You're in a Speedo about to jump into cold water, too?

> Nope. Long-sleeve
> pajamas covered with
> cat hair.

> Sexy . . .

Well, well, well. George Wickham was texting again, possibly coming back through town. This could make for a very welcome distraction from the perpetual annoyance of Ricky Collins.

Sunday, August 19th

"Are you sure you want to put this online?"

Charlotte leaned over my shoulder, watching the playback of the video I shot today. I'm currently rocking back and forth, such is my shock and anger. On tomorrow's video, I was supposed to be talking about how my mother is crazy and trying to push me and Ricky together—heck, she even mentioned "partnering" with him, which ew—when, suddenly, Ricky himself was making the same proposal.

While I was filming my video.

Yes, I got proposed to by Mr. Ricky Collins. On camera.

Except, what he asked me was not for my hand in marriage (his hands already being full with his as-yet-unmet Canadian fiancée), but instead, my hand in business.

He asked me to be his business partner at Collins & Collins.

Apparently, it was his objective in coming here all along. Packing up his mother's house was the excuse. His primary investor, Catherine De Bourgh, had advised him to get a business partner, presumably someone who knew about this "Internet video craze and how to monetize it." Ricky, having run into Charlotte and me at VidCon, and been impressed by my videos' viewership (he even asked to see my analytics, which felt a little invasive. Like, if when you went to the doctor, he took down your address and then asked how much you pay in rent. But I digress.), decided that I would be the perfect person to . . . how did he put it? "Share this most important part of my [his] life."

Someone should point his fiancée to my videos. They would be educational.

Regardless, the lack of background and education that Ricky

has in Internet video is surpassed only by the lack of respect he has for me, if the way he went about offering this proposition shows me anything.

First, he said that my lack of connections in the industry were a hindrance.

Secondly, he said he would have to compensate for my lack of business acumen.

Then, he said that I would have to give up my pursuit of my degree, and while that was a huge sacrifice (for him—not having a business partner with an advanced degree would be shameful), it was one he was willing to make.

All of this . . . for the chance to make corporate how-to videos with the hopeful future prospect of bad reality TV.

My gut churned as I listened to him. And the only thing I could do was listen because he, as per usual, did not let me get a word in edgewise. Finally I had to interrupt—well, yell at him.

I told him no. It took him a few times to get it; thinking I was negotiating, he offered me benefits, and a signing bonus, bigger and bigger manila envelopes of corporate compensation, and . . .

I couldn't do it. Maybe if I could have stomached Ricky or stomached his business model I would have considered it—but I can't stand either. So I told him off, as forcefully and finally as I could.

"I am well-connected, funded, and offering you a respectable position," he'd bristled. "As charming as you are, you are unlikely to ever be offered anything comparable with your connections and degree."

Read: I was turning down the best if not only offer I'll ever get and am ruining my life in doing so.

There are times you have to be reserved. Circumspect. And then there are times you need to forcibly eject a guy from your bedroom—which he barged into without asking in the first place.

Oh, no, wait—that's not true. He did ask permission to come

into my room and interrupt everything with his insistent proposal. He asked it of my mother.

I'm pretty sure my mother has been in on this scheme for a while now. She must have known about his intentions toward me—it certainly explains all those hints she dropped about "partnering" (still ew).

It also explains why she was waiting for me at the bottom of the stairs after Ricky left.

"Lizzie! What are you doing? I just saw Mr. Collins and he said that he offered you a job and I said congratulations to him and to you . . . and then he said that congratulations would have to wait until he'd convinced you to take it! What did you tell him?" she asked, barely letting my foot touch the bottom stair.

"I told *Ricky* no, Mom."

She looked at me as if I had just admitted to murdering a penguin. "You go after him right now, and you tell him you changed your mind!"

"No, Mom. I don't want to work for him."

"I DON'T CARE!" my mother screeched. After this there was some incoherent yelling and badgering, punctuated only by the words "Wait until your father gets home!" and the occasional sob and threat to march across the street and bring Ricky Collins back here.

I sort of wished Jane would walk through the door. Her presence, and likely Bing's, would have quelled some of my mom's more overt histrionics. Since we came back home, Jane and Bing seemed to be back on track—the little bump in the road of overstaying our welcome (and other things) long in the past. He'd even resumed driving her to work—but since we're no longer at Netherfield, they've stopped calling it "giving a ride" and have termed it "carpooling."

Heck, I would have taken *Lydia* walking through the door then. But Lydia has an uncanny ability to sense when Mom-drama might be unfolding, and to stay out of the way.

But finally, what ended the situation—or rather, brought it to a head—was my father coming home.

He was very quickly attacked by my mother.

"My dear, I can't understand a word you're saying. Let me put my bag down at least." He went into his den, and Mom and I followed.

"Your headstrong middle child has decided that she would rather not take a good job in her field working for a respectable man with money and connections," my mother harrumphed.

"What she means is that I would rather not give up my degree or my dreams of having a satisfying career creating narrative and influencing the world to go make corporate videos for Ricky Collins!"

My dad looked from Mom to me. "Ricky Collins. The dickhead?"

"No, honey," my mother clarified through gritted teeth. "The nice young man who has his own company, and offered your daughter a partnership. And she won't even give it a chance!"

"I don't understand why you want me to work for him so badly!" I blurted, finally losing my temper. "It in no way leads to me finding a husband, which is all you usually care about!"

"Because, husband or no, it's the first step!" my mother cried, her eyes going steely. "Whether you choose Option A or Option C, you have to start somewhere."

I was so shocked, I'm pretty sure my mouth fell open. My dad's, too. My mother raises her voice all the time, but this was different. This was . . . cold. And honest.

"God, I am so sick of everyone in your generation holding out for something perfect," she continued, beginning to pace. "Your sister Jane working that tedious job for no money when she could be doing something easier that pays better, with less stress, and still have enough time to wrap Bing around her finger. God knows what Lydia will do, but it won't be to settle for something she doesn't know she wants. And you think your ideals are so precious that when you step out into the world, everything has to be as exact as it is in your head. Well, it won't. You have to work for it. And taking a decent job—however unworthy you find it—is the first step."

She turned to my father. "You know I'm right. You know having one girl out of the house and supporting herself would be a godsend. So talk to your daughter, and tell her so." Then, she marched out of the room.

And the thing was . . . my mother *was* right. She was right about me wanting the perfect job when I leave school. Right about me being idealistic—perhaps too idealistic. But I hadn't even considered what a relief it would be to my parents. Out of the house— one less mouth to feed. Dad's mortgage meeting last week. Mom tearing apart the kitchen to get it up to code so we can sell if necessary. The coupon club replacing bridge.

God, was I being too selfish? I could feel my eyes stinging . . . and my resolve crumbling.

"Well, Lizzie. It sounds as if you have a decision to make," my dad said with a sigh.

"Dad . . . if you tell me to take this job, I will."

My dad just looked at me for a moment, considering. "Do you want this job?"

"No!" I sniffled. "It would be terrible. But if you need me to—"

"Then don't you dare."

His words came out fierce—fiercer than I've ever heard in my entire life.

"Your mother's and my financial problems are our own. You don't get to carry that burden. You'll have your own as soon as your student loans come due, so don't worry about us."

"But—"

"You have dreams, Lizzie." He laid a hand on my shoulder. "Goals. Now is the time in your life to pursue them. Don't put them on hold. Because if you do, pretty soon you'll be middle-aged with three children, working a job simply to pay the bills. And you'll have forgotten what those dreams were."

I hugged my dad. Long and hard, the way dads deserve. Then he said he would take care of Mom, and that maybe I should go have dinner at Charlotte's. So I grabbed my data card out of my camera and headed over to her family's apartment.

"Lizzie," Charlotte said again, poking me in the shoulder. "Are you sure you want to post this?"

I understand Charlotte's hesitation. This is the first time something has actually *happened* on my videos. Not me talking about it after the fact. Not a reenactment. It's raw and real. It might even be a little too harsh.

But I made my decision. I'm not giving up my dreams for Ricky Collins. Not for his base pay, benefits package, or signing bonus. And by putting my decision on the web, in my way, I'm sticking to it.

"Absolutely," I replied. And hit the button.

Tuesday, August 21st

My mother is relentless. No matter what my father and I have said to her, no matter how Jane tries to placate her, she does not take no for an answer. And she's been encouraging Ricky to do the same.

"Oh, Miss Bennet!" he said, practically attacking me in the brief span of time in between leaving my car and making it to the house. "There you are—I was afraid you were going to miss our appointment!"

"We had an appointment?" I couldn't help but ask.

"Yes! Your mother said that you would be pleased to assist me in packing up the last few boxes of my own mother's abode!" His eyebrows waggled. Yes. Waggled.

"No, Ricky." This must have been the forty-seventh time I've said "no" to him, not that you'd know it by his pushiness. "Besides, don't you have movers?"

"Sadly, the men hired for the task do not take instruction well and have more than once raised my ire by placing kitchen linens in with bathroom linens . . . They have not deigned to show up today."

This would explain why I saw my mom taking cranberry green bean gelatin out to the movers yesterday. One can only assume they are all at home with a stomachache.

"Thus your mother volunteered your services!" Ricky continued. "And perhaps in that time, I can convince you of the more improving aspects of working at Collins & Collins. I am given to believe that such a thing is possible, and of benefit to you."

All I can say is, thank God for Charlotte. As soon as she closed the passenger-side car door, she swooped around and got in between Ricky and me. Come to think of it, this might have been more for Ricky's protection than mine. I was pretty aghast. And you wouldn't like me when I'm aghast.

"Actually, Mr. Collins, Lizzie and I just came from class registration," Charlotte began, laying a calming hand on my arm. "So she has a lot of stuff to do. But I'm free. And . . . I can help."

"But Mrs. Bennet said—"

"Mrs. Bennet didn't realize that Lizzie's . . . carpal tunnel is acting up again, thanks to filling out all those forms. But there's nothing I love more than . . . lifting heavy boxes. All day."

Charlotte really knows how to take one for the team. That's martyr-level sacrifice right there.

"Don't worry, he'll be gone soon," Charlotte whispered to me.

As I watched Charlotte maneuver Ricky back to his house, I couldn't help but feel a little overwhelmed with everything. School starting back up in a little over a month, Ricky's proposal, Mom and Dad's fight over it. Plus, that last video I put online certainly made an impression. I'm getting a lot of tweets and comments about it.

Maybe I need to take a break—from what I can, anyway. Scale things back, stay off the Internet for a week or so. Just until things calm down and I feel normal again.

Sunday, August 26th

I just got home from a day of errands with my dad — and only my dad, thankfully, Mom's passive-aggressive griping having reached whole new levels of Southern-fried crazy — to find Charlotte in my room.

"Hey!" I said, seeing her sitting there, thumbing through a booklet and some papers from a big manila envelope. "What are you doing here?"

She seemed startled to see me. Even though it was my room. She quickly gathered up all the papers and stood.

"I was doing your video today, remember?"

"Have I thanked you for that yet?"

Seriously, Char took my desire to go a little off the grid and made it a reality. I didn't have to worry about filming today, so I could spend it out of the house, away from the stress of my mother and Ricky. It let me worry about other things, like my impending last year of school and my formal thesis proposal, due much too soon for me to want to think about.

"So what was the video about?" I asked. They are my videos, after all; best if I'm versed in them.

"Actually, Ricky came by and helped me out," Charlotte replied.

"And have I thanked you for *that* yet?" Charlotte has basically tied herself to Ricky this past week. She must have put a tracker on his phone, because whenever he showed up at our doorstep, Charlotte was there, ready to whisk him away. "Although I'm not certain how I feel about him being in my bedroom again. He didn't sniff anything, did he?"

"No. Lizzie, I have to talk to you about something," Char said, holding the papers in front of her like a shield.

"What? Is everything okay?" I asked, sitting down on the bed.

"Yes. Sort of. It's about the job Ricky offered you."

"Oh, God, not you, too," I groaned, putting my head in my hands. "Please don't try and convince me to take it—I can't handle that coming from my bestie. Just back me up on this one."

"No, that's not it. He's not going to offer it to you again."

"Oh. Good." I sighed, relieved. Charlotte glanced down at the papers in her hand, the manila envelope.

A manila envelope that suddenly seemed really familiar.

"He offered it to me," she said simply.

"Stunned" is not word enough for what I was feeling. "And what did you say?"

"I told him I have to think about it."

"Good." I exhaled. "But you don't really have to think about it, right? That was just a way of letting him down easy?"

"No. I don't have to think about it," she said, unable to meet my eyes. "I'm going to take it."

Tuesday, August 28th

I am calm. I am calm I am calm I am calm. I in fact have been calm the last two days. I told Charlotte that I understood, but she should think about it some more. That taking Ricky's job offer will alter the course of her life irrevocably, and quitting school with only a year left before getting her degree is something that she could very well regret in the future.

Charlotte listened, nodded, and then took that malicious manila envelope and went home. To think about it. Or so I thought.

What she really did was call Ricky Collins and accept his offer.

So I decided I would talk it over with her. Calmly. Rationally.

"How could you?" I said, when Charlotte came over today to film the next video—and hopefully to explain everything.

"Lizzie, it's my decision. And it's already made."

"I DON'T CARE!" I screeched.

"Wow." She blinked at me. "Sound like your mother much?"

I narrowed my eyes. "You can't take the job, Char. You just . . . you can't. It's ridiculous."

"Why is it ridiculous?" she asked. "And I *am* taking the job. I have to. I need to."

"You don't need to."

"Yes I do!"

"Is it the money? I know it's tight right now, but there's only one year left, and you have your aunt to help you, and—"

"Aunt Vivi can't help anymore."

My eyes flew to her face. "What?" Char was her aunt's favorite. She's always helped with Charlotte's education. It wasn't a lot, but it was something.

"A couple of months ago, when she got sick? She actually fell down the stairs. Broke her hip."

"Oh, my God."

"She's fine, but she couldn't work for a while. And there were a lot of bills. So I told her not to worry about my school anymore."

"Charlotte—"

"And if I move out of the apartment, my aunt can come and take my room, and live with my mom and Maria."

I felt for Charlotte, I really did. She's in a tougher position than I am. But . . .

"Does your family want you to sacrifice your education for this job? To make their lives easier?"

"No, but . . ."

"Then don't do it!" I wrapped my arms around her. "You work two jobs and have student loans *to get your master's*. If you leave school you're still going to owe that money, and you won't have the degree to show for it."

"What good is the degree, anyway?" she asked me. "You're the one who said we're doomed to unemployment. Hell, at least it's a job in our field!"

"But not what you want to be doing!" I knew I was yelling, but I didn't care. "You have dreams—goals!"

"Lizzie, right now my biggest dream is for my mother to not have to take a job flipping burgers when she's seventy-five." Charlotte threw up her hands.

"That's not what they want for you! That's not what *I* want for you!" I pleaded. "Charlotte, if you take this job, I'm never speaking to you again."

Then, my eyes fell to the camera. All set up and ready to go. And my mind went to the only thing I could do.

I threw my arms around Charlotte, held her in place.

"What are you doing?"

"If your family can't stop you, and I can't stop you, maybe *they* will," I said, as I turned the camera on.

Friday, August 31st

It didn't work.

Charlotte is gone.

She walked away from her degree, from the videos, and from her best friend.

I don't know what to do anymore.

Tuesday, September 4th

When I don't know what to do, it turns out, Lydia does.

Yes, Lydia.

I had been slinking around the house, dodging Mom, whose disparaging looks and passive-aggressive attitude can get surprisingly grating after the first dozen interactions. Dad does his best to mollify Mom, and Jane is constantly bringing me tea.

I just wanted to avoid life for a while. Because if I did face up to what happened, Charlotte would really be gone and I would really have been a terrible best friend for not seeing things from her perspective.

I still can't believe she did it, though. Gave up on her dreams of being a documentary filmmaker just to be No. 2 at Ricky Collins's company. Comfortable or not, she's still depriving herself—just in a different way.

Anyway, it was just me and my melancholy thoughts on this subject until Lydia burst in and insisted we go out to Carter's as a distraction. Remarkably, Jane was behind this plan as well, offering to call up Bing and Caroline and have them come, too. But the coup de grâce that got me out of my sweatpants and out of the house was the fact that George Wickham emailed me, saying he's back in town and was waiting for me with an ice-cold beer in hand.

Talk about a distraction.

I swear to God, that man was made for a commercial on the beneficial effects of spending six hours a day in chlorine. The minute we walked in, he turned away from the girl he was chatting with and focused his laser-beam baby blues right on me.

"Hey, peach." He smiled as we approached, and he wrapped me in a bear hug. "And the peach sisters!"

"Hey, George," Lydia said, putting herself forward—and by that I mean her boobs. He had met Lydia before, at least. I like to think she doesn't immediately preen for complete strangers.

"Hey, Lydia." He winked at her. "You gonna cause trouble to-night?"

"Are you offering?"

"Okay, that's enough of the Lolita act," I said, enjoying the feeling of George's arm around my waist.

"And this must be the lovely Jane." George then turned on the charm by raising her hand to his lips, a paragon of gallantry.

"It's so nice to meet you," Jane said. "I've heard a lot about you."

"Have you?" He looked at me then, all flirty. "Well, I'm flat-tered to have been thought worthy of mention."

"Worthy?" Lydia snorted. "You're the most interesting thing to happen to Lizzie in, like, *years*."

"Lydia . . ." Jane warned.

"Hey, look, a free table!" Lydia pointed, and shoved us toward it. "You guys hold it down—I'll get drinks!"

Lydia dodged her way through the Saturday night crowd and tried to elbow her way to the bar, without much success. We Ben-nets inherited our mother's petite frame.

"I'll go help her," George offered, as he held out a chair for me (!!). "And the first round's on me."

As George moved off, Jane caught my eye. "Well, I can cer-tainly tell what you see in him."

"He's pretty great, right?"

"Handsome."

"And charming," I replied. "If only he were rich, we would have hit the mother-trifecta."

"Don't let her hear you say that—at this point she might be willing to take two out of three." Jane laughed. Then her ridic-ulously perfect brow came down in confusion. "Wait, does that mean you're thinking about George . . . long-term? Hitting the mother-trifecta?"

"God no!" I replied immediately. "We've just been texting. You can't think long-term about anyone like that when you're limited in communication by your data plan." But . . . "He's interesting to me, though." I smiled.

The thing is, Lydia was not wholly wrong. George actually *is* the most interesting this to happen to me in years . . . at least guy-wise. I don't let people get close to me easily. It's just not my thing. Jane becomes best friends with everyone within five minutes of meeting them, and Lydia gloms onto people with the fervor of a chipmunk on a sugar high. But I've always been a little standoffish. A little suspicious, I guess. So the fact that I'm talking to a guy, liking a guy, letting that guy buy me and my sisters a round of drinks, is kind of a big deal.

While I was contemplating the big deal that was currently leaning against the bar and showing off an incredibly perfect . . . pair of jeans, Jane's phone buzzed.

"Oh, no," she said, her entire posture falling.

"What is it?" I asked.

"Bing's not able to come," she sighed. "But Caroline says she's on her way."

"Oh, that sucks—you guys haven't seen each other in forever."

"I know. His school is going to start up soon, and they've been giving me so many extra hours at work, which means I can't carpool with Bing . . ." She shrugged, letting it drift off. But I had to wonder. Bing's school is in Los Angeles. What was going to happen when he had to go back? A long-distance relationship? Jane making frequent trips down I-5 on weekends? He seems to really like it here; would he transfer?

"Excuse me," a guy from the next table leaned over, "but didn't we go to high school together?"

Jane turned around, startled. "I think so. It's so good to see you!"

Jane and the guy started talking, and he introduced her and me to his friends around the table. That's how we were situated when Caroline and Darcy walked in the door.

Ugh.

I hadn't actually seen Darcy in the flesh since Jane and I left Netherfield. He didn't seem worse for wear. In fact, he actually . . . smiled at me. *Smiled.*

I think I may have approximated something vaguely smile-like in return, because as Caroline went over and air-kissed Jane, wedging herself into the seat next to her, Darcy came and sat next to me.

"Hello, Lizzie."

"Hello." Yes, I do have the ability to mask my feelings and be polite. "How have you been?"

"I have been well," he said, his posture completely perfect. Seriously, even his bow tie was perfectly pointed at the corners. It was ridiculous. "And you?"

"Fine."

"Er, how are your students? The ones you tutor?"

"Good," I replied. "Although for most of them school has already started, so our sessions are over."

"Oh. So you're not teaching them anymore?"

"No—I only tutor in the summer—because of my own workload with grad school." Which will be starting up again soon enough. And I won't have my regular partner in crime anymore . . . but let's think about that later.

"Oh, that's too bad," Darcy said. "Not because you won't be . . . I'm mean it's . . . I just find what you teach interesting. That's all."

"What I teach?" I asked, a little bewildered by his inarticulateness. Usually he knows the most cutting thing to say at all times. "You mean English?"

"Yes. Especially for someone studying communications."

"I'm getting my grad degree in mass communications, but my bachelor's is in English," I said defensively. "If my understanding of literature wasn't sufficient, my former teachers would not recommend me to their students."

"That's not what I meant," he said quickly. "Just that it must give you an illuminating perspective about . . . Tolstoy."

"Tolstoy?"

"Yes! I was thinking about how you were saying that Tolstoy thought Shakespeare was a poor dramatist, and that as a communications student you must—"

Darcy stopped talking, mid-sentence. His eyes fell on something—or someone—behind me. I turned around. George was standing there, four beers in hand.

"Here you go, peach," he said, putting the beers on the table in front of me. "I got you the same kind you had last time."

What was really amazing was that George did and said all of this while keeping his eyes locked on Darcy's.

You know how I was saying I have the ability to mask my feelings and be polite? You know who doesn't?

Darcy.

And at that moment, I could read everything on his face.

"I'm sorry," he said, his jaw working overtime. "I have to go."

Then . . . he just stood up and walked out of the bar.

"Darcy, wait!" Caroline cried, clearly flummoxed. "Um . . . he's my ride. I'm sorry, Jane, I'll see you later?" And without bending to air kiss, Caroline was out the door on Darcy's heels.

Out of all the weird things that Darcy has done in my presence, this was by far the weirdest.

And George Wickham is the cause of this weirdness. From the look on George's face, he wasn't pleased to have seen Darcy, either.

"What was that about?" I asked under my breath.

"Nothing," George said, taking Darcy's vacated seat next to me.

"That wasn't nothing," I replied.

"William Darcy and I have . . . a history. That's all." He looked down at the beers in front of us. "But let's not let him spoil our night! I want to hear everything you've been up to since I've been gone."

If George didn't want to talk about it, that was fine; I wasn't going to push him. But obviously my curiosity was piqued. How could it not be, with such an enigmatic statement?

Jane might say that my curiosity was a little *too* piqued, because I did make a late-night video (not that kind, ew) about it. But come on, it's too juicy to ignore:

George knows Darcy.

Darcy knows George.

And given his actions, Darcy hates George.

I can't help it—I have a curious nature. And as my old DVD copy of *Harriet the Spy* as my witness, I am going to get to the bottom of this one.

* * *

I had just closed this journal when our doorbell rang. Thankfully Mom wasn't home, because I can only imagine the freak-out that would occur upon seeing one Mr. George Wickham on the other side of the door.

"Hey," he said. "I was thinking about going to the beach today. And I thought, maybe I could use a local tour guide? Someone who knows all the best spots?" He grinned wide. "You interested?"

George Wickham at the beach? In a swimsuit? Yes, please.

"Let me grab my suit," I said, and ran upstairs.

I have to admit, George is in town for three days and already, things are a lot more interesting around here.

SUNDAY, SEPTEMBER 9TH

George just left my room. I was making a video, and he was curious about it, so I let him come in and be on camera today. But what I learned . . . turns everything I thought I knew about Darcy on its head, *and* confirms him as a worse person than even I had previously thought.

George and I have been hanging out pretty much every day this past week. He doesn't start with his swim clients until Monday, and my classes don't start up for a little while, so might as well make the most of it, right?

And it's been *great*. *He's* been great. I know that it may seem a little fast, but . . . I like him. He's funny and ridiculously hot and charming. Granted, I don't think he's read any book longer than a *Men's Health* magazine, but since when are common interests and tastes the basis for good relationships? Whatever happened to opposites attract?

If Charlotte were here, she would be freaking out that I was getting too involved with him, but 1. She's not here, and 2. I'm not getting that involved. We're keeping it casual. Casually going to the beach. Casually meeting for a movie. Casually making out in the back of my car like ridiculous teenagers who can't afford a hotel room. (Although we actually can't, come to think of it. Plus, he has roommates and I live at home, so no wonder I never date.)

But I don't see anything wrong with enjoying myself a little. School is going to start soon enough, my life will be consumed by my final year, and my thesis and then getting a job/probably moving/real life will invade. If I was ever going to have some fun, now's the time.

George is a great partner for it. And he listens to me. He's interested in me. Which is why, when he said he wanted to see me make a video, I let him be on camera.

I also figured it would be a really good time to put him on the spot and ask him about all the Darcy drama at Carter's the other night. Hey— I had waited patiently for a *week* to know the answer. That speaks to a level of maturity I did not know I was capable of. Perhaps I *am* ready for the real world.

Anyway . . . while we were filming, I asked him. About the "history" he has with Darcy. He was pretty reticent to tell me, especially while the camera was on. So, I turned it off.

"Listen," he said, "I don't want to tell tales out of school, or denigrate someone who isn't here to defend himself. But honestly, Darcy really doesn't have much of a defense for what he did."

"If you're worried about impeaching one of my friends, don't be," I said quickly. "We only know Darcy because Jane is dating a friend of his, but that doesn't mean he's her friend, and it certainly doesn't mean that he's mine."

"And he's not one of mine, anymore," George replied.

"How long have you known each other?" I asked.

"Pretty much my entire life."

Wow. I hadn't expected that. Which must have shown on my face, because George continued. "I know. It's hard to believe. But there was a time when we were best buds. My mom was his parents' housekeeper. When my dad skipped out on us, Mom and I moved into an apartment on the Darcy estate, and Mr. Darcy stepped up, sort of taking me under his wing."

I hadn't known his mother was a housekeeper, or that his father had left them. He said it so matter-of-factly, but I could tell he was sad underneath all the charm and smiles. I just wanted to hug him. But instead I let him talk.

"William and I grew up together, always hanging out, waging fake wars in the woods, basic boy stuff," he continued. "I was pretty much a second son to the Darcys. So much so, Mr. Darcy promised that he'd cover my bill for college.

"Anyway, my mom retired from being a housekeeper when I was sixteen, and we moved out of our little apartment. Darcy and I didn't see each other all the time anymore, but we were still tight. At least I thought we were. Then . . . Mr. and Mrs. Darcy died in a car accident."

"Oh, my gosh," I said quietly. I felt for him. And I actually felt for Darcy, too. It does kind of explain why he's so closed off. But it doesn't excuse what George said next.

"I tried to be there for my friend, but he just cut me off. Finally, it was time for college, and I got into a great school, with the most incredible swimming program. But when I went to Darcy, and reminded him of his dad's promise, he said no."

"He said no?" I blinked, a little in shock, even though I was expecting it. "Just flat out?"

"Just flat out." George nodded. "I couldn't believe it. But Darcy . . . he'd become really cold, and snobby. He didn't want to play with the housekeeper's kid anymore."

"So . . . what did you do?" I asked.

"What could I do?" he replied. "It's not like there was anything written down, so I didn't have a legal leg to stand on. Which Darcy told me in so many words. So I applied for loans, financial aid, I even got a little swimming scholarship—it wasn't much, but it helped. Still, with all that, I only had enough money for a year of school. So I had to drop out and piece together a career coaching swimmers."

"Wow," I said after a moment. "I just . . . Wow. I don't really know how to process this."

"Can I confess something to you?" he said, putting his hand over mine. "I've been watching your videos."

"Well, I know," I said. "Since you wanted to be in one and all."

"Not just recently. You told me about them the first time we met, and I looked them up. They were so cool and addictive I kept watching, and then you mentioned this Darcy guy. I just didn't think that your Darcy and my Darcy could be the same person. Because the one you describe doesn't match my memories of the friend I used to run around the woods with as a kid. But it was. And now I can see that he's only gotten worse with time."

"Was Carter's the first time you've seen him since you were eighteen?" I asked.

"No. I've seen him once or twice, just for a minute, though. His sister Gigi, too—she used to be such a sweet kid, but last time I saw her, she was becoming a lot like her brother." His eyes hit mine and I melted into a puddle. "But it was still kinda shocking, seeing him here with you."

"Not with me," I quickly corrected. "Christ, he must have stalked out of the bar that night because he was ashamed of what he did to you."

"I don't know why he left the bar, but it wasn't because he was ashamed. That would mean he felt guilt. Hell, that he felt anything about how he ruined my life."

"George—you have to let me tell my viewers this. Darcy doesn't deserve to be walking around free of guilt. The world needs to know what kind of person he is."

He seemed to think it over. "Well, you can tell them if you want—but you should protect yourself. The Darcys have a bunch of lawyers, and if they found out, and decided to sue . . ."

"I think we can find a way around that," I replied.

So we turned the camera back on and told the Internet a "hypothetical story" about two boys who grew up together, and one betraying the other. Then, after Lydia came in and spilled water all over George—executing a convoluted plan worthy of Mom to get him to take his shirt off—he kissed me good-bye, and we made plans to meet up for lunch tomorrow.

I'm still having a lot of trouble processing what George told me.

I'm willing to believe a lot of bad about Darcy, having personally witnessed his terribleness, but this? This is not just being insulting and rude. This is actually negatively affecting someone's life. How could anyone do something like that? Especially to someone he once called a friend.

I sort of wish Charlotte were here—even though I'm still mad at her for giving up on her dream. I could use another person's perspective, and she's always been my trusty eyes and ears. But you know what? Charlotte would probably try to play devil's advocate and justify Darcy's actions, or take George down a peg for making muscle tone a priority in his life. And that's not what I want right now. I want someone to be outraged with me.

And besides, as stated previously, Charlotte is most definitely not here anymore.

TUESDAY, SEPTEMBER 11TH

It's very quiet in the library today. Which is, I suppose, as it should be. I don't have any tutoring students anymore; they're all back in school. And I don't have any classes of my own yet, and won't until October. The thing is, I could use some distraction in the form of droning lectures right now. It makes me wish my course curriculum had offered the last few classes I need for my degree during the summer session, just so I didn't have to be alone and ponder right at this very moment.

But days like today lend themselves to reflection. Especially days with this date.

So I *should* be pondering. But the problem is, I should be pondering more substantive things. About the state of the world, the sacrifices we make for privilege, and the hope for peace. But instead, I'm thinking about guys.

Way to be enlightened there, Lizzie.

Specifically, I'm thinking about George Wickham and William Darcy. It's not hard for me to reconcile what George told me with the Darcy I have come to know—just the opposite, in fact. The problem is, it's hard to reconcile *anyone* doing something so egregious to someone else outside of a mustache-twirling cartoon villain. How can he, who destroyed a friend's life on a whim, even get to exist among us more civilized yet common people?

George hasn't talked about it since, really. We hung out yesterday, and he was his normal "everything is awesome" self, but sometimes he would get quiet and look out into the distance, and I could tell he was thinking about it. I asked him, and he made a self-deprecating comment about how his life was ruined, but his smile didn't reach his eyes.

I don't know if George has been thinking about it for the past—what, eight, ten years?—or if it's just gotten all churned up because he saw Darcy in town. But either way, it's something that still really bothers him, and it's something I can't make right.

Maybe I'll confront him about it. Darcy, I mean. After all, Bing's birthday is coming up this weekend—which will be a fine opportunity for forced interaction with everyone's favorite killjoy. It promises to be a doozy of a party, too. Although I don't know if Caroline knows how to throw anything other than a doozy of a party. But this time, Bing's not only inviting us "young folk" but our parents, too. Caroline also said that her parents are coming into town, as well as some other relatives and a bunch of Bing's friends from college.

Oh, God—I just realized . . . what if this is Bing's way of introducing Jane to his parents? And introducing his parents to our parents? Or what if it's a secret wedding that he and Jane have been planning this whole time?!?

No. No, that's not possible. I just channeled my mom for a second, that's all. Besides, Jane would have told me. She really can't keep a secret, and especially not one like that. All that she's said is that she's looking forward to the party because she and Bing still haven't had much opportunity to spend time together lately, what with him having to fly out for med school meetings (admittedly, I know nothing about med school, but I didn't think it involved so much travel) and Jane's doubling down at work, sadly suspending the Cutest Carpool Ever (™ me, because I'm sappy like that).

Here's the thing, though—if I had the "meet the parents/surprise wedding" idea skitter through my brain, you KNOW my mother has latched onto it with the ferocity of a bulldog. Perhaps I should bring reinforcements to the party, just to distract Mom from her convoluted planning.

I could ask George to be my plus-one. He's a solid possible-son-in-law-sized distraction. But would he want to go with Darcy there?

Actually, maybe I'm thinking about this wrong. Given that Darcy was the one who ducked out of Carter's in shame, it could be Darcy who avoids the party if George is there. Granted, this means that I wouldn't get the pleasure of confronting him over George's grievances (if I have the guts to do it, which is in no way a guarantee), but I would instead have the pleasure of slow dancing with the ridiculously hot guy I'm seeing.

Now, that's something worth pondering.

Sunday, September 16th

Another party, another 2 a.m. journal entry. And another reason I can't sleep. And no, Lydia isn't passed out in my bed due to over-indulgence, nor has Jane stayed out all night with Bing. No, this time, my anxieties rest squarely on my own shoulders. Because only at 2 a.m. can I wonder about what's so wrong with me that a perfectly nice guy would stand me up?

George didn't make it to the party tonight. And I guess I would have understood if I'd had some warning, but he not only didn't show, he didn't call or text to let me know that he wasn't coming. If he didn't want to come, he could have told me. Instead he said that he wouldn't miss it for the world, Darcy or no Darcy.

I still haven't heard from him, and trust me, I've sent the maximum allowable number of texts someone with dignity can send (four) to find out what happened.

Then I was thinking, what if something did happen? What if he got in a car accident, or fell and is in a coma? What if he's injured and unable to call for help?

That's when Lydia's voice popped into my head and told me I'd been stood up. Except, it wasn't her voice in my head. It was her voice, next to me at the party.

"G-Dubs better have a solid excuse for ditching you, because no Bennet should put up with the ghost act. Not even the lame Bennet," Lydia said, as she put a drink in my hand. How she carried a drink to me when she was already double-fisting two of her own is unknown, but Lydia does possess unseen skills.

"I can think of only one reason," I said, my eyes finding Darcy as he stood awkwardly on the other side of the parent-sanctioned room.

It was pointed out that having a party with twenty-somethings and their fifty-something parents was a recipe for awkward, and a solution to this might be to utilize the echoing vastness of Netherfield and have essentially two parties. The older crowd mainly stayed in the lounge and patio area, where a jazz trio (I think it was the same one from the Gibson wedding) was set up for those inclined to foxtrot, while we younger folk had a nightclub-type setup with a DJ in the rec room and finished basement area.

We all came together for cake.

It was a bit like those parties we had when I was in eighth grade, where all us kids watched a movie and had pizza in Dad's den and the parents drank wine in the kitchen and gossiped. But on a massively different scale.

Anyway, it was getting later and later, and I had migrated upstairs to the parent-sanctioned area, mostly because it provided a sight line to the front door. I had just sent my fourth text to George when Lydia came up to me.

"Ugh, Darce-face." Lydia scowled, seeing my line of vision. "Why do I get the feeling you're already plotting the next mean thing you're going to say about him on the Internet?"

"You know me too well," I replied.

"Hey, I fully support you in this endeavor," Lydia said. "I mean, if *Darcy* is the reason we are denied the sight of a sweaty George Wickham dancing downstairs . . . and it gets too hot, and he has to take his shirt off . . ."

"Stay on topic, Lydia," I replied.

"Right, whatevs. Anyway, if Darcy's to blame, give it to him with both barrels. God knows you keep them loaded."

I didn't ask what Lydia meant by that.

"What are you doing up here, anyway?" I said instead. "Shouldn't you be downstairs rubbing up against some of Bing's college buddies?"

"Obvs," she replied. "But I had to come up here and find you or Jane."

"Why—what happened?" My radar immediately started going off. I glanced around the lounge. No Mom. Oh, no. In my worry over George, I had let her out of my sight!

"Nothing much," Lydia hemmed. "Just, you know, Mom wandering down to the kids' party. Talking to people. Telling everyone about the wedding arrangements."

"Oh, my God, did you stop her?"

"Stop her? I took video!" Lydia held out her phone and treated me to a reenactment of my slightly tipsy mother talking to a couple of baby stockbrokers about how she was "the inevitable future mother-in-law of the host," and "do you have any advice for investments once the couple settles in?"

"Oh, Lord," I moaned.

"I know, right?" Lydia grinned at me. "It sucks that Dad came down and stopped her then, but I'm so going to post the first bit on YouTube. Just so our audience knows that we aren't exaggerating about Mom."

"First of all, it's my audience, and secondly . . . can I see that a sec?" I asked sweetly. Lydia handed over her phone, and I let my thumb *accidentally* slip to the delete button.

"Aw, look at that, it's gone. Sorry, Lyds," I said, handing the phone back to her.

"I can't believe you did that!"

"Of course you can," I replied. "Think about it. What would Jane say if she saw that video posted online?"

"Huh," Lydia replied, obviously not having considered Jane's feelings and embarrassment. "Where is Jane, anyway? I haven't seen her all night."

"I think one of Bing's friends had too much to drink. I saw her and Caroline helping him down the hall."

I don't think Jane had a very good night at the party. She'd had her hopes so high, getting to finally spend some quality social time with Bing, but every time I saw them get within a few feet of each other, Caroline or their parents or one of the out-of-town guests would pull him away to play host. And when Caroline was free, she certainly tried to be by Jane's side, but she's a poor substitute for her brother.

But Jane is nothing if not resilient. She put a smile on her face and chatted with everyone she didn't know, delighted to make new friends as always.

"Maybe we should go find her," I said idly. "See how she's doing."

"OMG, yes," Lydia said. "Anything's better than standing around pathetically staring at a door or at Darcy. Speaking of which . . ."

I followed Lydia's gaze. To find William Darcy headed right for us.

"He's coming this way," Lydia squealed through her smile. "Now's your chance!"

"My chance for what?"

"Both barrels!" she said, and she shoved me forward.

I nearly tripped straight into Darcy's chest. But I caught myself.

"Lizzie," he said.

"Darcy," I replied. "Hello."

"Would you care to dance with me?"

Out of everything he could have said, I did not expect that.

"Dance? Now?"

"Yes. If you're willing."

"Umm . . ." I was caught completely off guard. By the events of the party, by Lydia pushing me, and now by Darcy. That is the only justification I can give for having said, "Okay. I mean, sure."

As he led me out onto the patio, I glanced back at Lydia. *Don't you dare video this*, I mouthed over my shoulder. She pouted, but she put her phone away, and then flounced off to cause trouble somewhere else. Leaving me with Darcy.

A few other couples joined us on the dance floor. If we had been downstairs, the music would have been so loud and fast that we wouldn't have been able to talk. But instead, the jazz trio struck up an easy mellow number, and as Darcy's hand came around my back, the silence had to be filled.

"You have to let me lead."

That Darcy. Full of conversation.

"What makes you think I wouldn't?" I asked as we began to move.

"Experience."

Oh, yes. We'd gone through this whole farce before at the Gibson wedding.

"Perhaps it's best to not judge a person on one dance alone. After all, if I had done that, we wouldn't be dancing now." In reality, I *should* have done that, but . . . yeah, caught off guard.

"Point taken," he said, and guided me through a turn surprisingly well. I wasn't entirely sure, but I think we were waltzing. "However, I am glad you danced with me, and gave me this second chance."

I could see that he was trying his best to be agreeable, but given the fact that I was determined to hate him, I really wasn't in the mood for it.

"I find second chances to be a very good thing. Don't you?"

"I suppose. If they are deserved."

"Aren't they usually?"

"Not in my experience," he replied.

"So in general, you find your first impression to be correct."

"Don't you?" he echoed.

"Yes . . . but I like to think that I give people the benefit of the doubt, initially at least," I said.

"I am more than willing to give people the benefit of the doubt when I meet them," he replied. "But if they show themselves to be not worth my time, I have no desire to have them in my life."

"That sounds . . . very clean."

"It is."

"And lonely," I added, pleased to find that I'd caught him off guard for once. "So, you are willing to admit second chances are a good thing for those who deserve them, but you don't grant them yourself."

"I . . . can think of very few times they are deserved."

"George Wickham comes to mind."

Darcy turned a deeper shade of snobby, if that's possible, when he said, "George Wickham doesn't deserve to even have his name spoken aloud."

By you, I thought. *To have his name spoken by you is too much give on your part, you conceited, suspender-wearing one-percenter.* But unfortunately, I didn't say any of that out loud. For some reason, both my barrels were failing me when I was smack-dab up against my target. I tried to rally. To bring the red out of my vision and return my voice to ice cold.

"You were very rude to him at Carter's the other night," I said, challenging. "Dare I say you hurt his feelings?"

"I'm really not concerned about George Wickham's feelings."

"I am," I replied. "I consider George a . . . friend." More than a friend, but I wasn't about to admit that to Darcy. For some reason, the way he loomed above made holding on to my bravery very difficult.

"George is very capable of making friends. He's even more capable of using them."

Spoken like someone who wouldn't recognize a true friend if one came up and tapped him on the shoulder.

"He's been unlucky, then, to have called you a friend once upon a time."

I let my eyes fall to the front door again, across the lounge and inside the house.

"He's not coming, Lizzie." Darcy's voice was a whisper in my ear.

"You don't know that," I said, whipping my gaze back to him. "I invited him. He could—"

"That man will not make an appearance. Of that I'm certain."

And with that, Darcy confirmed my paranoid theories about why George wasn't there at that moment. It was all his fault. Of course it was. There was no other explanation.

"I'm sorry," he said.

"Are you? I wouldn't think so." One thing I would not tolerate was his pity.

Silence reigned over us then. Just moving in time to the music, and willing it to end. For me at least. Darcy, however, had his mind on other things.

"May I ask," he said, "to what does your previous line of questioning pertain? About second chances, that is."

"Just trying to figure you out, Darcy," I said, suddenly tired. "You're hard to read."

"You're not an easy read, either," he said under his breath.

"Perhaps we are better off if we stop trying to read each other," I replied. "And just say what we mean."

I waited. Waited for the guts to come out with both barrels blazing and tell him off to his face. Waited . . . for him to say something first.

Apparently, I waited too long. Because as I was holding my breath the music stopped, and Darcy took his hand off my back and let me go.

"Thank you for the dance," he said before he bowed (yes, *bowed*) and walked away.

I would have given anything to have Charlotte there then. To have someone to run to and talk everything over with. George would have been good, too—although, if he'd been there, I would never have ended up dancing with Darcy. I would have even taken Mom at that moment, my desperation to not be alone with my thoughts was so acute. However, the flip side of the coin is I can be thankful that my mother did not see me dancing with Darcy, lest she suddenly decide to stop disliking him and start planning fictitious wedding number two.

As it was, I wandered. Looking for my Jane, who would hopefully provide some relief. But she'd been missing for a little while.

She wasn't with Bing. He was in the lounge talking to his parents, a forced grin on his face. Nor was she with Caroline, who I saw leading Darcy down a hallway, presumably to a place where he could fake text in a corner to his heart's content.

My last hope was Lydia. I found her downstairs, surrounded by guys, dancing—she was definitely enjoying herself too much to see me. (Luckily, Mom was not down there anymore. I think Dad took her for a walk to get some air.) And, I decided, in about one more drink she was going to get cut off—by her big sister, if not by the bartender. I'm better at recognizing the signs.

I wandered back upstairs, letting my feet soak in the pool for a moment. I wasn't in the mood for a party anymore. I was sad and tired and I wanted to go home. I was even considering roping in Lydia and getting my car from the valet, when I saw Caroline and Darcy walking quickly back into the lounge. Followed a few moments later by Jane.

"Jane!" I called out, grabbing my sister's attention. She smiled when she saw me, but there was something a little off. Her face was a little too flushed. "Are you okay?" I asked.

"Me?" she replied quickly. "I'm fine. How are you?"

"Fine," I said. "I guess. I just danced with Darcy, if you can believe it."

Jane smiled. "You danced with Darcy. Willingly?"

I laughed. Jane just has that effect on me. Three seconds of her attention and the world feels 100 percent kinder.

"Hey," Bing said, coming over to us and putting an arm around Jane's shoulder. "There you are!" He looked like he'd really missed her. He also looked a little tipsy. I guess I wasn't the only one feeling a little stressed by this party. "Are you having a good time? I have to make sure all my guests are having a good time."

"Of course we are," Jane answered sweetly. "We're having a wonderful time. Right, Lizzie?"

Given the lack of Wickham, the insanity of my mother, Lydia filming it, and the agitation from my dance with Darcy, there were a few choice things I could have said about this party.

But I just said, "Right. A wonderful time."

WEDNESDAY, SEPTEMBER 19TH

from @bingliest: Small towns are great but back to the big city. Hello
   Los Angeles!

—Sunday, September 16th

Bing's left town. No one can get in touch with Caroline—except
for one text she sent me:

> Sorry we left so suddenly, but
> I'll see you soon! XOXO.

No one has any idea what happened. Least of all Jane.

One minute, she's dropping off birthday cookies at Netherfield
and the next she's getting a message via Twitter—not even to her
personally, but to social media at large—that Bing's gone back to
LA.

And it doesn't look like he's coming back. Mom did a drive-by
of Netherfield (okay, I went with her, I was so worried), and we
didn't even get past the gate. But at the top of the drive we could
see a moving van being loaded up with all their things.

Mom drove straight home and promptly collapsed on the
couch, wailing that life was over. Not just Jane's life, or her life,
but *all* life.

As for Jane . . . she's called in sick to work the last two days.
She hasn't come out of her room. She must be sneaking out in the
night to refresh her tea supply and use the bathroom, but other
than that, I have no idea what's going on. She's gotten no answer
from Bing. And it's really starting to worry me.

I don't think she ever told Bing about her forty-eight hours of worry. But if she did—and he still left? That would make him a bigger schmuck than I'd even thought possible.

It would also certainly put a lot of other things into perspective. Such as getting stood up at Bing's party is not the end of the world. Even when George finally called yesterday, and told me that he'd ended up taking a friend to the hospital and his phone got stolen, I just told him it was fine, but I couldn't really talk, since I was too busy worrying about Jane.

How can someone be tossed aside like that, so carelessly? How can someone who I'd grown to like and respect treat anyone, but especially Jane, like something disposable?

Maybe Darcy's predilection for discarding people rubbed off on him.

It makes me wonder if I knew Bing at all. If Jane knew him at all.

Saturday, September 22nd

"What about this one?" Jane asked, clicking on the link. "They're looking for a third roommate—I'd get my own bathroom. Oh, no, wait . . . it says I'd get my own bathroom *key*." She looked up at me. "What does that even mean?"

"I don't know, and I don't want to know," I said, closing that link and going back to the search page. "Are you sure you don't want to just stay with Aunt Martha and Mary?"

"They only halve the distance between Los Angeles and here— it's still going to take me over an hour to get into my new office in the morning," Jane said. "It will be fine for the first week or so, but I am going to find my own place."

When Jane finally emerged from her room, and stopped pinning sad puppies on Pinterest, she still hadn't heard from Bing. She was so confused and heartbroken, I knew this wasn't going to be solved with ice cream and tea. So I made the suggestion that she go down to Los Angeles to try to find him and talk to him.

What I didn't suggest was that she transfer to her company's Los Angeles headquarters and move there.

It's actually a very good thing for her, career-wise. Jane and her boss had been talking about it for the past month or so—which makes me wonder if Jane was planning for the possibility of moving to be with Bing, in an entirely different scenario.

It's a step up both in title and salary, so Jane could possibly take her student loans out of deferment finally, provided she's willing to live either with Aunt Martha or in a hovel. And our parents are surprisingly supportive. Dad is happy about the new job, that she won't just be fetching samples and coffee, and is taking her car into the shop to get it up to code. (I heard my parents whispering about how much they can help Jane, and it turns out, not much. But Dad insisted on the car thing. He says it's something dads have to do.)

And Mom is absolutely certain that Jane will find Bing and come back home married with toddlers. Which she would presumably have found on a street corner somewhere, considering Jane is planning on coming home for Thanksgiving.

I'm a little less enthusiastic. Not to Jane's face, of course. To her face, I'm the world's most supportive sister. But I feel it's all a little rushed. A guy breaks up with her and a week later she's moving. That's a lot of life changes incredibly fast. Worse, this is the guy that she fell for—hard. That she realized she was in love with a month before he decided to skip town. I just don't want her to make a hasty decision that turns out to be painful or wrong.

And one of the worst, most painful decisions she could make is to live in a place where you need a key for the bathroom.

"The prices in the Valley look a little better—let's see what we can find there," I said, taking over the computer.

"Ugh, the Valley? Who wants to live in the Valley?" Lydia groaned as she burst into my room and flopped onto the bed.

"People who don't want to live here," I replied.

"OMG, Jane—you should try and find roommates who are also models. That way, you can use them as dummies when you're designing stuff."

"That's not a bad idea," Jane said kindly.

"Hot guy models preferably."

"Yeah . . . probably best not to type 'wanted: hot guy models' into Craigslist," I cautioned. "You don't want to see what that brings up."

"Says you," Lydia countered, as she grabbed for my computer. "Gimme that."

I nimbly held my computer out of Lydia's reach, but our little game of keep-away was interrupted by Jane's phone buzzing.

She grabbed it immediately, hopefully. She still wanted it to be Bing and jumped whenever any phone rang.

"It's work," she said, a little deflated, reading the caller name. "I'll be right back."

As Jane stepped out, Lydia came over to me.

"Okay, we have to find her the cutest, most awesome place to live, because when Bing finally shows his ugly, stinking face he does not get to see her being anything other than awesome and happy."

"Wow," I replied, unable to hide my shock. "That was remarkably succinct, and actually makes a lot of sense."

"I know, right?" Lydia leaned over my shoulder and started typing. "Let's ditch the Valley and look at Beverly Hills."

"She also has to be able to afford it."

Lydia frowned, displeased with the thought of anything practical. But then she just shrugged. "Well, Bing will just have to come to her. She probably doesn't want to be living too close to Caroline and Darcy, anyway."

"I suppose," I said, a little confused.

"I never got why you liked Caroline so much—she's a complete fake," Lydia said as she took over my computer, typing away. "And Darcy? He totes got inside Bing's head—I'd bet money on it."

That got me wondering. Had Darcy gotten into Bing's head? I know I speculated that his judgmental ways might have rubbed off on Bing. But what if this wasn't casual influence, but a more direct meddling in his life . . . the way he had directly meddled in George's?

Why would he do that? And how?

"Oh—you should buy these tickets!" Lydia jerked me out of my thoughts and my eyes to the screen.

"Wait—what page are you on?" Lydia had somehow clicked over to a page where tickets were being sold—featuring a music festival nearby, next weekend.

"George likes this band. It would be an awesome surprise for him!"

Next weekend. By next weekend, Jane would be gone to LA. I would be a week closer to school, and no doubt we would still have no idea what happened with Bing. So many changes . . . and so much staying the same.

And I haven't seen George in a couple of days, what with all the Jane worry. Maybe I should take a little time out for us. See where we're going. Better that than getting my heart handed to me with a shoe print on it like Jane did.

"Good call, Lydia," I said.

"Oh, goody—get a ticket for me, too?"

"Get your own boyfriend," I replied. "Come on—let's find Jane an apartment."

Tuesday, September 25th

Just another dreary day. Everything is running together in boredom and loneliness. Which is not my normal state.

Jane's gone. Left Sunday evening to drive down to our aunt's and start her new job in LA bright and early on Monday morning. I've already heard from her—she loves the new position, has a couple of decent leads on an apartment, and emailed Bing to let him know she was in town. She hadn't heard back yet as of today. I'm beginning to worry that she won't hear back as of ever.

You'd think I would find solace for my sister leaving in the arms of my quasi-boyfriend/guy I'm hanging out with, but he's up and left town, too. Yes, that's right, George Wickham has abandoned our little hamlet to coach a club team in Meryton. So glad I bought those music festival tickets for nothing!

On the one hand, at least he came and said good-bye. On the other, I guess I have the answer to my as yet unasked question about where our relationship is going. Oh, he says he'll be back in a few weeks, but I don't foresee a lot of staying in touch in the interim. Why bother with the girl who's far away when there are plenty of others nearby? He's a very out-of-sight, out-of-mind kind of guy—and it was fun while it lasted.

That's what I'm going to keep telling myself, anyway.

So now, without Jane, George, Charlotte, Bing, Caroline, or even Darcy, it's just me at home, staring down my last two semesters of school and no certain future beyond it. Well, me and Lydia.

Oh, God. My entire social sphere has been reduced to Lydia. This cannot bode well.

Friday, September 28th

"I can't believe you're leaving me, too." Lydia pouted as we settled ourselves on the lawn at the music festival. We had just spread our blanket out and begun to listen to the strains of . . . something. I think it was a ukulele, but we were pretty far away.

"Don't worry—I'll be back in a couple of weeks. I can't miss school."

"No, but apparently you can miss *me*," she grumbled.

What a difference three days (and one phone call) make! To think, only seventy-two short hours ago I was lamenting my lonely existence, resigned to my fate as Keeper of the Lydia (™ me, weeping into my keyboard) and a long, lonely year in the library or in front of a camera with nothing to say. Now, after the music festival with my rambunctious baby sister, I have to pack for my trip.

Because tomorrow, I'm going to go pay a visit.

And not to George. No, he's free to flirt with whatever swimmer girls he happens across in his various ports of call. I thought I would care more that he left, but beyond that first day? Not really. But then Charlotte called me.

I couldn't believe how much I missed the sound of her voice. It's only been a month since she left—since we spoke—but as soon as she said, "Hi, Lizzie," I was flooded with homesickness. And bear in mind, I was the one still at home.

We talked for over an hour. It turns out I needed to talk to my best friend about how crazy this past month has been. And it sounds like she's doing really well. She's settled in at Collins & Collins and her new apartment. Her little sister Maria was up interning for the summer. Charlotte hadn't been watching my videos, trying to stay as mad at me as I deserved, but Maria had a hand in getting her watching again. She called because she was worried about Jane. And worried about me.

She invited me to come visit her at Collins & Collins for a week, just before school starts. And I'm going. I need Charlotte's perspective, and I need my friend. And as we talked, I realized just how wrong I'd been. I was definitely the stupid one here. I should have tried to see things from her point of view and been happy for her new job.

Just a couple of days ago I didn't know what was going to happen next, and now . . . I can't wait until tomorrow.

"Whatever," Lydia said, brushing off her previous petulance. "I'll still know everything going on in your life, because one, you have nothing going on in your life, and B, you can't help but post that nothing on the Internet."

"True enough," I said dryly. I'm bringing my camera with me to Collins & Collins, of course. I have a thesis to do, after all.

"And your loyal viewers will not lack for adorbs if I do my own videos!" Lydia crowed triumphantly. "Don't worry, I got your back, sis."

"Thanks ever so much," I replied. Yes, Lydia is planning on resuming her own *interesting* entries into the docudrama of our lives lived on the Internet. One can only imagine the trouble she'll get into with her iPhone this time. I just hope she doesn't end up vandalizing someone's car. Again.

I do worry about leaving Lydia to her own devices. But again, it's only a week or so. I'll be back in time for school. Lydia's classes at the community college are keeping her busy this year, in that she has actually been going to class so far this semester. And I really want to see Charlotte. Besides, what's the worst that could happen?

Saturday, September 29th

I am here at Charlotte's place, one bottle of wine split between the two of us, and I have not felt this happy in a very, very long time.

The minute I arrived at the apartment complex, I was so giddy to get out of the car and see Char that I accidentally left my car unlocked and the keys in the ignition. Luckily, she lives in a pretty decent building, and no one stole it. Perhaps the fact that it's a ten-year-old Honda Civic with windows you have to manually roll down disguised its value. (Actually, I am lucky. I did have my camera in there.)

Charlotte and I just ran into each other's arms (if there was a field of flowers behind us I didn't notice) and did not stop talking until she sacked out for the night. And I turned in to *my* bedroom, with my journal.

Yes, that's right, it's a two-bedroom.

"New construction!" Charlotte said to me, showing me around the place. "New carpets—new appliances, and the pièce de résistance . . ." She opened up a pair of shuttered doors off the kitchen.

"No way!" I exclaimed. "You have *your own washer and dryer?*"

I had done enough research online for Jane last weekend to know that this was a big deal in the modern apartment landscape.

"I know!" she said with glee. "I haven't had a washer/dryer in-house . . . since my family moved out of the house and into the apartment! Lizzie, you have no idea how incredible it is to have my own stuff, my own place, with enough room for guests and to not worry about the money, and . . ."

Charlotte smiled, relaxed. And I realized I hadn't seen Charlotte fully and completely relaxed since . . . before high school? Before hormones, the pressures of daily life, and the difficulty with her family's finances set in. As hard as it was for me to accept Char's giving up on her documentary dreams and degree, the fact that she didn't have to hold on so tightly to the tethers that were pulling her in opposite directions was amazing.

Soon enough, the wine was opened and we were on Charlotte's couch. And we *really* started talking. All about how she'd felt marginalized by the videos' success, how I didn't think of her as a sidekick, and how much she's enjoying life outside of higher education.

Then I told her all about George, and my disappointment that I had been dropped—I mean really, a girl can take a hint—and she just looked at me like I was an idiot. "Well, he wasn't really your type, was he?"

"I know he was a little out of my league, but . . ."

"Out of your league?" Charlotte scoffed. "Why, because he spent four hours a day at the gym? Please, you were so outside of *his* league I consider your foray into dating him slumming, caused by temporary insanity."

"Temporary insanity?" I cried. "He was hot and charming."

"He was also full of it," Charlotte replied. "I watched your videos. I mean, you *know* that he didn't come to Bing's party because of his beef with Darcy."

True, I had come to that conclusion.

"Yeah, but—"

"So why let him get away with a stupid lie?"

"Well, maybe it wasn't totally a lie . . ."

"If his phone was stolen, how did he call you?"

"He . . . got a new one?" Except he hadn't. I had seen him, and I saw his phone. Same "Ryan Lochte is my Spirit Guide" phone case. Which I used to think was meant to be ironic, but now . . .

"Maybe they found the guy who stole it and he got it back," I tried again, but it was weak. I was tired of defending him, and there was no need, anyway. Not my boyfriend, never was exclusive, and he's off enjoying other young women who are having momentary bouts of insanity.

"Let's talk about you!" I said cheerfully instead. "How's Collins & Collins? What's it like to work for . . ." I couldn't keep the dread out of my voice. "Mr. Ricky Collins?"

"First of all, I work *with* Ricky Collins, not *for*," Charlotte corrected me. "And it's going really well. It's a lot of work, but I'm—dare I say it—enjoying myself."

"Enjoying yourself?" I was skeptical. "Making Better Living videos where you teach people how to screw in a lightbulb?"

"The Better Living videos were commissioned by Catherine De Bourgh. They pay the bills," Charlotte remonstrated. "Which allow us to start creating our original content."

"Which is?"

"Game of Gourds!" she cried, and grabbed her computer. "Come on, let me show you what we've been working on."

"Well," I said, after viewing the rough cut of the first few installments. "That is a very emotionally wrought competitive cooking program."

"I know," Charlotte replied. "At least it's cooked butternut squash they're flinging. If it were raw, it would cause a concussion. I need to tweak these episodes tomorrow, before we present them to Catherine De Bourgh for funding approval."

"Wait, tomorrow?" I said. "But tomorrow's Sunday."

"We're a start-up, Lizzie." Charlotte smirked at me. "We work eight days a week. I took this afternoon off to be here when you arrived, but I basically live at my office."

"But then when are we going to see each other?" This sucked. I had only a week with Charlotte before I had to go back for school. I knew she would have to spend Monday through Friday at Collins & Collins, but I thought we'd at least have the weekends, and after work.

"I was hoping you'd be interested in seeing the offices," Charlotte replied, twisting her fingers in front of her. "I think you'll find it enlightening. I have an empty office where we can put a desk in for you."

"Well . . . okay. I mean, sure, I'd love to see the offices, but I don't want to be in anybody's way . . ."

"You won't be!" Charlotte replied, flinging her arms around me. "You'll love it, I promise. I hope you brought your one suit jacket. This is gonna be so much fun!"

WEDNESDAY, OCTOBER 3RD

So, I had a phone call with Dr. Gardiner a little while ago. It went . . . surprisingly okay.

"Hi, Dr. Gardiner? It's Lizzie Bennet. I'm calling from Charlotte Lu's new offices! . . . Yes, she's doing great, and we are having a wonderful time. Actually, she had an idea that I thought . . .

"See, that's the thing. What if I *didn't* come back for classes next week? . . . No! No, absolutely not, I am not dropping out. But what if instead of taking my last four lecture classes, I turn those into four independent studies? . . . Well, they would focus on shadowing four separate new media companies, learning about their initial goals and then what the company evolved into, as well as analyzing their business practices. . . . Of course, I'll still be doing my videos for my thesis at the same time.

"In fact, Charlotte graciously offered up Collins & Collins to be the first new media company I shadow. . . . Yes, that is remarkably convenient. But I don't think it's—

"No, it's not just a ploy to stay with Charlotte. Although I would be staying with Charlotte . . . Dr. Gardiner . . . Dr. Gardiner, listen. I think it would be really good for me. On-the-ground experience before I actually get on the ground, as well as providing an in-depth study of the business side of new media theory. If you think that I am better served coming back to campus and taking those last four lecture classes, then that's what I'll do, but I think you know I'm right. This could be a great opportunity. . . .

"You will? I can? Thank you, Dr. Gardiner! Thank you so much! I promise, I won't let you down."

* * *

Since everything's squared away at school, looks like I get to have a new adventure! Now, to the other phone call.

"Hi, Mom, it's Lizzie. . . . No, everything's fine. Charlotte sends her love. . . . No, she's not married yet. . . . Because she's working very hard and doesn't need a man to define her? . . . Mom, could you please drop it with the Option C stuff? I actually wanted to talk to you about something. About maybe visiting with Charlotte a little longer than planned . . ."

Friday, October 5th

I'm enjoying it here at Collins & Collins a lot more than I thought I would. Charlotte is the power behind the throne and Ricky Collins is proving to be a bit more tolerable when on his home turf. So much more tolerable, in fact, that when he suggested I stay longer than my allotted week, and when Charlotte pitched an idea that took me out of the classroom for my last year of grad school, I actually did it.

Honestly, I thought that Charlotte's idea would be nixed on all sides, but Dr. Gardiner actually went for it. And my mom—once Dad took the phone away and I presume talked her down—was fine with it, too. So now, it's actually happening. My last year at school will not be spent safely on campus; instead, I'm going to be shadowing four different companies and writing up a prospectus (prospecti?) for each—the first of which is Charlotte's. And I have no idea what the other three will be. But I am researching like crazy, using those contacts I gained at VidCon, and Dr. Gardiner said she would pull a few strings if needed. Not to mention, I am yet *again* thankful for the fact that I've been keeping this journal. No doubt it will come in handy for my independent studies as well as my thesis, as well as helping me to stay sane.

Four independent studies. And a thesis. All on my own.

Oh, Lord.

And the truth is, looking back through these pages, I can now see that I wasn't really looking forward to going back to school this year. Part of it is because it's the last year—oh, dear, I'm going to have to grow up soon, let's delay that as long as possible—but the bigger part is that it wouldn't be the same. Not with the videos becoming such a big thing and everyone at school knowing about them. (Recording your life and putting it on the Internet invites scrutiny from people, you know, whodathunk?) And certainly it wasn't going to be the same without Jane at home, and without Charlotte at my side in school. Either I'm changing very quickly, and everything is standing still, or I'm the one standing still and everything is changing around me. Either way, I'm out of joint with the world.

So apparently, to get myself back in joint with the world, I'm going to have to take part in it—at least on a temporary basis. Out of the nest. Wild and free.

No, it's not scary at all.

But I have to say, seeing my bestie handle herself in the corporate climate of Collins & Collins has been inspiring. And from what I've seen of the division of labor between her and Ricky, Charlotte pretty much runs the place.

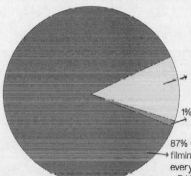

12% Ricky's work—schmoozing Catherine De Bourgh, learning new corporate-speak, employee morale, beard maintenance, inexplicably going to Canada to meet his fiancée (for the first time)

1% photocopier

87% Charlotte's work—putting together projects, filming, reviewing cuts, managing Ricky, telling everyone what to do and getting it done, being a BAMF

Ricky considers himself more of an "ideas" man. However, I haven't heard him say one idea yet that didn't come from his primary investor, Catherine De Bourgh, who got it from a corporate culture platitude book. I haven't met the infamous Catherine De Bourgh yet, but Ricky keeps threatening—er, I mean promising to take me along on one of his and Charlotte's business dinners at the De Bourgh estate. I don't think she actually lives around here—this far-out corner of the tech valley is not very swanky yet. (Hence why Ricky can afford office space and Char can afford a two-bedroom.) But she sure keeps a close eye on her investment. Considering that I'm shadowing this company, I doubt I can say no. Besides, it will make for a good paragraph in my Collins & Collins prospectus: *How One Secures Funding, and What Asses They Must Kiss to Keep It.*

But who knows, maybe I'm wrong—I've been wrong about a lot of people recently. Maybe Catherine De Bourgh is a pleasant yet shrewd businesswoman who will take me under her wing and teach me about this business.

See? I'm learning to be less judgmental already.

Tuesday, October 9th

I have dined with De Bourgh. I have been blessed by the Holy Venture Capitalist on High by being permitted into her presence while she masticates and imbibes. I was warned in advance not to think too lowly of myself, since she would not expect me as a poor grad student to have anything stamped in designer labels to my name, but that as long as I put together a neat appearance and was duly humble, I would be fine.

I was so warned by one Mr. Ricky Collins during the entire hour's car ride to her house.

I was not warned, however, that Catherine De Bourgh would have other guests as well.

But let me back up. Let me indulge in reliving the entire night, from tempestuous beginning to bizarre middle to the relief of it having ended.

It was an hour drive to Catherine De Bourgh's place, as she lives in the more established side of Silicon Valley. Not that where Collins & Collins is isn't nice, but the area is what Ms. De Bourgh would term "developing"—which apparently involves a lot of chain restaurants and reasonably priced office space.

Apparently, Ms. De Bourgh's neighborhood is the ritziest of the ritziest and boasts some notable neighbors. Ricky said that when Mark Zuckerberg moved in down the street from her, he tried to buy up all the other houses on the block. But—again, according to Ricky—the request was "quickly withdrawn, when he realized the estate in question belonged to the venerable Catherine De Bourgh!"

I'm not going to lie: When we turned onto her street, I kept my eyes peeled for a curly-haired guy in a hoodie.

And when Ricky called her home an "estate," he wasn't kidding. You know how Netherfield was the biggest house in the nicest housing development in our small town? The De Bourgh residence is twice as large, with fences three times as high. She has a guard at the gate. His whole job is to sit there and let people in. And honestly, who's going to try and break into the house? It's half a mile away from the road! I doubt Mark Zuckerberg is going to make that trek.

But anyway, we arrived, we were admitted (we were told, however, to park in the visitors' lot, a hundred yards from the house), and Ricky, practically bowing, pulled me forward to be introduced to Catherine De Bourgh.

"Do you go by Lizzie or Liz?" she asked.

"Well, usually it's—"

"Of course it's Liz. No grown woman would *ever* go by such a juvenile name as Lizzie. Liz, I've heard so much about you. Mostly because you were Collins's first choice for a partner but you decided against accepting a rather generous offer to come work for me, I understand. Must be nice to have such freedom of choice in your future prospects. Or are you one of those that simply don't want to work?"

I heard a sound. It was the sound of any hope I had for finding a welcoming-yet-powerful businesswoman to learn from dying. Also, it was the sound of the thing Ms. De Bourgh was holding in her arms gasping for breath.

"Oh, poochie, you want your din-din, don't you? Don't you, my little Annie-kins?"

The thing—a decrepit, one-eyed rat-sized dog of some indeterminate but probably overly pure-blood breed—growled and shivered in response.

"Anakin?" I asked Charlotte in a whisper. "Like Darth Vader?"

"No, like Annie-kins," she clarified. "Like she's Daddy Warbucks and that's her orphan."

"It's so heartening to see you rejoicing in the love only a canine companion can bring," Ricky piped up, mostly to cover my unfortunately timed snort.

"Annie-kins is not a pet, Collins. She's practically my business partner. Just like Miss Lu here is yours."

"Uh, of course!" Ricky said hastily, ignoring the look of alarm from Charlotte.

While Ms. De Bourgh was busy air-kissing her dog, Ricky was busy rhapsodizing about the virtues of pet ownership, and I was wondering if she was being hyperbolic or if Annie-kins was on the CDB Venture Capitalist board, a door opened behind us.

"Aunt Catherine, the chef says dinner is ready. Oh."

I turned. And saw one Mr William Darcy.

Seriously. Talk about being blindsided.

If it was any consolation, he seemed to be as surprised as I was. I'm taking it as a given that his displeasure was equal to mine.

"What are you doing here?" I couldn't help but blurt out.

"I . . . I'm having dinner with my aunt," he replied. Then he coughed and cleared his throat. "I'm passing through, on my way back to San Francisco. . . . And you?"

"I'm . . . visiting Charlotte."

"Mr. Darcy!" Ricky Collins cried and rushed forward to pump the unsuspecting man's hand. "I am Mr. Collins, of Collins & Collins, your aunt's latest investment! I have heard so much about you, especially from Miss Elizabeth's many wonderful—"

"Mr. Collins!" Charlotte stepped forward, rushing to my aid. God help me—God help us all—if Ricky accidentally told Darcy about my videos. "Um, you have to give Darcy here a chance to, um . . . greet us first?"

"As always in matters of proper corporate decorum, you are correct," Ricky said, deferring to Charlotte.

Darcy seemed to take this as his cue and nodded to Charlotte. "Good to see you again, Charlotte. And you, Lizzie."

"Gracious, does everyone here already know each other?" Ms. De Bourgh piped up. "How disturbing. And how very fortuitous for you, Liz. Knowing important people like my nephew. One would not expect it of someone whom I'm assuming went to public school."

Darcy took his eyes off mine for long enough to spare his aunt a glance. "We met this past summer, while I was staying with my friends the Lees."

"Oh, the Lees! You must tell me how Bing is doing back at medical school in Los Angeles—and that darling Caroline, have you snapped that one up yet? She's almost too good for you, what with her accomplishments and beauty—and she knows absolutely everyone worth knowing . . ."

It might have been a hunger-induced hallucination, but I think I saw Darcy blush.

"Aunt Catherine," he said, a little warning in his voice. "The food must be getting cold."

"All right, all right—we'll go in now." Ms. De Bourgh sighed. "Come on, Annie-kins, my sweetie pie. Let's see if chef made our favorite nibbles."

I'm going to assume that the food was delicious. I barely got to eat. I was so busy answering Ms. De Bourgh's questions that by the time the meal was over, Annie-kins had eaten more than I had.

Sometimes Charlotte sent me sympathetic looks, but she'd already been through an invasive questioning like this before. She knew the only way for me to get through it was to lie back and think of England.

"Liz, do you play polo?"

"No."

"Dressage?"

"No."

"Anything horse-based at all?"

"No."

"Goodness, what are they teaching young women these days?"

"I . . . used to play tennis."

"And then gave up on it, one assumes—so typical." She sighed.

"I preferred to focus on my education."

"So, Liz, what are you studying?"

"Mass communications, ma'am."

"What about mass communications is so important that you decided against becoming Collins's second-in-command?"

"Um . . ." I began nervously, "considering the speed at which the world is changing in terms of how we talk and relate to each other, I consider mass communications to be vitally important."

"Hmm . . ." Ms. De Bourgh's lips compressed into a thin line. "Well, I suppose I can admire your desire to finish your education. But isn't your family quite poor?"

"I . . . um . . ."

"How many sisters do you have?"

"Just the two."

"And you all still live at home?"

"Well, Lydia's only twenty, and Jane actually just took a job in Los Angeles and moved out."

"You say 'only twenty,' I say 'already twenty.' It seems rather stunted to me to have full-grown daughters still living at home with their parents. What a tragic commentary on the declining work ethic of today's younger generation. I have always felt the middle class has been too coddled. I do hope you're not one of those who are jealous of people with money. But we do work so much harder than you."

"Of course you do," I said. I think she missed the sarcasm, because Ms. De Bourgh just kept talking, blissfully unaware.

"Life must be pretty good if you're willing to turn down a job with career growth potential. Of course, I prefer getting out there and getting my hands dirty, but that wouldn't concern someone like you, who is content to sit at home and play with a camera and a computer and call it education."

"But I don't," I said, unable to hold it back anymore. Charlotte's hand squeezed my arm under the table. "I don't 'play'—I take it very seriously. And considering that you have invested in a new media company like Collins & Collins, you seem to take it seriously, too."

I managed to do something amazing. Ms. De Bourgh stopped talking and actually looked at me. As did everyone else in the room. Darcy stopped with his fork in midair, his eyes keenly on mine.

"I mean . . ." I continued, suddenly nervous. "Surely, for someone who appreciates hard work, you can see that creating content and cultivating an audience are hugely difficult endeavors that are worthy of the time and effort it takes."

"The advertising revenue is what makes it worthwhile—and quite honestly it's the only thing the Internet is good for. Don't you agree, William?"

Darcy, whose eyebrow had gone up while he stared freakishly at me, put his fork down. "The advertising is only as valuable as the audience watching—which responds to content quality."

Wow. Did Darcy just back me up in my argument?

But before I could so much as blink, Ms. De Bourgh blew out a breath of frustration. "Of course you're right, William. You always make the best sense. Just like my darling Annie-kins here. And of course like Caroline. When is that girl coming to visit again? You should bring her with you next time. Luckily, her work schedule is so flexible, such a complement to your rigid one."

As Ms. De Bourgh kept extolling the virtues of Caroline and matching her and Darcy's accomplishments (I believe something was mentioned about how Darcy playing the trumpet in middle school equaled Caroline having once sung for the Commander of NATO), Charlotte leaned over to me.

"Well done," she whispered.

"What?" I replied, equally low.

"Keeping your cool with Catherine—I half expected you to hulk out."

"I'm not going to hulk out in front of your boss, Char."

"Really? Your fork says otherwise."

I looked down. My fork was gripped in my hand pretty tight. And now bent slightly. Oops.

"Liz? Oh, Liz!" Ms. De Bourgh called out. "I was just saying to William here that I hope your sisters are better prepared for life than you are."

"I believe we are all as prepared as we can be," I spoke with assurance. Hey, I can balance my checkbook, which according to Bing is important. And Jane is managing fine. And Lydia . . . well, two out of three ain't bad.

"Really?" Her eyebrow went up—very like her nephew's. "I certainly hope you can cook. Meals of culinary excellence like this one will be few and far between for those pursuing starving artist status."

"I can heat a can of soup as well as the next person." Mom never got very far with me in the kitchen.

"Hmmm . . . Do you paint?"

"No."

"Fence?"

"No."

"Tell me, what is your opinion of the Monroe Doctrine?"

Believe it or not, it only got more farcical from there. I have no idea why Ms. De Bourgh was so keen on needling into my life and pointing out everything wrong with it. However, on those occasions when she was not feeding her dog caviar or gushing to Darcy about his self-importance, I noticed that she kept glancing toward Charlotte. I can only assume that she was trying to ascertain that her newest hire in a position of extreme responsibility did not consort with rabble? That she wanted to make sure Charlotte's friends were worthy of her? Or maybe she was comparing and contrasting Char and me in her own head and coming to the conclusion that Ricky had made the correct decision in hiring her—a conclusion I myself had come to a while ago.

It was just so bizarre that by the time we were on the ride home, I had to restrain myself from laughing—something I couldn't do in front of Ricky Collins, of course. He just kept going on and on about how fortunate it was to finally meet the revered Mr. Darcy, and how he hoped to entice him into a visit to the offices. Charlotte hummed nicely and made notes in her calendar, while also gently reminding Ricky to not tell Darcy about my videos.

"He would certainly be embarrassed. And we don't want to embarrass anyone as important as Ms. De Bourgh's nephew, would we?"

Got to love my bestie. Always thinking of the save.

If I were at home, I would have reenacted the entire thing for Jane. . . . Although Jane isn't at home, a fact that keeps fleeing my mind, and when I remember it, I get this small hollow feeling in my chest. I hope she's doing well in LA. She's sent me a care package already, and she seems to be really loving her job, but there's a pitch in her voice that tells me something is missing.

But, if I were to talk to Jane now, she would tell me to be nice. And that's exactly what I intend to do. I came here with the objective to see things more from Charlotte's perspective. And there's no reason to not extend that to Ricky Collins. Char seems to manage him pretty well, and while he can be annoying, he's never mean. He just tends to walk in without knocking and talk way too much.

And as for Catherine De Bourgh, she can't be that bad, either. After all, she . . . loves her dog?

However, I doubt I can extend my new open-perspective philosophy to Darcy. His defense of my (correct) argument aside, he was exactly the same tonight as he had been before: rude, standoff-ish, and probably thinking about what a trial it was to be forced to dine with such plebeians. So, yeah, that's a bridge too far. Luckily, he's just passing through. No reason to think I'll be forced into his company again.

SUNDAY, OCTOBER 14TH

I really should just never end my diary entry on phrases like, "I'm certain to ace that exam tomorrow!" or "Let's just keep driving over this cliff—we're bound to land on the other side!" or "Oh, I'm sure I'll never see him again!" It just doesn't go well for me.

A full week after the Shock and Awe of seeing Darcy at Catherine De Bourgh's dining table, and I hadn't given him another thought as I went about my life. Shadowing Collins & Collins is going really well—I get to be involved in (or at least watch) all aspects of production, from writing to filming to editing, not to mention endless meetings about corporate outreach, how to create buzz, selling their "Better Living" videos to clients who want them, and then selling advertising on their own productions, like "Game of Gourds." No wonder Charlotte works eighty hours a week, and no wonder we were spending another Sunday at the offices.

Well, at least *I* was. Charlotte and Ricky had a brunch with Ms. De Bourgh, where she was trying to foist a consultant on them (because Ms. De Bourgh is suddenly worried about Charlotte's lack of corporate experience). And apparently she succeeded, because Charlotte came back with said consultant. She was adamant that I meet him.

Who's him, you may ask?

Who do you think?

Go on, I'll give you one guess.

"Lizzie," Darcy said upon my entry to the conference room.

"Darcy." I tried to mask my annoyance with pleasant disinterest. "You're the consultant?"

"Yes. My aunt asked me to run through Collins & Collins's

numbers, to make sure that everything is progressing as it should."

Right. Progressing as it should. Meaning, making sure that Charlotte's lack of business experience was not a drawback to a company whose CEO has all the qualifications of an Internet-generated list of corporate buzzwords. The bonus, presumably, is to torture me. But Charlotte, with her spine of steel, did not look worried. She instead looked ready to face down the challenge.

"I'm certain you will find everything in great shape," I said, smiling at Char.

"Yes." He nodded. Then, "How is your family doing?"

Talk about a left-field question. Especially considering the entire room—consisting of several people—was watching us awkwardly shake hands. "They're fine," I replied. Then, I decided to put him under the same scrutiny he was applying to me and Collins & Collins, by asking the questions I hadn't been able (or had been too shocked) to ask last week.

"I mentioned at dinner the other night that Jane recently moved to LA. For work. You were in LA for a while, weren't you? Did you happen to see her?"

And I was rewarded by watching him squirm.

"No," Darcy replied. "Los Angeles covers a large area. I, uh . . . I did not see your sister."

"That's enough small talk; now let's get to the real reason you're here!" said the smiling, afro'd guy behind Darcy bouncing on the balls of his classic Adidas shell tops. "And that's to meet me. Hi—Fitz Williams."

He held out his hand. And when I took it he pulled me in for a hug.

"I am Darcy's better half and business partner in a few of his half dozen companies. And I have heard plenty about you, Lizzie Bennet."

"You have?" I froze, my eyes shooting to Darcy. He looked at his shoes. "That can't be good."

"Or, it could be great. You have no idea, and you'll just have to keep guessing, Lizzie B! Now, tell me all about yourself. Start from birth."

"Well, I was born in California . . ." I began, laughing, but then Darcy cleared his throat.

"I'm already riveted," Fitz said, taking his cue. "But we're gonna have to save it for dinner. You, me, my boyfriend Brandon, who is already going to love you because he has a thing for redheads. You in?"

How could I not be in?

If I'm forced to endure Darcy while I'm here, at least he comes with a side of Fitz. A cheerful, engaging guy with manners and charm. How is it possible Fitz is friends with Darcy? Then again, I find anyone being friends with Darcy inexplicable.

FRIDAY, OCTOBER 19TH

It's an interesting thing, shadowing a company that has recently been placed under the supervision of a consultant. Because basically, he's shadowing the company, too.

Which means that every photo shoot, every filming, every meeting, every editing session that I am observing, Darcy is observing as well.

He's everywhere. I can't escape him. If I try to arrive early to a meeting, he'll be loitering in the hall outside, insanely punctual and pleased to "escort me in." If I try to arrive at the last minute, he'll have held the meeting from starting so I could be shamed for my tardiness as I try to slip in unnoticed.

This has had the odd effect of making me very aware of Darcy, whether he's there or not. It's like my brain goes on high alert every time I'm in the Collins & Collins offices. Is he here? No? Then where is he? Knowing is the only way to avoid him!

This is normally where I would say thank God for Charlotte, but having Darcy here means she's now working 160 hours a week just to make sure everything is too perfect to possibly find fault with, so instead, I'm going to say thank God for Fitz. Fitz makes everything fun. You name it—meetings about show development, the interminable process of editing a "Better Living" video—if Fitz is there, it's already 1,000 percent better.

Heck, he even made this week's foray into Dining with De Bourgh (™ me, a couple of entries ago) enjoyable.

Well, tolerable at least.

I think I'm getting used to Catherine De Bourgh. She's just someone who wants to exert her influence on the world and is used to doing so because she has money to invest. And since she doesn't have children, she overly involves herself in the lives of her nephew, his friend, and her weird ratty dog.

And her niece. Because this time around, the game was Compare Lizzie Bennet Unfavorably to Georgiana (Gigi) Darcy.

"How's your sister Georgiana getting on?" Ms. De Bourgh asked Darcy, tacitly ignoring the rest of the table.

"Quite well. Actually, she's now nationally ranked in tennis."

"Splendid, splendid! You see, Liz, what dedication to an activity gets you? It's too bad you gave up on tennis, although you likely don't have the arm strength for it. You know, William, it was so unfortunate when Georgiana gave up swimming."

"It's for the best," Darcy said stiffly (more stiffly than normal, even). "She wished to focus her accomplishments."

"Such a work ethic! Liz, you should take notes—you girls today are much too prone to time-wasting."

Darcy slid a glance at me that could only be called sidelong before replying, "My sister certainly does not engage in time-wasting activities."

Again, if Fitz hadn't been there, making funny faces at me behind Ms. De Bourgh's back and talking to me like an adult about the finer points of business plans versus grad papers, I would have had a hard time keeping it together, even for Charlotte's sake.

Fitz is certain I would like Gigi. He thinks she's a cool kid, but from everything I've heard, she's as focused and driven and snobby as her brother. Although I did hear a lot of that from George, so . . . consider the source.

And given the choice between the two, I would much rather believe Fitz, and give Gigi the benefit of the doubt. But then again, I don't know if Fitz's judgment is sound when it comes to the Darcys. After all, he thinks Darcy is a good dancer, and that he charmed the pants off of the poor girl who was forced to dance with him at the Gibson wedding.

And for a guy who is so focused and driven and snobby, and not to mention anti–time-wasting, Darcy does seem to be spending a lot of time loitering in hallways, looking at his phone, and then putting it away in a hurry when he sees me. If he has better things to do, he doesn't have to be here, prying into Charlotte's business. And there is no definitive end to his "consulting." Fitz said it was only supposed to be a couple of days, but Darcy keeps wanting to stay and dig deeper.

I hope that doesn't mean Charlotte, or Collins & Collins, is in trouble.

MONDAY, OCT 22ND

It's no secret that I find Darcy strange. Annoying, aggravating, snobby, and pretentious, too, but mostly strange. But perhaps, yesterday was the strangest Darcy encounter of all.

I was in my little office at Collins & Collins, yet again on a Sunday. I could have stayed at Charlotte's, but she had a morning brunch with De Bourgh (the amount of time she and Ricky spend placating that woman's need to micromanage while she eats is amazing) and was coming back to the office afterward, so I decided I would just meet her here. I was in the process of setting up my camera for my regularly scheduled recording of my video, when who should walk into the empty office but Darcy.

"Oh. Hello," he said, as if he was surprised to see me. In my office.

"Darcy—what are you doing here?"

"I was . . . just passing, and I thought I might check with Charlotte . . ."

"Charlotte's at brunch with your aunt."

"Oh," he replied quickly. "I see."

"She should be back relatively soon, if you want to wait."

"Yes. Thank you."

And he took a seat. In my office.

Obviously, I should have clarified that I meant he could wait in the office that was assigned to him down the hall, not in mine. But I didn't, so there was little choice but to sit down as well.

"Are you filming something?" he asked, nodding toward the camera resting on its tripod.

"Oh!" I exclaimed. "No. That's not on."

"What's it for?" he asked.

There are times when it's okay to tell small fibs, massage the truth, if you will. Then, there are times when you have to outright lie.

"I . . . sometimes record things. Just notes. Documentation. To help with my, um, thesis."

Luckily, he seemed to buy it, and didn't poke all the obvious holes in such a lame excuse. In fact he just nodded, distracted, and looking out the window.

And said *nothing*.

"So . . ." I ventured after an uncomfortable amount of silence. "Were you hoping to talk to Charlotte about the operational report?"

"Yes," he answered, although it seemed like the idea had just occurred to him.

"But I thought it wasn't due until next week."

"It's not," he agreed quickly. "I just . . . like to stay on top of things."

And again . . . silence.

Clearly the onus of conversation was going to be on me, so I decided perhaps it was a good time to bring up subjects he had successfully avoided in the past.

"So, how are Bing and Caroline?"

"They are well."

"You, Bing, and Caroline all left the neighborhood in quite a hurry at the end of the summer."

That only garnered a stiffening of the mouth and furrowing of the brow.

"Do you think Bing might ever come back to Netherfield?"

"I doubt it," Darcy replied. "He's very busy in Los Angeles with medical school and new people."

I nodded and tried not to let the acid churn in my stomach, lest I get an ulcer.

"Well, if he's not going to come back, is he going to sell the property?" I asked.

"If he can. It was an impulsive purchase, considering the way the market is. For now he'll likely rent it."

Right. Impulsive to buy, impulsive to leave.

Darcy, probably sensing he was treading on thorny territory, tactfully changed subjects.

"Your friend Charlotte seems to have settled in well here at Collins & Collins."

"Yes, she has." I couldn't help but smile. "I wasn't very support-ive at first, but it turns out I was completely wrong. She's doing very well, and I am incredibly proud of her."

"Must be useful, too, to be working so close to your home-town."

"Close?" I scoffed. "It was a four-hour drive."

"Close is relative," he replied. "A four-hour drive means she can make it home if she's needed. Or if she just wants to visit for the weekend."

"True," I mused. "But it's also not *too* close. That way she doesn't get sucked back into the minutiae of daily life there, and she can make her own life here."

"Exactly," he agreed, and weirdly was almost smiling. "Not too close and not too far is ideal. Your friend likely prefers it. You would probably prefer it as well. You could even move farther away."

I had—and still have—absolutely no idea what he meant by that. Did he mean I would be happy living in Siberia? Or that I was destined to move up here and eventually go to work for Char-lotte?

My confusion must have shown on my face, because he blushed and looked out the window again. Then, after a lengthy pause, he suddenly stood up.

"I should go."

"Really?" I stood up, too—it seemed like the thing to do. "But Charlotte should be back—"

"No, I'll . . . I'll see her tomorrow. It wasn't important."

Before I could ask if the operational report was so unimportant, why was Charlotte killing herself over it, he had stalked out of the room and was gone.

Leaving me *completely* perplexed. But at least it made for a good video, once I was certain he'd actually left the building.

It seems like the more I'm thrown into Darcy's company, the less I understand him.

Thursday, October 25th

I am LIVID. I don't even know where to start.

No, that's wrong—I do know where to start. Start at the place that all of my problems originate lately: Darcy.

Why am I so livid at the person who just days ago was vaguely strange, mildly irksome, but tolerated for politeness's sake? Because now he's not vaguely strange and mildly irksome. He's the WORST HUMAN BEING TO ROAM THE EARTH. No, check that—HE DOESN'T EVEN GET THE TITLE OF HUMAN BEING. HE IS PROTOZOAN POND SCUM.

Because now I know that it was *Darcy* who decided that Jane didn't deserve Bing, and broke them up.

And I got it straight from the business partner of the horse's mouth.

Fitz told me. We were hanging out, and he thought he was defending Darcy—since it is not a secret (at least to Fitz) that I am slightly unimpressed by his friend. He was telling me how Darcy is actually a really good guy. And if you're his friend, he'll do almost anything for you. Then I asked for an example.

"Last month, he warned a friend about a girl he was seeing. He pulled him away from the whole situation. He warned him that it was . . . unhealthy. She was bad news."

"Who was the friend?"

"Bing Lee."

It was like the world was shifting under my feet, and all I could do was hold on to my chair. When I managed to put two words together and ask what reason Darcy gave for wedging himself into the lives of Bing and the as-yet unnamed girl, he said that the girl was a gold digger—not being real, and only in it for the money.

So to recap: DARCY thought JANE was the insincere one. That she was only with Bing for his money.

Now, my sister has been called a lot of things: sweet, kind, a living Disney princess, but none of those things imply that she would ever date someone just for his money.

I know I speculated in the past about Darcy's involvement in somehow breaking up Bing and Jane. But it's one thing to wonder; it's another thing to know.

And I don't want to know this! That must be the case, right? How else to explain why I have been paralyzed from doing or saying anything since I found out yesterday? All I've done is dodge Darcy in the hallways and tried to process this new information.

I don't want to know that people exist who could possibly think that badly of my sister. I don't want to know that Bing is apparently so incredibly wishy-washy that he would believe his "friend" over someone who loves him like Jane. And I don't want to know that people like Darcy get to roam free. I prefer to think that life is like a superhero movie—good prevails and the bad guy's facing twenty-five-to-life for general dickishness.

But sometimes the bad guy does get away with it. Sometimes, he does get to destroy other people's lives. Like Jane's. Heck, like George's.

Why am I such a coward that I can't confront him with this? Why am I so afraid to even tell Charlotte? It's simple—he has the ability to ruin my friend's career. She's all wrapped up in operational reports, and he has his aunt's ear.

I was stuck with my feelings balling up, powerlessness rendering me frustrated to the point of shaking, so when I got back to Charlotte's tonight, I resolved to tell someone. Thus I called the one person who most deserves to know.

"Hey, Lizzie!" Jane picked up on the first ring. "It's so good to hear from you!"

"Hey, Jane. Good to hear your voice." And it was, too. She

sounded at once bemused and happy and engaged. Like a steaming cup of tea. All of my anger temporarily dissipated.

"Did you get my care package?"

"Yes," I replied. Jane had sent me yet another care package, full of warmth and love and home. It made me smile and my chest all hollow and achy. "It was fantastic. I love the postcards of LA in the thirties."

"I knew you'd like those," she replied. "So what's up?"

I could have told her right then. But instead, my resolve had dissipated with my anger, and I ended up chickening out. Like the coward that I was.

"Nothing," I mumbled. "I just . . . wanted to hear your voice, is all."

"Wow," Jane said, and I could hear the smile in her voice. "Everybody wants to talk to their big sister today."

"Why? Did Lydia call?"

"Actually, Lydia turned up on my doorstep."

"Really?" I sat up straight. "Wait, doesn't she have midterms?"

"Yes," Jane replied very carefully. "That she does."

"OMG, is that Lizzie?" I could hear Lydia in the background, practically bouncing off the walls. "Tell her that we are going to have the awesomest time in LA and she should hop in her car and come down here and haaaaaaang!"

"Did you hear that?" Jane asked.

"Yes. Tell her that I would love to." And I would, I realized. I would like nothing better than to hop in my car, drive through the night and wind up on Jane's doorstep tomorrow morning, and spend the weekend with my sisters. "But unfortunately I have to stay here."

"I'll try to convey your disappointment." Jane replied kindly.

"Jane, can I ask you something?" I girded my strength. Tried to find my resolve.

"Of course, Lizzie."

"Have you heard anything from Bing?"

There was a long pause. I had never really asked Jane this directly. I always talked around it, and she talked around it, but now I had to know.

"No. Lizzie, that's . . . that's over." For once, Jane let her sadness show through. But also, her resignation. She had accepted it. It was over between her and Bing. Nothing to do but move on.

"Did you ever tell him about . . . you know. The forty-eight hours of worry?"

"No." She sighed. "By the time it had happened, there was no point. He just . . . he pulled away from me. That's all that happened."

All that happened was, just when Jane had realized that she'd fallen in love with him, Bing had pulled away. No, check that. Bing *was pulled* away. By someone who he thinks is his friend.

I fell back on my bed. The tear that had been threatening to fall all day slid out of the corner of my eye.

I wanted to yell. I wanted to scream the truth. But I couldn't.

If I told Jane what I knew, it would just drag her back to a place she'd decided to leave behind. A place I didn't want to see her, locked in her room for three days, picking over every aspect of their relationship. She didn't need or want that.

But I was still stuck knowing this thing I didn't want to know.

"So, how's work?" I asked instead.

"*Crazy*. But great," Jane said.

We talked for a couple more minutes, but since I couldn't say what I wanted, I got off the phone pretty fast.

Now, I'm still stuck not knowing what to do. I hate this. And I hate, I hate, I *hate* Darcy.

I guess I have to do the only thing I can. Keep it inside. Somehow. Avoid Darcy like the plague, and hope this doesn't bubble over into a rage filled tirade that costs Charlotte her job and me my dignity.

Sunday, October 28th

Well, *that* was interesting.

I can't even begin to describe what just happened.

Luckily, I don't have to. I have it all on video, and can simply transcribe it.

LIZZIE: Okay . . .

DARCY: Two parts of me have been at war. Your . . . odd family, your financial troubles—you're in a different world from me. People expect me to travel in certain circles. And I do respect the wishes of my family, but not today. I've tried to fight it for months now, but Lizzie Bennet . . . I'm in love with you.

(pause)

DARCY: I can't believe it, either. That my heart could completely overwhelm my judgment.

LIZZIE: Well, I hope that your judgment will be some solace in your rejection, because these feelings are not mutual.

DARCY: You're rejecting me?

LIZZIE: Does that surprise you?

DARCY: May I ask why?

LIZZIE: May I ask why you're even here despite your social class, the wishes of your family, and your own better judgment?

DARCY: That was badly put, but that's the world we live in, you can't deny it—social classes are a real thing. People who think otherwise live in a fantasy.

LIZZIE: And that is just the beginning of a substantial list as to why I am rejecting you.

DARCY: Such as?

LIZZIE: Such as . . . the nicest thing you've ever said about me was that I was "decent enough." You act like you'd rather have a hernia repaired than be around me. You have a checklist of what makes for an "accomplished" woman. And don't even get me started about what you did to Jane.

DARCY: What about her?

LIZZIE: You took the heart of my sister, the kindest soul on the planet, and tore it in half!

DARCY: I . . . didn't mean . . .

LIZZIE: Why did you do it? Why, Darcy? Does causing pain to those lower than your social standing bring you joy?

DARCY: No, I simply doubted her long-term faith in the relationship. I watched her dealings with other men. At your local bar that night when he was away. She was being very social.

LIZZIE: That's because she's nice! Have you not met Jane?

DARCY: And what about his own birthday? Her indiscretion.

LIZZIE: Indiscre—?!

DARCY: While he was entertaining his guests. She was . . . engaging with another man. I saw it with my own eyes.

LIZZIE: That's not true!

DARCY: It was then clear to me that Jane's feelings for Bing were fleeting and that she never truly cared for him as he did for her.

LIZZIE: Are you kidding me?!

DARCY: From that point, I never believed that her feelings for him were any more than simply her kindness. I was protecting him.

LIZZIE: Protecting him or protecting his wealth? Did you really think that she was dating Bing for the money?

DARCY: Well, it was made pretty clear to me that this would be an advantageous relationship for her!

LIZZIE: By JANE?

DARCY: No! But by her family, YOUR family.

LIZZIE: My . . . family.

DARCY: Your *energetic* younger sister, and especially your mother.

Every discussion, every moment I observed her, she would blabber about Jane and Bing—it defined and consumed her life.

LIZZIE: I . . . I'm . . .

DARCY: I'm sorry, I never thought of *you* that way.

(pause)

LIZZIE: And what about George Wickham?

DARCY: What about him?

LIZZIE: What imaginary act of friendship caused you to do what you did to him?

DARCY: You seem unnervingly interested in his concerns.

LIZZIE: He told me of his struggles.

DARCY: Oh, yes, his life has been quite a struggle.

LIZZIE: You destroy his life and joke about it?

DARCY: So this is what you think of me? Thank you for explaining it all so eloquently.

LIZZIE: And thank you for proving time and time again that your arrogance, pride, and selfishness makes you the last man in the world I could ever fall in love with.

DARCY: I'm sorry to cause you so much pain. I should have acted differently. I was unaware of your feelings toward me.

LIZZIE: You were unaware?! THEN WHY DON'T YOU WATCH MY VIDEOS?!

(pause)

DARCY: What videos?

END RECORDING.

I . . . It's been two days and I still can't believe he said that—and I can't believe how I responded! Oh, shit—I told him to watch my videos. *Watch my videos.* If there was one person in the world who I never wanted to find out about them, it was Darcy.

I manage to be polite when forced to be in company with him—sometimes even amused—but I don't exactly hold back in my videos. At this point, I'm betting he's watching through the events of the Gibson wedding and our stay at Netherfield and realizing just how much restraint I practice in face-to-face situations. And some of the things I say . . . they're not untrue, but they are likely considered defamatory.

I could get sued.

I'm going to get sued.

Oh, shit.

And what am I supposed to do now, at Collins & Collins? Just go through every day pretending it didn't happen? That Darcy didn't confess his (erp) *love* for me, and he doesn't know about my vague Internet fame and his sort-of-vague Internet fame because of it? That is going to make for one awkward budget meeting.

I can't pretend everything is the same as before because nothing is the same. I'm not that good a liar. And . . . I can't go on camera and pretend to all my viewers, either. This is just too big to ignore.

I really want to talk to Charlotte. And she can tell something is wrong by the way I give monosyllabic answers and change the subject when we get back to her place at night. But I'm not sure I can—I'm not sure how.

Hell, I could just show her the video . . . since Darcy decided to walk in and make his declaration while I was filming. I could show the world the video, and not go through the pain and awkwardness of having to explain it to all of the viewers.

I'm of two minds about this, though. Part of me, knowing he's watching, wants to spare him any further embarrassment—as distasteful as I find him, I'm not vengeful. Plus, I'm not at my best, either. But then the other part of me knows that I have a contract with my audience. They are, frankly, expecting to see what happens in my life. And this is a big, big thing that happened. A reenactment wouldn't do it justice. And hey, he knew I was filming. What he did afterward on camera is on him.

Also, 95 percent of my comments are asking, "When do we get to see Darcy?"!

Sigh. Deep breath, Lizzie. Deep breath.

What it comes down to is this: any reservations I feel be damned. I wouldn't be honest in my communication with the world, and that's what this entire project is about, right? So, how I come off, how he comes off—that doesn't get to matter.

What matters is that I express the truth. In the clearest way I know how.

Well, everyone wanted to see Darcy—now they get him.

Friday, November 2nd

Darcy came by. I was filming Charlotte's reaction to my last video when he just showed up. The bad news is, yes, he's watched all the videos. The good news is, he promised not to sue me. But the terrible news is that he handed me this letter.

And . . . I think I may be wrong. About everything.

Lizzie—

Don't be alarmed. This letter is not meant as a reiteration of the feelings I expressed to you previously—and as I now know, on video. I won't do us both the insult of replaying that scene. But you once asked me to simply say what I mean, and though I made that my goal when I approached you last, apparently I had not expressed myself well before that. You charged me with two very different crimes last night, and I feel I have the right to answer those charges.

The first is that I intervened in the relationship between your sister and my friend Bing. I admitted this freely, and I stand by what I said—the reservations I expressed about your family (specifically your mother and younger sister) and our fundamental differences apply equally to Jane and Bing. But most especially I stand by what I saw when they interacted. Bing is a person who falls in love easily, be it with a girl or a house in a remote town in central California. I have seen it happen half a dozen times, and it never lasted. But Jane seemed to be different for him. Which is why it was painful for me to see that she didn't seem to be as invested

in their relationship as he was. The way she looked at and spoke to him was pretty much the same way she looked at and spoke to everyone, including myself.

I will admit, I cannot account for Bing and Jane's interactions in private moments and, having watched your videos now paints their relationship in a very different light. It is possible Jane's feelings for Bing were deeper than I initially thought. That said, it does not justify her indiscretion on the night of his birthday party, nor does it negate the fact that Bing was so easily separated from her. If his feelings were as engaged as Jane's, it would have been a much more difficult task. His summer was tumultuous, anyway; it was time for him to get back to the reality of his life. Like I said, Bing falls in love easily. He also falls out of love easily.

I am sorry for any pain your sister may have felt, but perhaps it's best in the long run. I am very cautious of situations where one of my friends might be getting used. You will see why in a moment.

The second charge you lay at my door is that I ruined George Wickham's future, by ignoring my father's wishes for his education after my parents' deaths. While you may feel the weight of your accusations about Jane and Bing heavier, this one is the far worse, in my opinion. Because it is patently false.

I'm sure it doesn't surprise you that I didn't have many friends growing up. But one friend I did have was George. He was the son of our housekeeper, and she was practically family, having the charge of both my sister and me when we were young and our parents had to be away on business. As we got older, George and I started to go to separate schools and run in different crowds, but I still considered our friendship bedrock.

My parents died when I was a freshman in college. Technically, I was an adult, but I didn't feel like one. Suddenly I was the head of my family's company, and the guardian to my little sister. George— who since his mother had decided to retire had been less and less in our lives—came to me the day after my parents' funeral. He asked, as he'd been recently accepted to college, if he would still be able to go, as my father had promised to pay for his education. I told him of course—I was aware of my father's request and intended to honor it. But when I asked that George have the school send the bills to me, he said that he didn't want to bother me with paperwork when I obviously had so much going on, having to deal with the company and my sister on top of being in school. I must have been run over with grief, because I agreed to simply transfer $125,000 to his bank account.

I didn't hear from George again—which was unfortunate, because I could have used a friend then—until near the end of his first year. He said college cost more than he thought, and could he please have some of the tuition bills sent my way, as my father no doubt had wanted?

I have no idea how he spent all the money, but there's not a school in the country that costs $125,000 a year. I told him no.

Our relationship suffered after that.

I know, again from your videos, that this is not the story you were told by George. And also that your relationship with him was closer than that of mere friends. So before you discount what I say as stemming from jealousy, please consider that I do have proof— bank statements, etc. I have also known George much longer than you have. And while he can be charming, he can also be ruthless.

But I didn't know how much he hated me—and had probably hated me for a while—until he took things to the next level and involved my sister, Gigi.

As George was around when Gigi was growing up, she naturally looked up to him. She even developed a bit of a childish crush on him, but as George was our close friend, it was considered by all parties involved rather harmless.

Gigi grew up, and began college herself a few years ago. I hadn't thought about George in quite a while when suddenly (and more recently than I think would make you comfortable) I received an email from him.

It was full of the usual cordialities. He was simply "saying hi," was eager to catch up the next time I was in San Francisco and put the "ugly financial matters of the past" behind us. Then he included a photo. It was a penthouse apartment deck at sunset, with a girl in a hot tub. I knew that deck, that view, and that girl. It was my sister Gigi, and the photo was taken at her apartment in the city.

I left for San Francisco immediately. When I arrived at the apartment, Gigi was—to put it mildly—surprised to see me. She knew nothing, and still knows nothing, about the email George sent, which was as blatant as a ransom note. George was waiting for me to pull out my checkbook, so I did. He must have been hard up for cash, because it took significantly fewer zeroes for him to remove himself from our lives this time. But as glad as I was to see him go, he left my sister devastated to realize that the man she was falling in love with had just been using her.

I still don't think she's fully recovered.

I kept this quiet for my sister's sake, even when I knew he was

maligning me far and wide, buying friendship with a smile and a round of beers. But if you want a secondary source, ask Fitz. He and Gigi are close and she confided in him everything, especially during that period when she was refusing to talk to me.

This was a very hard letter for me to write. And you may choose to not believe me. You can rip up this letter—and actually, I hope you will when you are done with it. But as you allowed me to be privy to the truth of your perspective through your videos, I hope you will be accepting of mine.

Thank you for your attention, and giving this letter the benefit of the doubt.

Sincerely,
William Darcy

Thursday, November 8th

"Charlotte, have I gone too far?"

"What do you mean?" she asked. We had just gotten back to her place after another long day at the office—where we would likely be again in less than eight hours. The life of a start-up. "I thought you decided to not reveal the contents of the letter in your video. Or to me," she added, pointedly.

"I have, and I'm not going to," I replied, letting my bag thud to the ground. "But did I go too far before? Telling every little aspect of my life, hell—posting Darcy's video . . ."

"The views you got off that video were insane," Charlotte countered.

"I know. But still . . ." I hesitated, and took the glass of wine she had poured for me. It had been that kind of a day. "I was so wrong. About everything."

Charlotte took a sip, thinking. "You have been showing events from your perspective. There's nothing wrong with that. But now, because of Darcy and presumably the letter, your perspective has changed."

Yes, my perspective has changed, with every subsequent reading of the letter. I've pored over it at least half a dozen times, and each time, my worldview gets knocked a little more out of alignment.

On the first read, the part about Bing and Jane basically had me seething, and convinced that his snobbishness and superiority made him blind to the true love they had for each other. I was ready to write the entire letter off as completely self-serving, and its author a prime example of a jackass.

But then I got to the part about George Wickham . . . and

while I scoffed at the notion of George being so callous as to ask for money the day after Darcy's parents' funeral, a couple of little alarm bells started going off in my brain. Then, when he talked about his sister Gigi . . . You don't make up something like that about your sister.

And Darcy may be many things, but I have only ever heard him speak with pride and love about Gigi.

On second reading, I ignored the queasy butterflies that kept popping up in my stomach as I read the Jane and Bing section and skipped right ahead to the Wickham part. And I began to realize . . . I had only ever heard George talk about his and Darcy's past. He didn't offer any proof, he just told a story, and I believed him. Because I was happy to hear anything denigrating Darcy. And then . . . I told everyone else, the entire Internet, without ever questioning it. Was I that blinded by a smile and a set of abs? He had me completely snowed—everyone completely snowed. And here I was, priding myself on being the shrewd Bennet.

On third reading, I forced myself to go back over the Jane and Bing section. And as I did, I tried my best to recall the moments that I had seen Jane and Bing truly happy together. And while there were a few, I also recalled how Charlotte once said that Jane is too nice to everyone, so that when she really likes someone, it's hard to tell. Also, I recalled how for the last month or so they were together, Jane was working like crazy and Bing was being pulled away to do interviews. If their relationship were on better footing, maybe they wouldn't have been so easy to break up.

God, even his arguments about my family held up in this new light! As much as I love them, how often had I been the one to try and filter Mom, or driven a drunk and rambunctious Lydia home from the bar?

Basically, I've been blind. Partial. Prejudiced. Absurd.

I wanted to curl up into a ball and hide in the corner, thinking about how I acted toward Darcy. And while in my little mental ball, I had to figure out what to do about the videos. And I realized—I couldn't tell the entire Internet about the contents of the letter. *Especially* not the parts that involved George and Gigi. And no, this was not about protecting George, or protecting my own self-image online. It was about protecting the details of the life of a young woman I've never even met.

And yes, I have *talked* about people before, without them knowing, but at least I knew them. And had interaction with them. I wasn't trading in hearsay.

Way to split hairs there, Lizzie.

But the gist of everything is . . . this story isn't mine to tell. I won't disrespect Darcy, and especially not Gigi, that way.

Charlotte disagrees with me. She would have me talk about it to the audience, "maintain the authenticity of our connection." Or at least to her. But I don't want to talk about it with them. In fact, the only person I wanted to talk about it with was Darcy.

Yes, that's right: after a couple of days of chewing over this letter, I was actually *hoping* to run into Darcy in the halls. Hoping and dreading. Because . . . I don't know why. Because I wanted to ask him for more information? To apologize for being so wrong, at least about George? Get a solid explanation about Jane's supposed indiscretion? (Seriously, what is that about?)

But unfortunately, he's gone.

He and Fitz gave their final report to Catherine De Bourgh (a very favorable report; Charlotte passed with flying colors) and flew back to Los Angeles yesterday.

We even had to sit through a "celebratory" dinner with Ms. De Bourgh last night, and the entire time she was lamenting the fact that Darcy had to leave, but "of course he's so important and busy, moguls like him simply don't visit for weeks. He did that as a favor to me, and it shows just how strong our connection is."

And all I could think was, If only you knew. If I had taken Darcy up on his offer to . . . what? Date? Be his girlfriend? Regard less, if I had, that dinner would have been entirely different. And perhaps with less condescension about my life choices. Which, admittedly, would have been fun.

But considering I still don't know what my feelings are toward Darcy—because come on, he's still an unforgiving jerk who hates my family and destroyed my sister—it's probably a good thing he left town. If I did get the chance to talk to him, to ask for clarity or an apology or to apologize myself . . . I don't even know where I would begin.

Saturday, November 10th

You know, I was looking forward to a little bit of drama-free time. I do have an independent study prospectus to write up, which needs to be turned in remarkably soon. Also, I could use a small stretch of time that is completely normal and boring so I can perhaps find my feet again. And now that Darcy had left, I thought I was going to get it.

But apparently my life doesn't work that way. If this past year is any indication, my life is going to be constantly reeling from one unexpected visitor to the next.

"Lizzie!" Caroline Lee cried, as we once again entered Catherine De Bourgh's compound. "How are you! I've missed you!"

She attacked me with air kisses.

"Caroline," I said, sending a shocked *What the hell?* look to Char. "I'm surprised to see you!"

"Why?" Caroline asked, cocking her head to the side, causing that curtain of black hair to wave in the nonexistent breeze. "Lizzie, surely you know just how good of friends Catherine and I are."

True. In all the times we dined with De Bourgh (how many was it? Eight? Nine?), rarely a monologue went by when Ms. De Bourgh did not mention Caroline.

"And it's too bad that she arrived this week and not last, isn't it, Annie-kins?" The lady in question came forward, letting Annie-kins lick her face like she was a dropped treat on the floor. "We so enjoy seeing Caroline and Darcy together, don't we, my sweetie? Yes, we do. Yes, we do."

"Miss Lee!" Ricky moved in between Caroline and me, and for once I was glad of it as he took her hand and bowed over it. "It is such a pleasure to meet someone spoken of so glowingly by Ms. De Bourgh, as well as my business partner, Charlotte Lu."

Charlotte's look did not seem to say that she had ever spoken about Caroline in terms even close to glowing, but Ricky's profuse, if erroneous, compliments did the trick, because Caroline smiled at Charlotte and seemed to relax.

Then, she came over and attached herself to my arm.

"Now, you simply have to tell me everything that's going on with you! I feel like it's been too long. It's just so lucky that I found you here, Lizzie!"

I bet you can guess how dinner went.

"Liz, look at how Caroline wears her hair. Perhaps you can try to wear your hair like that, although yours will never be as shiny."

Well, after having had to give me life advice for the past few weeks without the benefit of an in-house paragon for contrast, having Caroline around must have been a nice refresher.

"Oh, Catherine!" Caroline blushed. "You said the same thing to the Empress of Japan. And her hair came out just as shiny as mine, once we were done with her."

"And I'm always simply agog at how you manage to look so breezy and relaxed, Caroline, especially considering all the hard work that you do," Ms. De Bourgh continued. "You should give Liz the name of your masseur. She always looks so miserable."

"What is it that you do, Caroline?" Charlotte piped up. All eyes flew to her. Apparently, since getting high marks from Darcy, she was feeling a little bit ballsier. "I don't recall what kind of a job gives you five months off in summer to hang out with your brother."

Caroline's smile froze in place. "I work in publicity."

"And fine work she does there, too," Ms. De Bourgh said haughtily. "It takes a certain level of class to be able to move in the circles we do. Where the decisions are made. It's not for everyone. Now, Caroline, you must let me tell you all about my nephew's recent visit. He was a delight except for the times I mentioned you, when I could tell he was just a smidge lonely—"

If only we hadn't been under the scrutiny of Catherine De Bourgh! I could have pounced on Caroline for answers to all the questions! Questions like: Why did you leave so abruptly? What's up with Bing ditching Jane? Why the hell are you here?

Granted, I know a lot of these answers now, thanks to Darcy, but still . . . I would find what came out of her mouth interesting.

I guess I have to chalk it up to a missed opportunity. And my cowardice, returning in full force when faced with fancy dinners and people who think they are superior to me. Besides, I'm still so unsettled by what Darcy told me in that letter, I'm not certain what Caroline could possibly tell me that I would want to hear.

Sunday, November 11th

"Okay, what is Caroline *doing* here?" I asked in a rush, closing the door to Charlotte's office. Once again, I thought that one dinner with De Bourgh would be enough to send the unwanted scurrying away, and once again I was wrong.

"She's here? Now?" Char asked, jumping out of her chair. "Where?"

"She didn't like the questions I was asking, so she pawned herself off on Ricky. He's likely giving her the office tour."

Charlotte paced back and forth in front of the door for a second.

"God, I hope she's not another consultant Ms. De Bourgh hired."

"I doubt it," I replied. "Unless you need someone who 'works in publicity.'"

"Did she say what she wanted?"

"To catch up, apparently." Caroline had actually burst into my office and said that she was there to visit me. Considering I hadn't heard from her in months—and trust me, I'd been trying to reach her—that is highly suspect. "But really, I think she wanted to know what's in Darcy's letter."

The letter. Which Darcy gave to me on camera.

"So, she's been watching your videos," Charlotte replied.

"She says she hasn't, but it's obvious that she has." There is no way Caroline turns up here, now, without knowing all about the recent drama. She couldn't like me that much. She probably never did.

Char began pacing again, now pulling at her lip, which is what she does when mulling something big over.

"She wants to know what's in the letter," she repeated.

"Yeah," I said. "Whodathunk she wanted to know Darcy's secrets so badly?"

"I don't think that's why she wants to know what's in it, though," Char replied.

"What do you mean?"

"She's afraid. Afraid he said something about *her*."

"Okay." I was happy to play along with Investigator Charlotte (I am, after all, Lizzie the Spy). "But what could Darcy have to say about Caroline?"

"You said you asked her questions. What did you ask?"

When Caroline burst through my door, I had used the opportunity (and the glaring light of my camera) to ask all those questions I couldn't delve into the night before. I quickly repeated the whole list to Charlotte: Why did they leave so quickly this summer? Did we do anything wrong? What happened at Bing's party, the indiscretion?

"That's it," Charlotte interrupted me. "The indiscretion — did she tell you what it was?"

"No, she skipped right over that."

"She knows what it is, it involves her, and she wants to make sure Darcy didn't spill that secret."

I blinked at Char. "That seems a bit of a stretch."

"Think about it." She came over and sat down next to me. She had that gleam in her eye like she'd figured out an Agatha Christie whodunit. "It's the straw that broke the Jane and Bing's back. If she had something to do with it, whatever it is . . ."

"Why would she care if I found out now? Jane and Bing are already broken up." And from what Jane has said, it's permanent.

"Maybe she doesn't care about *you* finding out." Char pulled on her lip again. "Maybe she cares about *them*. Your viewers."

I let that sink in for a second. "You know, she did burst into my office just when I was filming. Quite the coincidence, don't you think?"

Char nodded. "And she knows your filming schedule. That you generally shoot your videos on Sunday and post them on Monday, film on Wednesday and post on Thursday."

"Okay, but . . . she cares that much about what people think about her?"

"When you were at Netherfield, Caroline made sure she was seen as your friend on the videos," Char argued. "But what did she do when the camera wasn't on?"

"She was fine to me, and Jane, but . . . more often than not, she was making snarky comments in the corner with Darcy." Meaning that Caroline never did like us. She was just playing nice for Bing's sake, and for the sake of the camera.

Charlotte smirked in triumph. "As someone who quote-unquote works in publicity, she would know that there *is* such a thing as bad press."

It all fit. With Charlotte's logic and hindsight, I could see everything. Caroline being nice to me at Netherfield (she knew about the videos, and didn't want me saying bad things about her anymore), egging me on to vent my Darcy frustration (she wanted it recorded that I hated him, because she had some idea of how he felt about me), her saccharine quality whenever we met out in the world (barely hidden disgust), and her lack of communication once they left town (Bing was free from the little people, back to the big city).

Oh, and those snarky comments in the corner with Darcy! She was ingratiating herself to him. With the benefit of hindsight, I can see that Caroline's crush on Darcy was pretty ill-concealed. There's a reason she's Catherine De Bourgh's favorite potential life mate for her nephew.

"Excuse me," I said, rising, acting as dignified as I could manage. "But I have to go tell off Caroline, in terms my mother would describe as unladylike."

"No, wait!" Char blocked me from the door.

"What for?"

"Why tell off Caroline, and only have satisfaction for yourself, when you can get her to reveal her true colors on camera, and expose her to the world? Then, we may have a chance of getting real answers, too."

I paused.

"Charlotte Lu. I do enjoy your devious mind." I sat back down. "But how?"

"We have until your Wednesday filming to figure it out."

I sighed. "Okay, but after this, I really do have to start working on my prospectus."

Friday, November 16th

Well. That was fun. Caroline came to see me on Wednesday *just* as I happened to be filming. Shocking, that. And she *just* happened to apologize for lying and saying that she hadn't been watching the videos; she was *just* so worried about me, given recent events, and wanted to be here for me.

Of course she did.

Charlotte played her part like a pro. I think for Christmas I'm going to sign her up for community theater. She called Caroline out on her coincidental propensity to come and see me when I'm filming, as well as her "helping" to keep the videos from Bing and Darcy. That flustered her enough that we actually got to see the Real Caroline Lee for once.

And the Real Caroline Lee? Not so nice.

She admitted that she deliberately didn't tell Bing that Jane loved him when Darcy pulled Bing away, because she thinks Jane is unworthy of her brother. That Jane's career is going nowhere and that Bing has more responsibilities than prancing around being in love with someone who comes from a family so very far beneath him. Of course, she rationalized this by saying she did it out of love for her brother. She would do anything for the preservation of her family, and their "happiness."

I meanwhile restrained the urge to slap her.

So there you have it, Caroline Lee — crappy sister, no friend to the Bennets. Glad we got that one cleared up.

Alas, we still didn't get any answers about the "indiscretion" (which, yes, I should just ask Jane about, but . . . I don't want to put her into the past again. She's moving forward. Besides, if there was no "indiscretion" she wouldn't know what they're talking about, anyway.), and we didn't get the real reason Caroline wanted to see the letter. But she did give up hope of ever seeing it by calling my mother inconsiderate and belligerent and Lydia an embarrassment to everyone, and then storming out of the building.

We haven't seen her since. And hopefully never will.

Please, universe, please say that is the last of the drama I can expect for a while. I could use some normal. I have a prospectus to write, and I would really like to make some serious headway on it before Charlotte and I hit the road home for (woo-hoo!) Thanksgiving next week.

Tuesday, November 20th

Ladies and gentlemen, we are ready to leave the building. And I am so ready to go home.

Tomorrow, that is. Charlotte still has some last-minute adjustments to make to the Game of Gourds online trailer for its Thanksgiving release. Ricky has already left the building and fled to the great northern paradise of Winnipeg, Manitoba, where he will spend the holiday in a country that celebrated their Thanksgiving weeks earlier. But he's calling every fifteen minutes or so, and relaying instructions from Ms. De Bourgh about the best font and filter. (Note, the best font and filter were chosen and locked a month ago, but hey, let's question everything last-minute.)

Actually, I shouldn't be too harsh on Ricky. I've gotten to know him a lot better over the course of these past two months, and he's not that bad. He's . . . he's actually pretty nice, in a vaguely disconcerting way. He even offered me a job upon graduation.

"Should you have no other means of supporting yourself, of course," he clarified. "And it will not be nearly as lucrative as the package you refused and Ms. Lu accepted lo these many months ago, but your talent would be an asset. Especially at a cut rate."

Believe it or not, I'll miss Collins & Collins. The cheesy Halloween and Thanksgiving decorations I put up. The morning meeting and the coffee room. Of course, I'll miss Charlotte the most. I am thoroughly convinced I did the right thing in not taking the job, but being at Collins & Collins has been an eye-opening experience. Heck, I'll even miss Ricky Collins, a little.

But I won't miss Ricky enough to go along with his plan to force Charlotte to stay here through Thanksgiving, just to make certain the Game of Gourds trailer gets uploaded as scheduled.

(First of all, it's scheduled within the system, so it should go off without a hitch. And secondly, it's a task that can be monitored from literally any computer *anywhere*.) Nope, now that Ricky is out of the building and out of the country, I fully intend to whisk Charlotte out the door, tomorrow, for a well-deserved holiday. No matter how many times he calls her and asks for minuscule changes to the trailer.

It's going to be turkey, stuffing, and Mrs. Bennet's southern sweet potato pie. Home, here we come!

THURSDAY, NOVEMBER 22ND

"Too . . . much . . . pie . . ."

That was the refrain from all three Bennet sisters, as we lay on the floor of the den, slipping in and out of our Thanksgiving turkey comas. We'd just finished with dishes duty, Dad had commandeered the living room TV for his annual re-watch of *Planes, Trains, and Automobiles*, and Mom was lying down, exhausted from the intense schedule of cooking, serving, and passive-aggressively questioning her elder daughters about the state of their lives.

"That's my Jane, looking lovely as ever," Mom had said as she ladled out more mashed potatoes. "But I'm just so worried about you in Los Angeles! Why, your car!"

"My car will be fine, Mom," Jane replied with characteristic patience. "It was parked, and the side-view mirror got knocked off; insurance is taking care of the repairs."

"Until then, I am happy to ferry you to and from the train station," our dad interjected.

"But you are not eating enough in Los Angeles, are you?" Mom had continued. "When girls move away from home they never eat enough. Unless they have a nice boyfriend to take them out for fancy meals. I don't suppose you ever ran into Bing in the city?"

Way to be circumspect, Mom.

But Jane handled it well. "No. I'm busy, he's busy. Can I have more green beans, please?"

"Oh, me, too!" Lydia piped up, and shoved her plate under Mom's nose.

Mom could never turn down a request for more food.

"What about you, Lizzie?" Mom then said. "How is Charlotte doing at Collins & Collins?"

"She's doing great, Mom."

"Oh, so you mean her life *wasn't* ruined by taking the very generous job offer in her field?" she replied, her voice more tart than cranberry sauce. "That's so strange. I could have sworn that's what you thought would happen to you."

"It *is* what would have happened to me," I answered back. "Can I have more green beans, too?"

"Yes, my dear, it seems Charlotte and Lizzie are actually different people," my dad piped up between mouthfuls of stuffing. "I know you think they might have gotten switched at the hospital, but I'm afraid Lizzie is ours—she has the Bennet ears."

My mother sent my father a look that said he wouldn't be getting any green beans.

"What about Mr. Collins?" she'd asked instead. "Is he still unmarried?"

"He's *engaged*, Mom."

As my mother chattered on about how "engaged isn't the same thing as married," and "Canadian women have no idea how to keep a man happy" (meanwhile, the entire nation of Canada might have something to say about that, but I digress), my dad leaned over to me and whispered in my Bennet ear.

"I don't know if you're glad to be back, but I'm certainly glad to have you. It brings the relative amount of silly back down to tolerable levels."

"Thanks, Dad."

"Don't thank me—it also swings her attention away from me to you."

Even in the midst of my self-absorption (the Darcy thing was practically ringing in my ears all through dinner; I wanted to shout it at Mom when she started in on our love lives), I had noticed that

Mom and Dad have relaxed a bit in our absence. Dad mentioned going to bridge at the club again. Mom winked at him while she served the cranberry sauce. And she wasn't forced to skimp on the turkey.

Seriously, it was a thirty-pound turkey.

As we were clearing the table, and Mom was having her well-deserved glass of wine and putting her feet up—she would be snoozing in minutes—I pulled Dad aside.

"So . . . how have things been?" I asked him.

"I think you'll find we've been chugging along without you, my dear—although I do enjoy having you back."

Maybe it was the fact that I had been away, and I could see things a little clearer with distance. Maybe it was my recent introduction to direct confrontation via William Darcy, but I decided not to tiptoe around my father.

"Have you been having any more problems with the bank?"

There, I said it. Bold as brass, like an adult. And my dad looked up from his load of plates like he was realizing I was one for the first time.

"I sometimes wonder if we should have made you so smart and observant." He shook his head. "Perhaps we would have been better served letting you play video games all day long."

"Dad . . ."

"The wolf is no longer at our heels, Lizzie, if that's what you're worried about."

It *was* what I was worried about—and had been for a while. But it felt so good to have an actual answer for once that I couldn't just leave it at that.

"How?" I asked.

My dad began to load the dishwasher. Lydia and Jane were collecting the table linens in the dining room, so I knew I had a little time.

"Did you know we'd almost had the house paid off?" he finally said.

That was surprising, to say the least. "You did? When?"

"Five years ago—before my company downsized. It was either leave and try to find a different job in my fifties, or take a pay cut and hope for the best. I'd never saved for retirement. The house was going to be our retirement. Since it was almost paid off, your mother and I thought that if we could make it through the next few years, when you girls would be out of the house, we could simplify then."

I'd known about my dad's job, of course, and that having us three still at home long past our move-out dates was a burden. But I was feeling a little bit from hearing my dad talk about it so bluntly.

"So we took out a new mortgage on the house, freed up some funds, and resigned ourselves to paying for it for a decade or so longer than expected. Then we made the mistake of carrying on like nothing was different for five years."

"So . . . over the summer . . ."

"Over this summer we fell a bit behind, and we had to have some conversations with the bank. That's all."

"God." I took a deep breath. "No wonder you got so mad about Mom buying out the grocery store. I can't believe she remodeled the kitchen, too!"

"Actually, remodeling the kitchen was a stroke of brilliance on your mother's part. Once it was done we had the house reappraised, and discovered we had more equity in the home now."

I was going cross-eyed trying to keep up with all these real estate terms. Adult conversations are tough. "So what does that mean?"

"Basically, that means since the house is worth more, we owe less on it. And it's kept the bank off our backs." My dad closed the dishwasher and set it to run.

"Dad, that's . . . great. You have no idea how great that is to hear. But—it could happen again pretty easily, right? I mean, should you be back playing bridge at the club?"

"Allow an old man his foibles, Lizzie. I don't have to justify every expense to you." He winked at me as he said it, but it was a dismissal in every sense of the word. I just shook my head. It's awfully hard teaching old dogs new tricks, and if Mom and Dad hadn't learned from this close brush with foreclosure, then when would they ever?

"We will muddle through, kiddo. We always do. And one of these days your mother will finally convince me to sell, and we'll get a smart little condo on the other side of town. Just big enough for two empty-nesters, and your quibbles about bridge at the club will seem silly."

"Wait . . ." I said, confused. "*Mom* will convince you? Not the other way around?"

"Well, where on earth would I house my bonsai or train collections in a condo? Not to mention my daughters." He smiled at me and shook his head. "I want you all to have a home to come to. It's not the same without you. And even in spite of your mother's inquisition, and my sad financial planning, I hope you find coming home worth it."

So that was pretty much Thanksgiving dinner. Conversations big and small. But as we girls lay on the floor of the den post-dishes, I knew Dad was right: the four-hour drive home with a Men At Work tape (yes, tape) stuck in the player, and the entire meal's worth of Mom's cross-examination and then Dad's adult talk, had been worth it. Because I was home again.

"But if I never see another slice of turkey again, I'll die happy," I moaned.

"Don't speak too soon—if I know Mom, there will be turkey soup for the next week," Jane replied, causing both me and Lydia to groan loudly.

"Don't forget the stuffing," Lydia whined. "OMG, if our viewers could see us now."

"You mean *my* viewers?" I slid Lydia a look—although there wasn't much to it; turning my head took more effort than I was willing to expend.

"No, *ours*—duh. My videos got views, too."

Oh, yeah. Lydia's videos. While I was away, she filmed some more of her own, and roped not only Mary but Jane into being on them. Also, her little trip to Los Angeles to visit said Jane? Mom and Dad were unaware of it until Mom noticed her car was gone. Luckily, Jane called them, and then made Lydia call her professors.

But Lydia didn't get interrogated at dinner, did she?

"Right. Your videos."

"You haven't watched them, have you?" Lydia asked, sitting up.

"I'm going to!" I said. "I've just had a lot of stuff going on."

"They're two minutes each."

"Lydia," Jane cautioned. "You saw how busy I was at work? And I haven't had time to catch up on Lizzie's videos. I promise you, Lizzie was working just as hard."

A little pool of dread began to form underneath all the food in my stomach. I knew Jane wasn't caught up on my videos yet, because if she was, we would have talked. But she's going to have to be now. And I'm afraid that her heart is going to break all over again when she sees Darcy admit to what he did to her and Bing. And what Caroline said about her? She'll have to face the fact that we were completely deceived by Caroline—she was never Jane's friend. Or mine.

I wonder if I should tell Jane about the contents of the letter. Or will it make any difference to her? Darcy doesn't exactly apologize for what he did regarding her and Bing. In fact, he outright defends himself.

That might hurt too much.

"Whatevs," Lydia was saying, as she dug her phone out of her pocket and began texting. "You should totes watch my videos. The Los Angeles Adventures are particularly awesome. I got *lots* of views. I made like enough in advertising to get some pretty cool Christmas gifts for certain someones," she teased.

"That's so sweet, Lydia," I began, only to have cold water thrown over me.

"I know, right? I've been dying to get Kitty a super-awesome cat condo, so she'll stop shredding my jeans. It's not a good look."

"As the fashion aficionado in the house, I have to agree," Jane said, smiling at me. Then, as Lydia was distracted with her phone, she said low to me, "You really should watch her videos."

"I know," I replied. "I will. First I'm going to die from overeating, though."

"OMG!" Lydia bounced up out of her prone position on the floor, staring at her phone. "It's Harriet—I have to take this!"

As Lydia jumped to her feet and began to jabber, I couldn't help but feel wistful to have the food coma rebound capacity of a twenty-year-old. And I'm not that much older.

"Who's Harriet?" I asked Jane.

"One of Lydia's friends from school this year," Jane replied. "Lydia's been doing pretty well in her classes, you know."

"That's good! Is that Harriet's doing?"

"Honestly, I think it's Lydia's. And Mary helped her with math tutoring."

"Well, I'm glad she has some good influences," I remarked. "What with her penchant to run off to Los Angeles at the drop of a hat and all."

"They *saw*? Well of course they saw, my videos are online to be seen, bitches!" Lydia was laughing loudly into her phone. "Hells yes, I'll go out and meet your friends . . . Are they cute? . . . Tomorrow? Totes! . . . Anything for my *fans*."

"Although that's a little more concerning," I said under my

breath. "Jane? Do you think Lydia's a little . . . rambunctious? Like too much?"

Maybe it was because I was away so long, but now that I'm back in the bosom of my family, I can't help but be a little concerned. Ever since I got back, my baby sister has resembled nothing so much as a pinball, ricocheting from one thing to the next, making a lot of noise and flashing lights on the way.

Like Caroline said.

Like Darcy said.

I felt like the worst sister ever for thinking that way, but it just kept popping up in my mind, unbidden. I didn't know how to stop it.

But Jane simply watched Lydia, considering. "I just think she's Lydia."

According to Lydia, George Wickham is back in town. No idea why—swim season is long over; the community pools are covered. If he's back, one can only assume that the conditioning job with the Meryton Marines Club team didn't pan out. As per Lydia's sources, however (let's assume he met some of her classmates at the bars he frequents), he will only be around for a couple of weeks. Let's hope.

But as George is in town, I've got George on the brain. And so does Charlotte. She just blackmailed me into revealing part of the letter to my viewers. Not the part with Gigi, but the part where George spent $125,000 in one year of college. (How? Did he put a down payment on a house?) Since it was a rebuttal of what George (and okay, I) previously said on the videos, it was only fair that I give the other side airtime, too.

But still, I feel a little nervous. About betraying Darcy's confidence. About . . . actually admitting to myself that I 100 percent believe Darcy's version of events. Or maybe I'm just still wrestling with how wrong I was about George before. And how wrong I was about Darcy. Because if I was wrong about him for this, I could be wrong about other things, too. I'm not saying that I think he's anything less than a stuck-up rich hipster, but . . . stuck-up rich hipsters are people, too, aren't they?

I think part of this seismic brain shift is that Jane finally caught up on all my videos. Including the ones with a certain hipster. And do you know what she said?

"Poor Darcy."

"Poor Darcy?" I repeated, in shock. "Not even you could possibly think I should have said yes to him, can you?"

"No, of course not," Jane replied. "But it must have been a shock that you turned him down."

"Yes, I would say so," I said flatly.

"It . . . it took a lot of guts for him to come to you like that and declare his feelings. The fact that he thought they would be returned was probably the only reason he managed to overcome his natural awkwardness and do it."

That's my sister Jane. Determined to find the humanity in even the most unlikely of scenarios. Also, she had no idea what "indiscretion" Darcy was talking about, as expected.

"But what about what he did . . . regarding you and Bing," I ventured

"That's . . . more troubling," Jane eventually said. "But it doesn't matter now."

"Jane . . ."

"Lizzie, I knew that Bing was under pressure, which is one of the reasons I didn't tell him about . . . you know. And yes, he trusted his friend's judgment. But if he trusted Darcy more than he trusted me, then . . . maybe we weren't meant to be after all."

Jane stood, straightened her shoulders, and took a deep breath. "Bing made the decision to leave. Not Darcy. Not anyone else. And that's all there is to it."

Jane has been different this past week at home. Of course, she's been her usual crafting, baking, birds-help-her-get-dressed-in-the-morning self, but there's an extra layer to her now. She'll talk about her Los Angeles friends, and how she's getting along with her new roommate (who apparently has a golden retriever that sheds like crazy, making Jane cheerfully Swiffer the house three times a day), and how she went to an underground midnight fashion show in West Hollywood.

But I think that extra layer is actually a little bit of a shell. She'd never been hurt before like she was by Bing, so it stands to reason there would be some scar tissue. But I wonder if she's ever going to be able to give her heart fully again. Or if she'll just be too careful to share it.

Just had an interesting meeting with Dr. Gardiner during her office hours. I was . . . what's the phrase? Oh, yes. Raked over the coals.

But at least Dr. Gardiner does it nicely.

"So, Lizzie," she said, upon my entering. "Where's this prospectus on Collins & Collins?"

"I'm working on it," I replied. "I have until the end of the year . . ."

"Technically you do, but I wouldn't recommend it," Dr. Gardiner cautioned. "You have three other companies to shadow, not to mention your thesis; it would be prudent of you to not put off everything until the last minute. I would also like to read about your experience so I know that these independent studies are a worthwhile reason to skip your final required courses."

"I know, and I haven't put it off, I swear," I assured her. "I'm 95 percent done with the Collins & Collins prospectus."

"Good. I look forward to seeing it on Monday."

Well. Looks like I'm spending the weekend at the library in my study carrel.

"What about your next independent study? Have you found a company to shadow?" Dr. Gardiner asked.

"Yes," I replied proudly. "I met with the co-founder of a company called Gracechurch Street when I was at VidCon. We've been exchanging emails and he's happy to have me shadow his company."

"Gracechurch Street . . ." Dr. Gardiner said thoughtfully, as she typed it into her search engine. "In London? They deal with licensing media to different foreign markets?"

"Yep. That's them."

"So when do you leave for England?" she asked.

"Oh, no!" I laughed. "I'm not going to England. It would be an online shadowing. But don't worry—their company is relatively small, and I have been promised full access. I'll be Skyping into all their business meetings, as well as getting one-on-one time with the co-founder. I'd be watching very closely what they do and how they do it."

But Dr. Gardiner looked less than pleased. "Lizzie." She sighed. "I thought the whole point of these independent studies was to become immersed in the culture of the company. You can't do that from afar."

"Well, if there is a media company close to home, then I'd be happy to approach them . . ."

"What about something not so close?" Dr. Gardiner replied. "I have a contact in San Francisco, who works for—"

"Honestly, Dr. Gardiner?" I said, trying to be polite. "I just got home. I don't think I'm ready to go back out on my own again."

But Dr. Gardiner just looked at me funny. "What do you think is going to happen when you graduate?" she asked.

I didn't have an answer for that.

"Gracechurch Street is a fine company, and adds some nice diversity to the businesses you're studying. And since the clock is ticking, I'll sign off on your shadowing them. But Lizzie . . ." She leaned forward, looking me dead in the eye. "I want you to think about what you're hoping to get out of this experience. And what you'll have to do to achieve it."

Like I said, raked over the coals.

But for now, I have to lay claim to one of the good study carrels in the library (as my grad school cubicle was given up for the independent studies). I have a Collins & Collins prospectus to finish, and a new company to get a head start on.

Jane left to go back to Los Angeles yesterday. And I'm sort of at a loss. Not because she left—that was expected. She got to stay for a whole week longer than anticipated, and will be back for Christmas. According to Jane, the fashion world is pretty quiet between Thanksgiving and Christmas, and everyone goes somewhere fun and exotic (like central California, yay!) before things kick back up in January, when they have to start prepping for the fall fashion shows. Which take place in the spring, and therefore make no sense.

But that's not the reason I find myself at a loss and ruminating on my life choices. It's because Jane pointed out to me the same thing Dr. Gardiner was trying to point out . . . namely, that I might be too comfortable at home, and a bit afraid to leave it.

She's so grown up. When did Jane become so grown up? She's always been older, and responsible, but I think of us as young girls with braids in our hair. Now, Jane is out on her own, working in her field, paying off her student loans, and branching out. And no matter how much I worry about her newfound shell, and can see that she's still hurt by the mention of Bing, she's resolutely moved passed it. (No matter how much I bring it up on my videos, because the viewers are obsessed with it, almost as much as they are obsessed with Darcy.) It all just makes me realize how *un*-grown up I am.

I spend all my time being petty, and obsessing over other people's love lives. I focus on everyone else's business Mom's craziness, Lydia's antics—so I don't have to face reality.

The reality that I'm going to have to leave home soon.

And even though I just spent two months with Charlotte, I was simply visiting the real world, not living in it.

And looking back over these pages, I . . . I have to admit, I've been hesitant. I like to think of myself as so put together and ready to take on the world, but in reality . . . I've never really spent that much time outside of my study carrel.

And in six months' time, I won't have that carrel any more.

Man, first Darcy and now Jane challenging my worldview? Who's next, Lydia's cat?

WEDNESDAY, DECEMBER 12TH

If I haven't already been labeled as such, I am the worst sister of all time. Not for not watching Lydia's videos or not initially being happy about Jane's moving to LA (although very happy that she's doing well now). No, this week's offense is that I forgot about Lydia's birthday, which is today. In my defense . . . Okay, I don't really have one. I've been living at the library in my cubicle doing my shadowing and research (mostly because it's the only quiet place in the world now that Dad's joined the usual Lydia/Mom melee by breaking out his Christmas trains), and I just feel so overwhelmed with everything that I let Lydia's birthday slip out of my mind.

Lydia didn't, though, and since our parents will be in Sacramento for a Hanukkah party over her twenty-first (Uncle Phil is our token diverse relative—otherwise, we are incredibly boring ethnically), she is insisting on throwing a rager. Or, in her words, "The most awesomest party in the history of ever!"

I'm exhausted just thinking about it. Heck, half the time I'm exhausted being around Lydia. I love her, but now that I'm the eldest daughter at home, it's even harder to look at her antics without wishing she would calm down. Take a step back before acting impulsively, and *think*.

But I can't get either of my parents to realize it. Mom just tuts that Lydia's young and having fun! And my dad . . .

"Dad, I can't believe you're letting Lydia have a party while you're gone!" I told him a few days ago.

"Can't you? It's what she asked for, for her birthday, and I saw no reason to say no."

"No reason to say no? How about that she has no self-control?

For Pete's sake, she invited the entire men's volleyball team from her school. Or my school. Or, all the schools!"

"And what would you have her do? Go *out* with the entire volleyball team instead?"

"Well, no, but . . ."

"I see no problem with Lydia throwing a party. We won't hear the end of it until she does, and at least this way she'll be home, and thankfully you'll be here to watch out for her."

So I'm now on official Lydia duty. You know, I think my parents still owe me money for all that babysitting I did when I was fourteen and she was ten . . . although they may have docked me for expenses when they had to have the screen door replaced that one time.

All of this aside, I am as prepared as I can be for the party of the century. What I was not prepared for was an unexpected would-be party crasher that I ran into just this morning.

"Hey, Lizzie!" George Wickham's voice caused a shiver of revulsion to go up my spine. I was in the paper-plate-and-napkin aisle of the grocery store, stocking up on the more practical aspects of party planning. I already had industrial-strength trash bags and all the paper towels in the world in my basket. "Looks like you're planning for a party."

"What are you doing here, George?" I asked.

"Shopping for groceries. As you do." He held up his little basket, which contained a six-pack of cheap beer and Cheetos. Then he shot me that smile that used to make my stomach flutter; now it just made it churn. "It's so awesome to see you, peach."

I managed to step back before his arms made it all the way around me, dodging his hug. I only knocked over three or four packets of plastic utensils in the effort.

"How've you been?" he asked, undeterred. "I'm sorry I never called, it's just I got so busy, I was like, whoa . . ."

"I'm fine, George. Never better, in fact."

"What have you been up to?"

"Oh, this and that." I paused. "I don't suppose you've been watching my videos?"

"You're still doing those things?" George acted surprised. "That's awesome for you. They're totally cute."

Well, that answered *that* question. When I still didn't say anything else, George gave me the puppy-dog eyes. "Come on, Lizzie, you're gonna hold a grudge because I didn't call when I got back to town?"

"Not at all," I hastened to assure him, putting on my politest smile. "I didn't expect you to call. In fact, I thought you were leaving town again."

"I am soon, but I wouldn't want to miss the chance to see you." George smirked. "I'm just glad fate brought us together in the paper products aisle."

"How so?"

"Well, you were out of town, too, right? I thought someone told me you were doing an internship or something? With your friend Charlene?"

"Charlotte," I said, trying really hard to not grind my teeth.

"Right, right. Learn anything?"

I considered him for a long moment before replying. Then I thought, what the hell. "Actually, I learned a lot. Ran into some interesting people there, too."

"Oh, yeah? Like who?"

"Like Fitz Williams. And Darcy."

I had the pleasure of watching George's permasmile falter. But he recovered quickly. "Darcy. Just the mention of his name gives me chills. What with his having ruined my life and all. Hypothetically, of course." He winked at me.

"Perhaps," I said. "But perhaps he has more virtues than you or I gave him credit for."

"Virtues?" he laughed. "You think Darcy has virtues?"

"Actually, Darcy's not so bad," I said. "He has more than some people I could mention."

George finally seemed to register the fact that I was giving him my iciest death glare, because his smile fell completely away, and I felt like I got a glimpse of the guy Darcy knows. The one with such a chip on his shoulder, he would come demand money of a friend the day after his parents' funeral.

"Well," he said, "sounds like I have some catching up to do."

Yes, I thought. *You do. Catch up. Watch my videos, and realize that you should probably avoid being in the same hemisphere as me from now on.* But George, for all his slick charm and street smarts, didn't know when to stop.

"But you can get me all caught up tonight at your sister's party."

"What?" I exclaimed, shocked. "You're not invited."

"Not officially. But I know a bunch of the volleyball guys, and it doesn't sound like it's invitation only—"

"You're not invited!" I stated, more forcefully than I would have liked. "You can't come tonight. And if you're wondering why, watch my videos. They'll explain everything."

And with that, I abandoned my cart of paper towels and plates and marched out of the store.

Of course, then I had to drive across town to a different grocery store for party supplies, but hey, they actually had napkins on two-for-one sale.

I'm so pissed at myself for having liked George. Whereas before I thought he was completely charming, now I can only see a total sleaze. I'm really glad that our backseat activities were restricted to groping and making out, and not actual sex, because there aren't enough showers in the world to scrub that off.

But right now, I'm not focusing on that. Right now, I have to mentally prepare for the onslaught of people about to invade my house. I've laid out the food and beverages, moved all the furniture, locked Dad's trains and most breakables in the den, and put a sign on my door that says "Not the bathroom."

All right, people, let's do this birthday thing. Happy twenty-first to my baby sister!

Friday, December 14th

Oh, my God, I can't do it. I can't go out for another night. Between school, online shadowing a company that's eight time zones away, and Lydia's insistence that we celebrate her birthday *week*, I have gotten approximately four hours of sleep in the last three days.

Lydia's party went pretty well, considering. The police weren't called, so that's a plus. I got to hang a little with cousin Mary, introverts that we are. Almost everyone was gone by dawn, and Lydia enjoyed herself so much, she doesn't remember most of it. Which is worrying. I'm not wrong to be worried when my sister gets blackout drunk, right?

I hadn't even had time to get Lydia her birthday present yet. (Although, for some, cleaning up the house and taking the heat from Mom and Dad for the garden gnome carnage should be birthday present enough.) However, I wandered into the bookstore today on campus and found something I think will be perfect. Jane sent along a present she picked out (and I paid for half of), but I really think this book will be the icing on the cake.

It's called *Where Did I Park My Car? A Party Girl's Guide to Becoming a Successful Adult*.

Honestly, I can't think of a better birthday gift for my party-girl little sister who I would like to see become a successful adult.

MONDAY, DECEMBER 17TH

Okay, that did not go as planned. Lydia did not like the book, to put it mildly, and has not spoken to me since I gave it to her.

Here's the thing. I'm not wrong about Lydia. I am NOT WRONG. I am one of the only people around here who can see her with clear eyes. Mom treats her like the baby and Dad—for as great as he usually is—has always just sort of thrown up his hands whenever it comes to Lydia. She's out of control, and no one is bothering to rein her in.

Let's look at the evidence. She got wasted at the Gibson wedding, throwing up in the bushes. I had to pull my sister out of Carter's when they were going to call the cops on her for stripping down with some guy in the back. For God's sake, she got blackout drunk just last week at her party! She steals Xanax out of Mom's purse, cuts school to drive to Los Angeles, and can't be alone for more than three minutes together. I'm not wrong for wanting her to look at her life and realize she needs to grow up. She's twenty-one now. She'll get charged as an adult. She's not a kid, no matter what Mom says.

And yes, Mom says that Lydia's grades are good this semester. And great—good for Lydia for going to class and paying attention for once and learning—because that's what she has the potential to do. She's not dumb, she just acts that way because . . . because it's fun, I guess. But that doesn't mean she gets a pass on everything else.

Okay, nobody's perfect. And Lydia called me out on the fact that I didn't give Dad a book on how to better manage our money and Mom a book on how to not overly involve herself in her daughters' lives, but Mom and Dad . . . I don't know if they can be fixed. It's probably too late for them. Lydia is still young.

One month of being eldest sister in the house and I've managed to piss Lydia off to the point of complete incommunicado. God, I wish Jane was here. I called her, yesterday, just to get her perspective.

"Hey, Lizzie," she said. "Before you say anything, Lydia called me already."

"What did she say?" I asked.

"She's hurt. She thinks you hate who she is."

"She said that?"

"Not in so many words, but . . ."

"I don't hate her!" I cried. "Not at all. But Jane . . . I just want her to be . . ."

"What?" Jane gently prodded. "Less 'energetic,' right? Not an embarrassment?"

"That's not what I said. And I would never—"

"But that's what she heard," Jane replied. Then she sighed. "I understand where you're coming from, Lizzie. But maybe the method of delivery was a little unkind."

Jane, as usual, was right. The way I presented the book couldn't possibly have been more ham-fisted.

I did accidentally call Lydia "energetic"—which is exactly what Darcy called Lydia when he came on my video and told me he "loved me, but . . ." So, she didn't hear "energetic," she heard embarrassment, I guess. That I think she's an embarrassment.

Maybe there's still a way to fix this. Maybe I can cajole my way back into Lydia's good graces. Hell, maybe another couple of days go by, Christmas fever hits, and she forgets all about this.

Maybe.

Friday, December 21st

Nope. Not fixable.

Lydia went too far this time. She's just . . . ARRRRRGGHHH! She's not listening! And now, she's just reaching out and slapping back at me and you know what, Lydia? It does hurt. And now she's just being a brat, and I . . . I don't want to deal with it. And honestly, I shouldn't have to.

I tried to explain to her a thousand times that I didn't mean the book the way she took it. I entreated, I cajoled, I bought her fro-yo! And how did it go?

"I just wanted to take you out today, to make sure that we're okay," I'd said, as we ladened down our double Dutch chocolate yogurt with the appropriate fruit and sprinkles.

"Hmm," Lydia replied.

"Like I said, I didn't intend for the gift to be mean. And I'm so sorry if I hurt your feelings."

"Hmm."

We wandered up to the cashier to pay.

"I'm just looking out for you. You're twenty-one now. Jane's gone to LA, and I'm going to be graduating soon. We won't be around to look out for you. You'll have to be more responsible, and look out for yourself."

"Hmm."

I paid for our yogurts and guided us outside toward a table.

"It's not a bad thing. I promise," I said. "I mean, you can't be like this forever. Change is good. It's normal."

"Hmm."

"So," I said, as I sat in my seat. "Are we good?"

Lydia remained standing. "No," she said, and strode over to the trash can, dumping her untouched cup of yogurt in the garbage, before walking away.

Okay, so she didn't accept that my gesture was well-meaning. I left her alone for a couple of days after that. But I'd thought it would eventually blow over. Lydia doesn't stay mad for long—more often than not, something comes up that distracts her from what happened before, and we move on. It's human nature. But this time, she didn't. No, letting it go would have been the ADULT thing to do.

Instead, she retaliated, using the only thing at her disposal.

The Internet.

Lydia decided the mature thing to do in this situation would be to create a list of things I can improve about myself and then post it in a video.

And she has plenty of people watching her now, thanks to me.

Lydia's List for Ways Lizzie Bennet Can Be Less Lame

1. *Update my wardrobe.*
   Whatever; I'm used to Lydia deriding my fashion sense. Hey, I prefer classic staples to her adherence to stupid trends. Besides, did she forget that we're poor, and probably shouldn't be going to the mall whenever we're bored? Actually, she probably did.

2. *Get a hobby.*
   Sorry. I don't have time to fritter away on other things besides the pursuit of my degree and career, but glad to know her priorities.

3. *Be better at stuff.*
   According to her, people like to be around others who are good at things. I suppose she would like it if I got better at drinking. Because then I'd be less lame in her eyes.

4. *Get a boyfriend—but not one that leaves town immediately.*
Thanks, *Mom*. And way to bring up the skeevy recent past.
Thank God I never told her the whole story about the real
George Wickham—I'd never hear the end of it. Oh, and I
notice you're fairly boyfriend-free there, too, little sister.

5. *Stop thinking that I'm better than everyone else.*
Which I do not. I don't. I don't think I'm better than anyone
else, because if I did I would never be able to admit to being
wrong, and I can't even calculate the number of times I've
been wrong in the past year alone. But it still doesn't mean
that I'm wrong about Lydia.

It's already gotten thousands of views.

You know, it's not the message—trust me, I get this type of criticism all the time, most of all from myself—it's that she took it to
the Internet instead of telling me. And that just shows me that she's
beyond immature and completely unwilling to change.

I certainly didn't intend to hurt her, but she is willfully trying
to hurt me. And you know what? It's working. Now she's saying
that she's going to Vegas for New Year's with friends, and nothing I
say will convince her otherwise, no hints I drop to the parents will
matter, so why bother? Why bother putting up with someone who
is obviously just trying to hurt me and drive me crazy? I have plenty
of work to do to keep me busy; I'd rather not have to deal with an
immature, needy, reactionary, pissed-off, substance-abusing little
sister, so I'm not going to. I'm not even going to watch her videos
while she's gone. Hell, I won't even follow her on Twitter.

I need to get on with my own life and stop worrying about hers.
You want incommunicado, Lydia? You got it.

Saturday, December 22nd

"Dr. Gardiner!" I called out, running down the hall.

"Lizzie," Dr. Gardiner said, startled. "You've caught me packing up my office for the next three weeks. What are you doing here? It's Christmas vacation."

"I know, but I wanted to talk to you—about my independent study," I said in between gasps of breath. I really do need to exercise more.

"Is everything all right? With the Gracechurch Street company?"

"Yes, great—in fact, I should have enough by the end of December for my prospectus. I was hoping to talk to you about the *next* independent study."

Dr. Gardiner stopped packing up her bag.

"You mentioned you had a contact at a media company in San Francisco? If the offer still stands, I think I would really like to check it out."

I held my breath as Dr. Gardiner considered it. "I thought you weren't looking to go that far away from home."

"I know. I hadn't been," I replied. "But you were right about broadening my horizons. I'm ready now."

Jane was right: I did need to go out into the world, and not be afraid. Besides, what do I have to stay home for? More of Mom's passive-aggressive comments about my love life and Lydia's silent treatment?

"I'll make a few calls, see if it's still possible," Dr. Gardiner finally said.

"Thank you!" I admit, I might have bounced a little bit.

"I'll let you know early next week if it's a go, but Lizzie—if it happens, it will happen fast. So make sure you have everything else cleared out of the way, okay?"

"Yes, of course," I said, knowing she was talking about having my second prospectus done. Which shouldn't be a problem. I'll just . . . not sleep until I finish. "Thank you again. And happy holidays!"

"Merry Christmas, Lizzie," Dr. Gardiner called after me, as I practically skipped down the hallway.

San Francisco, here I come.

TUESDAY, DECEMBER 25TH

Merry Christmas! Right now, we have reached my favorite part of Christmas Day: that pleasant lull after the presents are opened, the festivities done, and everyone goes to separate corners to play with their new toys. While I wait for my new four-terabyte hard drive to sync up (thanks, Bestie!), I thought I'd jot down my impressions of this year.

As Christmases go, it's been an above-average one, I think. Certainly better than when I was eight and I decided to help Mom make Christmas breakfast and ended up making the omelets with what I thought was blue cheese. But it turns out, this cheese wasn't supposed to be blue. We all ended up spending the holiday in line for our one bathroom, doubled over in pain.

This holiday was the first one where I felt like gathering together as a family was a special occasion. With Jane in LA and Charlotte at Collins & Collins, seeing them again (and yes, I know I saw them a month ago) filled me with all those warm holiday feelings the commercials preach.

Cousin Mary, Aunt Martha, and Uncle Randy came over last night. Uncle Randy isn't Martha's husband, but he's been her not-living-together boyfriend for so long we've always just called him Uncle Randy. (Dad claims he has long since stopped judging his hippie sister, but he still only shakes Randy's hand instead of hugging him. Although that might just be the overwhelming patchouli.) Mary brought her bass guitar as always and picked out "Jingle Bells," which is a true sign that it's Christmas, according to Jane. My mom took Martha for a last-minute whirlwind at the mall, and I would have thought that Lydia and Mary would have been thick as thieves, considering how much time they've spent together this past year (what with Lydia staying at Mary's all through August, and Mary tutoring Lydia in math), but no. Lydia pretty much stayed in her room, talking on the phone with her friends from school, whoever they might be.

Jane said I should give it time. Charlotte doesn't say anything, but I can tell she's concerned.

Unfortunately, Jane and Charlotte's visit is going to be shorter this time around—I guess extended Thanksgivings lead to truncated Christmas breaks, but I'll take what I can get. Especially with Lydia still giving me the cold shoulder.

I have decided that I can't care about Lydia's current snit. I just can't. I have my own life to focus on, and she shouldn't get what she wants simply because she's stubborn enough to hold her breath until she passes out.

So, yes, I can't care about it right now. Especially if Mom can't be bothered to care, either.

"Lizzie, I don't know why you're so hard on the girl."

"Because no one else is," I muttered beneath my breath.

"Her grades are up, and everyone deserves a little fun." She sighed wistfully. "I had fun in Vegas when I was a girl."

There's no need to get deeper into that, so I just shot my dad a look and continued cleaning up the discarded wrapping paper from our usual Christmas carnage (which didn't decrease at all this year, even given my parents' brush with foreclosure over the summer—maybe I really should have gotten Dad a book on how to manage finances).

"Your sister is just getting it out of her system," my Dad whispered to me. "I have a feeling that once she comes back from Las Vegas, everything will go back to our warped version of normal."

You're probably right, Dad. The problem is, I don't think our warped version of normal is very good for Lydia. Or for us.

Right now, she's in her room, packing for Las Vegas. Funded by her advertising revenue from her own videos and with Mom's permission to use their shared car, she's taking off in the morning. I doubt I'll get a good-bye out of her.

Which is unfortunate, because by the time she comes back, I'll be gone myself. And I have to admit, I'm surprisingly eager to say good-bye to this drama-filled year and move on to the next thing.

In fact, I just got an email yesterday about the next thing! I'm very excited, because come the first week of January, I'm going to San Francisco! I'll be apartment-sitting in the city (yay!) for a friend of Dr. Gardiner's, while I shadow a company called Pemberley Digital.

Hm. That name is vaguely familiar to me. I'll have to look it up.

Tuesday, January 1st

Nothing like starting off the year with a desperate phone call to your faculty advisor hoping to get you out of something you really don't want to do. Although this time, it doesn't seem like I was as convincing as I was with my bid to stay at Collins & Collins.

* * *

"Hi, Dr. Gardiner! I'm so glad I finally got through to you! . . . Yes, I realize that you're on vacation. . . . In Australia! Wow, that must be fun. . . . So it's about four in the morning there, isn't it? Okay, then, let me get right to the point—this company in San Francisco—that you have been so gracious as to set me up with—it's called Pemberley Digital, right? . . . Well, interestingly, and I'm sure you're going to laugh, that's the name of William Darcy's company, too. . . . William Darcy? The, uh . . . stuck-up hipster who I've mentioned in my videos? . . . True, I've more than mentioned him, and that's actually kind of my point. How am I supposed to shadow the company of a person that I haven't exactly been the biggest fan of—or treated very nicely—on the Internet?

". . . No, I don't have a backup company for my independent study, but I'm sure I could find one. . . . Yes, I understand that this is my last term, and that the independent studies are extremely truncated. . . . Yes, I understand that, but . . . No, of course not. . . . So, if I didn't go, I wouldn't be able to graduate on time? . . . Yes. . . . Yes. . . . No, I get it. You're absolutely right. . . . Actually, I'm headed up there in a few hours—I'll be in San Francisco tomorrow. Okay. . . . Happy New Year to you, too, Dr. Gardiner."

＊ ＊ ＊

Well. Looks like there's no getting out of it without jeopardizing my graduation schedule. So, I don't really have a choice.

To Pemberley Digital, therefore, I shall go.

Sunday, January 6th

I've been in San Francisco for four days now and I am already in love. With the city.

And, I have to admit, with my new independent study.

After I got off the phone with Dr. Gardiner, I accepted my fate. No, that's not true—I moped and worried and bit my nails raw the entire ride up to Charlotte's. My bestie offered to drive me to San Francisco so I could leave my car for Mom, who is without one while Lydia flits off to Vegas. (One could say that it's Mom's own fault for letting her go, but whatever. I'm the good daughter.) Plus, I won't have to worry about parking, and the apartment I'm house-sitting is within an easy mile of the Pemberley Digital offices. Besides, I like to walk.

We stayed over at Charlotte's place on Tuesday, and she dropped me off at the apartment the next morning.

"It will be okay," she told me, as we drove over the bridge into San Francisco proper. "Think about it—you were at Collins & Collins for two months and how often did you see the CEO?"

"Ricky?" I replied. "Almost every day that he wasn't in Winnipeg, Manitoba."

"Yeah, well . . . we're a much smaller company. Besides, you said that Darcy was in Los Angeles right now—even you, with your luck, would have difficulty running into him if he's in a different city."

That was true, and it was the only thing calming me down— Darcy's tweets place him squarely in Los Angeles for the foreseeable future (what good is social media if it can't help you avoid awkward run-ins with the guy who told you he loved you, who you then shut down?) and therefore I shouldn't worry about seeing him. Heck, he might not even know that I'm here.

Although I have to sort of assume that he does know I'm here. Especially if he's still watching my videos. Plus, wouldn't he have to have approved me shadowing his company?

"Not necessarily," Charlotte said, as we pulled up to the corner of Hayes and Octavia, in front of a sandy-colored three-story apartment building that was to be my home for the next couple of months. "Like I said, his company is bigger than Collins & Collins. Do you think the President of the United States approves all of the interns at the White House?"

Again, Charlotte knows exactly what to say to make me feel better.

We grabbed my bags and headed up the stairs to my top-floor apartment. When I found the keys and swung the door open, both Charlotte and I stood there for a minute, mouths agape.

"Okay, I'm not usually jealous of you," Char said, "but I'm getting a little jealous of you."

The apartment was gorgeous. Small—but what in a major metropolitan area is spacious?—and perfect for me. There were shelves and shelves of books that lined one wall, and an open kitchen with a huge table right before the room flowed into the living space. Big windows fed airy light to a few hanging plants. A bedroom beyond, and everything decorated with tasteful restraint. I couldn't have dreamed of a better apartment for me. Seriously, I don't even think Jane could design a space better, and she's the professional.

"The bathroom has a claw-foot tub!" Charlotte cried. "Okay, calming breath, calming breath—remember that you have a washer/dryer in unit."

"True. But Pemberley Digital has an in-house laundry service," I said, inspecting an antique writing desk.

The noise Charlotte made cannot be recorded by our current technology. "Who are you house-sitting for again?"

"A friend of Dr. Gardiner's who is taking a sabbatical in South America for the semester. She just wants someone to collect the mail and water the plants."

"And you get to live here for free?"

"Actually, I get a small stipend."

Charlotte made another non-recordable noise. Then, taking another few calming breaths, she pasted a smile on her face. "Come on—let's go check out that cute French café across the street and then walk around the neighborhood. I'll try to restrain myself from cursing your good luck in the meantime."

The neighborhood (the tourist maps call it Hayes Valley, near SoMa, which stands for South of Market, which is not a pretentious-sounding acronym at all) was delightful. Full of young people chatting, little stores with handmade things, and a wide breadth of boutique coffee shops. Charlotte and I wandered for a little bit, found a place to have lunch, and after one more Don't-worry-Pemberley-Digital-will-be-Darcy-free pep talk, Char got back in her car and drove home to her own apartment with a washer/dryer.

It felt strange being on my own for the first time . . . ever. It still does. In college I had roommates, and at home I share a bathroom with two parents and two sisters. This is the first time in my life I've lived alone. On the one hand, I have complete control of the remote. On the other hand, it is eerily quiet.

But I couldn't let myself get too weirded out by my newfound personal freedom just then, because on Friday, I had my orientation at my new independent study.

"Welcome to Pemberley Digital!" cried the very chipper tour guide, as she handed out badges to me and a group of fourth graders.

The entryway to Pemberley is a beautiful glass atrium, stretching all the way up through the center of the building, feeding natural light down to the fountain in the middle. People moved across glass walkways, saying hi to each other or asking questions in the open atmosphere. Everyone curious, everyone energized. It reminded me of the very best of college campuses. I was five minutes through the door and already I was in awe, stretching my neck to see all the way up.

"Lizzie Bennet," the tour leader said to me as she handed me my badge. "We are so excited to have you shadowing Pemberley!" Then . . . she hugged me.

Belatedly, I realized that was the first clue. At the time, however, I was simply surprised that Pemberley was such a huggy place.

"Now, everyone, Pemberley Digital is a new media and entertainment company that builds technology platforms as well as content. So, what does that mean?" She smiled at the fourth graders. "Well, our CEO, William Darcy—" She grinned wider when she said his name. And oddly, so did other employees within earshot. "—would say we are an innovative firm dedicated to the next wave of communication innovation. But basically it means we make stuff for the Internet. And yes, that's a real job."

That got a laugh out of the fourth-grade teachers.

Our tour guide walked us through the atrium and into the building proper.

"Is that a slide?" one of the kids asked. "And a ball pit?"

"These are some of the offices of our creative team," our tour guide said. "We encourage everyone to decorate their office as out-of-the-box as they want. Conformity doesn't often lead to creativity."

I'd say it was out-of-the-box—it looked like a jungle gym with desk space. The next office looked like an undersea pavilion. The fourth graders ohhed and ahhed. (And they weren't the only ones.)

"And these are our napping pods. Anyone can climb in and take a nap for a half an hour, whenever they need it."

I could easily imagine the noise Charlotte would make if she were here.

We moved on to the third floor.

"These are our production facilities," the tour guide was saying. "We have a stage, a wardrobe department—now, who wants to play on the green screen?"

A bunch of fourth-grade hands went up. And okay, mine did, too.

After that, we made our way through the cafeteria, the theater where new apps and programming are presented (with popcorn!), and up to the rooftop, where there was an Olympic-sized pool, an in-house masseuse, and topiary lovingly tended into the shape of dozens of animals.

"Is that . . . a unicorn?" I asked our tour leader.

She cocked her head to one side. "I've always thought it was a seahorse. Lizzie, I hope you don't mind being grouped with a bunch of kids. We haven't really had a shadower before, and I thought you would enjoy a tour first."

"I did!" I assured her, and watched her face break into the widest smile. "This place is pretty incredible."

"Great!" she replied. "You have no idea how glad I am to hear you say so. I have to take the kids down to the cafeteria for their lunch, but I'll show you your office first, and then come back to check on you. Sound good?"

Yes, my office. Not some corner that wasn't being used I could set up in. My office, with my nameplate next to the door. And it's *lovely*. Big windows, with such a view, a desk with a new computer, and a couch and . . . more than I could possibly have ever wanted.

I sat there in shock for a while, that this is my life now. This great apartment in San Francisco, this incredible opportunity to shadow one of the most impressive tech companies I've ever seen (although my purview is admittedly limited), and being treated like a welcomed and respected member of the team, not a lowly grad student/stranger looking for scraps from the knowledge table.

There was yet another thing that shocked me. Our tour leader? Happened to be Georgiana "Gigi" Darcy. William Darcy's younger sister.

I don't know what shocked me more: the fact that she, a Darcy, was this sweet, enthusiastic creature, or the fact that after admitting to having watched all my videos, she still liked me.

In fact, was very eager to like me.

Gigi Darcy being our tour guide simply brought back to the foreground of my mind the hipster shadow that had been lurking behind every napping pod and innovative company policy. Darcy.

He *has* to know that I'm here, right? No matter what Charlotte says when she's trying to alleviate my worries. The only way he wouldn't is if he stopped watching my videos. Which is a distinct possibility. Perhaps after he gave me the letter, he decided he'd seen all he needed to see.

Regardless, tomorrow is my first full day at Pemberley Digital, and I have to give it my full attention, so I can't give in to the temptation to worry over Darcy anymore. Especially since he's not here.

Wednesday, January 9th

Darcy is here. And yes, I shouldn't be too surprised. It *is* his city, and his company. I'm the one that's the intruder. But I still can't help feeling ambushed.

Although Darcy seemed pretty ambushed, too.

It was his sister who did it. Yes, it seems that the ebullient Gigi Darcy, watcher of my videos and amateur matchmaker, has decided that luring her brother away from Los Angeles to San Francisco and then literally *throwing* him into the same room as me would be the BEST IDEA EVER.

And to think, I had just been contemplating friendship with her.

I'm kidding. (A little.) But there I was, sitting in my office, making a video and killing time before I was scheduled to have dinner with Dr. Gardiner (fresh off the plane from Australia), when in came Gigi, dragging her brother by the arm.

One minute, I was there by myself, and the next . . . Darcy was right in front of me.

It was as awkward as I had feared.

I don't really remember what was said—although I could simply re-watch the video—but I know that he was as surprised to see me as I was him. He knew I was here. As I'd guessed, he'd have to have been informed, but I don't think he had any intention of seeing me. That is, when you find out the girl you professed love to basically thought you were scum, but then find out she is miraculously at your office, your natural inclination might be to avoid the pain and embarrassment of seeing her at all costs. And I can't blame him for that.

It was so odd just being in the same room as Darcy again. He looked . . . different. Not like he had a new haircut or a mustache or anything ridiculous like that, but he seemed to carry himself differently. Or perhaps I was just seeing him that way. After all, this was the first time we'd seen each other since I read his letter and found out just how wrong I was about almost everything.

People look different when you know their secrets. And they look differently at you.

As for me, after the initial shock wore off, I felt shame. As if I'd been caught doing something I shouldn't have—that my being here was essentially snooping into his business and life. But Darcy was so strangely nice about it. Well, nice in his way. He asked if there was anything he could do to make my stay more comfortable. Made sure that everyone was treating me well. The whole time I wanted to scream, "You shouldn't be nice to me! You should be angry I'm here! Or at least a little rankled!"

It's strange. I had been dreading for so long seeing Darcy, and now that I have . . . it sort of feels like I was actually *hoping* to see him. There's such a thin line between those two things.

However, my walk down to the Marina for dinner was not enough to settle my mind on the subject, and Dr. Gardiner called me on it.

"What is it?" she asked. "Is everything okay at your independent study?"

"What? Yes!" I said quickly, bringing my eyes up from my plate. "I'm being treated so well and given access to everything."

"What about the apartment?"

"It's amazing. And you can tell your friend that the plants are still very much alive."

"Then why have you picked apart three dinner rolls and not eaten a thing?"

I looked down at my plate. Sure enough, there was a pile of torn-up bits of bread, ready for me to throw to pigeons like the crazy lady who lives in the park and mumbles to herself. (Which, considering my dislike of birds, is not a good life choice.)

"If you're watching my videos, you're going to find out about it, anyway." I sighed. "Darcy is here."

Dr. Gardiner's academic eyebrow went up.

"I just saw him."

"Well," she finally said, "you knew this was a possibility."

"But that doesn't make it easy. It was very unexpected and uncomfortable on both sides."

Dr. Gardiner took a sip of her wine. "Is it more unexpected or more uncomfortable?"

I considered it for a moment. "Unexpected, I guess. In fact, he did everything he could to make sure I was *not* uncomfortable."

"Lizzie, you are going to encounter the unexpected in your professional life," Dr. Gardiner replied, smiling at me patiently. And personal life, I thought, but Dr. Gardiner continued. "Someone you interned with could be interviewing you one day, or your teacher could set you up to shadow a company that belongs to someone you'd rather not see. But you have to work *with* the unexpected, not against it. Who knows? The results might surprise you."

Once again, Dr. Gardiner was correct—as she tends to be. Things like this happen. You run into people, or work with people, you have a fraught history with. My history with Darcy might be a bit more fraught than most, but still—we are adults. I'm here to shadow his company, and that's all.

"Now, enough about the CEO," Dr. Gardiner was saying. "Tell me all about Pemberley Digital."

As I started going into raptures about the napping pods, our food arrived and I felt a little bit more like eating. But now that it's two in the morning, and I know that I will likely see Darcy again in six short hours, I'm back in my nervous, insomniac journal-writing mode.

I just have to keep remembering Dr. Gardiner's advice. This is unexpected, not uncomfortable. I just have to roll with it.

And who knows. Darcy might end up surprising me.

Tuesday, January 15th

They say things happen in threes. First, Gigi startled me by being my orientation tour leader and genuinely liking me. Then, Darcy startled me by showing up here and being gracious and kind. What could possibly be the third? The cherry on this Let's Shock Lizzie sundae?

Bing Lee.

He just showed up the other day. Walked into my office (I either have to get used to this as the norm or start locking my doors), saw I was filming, sat down, waved to "Charlotte." We talked, but mostly around things. It seems that he is still blissfully unaware of my videos, thinking I'm making video letters for my friend. He also seemed very eager to see me—and as if he'd come into Pemberley Digital for that express purpose.

So, another hit of the unexpected. That's okay, I can work with it.

But I still needed an explanation.

Right after I saw Bing, I ran into Darcy in the hallway. Or he ran into me. I might have loitered for a few seconds outside a meeting he had just been running.

"Lizzie, good," he said, pulling me slightly aside as the rush of Pemberley Digital employees exited the room. "I was hoping to see you."

"You were?"

"Yes." He cleared his throat. "I wanted to make you aware that a . . . mutual acquaintance is visiting."

"If you mean Bing, I just saw him."

"You did?" Darcy looked surprised. "I'm sorry if that disturbed you—Gigi must have told him you were here and I guess he couldn't wait to seek you out."

"I wasn't disturbed," I replied. "But why is he in town? Doesn't he have med school?"

Darcy blinked twice before answering. "He had some interviews, with local hospitals. He asked if he could stay with me."

"Oh. Well, like I said, seeing him didn't disturb me."

"Good," he replied. "I would hate it if you were made to feel uncomfortable."

"Yes," I smiled, sheepish. "You've mentioned that."

"I know that . . . well, with me here for a few days . . ."

"It's your company!" I interrupted, feeling my face go red. "You're the one who belongs here. You shouldn't be the one to feel out of place; it honestly should fall to me."

"I wouldn't want that," he said. Then he cleared his throat. "Are you enjoying your stay—gathering useful information for your prospectus?"

"Oh, yes—Pemberley is . . . amazing," I said. "I enjoyed the meeting you ran the other day—about the investment potential in creative outlets on the Internet."

I had tucked myself into the back corner of a standing-room-only conference room, where Darcy had been leading a discussion about all the creativity and talent to be found online, and how they can help foster those talents. Before I got here, I had been thinking that Darcy's company would be all about making the quickest, easiest buck. But really, Pemberley Digital's mission is to grow and create new things. Through mentoring and development in new media, to make the world just a little bit better.

But when I mentioned the meeting, it was Darcy's turn to blush. "Anyway," he said, changing the subject and walking me back toward my office, "I just wanted to make sure you weren't thrown by Bing showing up here."

Thrown? Yes, a little. But more than anything, I was confused. Why was Bing so keen to seek me out—especially if he hadn't seen the videos? And why on earth has no one told him about them?

And why, oh why, oh why didn't I ask him what the hell happened between him and Jane?

More than anything, seeing Bing just dredged up old feelings from last summer—remembrances of seeing my sister happy, sitting next to him on his couch at Netherfield, looking like the only two people in the world. And then flashes of despair, knowing how hurt Jane was by his leaving.

I've long since stopped being angry at him—it wasn't my place to be angry, and I know that it wasn't *all* his doing. But I still want answers, damn it.

I've gotten too good at letting opportunities pass me by. I have to stop dancing around the edges of the truth and actually be willing to get to the bottom of things.

And with Bing Lee here in San Francisco, maybe I'll finally have the chance.

Friday, January 18th

I just keep getting surprised by Darcy. Not "leaping out of the shadows at me" surprised, but more "revelations of character" surprised. Which can be just as disturbing as, if not more so than, someone creeping up to you in your high school hallway and scaring the bejesus out of you by pretending there is a bird on your shoulder, *Charlotte*.

Not that anything that alarming happened. Well, Darcy did voluntarily wear a newsboy cap and bow tie, which was a little shocking. But a few days ago, I was working late in the office, and no one else was there—except Darcy.

I had been hoping to get answers from Bing about why he left Jane, and how he could let his friend and his sister control so much of his love life, but since I hadn't seen Bing since he dropped by the office almost a week ago, my courage was waning by the day. However, I finally got up the nerve to ask Darcy instead.

On camera.

"Why didn't you tell Bing about my videos?"

I expected evasion. Hemming and hawing. Maybe outright indignation that I would question his judgment. (Hey, outright indignation is not a foreign concept to Darcy . . . or at least the Darcy I thought I knew before.)

But this is where he surprised me.

Darcy said he didn't tell Bing because he was respecting my confidence about the videos, the same way I respected his in not revealing too much of the contents of the letter. I'd never thought of it that way, but he's been keeping my secrets, too. Which is odd for people who are little more than acquaintances, right?

Darcy also said it was because it seemed like it would be cruel.

They've both moved on. Who knows if she would even take him back?

Maybe he's right. In fact, I think he is. Everything that Jane has said since she moved to LA tells me that she's enjoying life and moving on without Bing. But it still makes me so sad.

No, Lizzie, stop it. I shouldn't get involved. (In fact, that should be a belated New Year's resolution.) No good has ever come of it. Hell, I took a step back from Lydia's temper tantrum, on the auspice that I had to focus on my own life. And Jane is doing great on her own in LA. Why should the sudden reappearance of Jane's ex-boyfriend throw everything into a tailspin?

There is so much more going on here—I'm learning so much at Pemberley, I'm part of creative strategy sessions, and I was asked my opinion on color options for this new communications app they are developing. (I went with blue. Always go with soothing blue.) I've even been making friends, hanging out a little bit with Gigi and Fitz, who have threatened me with karaoke.

Everything at Pemberley is about creating something new and innovative, not rehashing the past.

I'm not here in San Francisco to obsess about my sister's love life.

So why is my mind obsessed with Jane and Bing? And admittedly, with Darcy?

TUESDAY, JANUARY 22ND

They say New Year's resolutions only last on average three weeks. So, this is the week to break them, right? Discounting the fact that I actually made my "policy of non-interference" resolution four days ago, it seems like I'm right on schedule. Because not only did I interfere in Bing and Jane's life again, I went and told Bing that Jane is still single.

To be fair, he asked. He came to say good-bye—his "interviews" had finished and it was time for him to go back to class. I can't imagine medical school is as lenient with their third years as my grad school happens to be, but Bing doesn't seem to be suffering for it.

He asked how Jane was doing. He was so earnest. And I realized it was the one thing he'd wanted to know since he saw me. It was the reason he walked through my door. So, as he fished around for information, I just blurted it out: "She's not seeing anyone." And, "If you have something you want to say to Jane, you should call her."

I know—I shouldn't have done it! I just hope Jane can forgive me for it. In fact, I talked to her earlier today, with the express purpose of confessing my interference. But once again . . .

"Studio and Design Services," she said upon answering.

"Jane?"

"Oh, hi, Lizzie!"

"Sorry, I thought I called your cell phone."

"You did—it's just rote now for me to answer it that way—there are so many different vendors to deal with, I've been giving out my cell so they can reach me 24/7. How are you doing?" she asked.

"Good!" I tried to sound cheerful. "Not as busy as you, I can guess."

"Yeah, it's pretty crazy here. I've just been given some new responsibilities—can you hold on a second?" The phone went muffled and I could hear her say something about mauve, not lilac, chiffon and her usual sweet "thank you so much!" before returning to me.

"I'll let you go," I said, chickening out. Now was not the time to dredge up old boyfriends, and how I told said old boyfriend she was still single.

"No, wait a second," Jane said. "I wanted to ask you something."

Oh, God, I thought. She knows about Bing. I was banking on the fact that she would be too busy to watch my videos (and, you know, having a life of her own), but even though she's being run ragged all day every day by her job—and loving it—she still knew that—

"Have you spoken to Lydia recently?" she asked.

"Oh." I paused. "No. No, I haven't."

I could hear Jane's disappointment in her silence. "I really wish you would."

"If she wants to talk to me, she has my number," I replied. Then, after a minute . . . "Have *you* talked to her lately?

"Only for a minute, I've been so busy. I think she met a guy in Las Vegas."

"Perfect." I rolled my eyes. "Well, Lydia can enjoy her random hookup. Maybe she can drive him crazy and not us for a while."

"Lizzie . . ." Then, her tone shifted. "Oh, hold on a minute. I have to take this other call."

"No, that's okay. I'll let you get back to work."

"Okay," she said, a little sad. "It was nice to hear from you."

"You, too."

Calls like that with Jane only throw into sharp relief how much I miss my sisters. Yes, that was plural. I do miss Lydia. I miss girl time, and girl talk.

But she's not the only one who can be stubborn.

Luckily, there *is* some girl talk to be found in this city. Gigi's invited me out to lunch, so perhaps that will fill some of the void. One of the true delights of being at Pemberley Digital has been getting to know Gigi. She's such a smart, fun, happy young woman, and every time I think about what George Wickham did to her I want to find and slap him all over again.

WEDNESDAY, JANUARY 23RD

"Darcy!" I called out in a whisper. I don't know why I whispered, but it was near the end of another busy day and there were still some people milling about, so yelling his name would have caused everyone to come to a dead stop. "I need to tell you something."

"What's wrong?"

"Nothing!" I promised. "But, um . . . I need you to be aware of something. In the interest of respecting your confidence."

He looked from side to side. "In my office?" he asked.

I nodded, and he gently took my elbow, guiding me down the hall into his office.

Which I hadn't been in before.

I instantly felt like I was intruding. It was his inner sanctum, after all. Everything in here was very Darcy. It was smaller than I expected, and messier, too. Then I realized this was not the office of a vanity CEO. This was the office of someone who worked.

Deep leather chairs faced a window that had a view all the way to the bay. Piles of books and papers sat on the windowsill. Everything was old school, except for his desk—which featured a computer that was probably two generations ahead of what was currently on the market. As well as . . .

"Is that a bobble-head?" I asked, noticing the green bouncing thing next to the hi-tech equipment.

"Yes," Darcy answered, blushing.

"Of Oscar the Grouch?" I said, stepping toward the desk.

"It is," Darcy replied. "Is that what you wanted to talk to me about?"

"No. I just . . . I never pictured you as the kind of person to have a bobble-head. Of Oscar the Grouch."

Darcy reached out and settled Oscar's bobbing head with a single finger. "Gigi gave him to me when we were kids."

"Right. Gigi." I took a deep breath. "That's actually what I wanted to talk to you about."

"What about my sister?"

I took a deep breath. No way out of it now. "A little while ago, I was filming, and Gigi . . . and please bear in mind I didn't ask her to do this, she did it voluntarily . . . Gigi came on video and told all of my viewers about what happened between her and George Wickham."

It was the one part of the letter that I had held back. Out of respect for Gigi, and also Darcy. We've become the keeper of each other's secrets, after all. I hadn't even told Jane or Charlotte about it. It had felt too personal.

Darcy leaned on his desk, for once his rigid posture bending slightly.

"Well," he said. "Thank you for telling me."

"I don't have to post it. I can film something else before tomorrow."

"No. It was Gigi's decision to tell her story. She must have thought it was something she needed to do." He sighed and rubbed his temple. "It doesn't mean I have to like it."

It was curious, but I felt for Darcy in that moment. There's a kind of frustration only little sisters can cause. So I felt for him. Was drawn to him. As he stood there, leaning on his desk and rubbing his temple, I had to tamp down the urge to reach out and comfort him.

Which is ridiculous.

"Well," I said. "I just wanted to give you a heads-up."

"Yes, thank you," he said, straightening. "Are you headed home?"

He nodded at the bag on my shoulder.

"Oh. Yes. I was going to try walking to Haight-Ashbury and see some tourist-y things. But that's kind of tough when it gets dark by four in January."

"You were going to walk to the Haight? From SoMa?" Darcy asked, one eyebrow going up. "I know you like to walk, but that's quite a distance."

"I guess that's not done?"

"Not after four in January," he replied. "You haven't had the opportunity to see much of the city yet, have you?"

"Not really," I admitted. "But I'm looking forward to seeing it this weekend, with Gigi . . . and with you."

Darcy's cheeks went bright red and he mumbled something under his breath. Something that sounded like "so am I," but I couldn't be certain.

We stood there for another couple of seconds before I realized I was in his office, and it was up to me to leave.

"Well," I said finally, "good night."

"Good night, Lizzie," he said, as I had my hand on the door. "And thank you."

Saturday, January 26th

What a marvelous day! What a gorgeous, exhausting, interesting, illuminating day! Plus, I got to see sea lions.

But it wasn't marine animals that made the day so special. It was, believe it or not, the Darcys.

Both of them. Gigi for her enthusiasm, and Darcy for . . . just being Darcy.

Once again, it was Gigi who constructed the plot. She asked me a few days ago if I would let her and her brother give me a tour of the city. As I haven't been able to be as much of a tourist as I would like, and I do enjoy spending time with Gigi, I said yes.

We met at a brunch place not far from my apartment.

"Lizzie!" Gigi cried, when she saw me approaching. She stood up from their table and waved like a maniac. Her brother rose, too.

"Are you ready for your epic tour of San Francisco?" she asked, as she moved chairs so I was wedged between her and her brother.

"It's an epic tour?" I asked, turning to Darcy.

"It's certainly comprehensive," he replied.

"William planned quite the itinerary for today," Gigi said, ribbing her brother. "I'm glad to see you wore your walking boots."

"I . . . know you like to walk, but if you prefer, we can have the car—" Darcy added.

"No," I interrupted. "It's too nice a day to not walk."

"Good!" Gigi chirped. "I agree. My tennis conditioning coach would love it if I walked everywhere, I'd have calves of steel."

"So, what's on the epic tour?" I asked.

"I thought we could go walk through Chinatown, then stop by Lombard Street, then down to the Marina," Darcy said. "Does that sound worthwhile—is there any place you'd rather go?"

"No, it's great!" I replied. "I've actually been dying to see the Marina. I only went once, for dinner, so it was pretty dark. And I got lost on the way back."

"Well, you're with natives this time," Gigi said. "Getting lost isn't possible. But now it's time to carb up! You should get the waffles here, they are A-mazing."

Gigi handed me a menu, and as I began to peruse it (and yes, the waffles looked to be the standout), I noticed Darcy looking my way. Gigi was doing something on her phone, so I decided to try something Darcy and I had never actually managed before.

Small talk.

"I think you out-hipstered yourself today," I said.

"Because of the glasses?" he asked, suddenly self-conscious. He took the dark Elvis Costello frames off, blinking to focus. "I know, I wouldn't have, but I couldn't get my contacts in this morning, and—"

"Darcy, it's okay. I was teasing. They . . . they look good."

They did look good. He put them back on and I couldn't help thinking—maybe the hipster aesthetic wasn't as unattractive as I previously thought. Some people could pull it off.

"Say cheese!" Gigi said, snapping a photo with her camera before either of us knew what was happening.

"Great picture!" she cheered, upon review. "I'm going to document this whole day!"

* * *

San Francisco's Chinatown is the best-known Chinatown in the world (outside of China, one presumes), and it earns that reputation. We walked from the famous green-roofed gateway arch to the top of the street, marveling at all the little trinkets sold in the shops. I bought a pink bamboo umbrella for Jane and a small cat figurine for Lydia. Maybe someday we'll be on speaking terms again and I'll be able to give it to her.

"Here, let me carry that for you," Darcy offered, gently taking the bag out of my hand before I could protest.

"It's not that heavy."

"Which is why I offered," Darcy said, with what might have actually been a smile. "If it weighed a ton, you'd be on your own."

Holy of holies. Ladies and gentlemen, William Darcy attempted a joke.

"I guess I shouldn't get a bonsai tree for my father, then," I replied, playing along.

"Those aren't bonsai trees. In Chinese culture they're called penjing." Then he stopped himself. "I'm sorry. Gigi says I lecture too much."

I looked around for Gigi—I'd been trying to pace the walk so all three of us would be together, but Gigi kept running ahead or falling behind when she saw something interesting. Right now she was across the street, admiring some beaded bracelets.

"Don't worry about it." I smiled. "Seriously, you shouldn't beat yourself up over every word uttered."

"It's a lifelong trait," he replied. "One I've tried to dispel."

My mind suddenly flashed to all the cruel things in the past I said about Darcy without so much as an ounce of regret. "And one I should probably cultivate."

Darcy's gaze slid to me. "I think you're fine."

I could feel my face turning red.

"I think you're fine, too."

We left Chinatown several (lightweight) trinkets richer, and made our way to the famously winding Lombard Street—where the hills were decidedly unforgiving and I have to admit even my preference for walking was being challenged.

Of course, I didn't say that out loud, but Darcy noticed, anyway.

"Don't worry," Darcy told me. "It's mostly downhill from here."

"Oh, thank God," Gigi said between breaths as she came up

behind us. "My coach is going to be so pissed when she finds out how winded I am. Still . . . it's awfully pretty."

The street was really lovely, with switchbacks to make it so the incline was less harrowing for cars, the road paved in red brick and greenery filling in the spaces in between. Plus the view from the top down to Coit Tower was amazing.

"Yes, it is," Darcy agreed.

"I take it you guys don't come here that often."

"Not really, no," Darcy said. "I suppose living so close to well-known places make them less special. No one thinks to be a tourist in their hometown."

"True," I said. "I live a half hour away from the beach and haven't been in . . . months."

He considered that. "I haven't been to the Marina in years."

"Well," I said, "let's not keep you two apart any longer."

"Hold on," Gigi called out, and we began our steep descent. "I wanted to take a picture of you on top of a hill!" Then, exhausted . . . "Oh, screw it. I'll take it at the bottom, when we've conquered it."

After that, we made our way to the Marina. We stopped at the fresh seafood market at Fisherman's Wharf, then went and looked out at the water. On a clear day like this, the Golden Gate was stunning. As were the tall ships in the harbor, Fort Mason, and Alcatraz (although unpleasant memories of a bad walrus joke marred its view). Gigi insisted on stopping and taking pictures, while Darcy insisted on indulging each of our whims. Gigi wanted to get hot chocolate at the Ghirardelli factory. Darcy stood in line, while we sat and rested our feet. I wanted to go down on the pier to see the sea lions. Done.

"Okay, you didn't warn me about the smell," I said once we approached Pier 39, which was no longer able to house boats, as the sea lions had invoked squatters' rights and taken over the whole thing. I whipped out my camera and took a few pictures. Luckily, pictures don't smell.

"Would it have stopped you?" Darcy replied over the sea lions' barking.

"No, but . . . forewarned is forearmed." I smiled at him. "So, do you still miss the Marina?"

"Actually, I do. I don't make as much use of the city as I should. Perhaps I'll make an effort to spend more time here." Just then, another tourist shouldered us to get a better view of the odiferous adorableness sunbathing before us.

"But perhaps when it's less crowded," I added.

Just then, another tourist bumped into us, and I dropped my phone. Not in the water, luckily, but hard on the dock, and in the center of a busy tourist thoroughfare.

"I'll get it," Darcy said, and ducked into the fray to retrieve my phone. He grabbed it and held it out to me.

"Here you go. No worse for wear, I think."

When I reached out and took the phone from him, my finger brushed his. And I *felt* it. A warm shock spreading from the point of contact up my hand. Not electric, but more of a tingly comfort. Easy. And right.

My eyes flew up and met his—and I could tell he felt something, too.

I quickly took my phone and shoved it in my pocket.

"Thanks," I mumbled.

"My pleasure," he replied in a similar mumble.

"William! Lizzie!" Gigi called out once we'd left the dock (she had stayed behind, avoiding the smells). "Come check out this fountain!"

The rest of the afternoon passed quickly. The shadows were growing long and so we headed back on foot toward my place. Along the way, Darcy would point out something interesting here and there, and more than once I caught Gigi taking a surreptitious photo of us. She'd make a terrible paparazzo or private detective.

It was dusk when we finally got back to my apartment building. At the door Gigi gave me a big hug, and Darcy solemnly handed over my bag of Chinatown goodies he'd been lugging all day, and then . . . shook my hand.

But that warm, comforting shock from before wasn't a fluke. It was still there.

And then we all stood there for a moment, not wanting the afternoon to be at an end.

"Thank you," I said. "The tour was indeed epic."

Darcy suppressed a smile. "You had a good time?"

"The best."

Once I got upstairs, I couldn't stop grinning. And it took me a little while to figure out why.

It was Darcy.

He was so different. He was attentive, and with his sister around, he's much lighter. I've known ever since the letter that my first impression of him was inaccurate, but I hadn't really been thinking of him as . . . as a *guy*. Until today.

And he *is* a guy. A smart, handsome, kind of shy one, who just took me around to all the tourist traps in the city on what has to be one of his rare days off.

Even after everything I've said about him, he still wanted to spend the day with me. He went very far out of the way to make me feel special. And that in and of itself makes me feel special.

But as I was contemplating Darcy, and reheating noodles for dinner, I got a phone call.

"Lizzie!" Gigi's voice was almost drowned out by the crowd noise and singing I heard in the background. "I know we just spent the day together, but I'm inviting you to impromptu karaoke! We're less than two blocks from you."

"We?" I asked.

"Fitz and Brandon and me . . ." The connection became a little garbled, but I managed to make out, "William had to catch up on paperwork."

"Oh." I was strangely (or not strangely?) disappointed.

"Come on! Sing one show tune with me!" she pleaded. "Fitz wants to ask you all about the day and is willing to ply you with mixed drinks for it. He doesn't believe me when I say you had a good time."

I looked at the clock. "Okay," I decided. "One song and drink."

Gigi squealed and gave me the address.

I have to admit, I'm happy for the distraction. As great as today was, it was also altering. The fact that Darcy wouldn't be there meant that I could relax

I'm relieved by it.

And yet, I'm not.

I find myself wanting to see him again. Only hours after he dropped me at my door.

Wow. Do I . . . do I *like* William Darcy?

No. No, Lizzie, don't go that far. Pull up on the reins of your imagination.

But I know I *could* like William Darcy. Which is strange enough.

Ode to a Broken Phone

I remember when we first met. You so shiny, so new, so
rectangular.
You promised the world to me.
A world of Internet and email, cat memes and Angry Birds.
Alas, I would always root for the pigs.

It was beautiful, the years we grew together,
the phone cases I clothed you in,
the pictures and videos we shot, then deleted.
You could incriminate me, yet you never did.
The notices, the texts, the dings and pings.
All of life's moments, big and small, we shared.

But our time has come to a sad end.
Gravity has parted us.
One fall on the dock left you seemingly fine, and yet.
And yet.

It began with a garbled connection. The decline.
Miss calls, dropped texts. The downfall.
Something in your insides scrambled, something no longer
wired right.

"Don't worry!
You will be going to a good home.
A farm upstate, with an open field that

will never allow for hard landings."
But I lie to both of us.

I would say you are irreplaceable, but let's face it.
We are in the hi-tech capital of the world,
and I can get a new phone as easily as a cup of coffee.

Good-bye, broken phone.
The time we shared has been so sweet.
And I consider your last act a kindness,
sacrificing yourself so two pairs of fingers could meet.
I will miss you —
the small scratch at your bottom left corner,
the volume button that won't go down.

Good night, sweet phone. Good night.

WEDNESDAY, JANUARY 30TH

I'm sitting on a plane bound for home. They've made us turn off all electronic devices and I can no longer keep calling Lydia. Although she's not answering. Twenty-four hours ago, home was the last thing on my mind. Hell, four hours ago, for a brief moment I thought I might be spending tonight at the theater in the company of someone who could be special. But that was before I got the call.

My phone had been on the fritz ever since I dropped it at the pier. The outside seemed fine, but calls quickly became fuzzy, then the type pad wouldn't work properly, and finally it just wouldn't turn on. I got a new one, and while I was offline waiting for it to activate and download my settings, the world decided to implode.

"Charlotte?" I said, immediately picking up the phone. "What's wrong?"

Something had to be wrong. The minute my phone turned on I could see that she'd called me seven times in the last hour.

"Oh, thank God, Lizzie." She exhaled in relief. "Where have you been?"

"My phone died and I got a new one," I tried, but she just cut me off.

"It doesn't matter—Lizzie, get on the Internet. There's a website."

"A website of what?"

"They say they have a tape of Lydia. A sex tape."

"A . . . a sex tape?" I couldn't believe it. There was no way Lydia would make a sex tape—but, would she?

"The website is asking for subscriptions, and they have a countdown clock, and . . . Lizzie, it's with George. They've been dating," Charlotte said.

"George. George *Wickham?*"

And that was when I knew it was real. A sex tape was not beyond the reaches of George's twisted imagination. And since he could talk an Eskimo into buying ice, I have no doubt he could talk Lydia into this.

"I'm forwarding the link. I think they're trading on her fame. They call her 'YouTube Star Lydia Bennet,'" Charlotte was saying. "I tried calling Lydia when I couldn't get through to you, but she didn't pick up. Lizzie, do you have any idea what's going on? Do your parents know?"

"No," I said. But I needed to find out. "No, I'm coming home. I'm coming home right now."

I hung up and just stared at my phone. Like a bomb about to go off—but it had already exploded.

"Lizzie, what is it?" Darcy asked, beside me.

Yes, because Darcy had been witness to the entire exchange. He'd come into my office to ask me if I wanted to go to the theater that night

With him. On a date.

After I hung up the phone with Charlotte, the rest is kind of a blur. Except for Darcy. He made me tell him what was going on. He asked me to let him help. But as I opened up that website on my phone, its garish, sparkly text and its picture of Lydia and George *smiling* at each other in bed, I knew there was nothing he could do. And the only thing I could do now was try to talk some sense into Lydia.

Darcy insisted on putting me on a plane immediately, getting me the first flight out. Which is how I got to here. Sitting on the runway at SFO, unable to keep calling Lydia or Jane (I tried her once but she doesn't seem to be picking up, either we Bennet sisters chose a *really* bad day to simultaneously go offline). Darcy put me into his car and instructed his driver to take me back to the apartment, where I packed up my things in ten minutes before running back out to the car again to make my flight.

I just can't believe Lydia would do this. That she would make a sex tape, and let George release it online. For what? For money? There's no amount of money in the world worth letting something that personal exist in the open, and forever.

And I'm at fault for this. I wasn't holding the camera, but I sure as hell didn't warn her about George. If I hadn't been so stupid and stubborn for the past month and actually *talked* to my sister, I might have seen this coming and been able to stop her.

But how, and why, would George go after Lydia?

She doesn't have anything, other than a marginal bit of recognition due to the videos—hers and mine.

And that's my fault, too.

I knew Lydia had been making videos while I was away. Viewers had been tweeting me, imploring me to watch them, but I didn't. I couldn't. I thought it would just be Lydia being Lydia, blithely irresponsible and floating from one crisis to the next.

I never thought she would ever do anything like this.

I tried to watch one of her videos with George while I was in the airport lounge, waiting to board. But once his smarmy face popped up I couldn't continue. I just wanted to break through the screen and strangle him. Everything he said was a line. A self-deprecating ploy. My insides were screaming at Lydia, asking why couldn't she see it?

But then again, I hadn't seen it at first, either.

I don't know what I'm going to do when I get home. I don't know what I'm going to say when I see Lydia.

I just know I need to see her.

Saturday, February 2nd

I don't even know where to start.

As bad as it was thinking that Lydia and George made a sex tape and released it, the reality is actually ten times worse.

My presumption that Lydia had known about the website—had signed off on it—was terribly, terribly wrong. If she had known, as disturbing as that would be, at least she would have had some control. Perhaps we would have been able to talk her out of releasing the video when the countdown expires. Which is in about twelve days. God, we only have twelve days to solve this.

No, as bad as my presumption was, that's not the nightmare scenario. The nightmare scenario is that Lydia *didn't* know about the website.

She knew about the tape, of course. She'd participated, but she never dreamed George would do something like this with it. That he'd try to make money off of baring her body and soul to anonymous perverts online.

Because she loves him.

When I came home, no one was here. Lydia still wasn't picking up, so the only thing I could do was wait. And when Lydia finally did come home . . . I got angry with her. Because I thought . . .

I can't believe I thought that she knew about it.

When I showed her the website, I watched something inside my little sister break. She became so small and so very, very young. She ran to her room and hasn't come out since.

That was three days ago.

Thank God I finally got in touch with Jane, and she came home, too. Lydia wasn't letting me into her room, but I knew she'd let Jane in. She's been going in once an hour, with ridiculous amounts of tea, just to make sure Lydia is okay.

That she's not hurting herself.

"Has she eaten anything?" I'd whispered to Jane, as she was preparing her fourth tea tray of the day in the kitchen.

"No, but she did drink a little tea," Jane whispered back.

"Is she talking to anyone?"

"I know she's tried to called George. Is still trying," Jane replied.

"He's not answering," I said.

"It's worse than that. I've heard her through the door. She still thinks this is some kind of misunderstanding. Like George got hacked. I think she tried all of his friends, too, but—"

"But he's nowhere to be found."

I knew this because I had done the same thing. I had called George's number a million times, wanting an explanation. I tried everyone I could remember was a friend of his . . . but then I learned he didn't keep friends very well. Two of his so-called buddies told me that if I found him, to let them know, because George owed them a couple hundred bucks each. I even went down to Carter's to see if anyone there might have an idea where George went.

Nothing.

"I don't know what to do anymore," I whispered to Jane. I was filled with so much impotence and rage. Without George, there was no way of getting the tape back and getting the website shut down. I'd even emailed the company that was listed as creating the site (Novelty Exposures, ugh), sending a DCMA takedown notice on Lydia's behalf, but didn't get a reply. Of course. Charlotte says Novelty Exposures is just a shell company, and there's an entire labyrinth of holding companies and false ISPs that are protecting it from view. We have no idea who actually has the tape.

"I know," Jane said. "Neither do I."

"How are we going to get her through this? How are we going to stop him?"

"Stop who?" my dad said from behind us, causing both Jane and me to jump.

"No one," I chirped, a little too brightly. "We were just discussing something . . . Jane and I saw on television."

But my dad just shook his head. "Don't lie to me, Lizzie. Not you." His eyes flew to Jane. "Why are you home? You have a full-time job and an apartment in Los Angeles." Then back to me. "Why aren't you completing your coursework in San Francisco? And why haven't I seen my youngest daughter or heard her voice in days?"

"Lydia's not feeling very well," Jane tried. But it was no use.

"Girls," Dad said. "Something's not right here. So, I'm only going to ask this once more. You are either going to tell me what is going on or I am barging into Lydia's room right now and asking her."

I looked to Jane. She nodded at me. It was time. We'd both run out of ways to fight this on our own. We needed help. We needed our dad.

But that meant he had to be filled in on some backstory. About the videos.

"Dad," I sighed. "I don't even know where to start."

"Start at the beginning," he said, softer now. "It will be okay. Whatever it is, you can tell me."

And so I did.

Tuesday, February 5th

I don't want to make another video. I don't want to expose the inside of myself anymore, or the inside of my family's lives.

That's what led to this. Right? My videos led to me being vaguely Internet famous, which led to Lydia being vaguely Internet famous, which led to George thinking he could make money off of her.

But I can't stop now—contract with my audience, and all.

Besides, the people who watch my videos are almost as invested in our family as we are. Everyone is commenting and asking if Lydia is okay. They care about her. More than I was caring about her for the past couple of months, it seems.

She still hasn't come out of her room. Jane is still going in there with tea and trays of food.

Maybe I can use the videos. Beg people to not subscribe to the website, and also beg them for help. Who knows, maybe some tech genius is watching and knows how to take down a website. That's what I keep praying for. In fact, it's gone down a couple of times now. But never for long. It pops right back up, like an evil hedgehog.

I don't know how to stop this from happening.

But Dad is doing everything in his power to try to fix it—which, we've discovered, is not easy. Dad talked to Uncle Phil—under the strictest of lawyer-client privilege so Mom, his sister-in-law, won't find out. Uncle Phil is a tax attorney, so I don't know how much he can help in reality, but he did some digging.

Since the website is subscription based, nothing illegal has been posted yet. Apparently authorities can act only after something happens, not before. Dad says he's going to talk to a friend who's a private investigator and see if he can find George. But George has practically disappeared off the face of the earth.

He is incredibly slick. More slick than I think I gave him credit for. I keep thinking back to when I challenged him to watch my videos in the grocery store, so he'd know how much I no longer liked him. Then I have to wonder, did he go after Lydia to get revenge on me for it? No. That's too self-centered. He just knew Lydia was an easy target for someone like him.

Because she was alone.

Because I gave her a book, and we got into a stupid fight, and I left her alone.

I just did the math and realized—the day the countdown ends and the website goes live? Valentine's Day.

As if we needed further proof that George Wickham is a sadistic asshole.

Friday, February 8th

Among the other shitty things to have happened recently, Jane lost her job. Her coming back home to help her family during one of the busiest times of the fashion year did not go over well with her new boss. Or her now new ex-boss.

She loved that job. And I bet more money than I have in my bank account that she was the best thing to happen at that office, too. However, even knowing how much losing her job sucks, I can't help but be grateful that she's here. She's the only one who makes any sense.

She's also better at handling Mom—who is still in the dark about most things, including my videos and the sex tape. While it is hard to believe that anyone could be so oblivious about the goings-on right under her nose, here is a sampling of things my mother said at last night's dinner table:

"With Lydia's hair and young George's physique, their babies will look just like Prince Harry. Oh, we'll have our own little princes and princesses in the family!"

"Do you see how distraught your sister is when her boyfriend leaves town for just a few days, Lizzie? That's what love looks like. Men like a certain show of devotion. Something you should learn."

"Now, Jane, I insist you take some of these mashed potatoes up to Lydia tonight. I know, I know, she's 'under the weather.' But I will not have her wasting away for want of her George."

While I was boiling over, Jane simply hummed to Mom her assent and deftly changed the subject to a more innocuous topic. Like global nuclear politics.

We've all been debating whether or not to bring Mom into the fold. Part of me wants her to know, so she would at least stop being

George's champion, but the other part of me knows how she'll react—if the wailing and couch-fainting she did when Bing left is any indication, this would be incapacitating. Dad agrees, because having to clue Mom in would simply hinder any progress on getting the website taken down.

I use the word "progress" liberally, because there has been none. George is still missing. The website countdown is still going on. And Lydia still won't let anyone in her room but Jane.

Which is another reason I'm glad Jane is here.

I feel so useless.

But Jane did something else. She challenged me to sit down and watch Lydia's videos with George. My previous aborted attempt ended with my stomach churning and me looking for a *Matrix*-like ability to climb through video screens and beat George bloody. But Jane says Lydia and I have more in common than we realize. That we're both stubborn, and would rather talk to the Internet at large than to each other.

So that's what I'm going to do. I've got the videos queued up, and I am as prepared as I can be.

* * *

Wow. I . . .

I need a minute.

* * *

Okay, now that I'm not crying anymore, maybe I can make some sense of this. Of how I'm feeling. But the hardest thing to admit is that . . . I never knew. I never knew anything about Lydia.

I never knew how much I hurt her.

At the beginning of Lydia's videos, when she's in Vegas, she is so defiant, ready to party even though "Lizzie would disapprove." Because she's "so irresponsible" and "crazy." She was lashing out—to hurt me in the way I hurt her. At the time I was too mad at her to see it. But now, with the benefit of painful hindsight, I know.

Also, I never knew how lonely she was.

I was gone, Jane was gone, Mary had her own life. Her school friends abandoned her in Vegas when she went overboard with the partying. Lydia felt left over. And that led her to the only person in town who seemed to want to hang out with her: George Wickham.

And I never knew how truly manipulative George was.

He had answers for everything. Sold my sister on a sob story about how yes, he did spend all the money Darcy gave him in his first year of college, because he was trying to impress his friends. When he admitted he'd screwed up, Darcy—the closest thing he had to family—wouldn't help. Totally plausible, totally reasonable. And if I hadn't known about his history with Gigi, I might have even bought it.

Whenever Lydia tried to joke with him, he would act hurt and make her back down. Make her doubt herself. He pressured her into commitment—saying that "someone has to look out for you" and getting her to declare that they were dating. Whenever they discussed me or Jane, he was always the defender, saying we don't care about Lydia. But *he* does. He would do anything for her. Lizzie and Jane? They don't need you—they have each other.

And she believed it.

And finally, I never realized that Lydia has never been told that she is loved exactly as she is.

That's what George honed in on about her. Lydia's never had anyone say they love her just the way she is. She's always too much, or not enough. Too crazy, too energetic, too wild. Not serious enough, not studious enough, not good enough.

I'm the one who told her that. That's my doing. With a stupid goddamn book. With every single disappointed sigh and disapproving look and trying to rein her in.

But I told Lydia a lot of other things, instead.

I scolded Lydia for getting drunk in public. You know who I didn't scold? Charlotte, when she got drunk at the Gibson wedding.

I admonished her for her sexual behavior. You know who I didn't admonish? Jane, when I caught her sneaking out of Bing's room at Netherfield, or when she told me about her forty-eight hours of worry.

I told Lydia time and time again she was being irresponsible. You know who I didn't think was being irresponsible? Me, when I turned down a good job offer from Ricky Collins.

How could I have never told Lydia that I love her? Just as she is? Exasperating, caring, crazy, wonderful, all of it. What the hell kind of sister does that make me? How could I be that person who just picks and picks at her until she's so starved for approval she'll take it from anyone and anywhere?

I feel like I don't know her at all.

And how could I have not seen her this whole time?

Monday, February 11th

I'm emotionally spent. The last day has been so hard, but so necessary. Lydia and I finally talked. She came into my room, and I was so relieved to actually see her in the flesh at first that I forgot about everything else. Almost forgot about the camera. But Lydia didn't. She wanted it on. And I think it's what allowed her to talk to me.

She's been broken by him, but not beaten. She was in love with George. And he used her, and threw her away.

And I'd been calling her selfish, and crazy, and a slut for the last ten months on the Internet.

We needed to talk. We needed to break down. I needed to tell her that I loved her.

There was a lot of crying and apologizing, and I don't know where to begin getting to know my sister again. The biggest thing I can do is to be here for her now. After our big crying session, I made Lydia lie down in my bed, and I held her as she fell asleep.

She was snoring softly after a few moments. I don't know how much sleep she's gotten this past week.

"How is she?" Jane asked me, ducking her head in.

"I don't know. A little better, hopefully, from here on out. You were right," I said.

"About what?"

"About watching Lydia's videos. She's . . . I've been the worst sister. There are no two ways around it."

"Lizzie, you're not the worst sister. You—and I, sometimes— just forget that Lydia hears everything we say. And underneath that bright, loud outside she wears, she's vulnerable."

"Pretty sure I still get the worst sister award."

"Fine. Then start making it up to her."

And that's what I'm going to do, from here on out.

"Dad's back," Jane said.

"Did his PI friend from college find anything?"

"Not really. Just a trail that goes cold at that company on the website."

"So we can't buy it back," I concluded in despair.

"I don't think so." Jane shook her head. "Besides, who's to say George doesn't have copies? Uncle Phil says we can try to sue them for not having Lydia's permission to release it, but they still have to release it first. And we don't know who to sue yet. Besides, it could take months to settle a case like that, if not years. And a lot of money we don't have."

I felt all the air leave my body.

"Dad must be so disappointed."

"I think he's more worried about Lydia. She hasn't talked to him, either."

It was at that moment that Dad appeared in my doorway. His trench coat still on, his hat in hand. Utterly defeated. He walked past Jane and me, and went to sit beside Lydia sleeping on the bed.

"I remember when she was so small," he said, brushing her hair out of her eyes. "Smaller than either of you two. She came early. Couldn't wait to greet the world."

Just then, Lydia opened her eyes. Blinked and saw Dad sitting over her.

"Lydia," he said, his voice breaking.

"I'm so sorry, Daddy," she said, bursting into tears again.

"No, my girl, no," he said, wrapping her in his arms. "It's not for you to be sorry. We'll fix this. You'll see."

Since then, yes, some things are fixed . . . or on their way to being fixed. Lydia's talking to us again, and eating more. Not at dinner, of course—Mom is still mentioning George every chance she gets. Dad wants to see if Lydia will agree to speak to a counselor. Someone objective, who can help.

But the sex tape . . . I don't know if it can be stopped at this point. At this moment, there are three days left before it goes live.

I'm beginning to fear that sometimes, the bad guy gets away with it.

Tuesday, February 12th

"Lydia, my love," my mom said as she was drying dishes in the kitchen, "bring in that serving plate to your sister. I'm so glad you came down to dinner tonight."

"Thanks, Mom," Lydia said softly, handing the serving plate to me. She let Mom embrace her and sneak in a quick feel of her forehead.

"You're still a little warm. But another day or two and you'll be well enough to go back to school, see your friends . . . and maybe invite that lovely George over for a meal sometime?"

Lydia froze in her tracks, unable to answer. So I did the only think I could.

I dropped the serving plate I was washing.

"Lizzie!" Mom cried, turning to me. "What has gotten into you?"

"I'm sorry," I said, as I bent to pick up the broken shards. Out of the corner of my eye, I could see Lydia snapping back to reality and escaping the kitchen while our mother's attention was taken.

"That's my good serving plate, too!" she cried. "I swear, between you and your father, I'm going to have to get an entirely new set of china!"

This particular trick was also employed this afternoon by my father, breaking a teacup to distract my mother. Great minds think alike.

"You're right, dear," Dad said, coming over to Mom. "Clumsiness comes from my side of the family. Now, I'll help Lizzie clean and you go rest your feet."

And with a kiss on her cheek, my mother was placated, and moved off to the living room.

"Thanks," I whispered.

"You're welcome," Dad whispered back.

"How long do you think we can keep this up?" I asked.

"How many dishes do we have?"

"Mom's going to have to be told something eventually. Especially when the website goes live." As oblivious as my mom is about the Internet, this is something that would get out. A friend of a friend would mention it, and it would make its way back to her. "She should at least be prepared."

"You're right," Dad conceded. "At the very least, she'll want to know why we are selling the house to pay attorney fees."

My head came up.

"Are you really going to do that? Sue the website company and George?"

"If George can be found," he grumbled. "But Lizzie, if that website goes live, there's no other choice. Lydia is our daughter. And I promise you this—your mother would agree with me."

"True." I glanced at my mom, sitting in the living room next to Jane. "Mrs. Bennet is a mama bear. Don't mess with her cubs."

She seemed to be going on and on about something while Jane knitted. I'm not sure, but I think I heard the word "Bing" in there. And then a deep, sad sigh.

"But let's spare ourselves the initial histrionics as long as we can," Dad said, cringing with the memory of the last boy who broke one of her daughters' hearts.

A wave of guilt washed over me. My dad must have seen it on my face because he said, "What is it? Something new couldn't have happened in the last three minutes, could it?"

"No." I gave a small smile. "Just . . . if I hadn't been making videos then Lydia wouldn't have been, and now you're talking about selling the house . . ."

"Don't. This is not your fault. Besides, I quite like the videos. Especially the ones where you dress up as me."

"You do?" I said, a little shocked.

"Yes. Although I'd been wondering where my blue bathrobe was, and I would like it back when you're done with it."

I blushed. "I ransacked your closet for your costume. Sorry, I thought you were done with it."

"A man is never done with a bathrobe, Lizzie." He smiled at me. "And while your caricature of your mother is a little overly broad, it's plain to see that you know she loves you. And that you love your sisters, and your friends."

"Dad . . ." I said, my voice going soft.

"I find . . ." He paused, cleared his throat, and then started again. "I know that I have not been the most attentive father. I let your mother do the hard, mundane work of parenting, not realizing how important it is. But now, through your videos, I can see what I've been missing. You've created something wonderful, and . . . I'm really quite proud of you."

I wrapped my arms around my Dad's waist, and we forgot about the shards of crockery on the floor. We'd get them later

But at that moment, I was just so glad to be able to talk to my dad again.

Thursday, February 14th

It's gone! It's down! The website is down, and I don't know how or why, but whoever did that, I could kiss you. Thank you, thank you, thank you.

Charlotte's looking into it. I'm looking into it, though my contacts and knowledge in this section of the web are limited. But someone out there just saved our family, and I want to know who to thank.

Lydia and I are . . . better. I've decided I'm going to stick around home for a little while, to be there for her. And she has her first session with a counselor tomorrow. Someone highly recommended, with more skills than we have to get her through this time. Dad's going to drive her. They could use some father-daughter time, too.

I feel like we just battled a dragon, and somehow the dragon just up and died on us, and all I want to do now is flop into a heap of exhaustion. We won the fight but have no idea how. And we still have to pick up the pieces and try to go back to our normal lives.

For me, that means grad school.

For Jane, that means looking for a new job.

For Lydia, that means . . .

"Well, Lizzie," Dr. Gardiner said when I came into her office for office hours. "I'm surprised to see you here."

"Yes," I said as I sat down. "I don't know if you've been watching my videos lately, but there was a bit of a family crisis, and I had to come home."

"I know," she replied. "And I'm very, very glad that your sister is doing better and that horrible website came down. But I would have thought you'd return to Pemberley Digital, to finish up your independent study."

"No. I've decided to stay in town for the rest of the school year. I'm confident I have enough from my month there to produce a thorough prospectus on the company."

"Are you sure? I would think that you'd be welcome—"

"I'm sure," I said. The truth was, I didn't know if I'd be welcome. I hadn't heard one word from Darcy, or Gigi, or anyone at Pemberley Digital since my abrupt exit. And if I did go back . . . it's not like we could just pick up where we left off, is it?

Besides, Lydia asked me to stay. So I'm staying.

Luckily, Dr. Gardiner didn't say anything else on the subject.

"Well, your last two prospectuses were very well received by the review board; I'm sure you'll do just as well with Pemberley's. And with your last one." She smiled at me. "Speaking of, do you have any idea what it will be?"

I took a deep breath. "To be honest, I have been hyper-focused on my family, so I haven't set anything up. I will try all of my contacts from VidCon, but not many of them are local enough to suit my needs. And I know you don't want another remote shadowing."

Dr. Gardiner nodded. "It would look a lot better to the gradu-ate board if you could avoid it."

"Well, I um . . ." I hedged. Finally I threw up my hands. "Dr. Gardiner, as my advisor, what would you advise I do?"

She gave me that patented inscrutable look.

"Lizzie, school will be over in a few short months. You will have to find a way to meet your credit obligations, as well as deliver your thesis. To come up with a final company to study at this late date . . . you might need to get creative."

I bit my lip and gave a quick nod. "Right. That makes sense. I'll work on it."

I have absolutely no clue what I'm going to do.

Wednesday, February 20th

With everything that was going on with Lydia, I'd forgotten about some things. Such as—Jane hadn't been watching my videos. Which means she didn't know about Bing being in San Francisco.

When I told her, she reacted . . . as well as I think could be expected. Stunned nearly speechless, but not completely thrown by it.

Instead, what completely threw her was Bing showing up on our doorstep a couple of hours ago.

I don't know how she handled it with that much class. If Darcy showed up all of a sudden, I don't know what I would do. Not that Darcy and I have a romantic relationship the way Jane and Bing did—or at all. Heck, we're not even really friends. I mean, maybe at one point in time . . . anyway, back to the real topic at hand.

I was the one to spot Bing as he came into the house. From my perch in the den I could see the door and the stairs, so I pulled him into the room immediately.

A few things have changed since the last time I saw Bing. Namely, he's found the videos.

Yes. About time, too.

And now, he knows how much he hurt Jane. I think he came here with the intention of apologizing, but I don't know how much Jane is going to be willing to forgive him.

Because at first, she wasn't even willing to see him.

"Jane, Bing is here."

She was with Lydia in her room, searching for jobs on her computer. But when I made my unceremonious announcement, her head came up.

"What?"

"Bing—the guy who broke your heart last year. He's here. I left him in the den."

Jane looked from Lydia to me with eyebrows raised.

"Um . . . I . . . I can't," Jane said, flustered.

"Okay," I replied. "That's okay. You don't have to."

"Are you sure?" Lydia asked her.

"Yeah. I can't. I'm sorry."

When I went downstairs and told him she was busy and couldn't see him, I'd never seen anyone so crushed. It was as if I'd killed a puppy. And the puppy was Bing.

But then, miracle of miracles, Jane came into the room.

"Jane!" he said, standing up.

"Hi, Bing," she replied quietly.

It was like watching them meet for the first time all over again.

I left them alone after that, ducking out to the hallway, where I found Lydia hovering on the stairs.

"Hey," Lydia whispered, "did she go in?"

"Yes," I whispered back. "What did you say to her?"

Lydia shrugged. "Just that she was owed an explanation for how she was treated. I'd want one."

And Lydia is right. As much as she claims to have moved on, I can still tell that Old Jane is underneath the New Jane exterior. And since she's lost her job, and is back home, she's pretty much in the same position she was when she met Bing a year ago. Except now she knows he's capable of breaking her heart.

We waited for a few minutes on the stairs, straining our ears for any clues as to what was going on in the den.

When we finally heard movement, Lydia and I both scrambled out of sight immediately. (We are our mother's daughters in some respects.)

"Thank you for stopping by," Jane was saying, as she walked Bing to the door.

"Thank you for seeing me," he replied. From our perch at the top of the stairs, we could see Bing reach out to touch Jane's shoulder, before stopping himself. "Hopefully, I'll see you again soon."

"I would like that," Jane replied. And then he was gone.

"You can come out now," Jane called up the stairs.

"We just, um—" I said, as I noticed Lydia had abandoned me to face Jane alone. "Or I mean, *I* just wanted to make sure everything went well."

"It did," Jane assured me.

"Good. Tell me everything," I said, no longer able to keep my curiosity at bay. Thankfully, Jane was more than willing to share.

Jane said he didn't beg for forgiveness.

Damn it, I wanted begging.

What they did do was talk, about how they couldn't take back the past, and can only move forward. They still care about each other. So, since Bing is going to be in town for a while (Netherfield is still not sold or rented, so it was easy enough for him to move back in), it seems they are going to try to be friends.

Jane and Bing are being awfully adult about the whole thing. Which I guess means that this is what an adult relationship looks like.

Saturday, February 23rd

"Bing—or should I call you Dr. Lee yet?—would you pass the potatoes, please?" my mother cooed across the table at dinner tonight.

She knows the answer to that question, by the way. She knows, because she's asked some variation of it every night for the past three nights. Because if one were to infer that the return of Mr. Bing Lee to our quaint little hamlet is of the most interest to Jane out of all the Bennets, one would be mistaken.

When Bing left our house on that first day, he ran into my mother, pulling into the driveway.

My mother promptly flailed all over him, like a prodigal son-in-law returned.

Okay, that might be a little over the top—I have no proof of any flailing. But she did invite him to dinner that night.

To Mom's credit, she restrained herself from pulling out all the stops this time. No trips to the store for forty-seven different possible entrées, no bananas flambé. She edited herself down to four simple courses—well, five if you counted the sorbet palate cleanser.

Dad had a hand in this newfound restraint. When I told him Mom needed to be clued in to certain things, he took it to heart. He didn't tell her about the videos—thank God, I have no idea how I'd handle first showing her how to play videos on YouTube, and then the ensuing conversation. But he did tell her that George Wickham not only broke Lydia's heart, but violated her trust. I'm not certain what other details he gave, but ever since then, my mom has been very supportive of Lydia, of her counseling, and of just keeping things calm around the house.

And that calm has included dialing back the enthusiasm she displays for her daughters' jobs, futures, and, most importantly, love lives. Hence, the restrained meal.

I'm really proud of Dad. He's been far more vocal as of late. He's been talking to Lydia a little bit every day—and I mean really talking, not just the basic "how was your day" and "did you do all your homework" we got most of our lives. And I know, could he have prevented it, he would have cancelled dinner with Bing to spare Jane the embarrassment.

The thing is, Bing was more than eager to have dinner with us. So much so that Mom invited him back again. And again.

Which is why he was passing Mom potatoes across the dinner table once more.

As awkward as it was, luckily none of us were called on much to contribute to the conversation. Bing and Mom did most of the talking.

"No, Mrs. Bennet, I'm not Dr. Lee," Bing replied.

"Not yet," she said with a smile. "But that school of yours has just the strangest schedule. Did you say you were going to graduate in April or May?"

Actually, Bing had never said anything about graduation. Which was smart on his part. If my mom knew the day, she would finagle tickets and be sitting front row center when his name was called.

Bing didn't answer Mom, and just turned to Jane. "Did you want any more pot roast?" he said softly, offering the meat (on a brand new serving plate!) to her.

"Yes," Jane replied. "Thank you."

"That's my Jane," my mother piped up. "She loves my home cooking. And she cooks just as well, you should know. Even though she's become so cosmopolitan in Los Angeles, she still knows how to make a house feel like a home." She smiled, and Lydia and I shared a glance across the table. "But I do have to say the city agrees with her. Have you two never run into each other in Los Angeles?"

"No," Bing replied. "To my infinite regret."

"It's a big city, Mom," I added, dipping my toe into the fray.

"It's too bad that her job let her go. I have no idea what she'll do now."

"Mom, you know I'm looking for a new job," Jane cautioned. "I even had some phone interviews last week."

"Your daughter is amazing, ma'am," Bing said, smiling at Jane. "I'm sure she'll find an equally amazing job in no time."

"I'm sure she will, Bing," Mom agreed. "But tell me, how long are you planning on staying in town again?"

"I'll be here for a little while," Bing replied, not taking his eyes off Jane. "I have some time, and . . . well, there are some things here that Los Angeles just doesn't have."

I am *shocked* that my mother managed to keep her fist-pumping subtle, and under the table.

The thing is, she might have something to pump her fists over. The way Bing looked at Jane all throughout dinner, and when I spy them talking alone, it's clear that he's not over her.

And the way Jane looks at Bing . . . I think she might be a little afraid of not being over him, either.

But Jane is holding fast to her principles. So far, they are just friends. Nothing more, nothing less. And I think it's smart. Why let yourself dream of something bigger, when you don't know if anything is going to come of it?

Tuesday, February 26th

"What about this one?" Jane said. "I'd have to find a roommate to afford it, but my friend says that's the safe part of Brooklyn."

"It's a studio," I replied, leaning over her shoulder to look at the screen. "How are you going to have a roommate in a studio? Rotating sleep cycles?"

"At least it doesn't have a bathroom key," Lydia said from the bed. "Does anyone else have a really weird feeling of, like, didgeridoo?"

"A didgeridoo is an Australian musical instrument. But if you mean déjà vu, then totally," I said, and Lydia threw a pillow at me.

Yes, there was a certain sense of déjà vu over the proceedings. Because once again, we were helping Jane look for an apartment. But this time, we weren't looking in Los Angeles.

No, Jane is moving to New York.

She got a job. A *great* job, from the sound of it. Since Jane lost her previous job, and since work is delightfully rare in this economy, she'd been applying everywhere, not just Los Angeles and California. The job in New York was a pipe dream, a wild "why the hell not?" shot in the dark, but they liked her. They liked her style, her lookbook, the recommendations she got from clients, and the referral she got from her old boss at the style firm here in town (hey, it turns out her newer ex-boss in Los Angeles has a reputation as an asshole; go figure).

Sometimes, when you go for the pipe dream, you actually end up getting the pipe dream.

I am incredibly happy for Jane. And I feel a lot better about her career advancement this time than I did back in the fall when she moved to Los Angeles. Maybe because this is how it's supposed to be, and I'm finally at peace with it. We are all growing up. And changing.

"Whatevs, wherever you live it has to have a spare bedroom for me when I visit after summer classes," Lydia said. "My counselor said it would be good motivation for me. Oh, you should totally get a collection of hats. That's what they do in Brooklyn, right? Wear hats?"

But thankfully some of us aren't changing too much.

I like that Lydia is sounding more like her old self. A less boy-crazy, more future-planning version, but the spark that is Lydia is peeking out from behind the scared, bruised outer casing.

"I'll make that my first priority," Jane replied. "Right after rent. Which is . . . alarmingly high."

"Well, your friend from college is letting you crash on her couch for a couple of weeks, so you'll have a better sense of the market and what you can afford then," I replied. "Plus, you're selling your car."

One of the first things Jane's college friend told her was that no one needs a car in New York City. And you know what they say: when in New York . . .

"Well, I'm not taking my car, but I'm not selling it, either," Jane replied.

"What are you going to do with it, then?" Lydia asked. "Just let it sit in the driveway?"

"I'm giving it away. To you."

As Lydia began squealing about no longer having to car-share with Mom, and crushing Jane's ribs in a hug, I noticed Jane's phone play a familiar personalized ring tone.

Bing bing bing bong. Bong bing bing bong. BING! BING!

Three guesses as to whom it belongs.

Jane heard it, too, and escaped Lydia's chokehold of gratitude.

She picked up the phone and, after a second, silenced it and returned to looking at apartment listings on her screen.

Lydia and I looked at each other.

"I'm . . . gonna go tell Mom about the car. She's going to be almost as happy as me," Lydia said, giving Jane one last squeeze before slipping out of the room.

"You haven't told Bing yet, have you?" I said quietly, once the door shut.

"No," Jane said, her voice small. "But I will."

"You're leaving in three days."

"I know!" She nodded, her eyes not leaving her computer screen. "And I'm going to tell him, but . . . I'm just getting to know him again. I don't know how to say good-bye. Especially since I never had the chance to say good-bye the first time."

I know why Jane is reluctant to say good-bye to Bing. Not because she doesn't know how. I think she's afraid that she won't be able to when the time comes. Especially considering how she felt about him before.

"Jane . . . you have to stop not telling him things."

She kept her eyes locked on the computer but was no longer looking at it. When she finally did speak, her voice was small, unsure.

"Do you honestly think if I had told him about the . . . forty-eight hours of worry, it would have made any difference?"

Now it's my turn to stare into space, thinking. Would it have made any difference? I don't know. Heck, it might have driven Bing away all the faster, especially if he was listening to a friend who was operating under the assumption that Jane was just using Bing. But then again, maybe it would have brought them closer. Made them open up to each other, and talk about the future in a way they hadn't been doing before.

I thought about Lydia, and how much I wished we had tried

to understand each other before Christmas instead of blowing up and getting angry. And yes, I thought about Darcy, too, and all we hadn't said.

"I think . . . that you wouldn't believe the problems that can be resolved just by people taking the time to talk to one another."

WEDNESDAY, FEB 27TH

"Mom, do not go in there."

"But I need to get your dad's socks out of the den."

I moved in front of her when she tried to dodge me, like a point guard blocking the shooter. (What? I know basketball. I went to college.)

"Mom, trust me, you do not want to go in there right now."

"For heaven's sake, Lizzie." My mother sighed. "This is my house, too. I know your father doesn't like anyone in his den, and now you've set up your secret little clubhouse in there—"

"Only because you turned my bedroom into your Zen meditation chamber. With an aquarium."

"—but if I don't get your father's socks out from under the chair, they will stink to high heaven by the next laundry day. Trust me."

She tried to get past me again. So I did the only thing I could. I told the truth.

"Mom, Bing found out Jane is leaving for New York, and he came over to talk to her, and they have locked themselves in the den. So . . . as much as I hate telling you this, it is possible that all your dreams for Jane's future happiness hinge on this one moment. So for the love of all that is holy, don't go in there right now."

Mom blinked at me. Then blinked at the door. Then back at me.

"Under those circumstances, I suppose I can come back for your father's socks later."

Mom moved on to the laundry room and I breathed a sigh of relief, holing myself up on the stairs to wait. Not to spy. Just in case there was screaming.

When Bing came in while I was filming, I didn't know what to do. In the kindest way possible, he demanded to talk to Jane. So, I just sort of . . . left them in the den.

I don't know what is going on in there (hopefully some abject begging), but I can't imagine it would go well if Mom walked in and saw them. Plus all of my camera equipment is out and . . .

Oh, crap.

I think I left the camera on!

SATURDAY, MARCH 2ND

Jane just called. She is safely ensconced on the couch of her friend from college in the grand and hat-wearing borough of Brooklyn (the safe part). And interestingly enough . . . so is Bing.

Not that he's ensconced on the couch. But he *is* in New York City. Because he and Jane flew off yesterday in side-by-side seats.

That's right. Jane and Bing went to New York. Together.

Don't worry. They're not engaged. If that were the case, my mother would be dead and we'd be planning a funeral.

Nor are Jane and Bing living together—Jane imposed some strict rules on his coming with her, I think smartly, and rule number one is separate residences.

But what they are doing is giving each other a second chance.

While I was hiding on the stairs (and yes, my camera was on, capturing everything), my sister and her ex-boyfriend were having the heart-to-heart to beat them all. And it turns out, Bing had been keeping some things from Jane, too—and from all of us.

For instance: it turns out, a third-year medical student doesn't have a lot of free time to jaunt off to San Francisco for "interviews," nor can he come to my quaint little hometown to spend time "just friends" with Jane. How did Bing get around this little issue?

He quit med school.

Months ago. In retrospect, it makes a lot of sense. The reason he was in San Francisco was that he was trying to get his head on straight and Darcy gave him a place to be right after he dropped out, so he could try to figure out what to do next.

I don't know if Caroline and his parents even know yet. Well, they'll know when they receive a call from him in their family's pied-à-terre in Manhattan. I can't imagine Caroline will be too pleased. But what can she do about it? It's his life.

After they came out of the den, my mother pounced on them. But it was okay, because they were so happy and smiling, no amount of maternal flailing was going to take it away from them.

"Oh, Jane! Think of all the wonderful restaurants you'll go to! And all the parties Bing will take you to!"

"Actually, Mom, since I'm the one with the job in the fashion industry, I'll probably be taking *him* to the parties," Jane replied.

"Darling, give the girl some breathing room," Dad said, wedging his way in between them, forcing Mom to turn her fawning squeals onto Bing. "Now Jane, I know you'll be happy—but I just want you to tell me that this is truly what you want. If so, I will be kind and welcoming, and take the irrevocable step of letting Bing view my train collection."

"Dad, I know what I'm doing." And she kissed his cheek. "Go ahead and show him your trains. It will be your last chance for a while, since we're leaving in a few days."

Jane . . . Jane just took the biggest leap of her life. A new city, a new job, and giving Bing a second chance.

He wasn't happy without her. He wasn't happy, period. He'd finally acknowledged how much he let others influence his decisions, and decided to make one of his own.

And while Jane managed to survive without Bing, she is flushed with love when he's around. But they are both different people from before, and I think it's a good thing they are away from their families and other influences while they try to learn how to be with each other the way they are now.

I'm so proud of her. And I wonder if I will ever be that brave. Because I don't know what's next for me. I have my thesis to finish, another independent study to come up with, but then what? What's in Lizzie Bennet's future?

I started re-watching my videos to see if I left myself any clues as to what my path should be (God, my makeup in the first few videos was horrrrrrrrible). But I'm just as clueless now as I was then. Sometimes all I think I've gained from the past year is a record of it.

That, and I'm a hell of a lot better at making videos now.

Actually . . . I'm really good at it.

Tuesday, March 5th

Charlotte is in town! My beautiful bestie, having finished production on Game of Gourds, has earned a spring break the likes of which this town has never seen! There will be beer bongs and wet T-shirt contests, and incredibly bad decisions being made!

Just kidding. I think we Bennets have made enough bad decisions this past year—why go back for more when we (well, Lydia and Jane at least) finally started making good ones?

But Charlotte is back for a couple of weeks, and I think the world is better for it. Except for one thing.

Since Charlotte has been following the drama in the Bennet house remotely, she is very eager to revisit all of it. Lydia (Char still hasn't found out who took down the website), Jane (she can't believe Bing quit med school!), but most of all . . . Darcy.

"Why do you keep bringing up Darcy?" I asked, exasperated. We were back in the library, back in our graduate school cubbies—although our original ones had been reassigned, and we were relegated to the back near the bathrooms where no one wanted to be. But still, it was just like old times.

"Because it's the one thing that's unresolved!" Char replied, loud enough to get shushed. "Oh, shush all you want, Norman—I don't go here anymore."

"Speaking of, you didn't have to come find me in the library. I was going to meet you at the theater."

"Yeah, but I knew you were here and I was early." Char shrugged. "Besides, I have to head to LA tomorrow for a couple of meetings and you are dodging the subject."

"And by subject I assume you are not referring to my thesis, which I am currently trying to compose?" I replied.

"Not unless you've changed your thesis to a 150-page report on the recently discovered virtuous aspects of one Mr. William Darcy."

"You know, I don't know if I like it when you have nothing to do. You turn into my mother."

"Lizzie . . ."

"Look, I told you—Darcy and I . . . we aren't anything," I finally said. "We aren't friends, and we aren't more than friends. There might have been a time when we could have been, but I haven't heard from him since I left Pemberley Digital, and I don't expect to."

"Why not?" Charlotte asked softly.

"Because . . ." I tried. "Because I don't."

It was just a missed opportunity. That's all. And it sucks, especially because it seemed like . . . it seemed like I might have not only missed an opportunity, but missed something important. But I can't go back in time.

"You know you don't have to accept that, right?" she said.

"Charlotte, can we talk about something else, please?" I said, shutting down that line of conversation. "What are these meetings you have in LA?"

"Shopping around Game of Gourds—we want to make it our launch series in our entertainment division, expanding out from our informational videos. It's an entirely different business model and we need to finance and market it accordingly."

"You should use the game platform itself," I said. "Package the first five episodes together and end on a cliffhanger, so the investors want to see what happens next."

"Not just one episode?" Charlotte asked, taking out a pen.

"No—the episodes are short; let them get sucked in," I replied. "That can work for your marketing strategy, too—launch with little expectation, let word of mouth build, and then once five or six episodes have aired, media blitz. This way people have something to binge-watch and get sucked into."

Charlotte smirked at me. "You want to take my meetings for me? You'd be good."

"Thanks, but I've got a thesis to finish."

"Heck, I should hire you right now—so you don't go and start your own company right under my nose."

I looked up from my papers to Charlotte. But her head was buried in writing down what I had been saying.

Meanwhile, it's what *she* had said that captured my attention.

* * *

"Dr. Gardiner!" I called out, racing down the hall. I don't know why I'm always running down this hall, but this time it seemed particularly important that I reach my faculty advisor in the greatest haste.

"Lizzie," Dr. Gardiner replied. She was used to my affinity for haste. "What can I help you with today?"

"I think I got it."

"It?"

"I mean, I think I figured out what my last independent study can be. My own company."

That got her attention. "You have a company now?"

"No . . . it would be a fictional company. But I would write up a full prospectus as if my videos and their success were the launch project for my own company. Initial start-up goals, five-year projections, market strategy, everything."

Dr. Gardiner considered me for a moment. An uncomfortably long moment.

"Well, that certainly qualifies as creative."

I took a deep breath. "Listen, the one overarching thing I learned at Collins & Collins, and Gracechurch Street, and especially at Pemberley Digital, is that I have the ability to do this," I said, boldly. "To be in this industry. Heck, to build a company myself. Dr. Gardiner . . . I can do this."

Dr. Gardiner considered it—and I quietly panicked—until her face split into a smile.

"Why not," she said, shrugging. "I've agreed to everything else this year."

"Thank you!" I gave in to the incredibly unprofessional urge to hug my teacher. "Thank you so much!"

She stumbled back a little bit with the force of my hug, but kept smiling. Finally, I realized just how uncouth this was and released her.

"Sorry," I said.

"That's quite all right," she said. "Lizzie, I want you to know, you have certainly made this past year interesting. As a teacher, you learn that good students are a dime a dozen. Interesting ones? They are what you hope for."

I blushed, and then took my leave, knowing Dr. Gardiner had just given me the biggest compliment she could give.

Now, I just have to live up to it.

"Hi, Mary," I said when I answered the door. "I forgot you were coming over."

My emo cousin just stared at me. "I'm helping Lydia catch up in her math class. She missed a couple weeks, what with . . ."

"Yeah, I know," I replied. "Actually, do you have a sec? I would like to talk to you about something."

I hadn't really forgotten that Mary was coming over. In fact, since Lydia mentioned it yesterday, it was all I had been thinking about.

Because it was possible that my humorless, dry, only-owns-the-color-black cousin Mary had some answers. And I had a lot of questions, most of them stemming from what Lydia told me a few days ago.

We've all been wondering who or what caused the Website That Shall Not Be Named (™ J. K. Rowling) to mysteriously disappear from the Internet just a day before it was intended to go live. Charlotte couldn't find anything, I didn't even know where to start looking, and Dad was so relieved, he stopped investigating and started focusing on Lydia's recovery.

But Lydia didn't forget. Lydia did some digging.

And she discovered that the website ceased to exist because of one William Darcy.

How did he do this? He bought the company that George sold the tape to. Novelty Exposures (or the company it was hiding) is now owned by Pemberley Digital. And in so doing, he bought all of their property, including the sex tape. The most amazing part is that George had not only sold the tape to the company, but universal rights to it. So if he ever leaks a frame of it anywhere, he will be in violation of his contract and sued so fast he'll have to leave the planet to escape extreme pecuniary damages.

Of course, this doesn't solve everything. George is still free to roam the world. Free to try to pull this stunt on other women, although I would hope that any woman in that situation would perform an Internet search history of George and see my videos. But I can't guarantee it.

Sometimes, the bad guy does get away with it. But at least this time, he didn't get away with hurting my sister.

However, my big question is—why would Darcy do that? Why would he save Lydia? He's never even liked Lydia, being that she's too "energetic" for his tastes. I've been thinking it over and over for days, and whether he did it because he still feels responsible for how despicable George is, or . . .

Or he did it for me.

Which is impossible to wrap my head around! While we might have gotten close to something happening at Pemberley, ultimately nothing did. And in the grand scheme of things, I'm still just the girl who shot him down and called him names on the Internet. I cannot fathom why someone in his position would do something so large for any reason, let alone me.

So I decided he didn't.

Lydia didn't reveal anything about how she found out. It could have been just from a friend of a friend through the grapevine of Internet life. But . . . Lydia assures me she's not wrong. So I need to check with my own sources.

"So, Mary," I began, more than a little unsure how to broach this subject. "How are you? I haven't seen you since Lydia's birthday party."

"Really? Because I was at your house for Christmas."

"Oh . . . yeah. I remember now."

"And I was here last week, hanging out with your sister. We

passed on the stairs, and you said, 'Hi, Mary, I forgot you were coming over,' much like when you greeted me just now."

"Okay, you make a solid point." I stopped her before she could list the few hundred times I've forgotten about her existence in the past twenty-two years. "But, um . . . that's sort of what I wanted to talk to you about. You and Lydia are close these days."

Mary cocked her head to one side. "I guess."

"So, did she tell you anything about how she found out . . . about who took the website down?"

Mary looked genuinely surprised. "You mean she didn't tell you?"

"She told me that it was Darcy, but not how she found out. And it doesn't make that much sense to me, so I thought—"

"It was him," Mary cut me off. "Our source is solid."

"Mary . . ." I sighed, suddenly tired. "I need to know. Please."

Mary glanced around quickly, then shrugged, putting her bag on the floor. "Lydia'd been thinking a lot about the website. Obsessing over it, really. The only conclusion she could come to was that George had taken it down, because he hadn't known how much it would hurt her. That somehow she'd gotten through to him."

I could feel my brow coming down in a flat line. "George didn't contact her, did he?"

"No," Mary assured me. "Her counselor told her that was a common hope in betrayal situations, but not likely. But I knew that she'd keep holding on to the hope until she knew for sure. So, I figured we should get into contact with the one person we know of that also knows the real George."

"Who?"

"Gigi Darcy."

"Wait . . ." I shook my head, trying to comprehend. "Lydia called Gigi?"

"No. There's no way Lydia was ready for that. So I friended Gigi on Twitter, and we messaged." Mary's eyes lit up with anger.

"She told us that her brother had immediately begun to search for George, the moment he heard about the sex tape. George had been hiding out in a beach resort when Darcy found him, sipping a margarita and cashing in on Lydia's pain."

I could barely breathe. "And then what did he do?"

"George wouldn't budge," Mary continued. "But Darcy did get the details of the sale to that porn company from him—who he actually sold it to, I mean. With so little time, Darcy knew the only way to stop the company was to buy it. So he did."

I stood there, in total shock for what must have been a full minute, because Mary began to squirm.

"Did you need anything else?" she asked. "Lydia's probably wondering where I am."

"Hm? Oh, right," I said, shaking off my haze. "No, I'm good. And thanks."

"No problem." Mary sighed the sigh of the long suffering.

And I was left to sort out my feelings.

There's no way Gigi would lie about her brother, so it has to be true. Darcy bought an Internet porn company, and dismantled it, to stop my sister's sex tape from being released.

I can feel that familiar queasiness in my stomach, as I am once again dancing on that thin line between dread and hope, thinking that Darcy might have done it for me.

But if he had . . . I would know, right?

Wouldn't he call me?

Maybe he'll call.

No, Lizzie. Stop being foolish.

. . .

. . .

Still, I should make sure my phone is fully charged. And the ringer on. Just in case.

MONDAY, MARCH 11TH

You know, I kind of hoped we were done with drama in the Bennet household. Things have been much calmer with Lydia taking some time to heal and Jane and Bing on the East Coast. Dad comes home after work every day and hangs out with his daughters. Mom is happily occupied dreaming of the day Bing and Jane get engaged and deliver her grandchildren, and I'm keeping my nose to the grindstone, writing my thesis and last independent study concurrently. So, all in all, things have been pretty calm around here.

All of that changed yesterday, when Caroline Lee barged into the den and confronted me.

Yes, confronted me.

About what, I'm still not sure. But she was incredibly angry when she came in and accused me of ruining her brother's life by encouraging him to run away with Jane, and now ruining Darcy's.

Let's put aside the fact that I have absolutely no say or influence over Bing's life — or my sister's. And I told Caroline as much. But to say that I ruined Darcy's life, when I have almost nothing to do with him at this present point in time, is frankly ludicrous.

But Caroline has been watching my videos. And she blew it out, point by point.

She said it was my doing, and my doing alone, that had Bing quitting school and running off with Jane. Jane wasn't strong enough, and Bing had never made a decision of that magnitude in his life, according to her. Of course, Bing didn't even find out about my videos until after he quit school, but in Caroline's mind, that's neither here nor there.

She also said that Darcy taking time away from his business

to go solve my younger sister's crisis looks extremely bad to his financiers. Especially his aunt, Catherine De Bourgh. Caroline claimed she was thinking of withdrawing her support, but since I worked at Pemberley, I know how well they are doing, and a businesswoman as savvy as Ms. De Bourgh wouldn't make such a decision on such a flimsy excuse.

Caroline kept going on and on about how terrible I was for her brother and Darcy, how it was *my* influence that was making them make terrible decisions.

Oh, yeah, Caroline? Decisions like making your brother break up with my sister?

That was when I decided to pull out the big guns. It was time to finally ask Caroline about Jane's supposed "indiscretion" the night of Bing's birthday party. Because if Jane has no idea, Bing wasn't sure, and it seemed like Darcy wasn't entirely sure, either (although he's the one who saw it), then Caroline is the only one who's left.

"You mean your sister never told you she kissed another man?" she said so smugly, I knew that if Jane *had* kissed another man, then it was Caroline who orchestrated it. After all, she'd been in Jane's company the whole night.

And she didn't deny it.

What Caroline did do was, at Bing birthday party, somehow fix it so that Jane was kissed by one of Bing's drunk friends, and Darcy saw, misinterpreting it as a betrayal of Bing. That's it. That's the big mystery. One that could have been cleared up by PEOPLE TALKING TO OTHER PEOPLE. Since I'm one of the people who often has trouble with such communication, I shouldn't judge, but I can't help but think of all the heartache that could have been saved had Caroline not been so desperate to get her brother away from Jane.

She had the audacity to say that she was simply doing what was best for the people she cares about. She "helps them."

And there she was, accusing me of interference!

I was so angry, and honestly exhausted by the whole thing, I did the only thing I could. I told the truth. With everything I had in my power.

"Well, let me help you with something. You know who's in charge of Darcy's life? Darcy. And you know who's in charge of mine? Me. The same goes for Bing and for Jane." I took a deep breath. "And now, despite the fact that you've come into my house and insulted me, and my family, again, please consider yourself welcome to stay for dinner."

I'm particularly proud of that last part. My mom's southern hospitality is born and bred in us, and it had the pleasant side effect of making me look like the better person.

She turned me down. And walked out.

It took only about five seconds for me to start to feel bad. And to feel like we weren't done. I mean, why does Caroline think she gets to control my life? Because that's what she was doing—she was there to make me feel terrible for her brother and my sister being happy together, and to make sure that I kept my greedy mitts off of Darcy. And if she's been watching my videos, she knows there is no call for such a warning, because he doesn't want anything to do with *me* anymore. But that didn't stop Caroline.

Yeah, we definitely weren't done.

Quickly, I jumped up and followed her out to her car.

"Caroline," I called out, stopping her from opening the door. She kept her curtain of shiny black hair in front of her face, blocking me from her view.

"You know, if you think you can barge into my life and start ordering me around, then—"

Her head whipped up then. She was . . . crying.

"Obviously I *can't*," she spat at me.

"Caroline," I said, much softer.

"You get your own life. Darcy gets his own life. Jane gets hers,

Bing gets his." She blew out an angry breath. *"THEN WHAT DO I GET?!?"*

"I . . . I don't know," I replied, shocked. "I think you have to find that out for yourself."

She looked for a second like she was about to say something else, but she just ended up mumbling under her breath, "Of course," before climbing in her car and screeching out of the driveway.

When I turned around, Lydia was standing in the doorway.

"What was that all about?" she asked, wrinkling her nose at the car fading into the distance.

"I'm not totally sure. It's complicated."

Lydia crossed her arms. "Explain it to me over fro-yo? I'll drive."

So I did. Over red velvet cake fro-yo with coconut shavings.

"It doesn't even make sense, right?" I said when I was done. "Her coming here and throwing all that stuff at me. Especially the stuff about Darcy. I mean, I know Caroline has a crush on him, but it's not like—"

"Yeah, that's not what this is about," Lydia said, swallowing a spoonful of yogurt.

"It's not?"

"It's about how everything was going fine in Caroline-land up until a year ago, then it all started to fall apart when Bing quit school."

"Wait . . . Bing quit school only a couple of months ago—not last year."

Lydia shot me a glance over the top of her sunglasses. "The first time he quit school, I mean."

I blinked. "The first time he quit school?"

"Lizzie, med students don't get five months off in the summer to just hang out. And people who aren't like in the midst of a *total* identity crisis don't just up and buy a house in the middle of no where. Bing dropped out of school. And Caroline and Darcy were sent up here to get him back on track."

Little puzzle pieces were beginning to fall into place in my head. Bing being able to simply leave LA and buy Netherfield. The looks his parents gave him at his birthday party. And toward the end of summer—all the pressure on him, the flying back to LA for "interviews," the lack of communication between him and Jane. He'd quit school. And he'd been pressured into going back.

"But if Caroline saw her brother was unhappy . . ."

Lydia shook her head. "Lizzie, if I told you I'm quitting school, starting a rock band with Mary, and moving to Mexico, what would you do?"

I answered without hesitation. "I'd lock you in your room until your passport expired."

"Well, damn, there goes that life plan," she smirked at me. "I actually really feel bad for Caroline. As bitchy as she is. Especially about me." She furrowed her brow. "Scratch that—I don't feel bad for her at all."

"Yeah you do," I replied, watching Lydia carefully. "Why?"

My sister shrugged, and focused on her yogurt. "I dunno. It's just . . . she's not the golden child. People don't have expectations of her. And that can really suck. Finally, she was asked to do something important and she proved herself. It was hard enough the first time to pull him away from Jane, but to have him go back—and quit school *again*—means she failed."

"How do you know all this?" I asked after a moment.

Lydia just gave me a look that spoke volumes about my current stupidity. "Because I watched them. Duh."

I let that settle over me as my yogurt melted. Meanwhile, Lydia finished hers and lobbed the cup toward the trash can in a perfect arc.

"Anyway, all the Darcy stuff stems from that. She can't get her brother to listen to reason, she sees her crush Darcy following the same path, and suddenly she doesn't have anything."

"Okay, all the Bing stuff makes sense," I reasoned. "But Darcy's not following the same path. He's not running away, or wildly altering his life to be with . . . someone."

"Right—'cuz most people buy companies for no reason." Lydia just sent me that smirk again. "You keep telling yourself that."

"He didn't—"

Lydia just eyed me and stood up from the table. "Whatevs. Are you done with that or do you want to grab a lid for it? Either way, I'm not letting you in *my* car with an open drippy yogurt."

Tuesday, March 12th

I've been doing a lot of thinking lately. About what Charlotte said, about what Caroline said, and about what Lydia said.

And I've come to absolutely zero conclusions.

Maybe because I haven't spoken to the one person in this situation that matters — Darcy.

I keep saying that Darcy and I are not involved, that it was a moment of possibility that passed. But I recently finished my re-watch of all my videos, and . . . maybe we are.

But if we were involved, why haven't I heard one word from him? Especially when he went through so much trouble to save my sister.

Unless he didn't want me to know.

Darcy has managed to completely bewilder me. Yet again. Go figure.

At one point, I thought I knew him, and I dismissed him. Then I got to know him, and I realized there was so much more.

I just don't want to sit here passively, wondering forever. Which means maybe I should take matters into my own hands.

Saturday, March 16th

"He hasn't called back yet, has he?" Charlotte asked immediately when I opened the door.

"Happy early birthday to you, too," I replied. "Why don't you come out of the rain before you start the inquisition."

"It's barely drizzling," Charlotte said, but she stepped inside and shook off her jacket. "And, happy early birthday!"

Tomorrow is Charlotte's and my mutual birthday. Our mothers went into labor at the same book club meeting, and delivered us about three hours apart. I don't think book club has ever been as interesting since.

Not many people can say that they've known each other their entire lives, but Charlotte and I can. Hence why Charlotte thinks she's earned the right to bombard me with personal questions the minute she walks in the door.

Which she probably has.

"So . . . did Darcy call back yet?"

Yes, amazingly, over the past couple of weeks I managed to forget that I don't live in the nineteenth century. And while I was biting my nails over the fact that I hadn't heard from Darcy, and wistfully cyber-stalking him, I conveniently forgot that telecommunications work both ways. (I blame the movies for this little gendered slip-up.) So, finally, at my wits' end, I gave Darcy a call. And ended up leaving a message.

"Hey, Darcy. It's Lizzie . . . Um, if you could call me when you get a sec, I'd like to . . . chat."

I don't think I've ever been lamer. And trust me, I've been very, very lame in my time.

That was three days ago.

"No, I haven't heard back from him," I told Charlotte. "Why do you have what has to be the entire freezer section of Ben and Jerry's?"

"I was hedging my bets," she replied. "Either you would be miserable over the lack of Darcy calling, or he would be here and you would be making out, in which case I would just go eat this all by myself on the way to the SPCA to pick out a cat. Maybe a ferret."

"It's the former," I said, taking a pint of Cherry Garcia.

After three days, a girl can take a hint. I don't know what I'd hoped for when I called Darcy. But I know that the idea of hearing his voice again got my heart beating faster, so the fact that I haven't can only be a disappointment. It's so strange. Not six months ago, I thought Darcy was snobby, rude, and stuck-up. I thought he was convinced that he was better than everyone else and that I in particular was beneath him, and worthy of scorn. So I scorned him right back.

But now my feelings have changed so much. Now I know he's shy, and strong, and loyal. Yes, a little socially awkward, but it makes his efforts all the more endearing. Now, I know he doesn't feel that he's better than me. But I know that he *is* better. And if I could go back in time, I would do everything differently.

So, yes, I'm a little sad. But I have plenty of other things to worry about. My final independent study, building out my prospectus based on my own fictional web video company, and finishing my thesis. The videos will have to end sometime soon so I can put the whole project together.

Wow. That's a huge part of my life for the past year, coming to an end. Another thing to feel sad about.

Maybe, instead, I can think of it as the next phase beginning, with me being a little wiser.

Not to mention older.

"So, what are you going to do when we turn twenty-five tomorrow?" I asked Charlotte. "I know . . . let's go rent a car for no reason!"

Charlotte laughed, and we moved to the living room and set up camp. In spite of my distraction and all the work I have to do, I had managed to pull myself together enough to get Charlotte a birthday present.

"Aw . . ." Charlotte said, unwrapping it. "It's a mug. From our grad school. You bought this in the student center gift shop, didn't you?"

"I did," I admitted.

"It's okay," she said, giving me a hug. "I understand you are lonely and despairing now, and therefore can't be counted on to do anything like groom and feed yourself. That's why I'm here."

"And me!" Lydia said as she entered. "Mind if I join you?"

"Sure, come on in," I said "Plenty of Chunky Monkey for everyone."

Lydia grabbed the carton of ice cream, then noticed the gift wrap strewn in front of Charlotte. "Oh, are we doing presents now?" she asked. "I'll be right back."

As Lydia bounced out of the room, I turned to Charlotte "What else you got in the bag?"

She fished inside and brought out two movie choices. "This evening's distraction. Do you want to watch pretty people fall in love or things blowing up?"

I eyed them both. "Do you have anything with pretty people blowing up?" I asked, and Charlotte threw a pillow at me.

This right here? This is why I have a bestie.

"I vote carnage," Lydia said as she came back in the living room, bearing gifts. "If that's okay with you guys, of course."

"Carnage it is," Charlotte said, and smirked at me as she moved to put the DVD in.

"Happy early birthday!" Lydia said, handing me the packages. "The green top is from Jane, and the necklace is from me—and

I also got you a book titled *Where Did I Leave My Pride? A Nerdy Girl's Guide to Making Lame Phone Calls.*"

I stared at Lydia open-mouthed until I saw Charlotte behind her, her shoulders shaking from suppressing laughter. And I burst out laughing, too. Then so did Lydia.

It's why I have sisters, too.

Sunday, March 17th

Today was . . . something incredible. And I think I'll let it speak for itself.

COMPLETE TRANSCRIPT OF EVENTS RECORDED ON SUNDAY, MARCH 17TH

LIZZIE: Thank God for Charlotte. And for Lydia. And for Jane. Who is still really happy with Bing in New York! And that's great. That they get to have this second chance and are running with it. And second chances . . . second chances are rare. I'm pretty sure I used all mine up.

(The door opens.)

LIZZIE: Hey, did you need money for the tip?

DARCY: Excuse me, Lizzie?

(I jump up.)

LIZZIE: I thought you were . . . Chinese.

DARCY: I . . . can understand the confusion. Would you . . . care to sit down?

(We sit. It's awkward.)

DARCY: Do you . . . film everything in your life?

LIZZIE: No, I swear. You just have impeccable timing.

DARCY: Well, I can't begrudge your videos, certainly. They have been very useful, from my perspective.

(pause)

DARCY: I was surprised to see Charlotte.

LIZZIE: It's our birthday.

DARCY: I'm sorry . . . I didn't know it was your birthday.

LIZZIE: No, I mean—why would you?

DARCY: I . . . Happy birthday.

LIZZIE: Thank you.

(pause)

DARCY: You called me.

LIZZIE: I left a message, yes.

DARCY: I was in Chicago, that's why—

LIZZIE: Oh, God—I didn't intend—I thought you would just call back; you didn't have to come here.

DARCY: Yes, I did. I needed to see your face when I asked you . . . why?

LIZZIE: Why?

DARCY: Why did you call me? I've been watching your videos. I know that you have found out . . . certain things about recent events.

LIZZIE: "Recent events"? You bought up whole companies to save my sister. For what you've done for my family, we cannot thank you enough.

DARCY: Your family owes me no thanks. As much as I have learned to respect them, I did not do it for them. I did it for you.

LIZZIE: My gratitude is there and it always will be.

DARCY: Lizzie, I have to admit to some confusion. Because you also said on your videos that we are not friends. And I realized you were right—even though we got to spend so much time together in San Francisco, we hadn't become friends. But then I thought perhaps you wanted to amend that.

LIZZIE: I do!

DARCY: So . . . you want to be friends?

LIZZIE: Yes! . . . Well, I mean . . . well. God, no wonder you're confused.

DARCY: Lizzie, I still feel the same way I did in the fall. More strongly, even, than I did then. So if you just want to be friends or say thank you for recent events, then I—

(Voices suddenly become muted, because I'm kissing him.)

LIZZIE: Does that . . . clear up some things for you?

DARCY: Some . . . I could use some further illumination on certain points, however.

(Muted noises, more kissing.)

LIZZIE: Just so you know, you're not the only one who was confused.

DARCY: Really?

LIZZIE: Well, we had been getting along at Pemberley, and then after I left there was nothing but radio silence from you and—I thought . . .

DARCY: I didn't know if you wanted to hear from me. I watched your videos and your focus was solely on your sister, as it should have been. I realized I would have just been an unwelcome distraction.

LIZZIE: Not unwelcome. I promise.

DARCY: Then, I heard what you said to Caroline, about my life being my choice and your life being yours, and it got my hopes up again. But I didn't know if it was because of what you found out or—

LIZZIE: I get it. Confusing. God, for two such smart people we can certainly act like idiots, can't we?

DARCY: One might even say it's our forte.

LIZZIE: Well, let me make things as clear as possible. William Darcy—I don't want to be just friends. And I don't want to be with

you because I'm grateful to you. I want to be with you . . . because of you. Got it?

DARCY: Clear as day, Lizzie Bennet.

(muted kissing sounds)

LIZZIE: Um, one sec.

END RECORDING.

Monday, March 18th

Happy. Just happy.

Tuesday, March 19th

Still blissfully happy.

WEDNESDAY, MARCH 20TH

Okay, one more day of just being happy and then I'm sucking it up and telling Mom.

Mom took it better than expected. Eventually.

"Mom, I've invited someone over for dinner tonight," I said.

"Of course, dear—you know Charlotte's always welcome," she replied, humming as she put the casserole in the oven.

"Actually it's not—" But at that moment, she flipped the disposal on, drowning out my words.

Well, I tried to warn her. In truth, I was kind of looking forward to seeing the look on her face when Darcy walked through the door.

And I wasn't disappointed.

"Mom, Dad," I said, guiding Darcy into the living room by the hand once he arrived. "You remember William Darcy."

"Mrs. Bennet, a pleasure to see you again," Darcy said, with only the slightest bit of nervousness in his voice. I'm pretty sure I'm the only one that could hear it. I've been making a study of it the past few days.

My mom looked from the bottle of wine he held out to her, up to his face, then down to our intertwined hands. Then she mustered up every ounce of southern hospitality she had in her being.

"Of course," she smiled, taking the bottle of wine. (I'm thinking Bing gave him pointers on what vintage to get.) "So nice to see you again." She cleared her throat and turned to me. Suddenly, her voice took on a high pitch not often heard outside of the Muppets. "Lizziewillyouhelpmeinthekitchenplease?"

I was pulled away so quickly I might have whiplash. I was barely able to overhear my father as he greeted Darcy. "Don't worry, young man—this will all be sorted out quickly. That, or my darling wife will have murdered Lizzie, but either way it's an exciting start to the evening, eh?"

Once in the kitchen, Mom launched into me.

"All right, Lizzie, is this some kind of joke?" she asked.

"No, it's not," I assured her.

"Because that's the only explanation I can think of for William Darcy being in my living room."

"Well, another explanation is that we're dating."

"Lizzie, do be serious."

"Mom, I thought you'd be happy!" I replied. "After all, he is . . ."

"Rich?" my mother finished for me. "Out of all my daughters, I thought you were the one who didn't care about that."

"Actually, none of us care about that," I quipped. "But perhaps I've been more vocal than Jane or Lydia."

"I thought you only cared about *character*," my mom rambled on. "I thought you would *never* want to be with someone as rude and snobbish as Darcy."

"He's not rude or snobbish," I replied. "I . . . we all misjudged him."

"He's nice, Mom," Lydia's quiet voice came from behind us. "You should give him a chance."

Mom's head whipped back and forth between Lydia and me, her mouth agape. Finally she turned to me. "You're really dating him."

"Yes," I said, catching Lydia's smile.

You could hear a pin drop in the kitchen. Until . . .

"Well for heaven's sake, why didn't you tell me?" she screeched. "You bring your boyfriend over to dinner and I'm serving a *casserole*?"

"One that I think will pair very well with that wine." But Mom was having none of it. She was already rummaging in the fridge for something more fancy she could prepare.

"Lydia, quickly—toast some bread. We need crostini appetizers immediately!"

Dinner went pretty well after that. I found Dad and Darcy engaged in a conversation about the arts of bonsai versus the arts of penjing. Lydia came out of the kitchen fifteen minutes later, bearing a tray of hastily arranged crostini.

"Hi, Darcy," she said shyly, having trouble meeting his eye.

"Lydia," he replied warmly. "How are you doing?"

She managed to look up at him then. "Better. A lot better now. Thanks."

"I'm glad," he replied.

Lydia looked aside for a moment, then ditched the tray and gave in to her impulse to hug him. Darcy was a little shocked, but he took it well.

I met my Dad's eyes. He simply glanced from me to Darcy, and then asked, "So, young man—do you like trains?"

The casserole actually did pair well with the wine. Dad only teased Mom twice about how the simple dinner had miraculously turned into a multi-course meal, and she only threw one dinner roll at him. Darcy seemed startled, but I squeezed his hand and let him know that this is just how family—my family—is: We tease each other.

After dinner, Dad pulled me aside into his den.

"How did your mother take it?" he asked, a small smile playing over his features.

"Dinner didn't speak for itself?" I replied. Mom should really be forced to cook on the fly more often. The vichyssoise was particularly excellent.

"I suppose so. I knew she'd come around quickly. Mind you, if I'd not had the advantage of seeing your videos, I might have been as bewildered by your choice as she was."

I blushed. "I know I've been a little harsh on him in the past, but . . . all that's changed."

"I know." My dad nodded. "And when I took him to see my train collection, I managed to thank him for what he did for Lydia. There is no possible way I can repay him for it, but I just want to make sure that your being with him is not *your* way of repaying him for it. Do you understand?"

"Dad, it's not," I stammered. "He's so much better than I thought . . . He's smart and kind, and thinks deeply about things. The people that he loves—his sister, his friends—they know that he's one of those people that you want to have at your side in case of a crisis. Or no crisis. He's the one person you want to see every day, no matter what."

"You mean, he's the one person *you* want to see every day," Dad said.

"Yes," I replied.

"You really like him then?"

"Dad, I love him."

There was nothing really to be said after that. My dad just wrapped me in a bear hug and kissed the top of my head. "Then I am very happy for you. I wouldn't be, mind you, if it were anyone less worthy."

He released me and stretched out his arms, as if hugging the world.

"Well, I'm quite at my leisure, then," he said. "Although I have no idea what your mother's going to do now, without Jane's or your romantic lives to fret over. And I won't allow her to bother Lydia with it." Dad looked thoughtful for a moment. "I don't think Kitty's been fixed yet. We can see about getting her a nice cat boyfriend and creating some cat grandchildren for her to fret over."

We went back into the living room, to find Darcy wedged in between Mom and Lydia, Mom going on about how "someone in technology should just make some kind of database of all information. Don't you think that's a good idea?" When he looked up and met my eyes, his face split into a wide, relieved smile.

I'm going to remember this forever, I realized. This moment, where William Darcy came to dinner and met my family. As my boyfriend. As the most important person in my life. And that he survived it with aplomb.

This is the beginning.

Friday, March 22nd

To: Lizzie Bennet (lizziebennet@. . . .)
From: Digital Investment Group (DIGroup@. . . .)
Subject: New Media Venture

Dear Ms. Bennet—
As a viewer of your videos, I was very interested to hear you discuss
your final project for school—creating a prospectus for your own Internet company. As a financier of similar ventures, we would love the
chance to speak with you about making such a company a reality. We
think you have great market potential . . .

* * *

To: Lizzie Bennet (lizziebennet@. . . .)
From: Cyberlife Fund (CyberlifeMarketing@. . . .)
Subject: Your videos

Dear Lizzie—
I was introduced to your videos by my daughter, who is a devotee.
I have long been an advocate of the Internet as the medium of the
future and find your videos funny, touching, and smart. You mentioned the possibility of creating your own company based off of the
success of your videos, and I would be very interested in such an
endeavor. Cyberlife is an investment group devoted to smart start-ups
with high growth potential, and feel that "The Lizzie Bennet Diaries"
would add greatly . . .

* * *

To: Lizzie Bennet (lizziebennet@. . . .)
From: New Global Hedge Fund (NGHF@. . . .)

Ms. Bennet—
I have never seen your videos, but my assistant has. I am impressed by your viewership numbers and your high positive rankings from your comments. My assistant tells me you will be forming a new company soon, and I find such investments interesting. Please contact me at your earliest convenience. Let's make some money!

* * *

What on earth are all these emails? I scrolled through my in-box— there are a half dozen more, all from hedge funds and investment groups. I mentioned on my videos a week ago that I would be doing my final independent study on my own fictional business . . . but half of these seem to think I'm actually creating a business. And they want to invest in it—or at least meet and talk about it.

They think my fake company is a real thing.

Could my fake company become a real thing?

"Lizzie, what are you doing?" Darcy asked.

"Just checking my email," I said.

"Lizzie . . ." he sighed, leaning down to kiss my shoulder. "Come back to bed."

I suppose emails can wait.

TUESDAY, MARCH 26TH

"Hey, Lizzie," Lydia said, approaching me. "Can we talk to you a sec?"

"Sure," I replied, blinking at my sister's voice and closing my folder. I'd been going blind all day putting my prospectus together. Not to mention the twenty pages of a section of my thesis I'd typed up last night. Add to that the constant delicious distraction that was Darcy, and I was a little out of it lately. "Hey, Mary—I didn't realize you'd come over."

"You're the one who let me in," she grumbled.

"Anyway," Lydia said. "We were hoping to talk to you about the future."

My eyebrows went up. "There seems to be a lot of talk about the future recently."

"Yeah," Mary said. "Specifically about you starting your own company and moving to San Francisco."

Even without the new boyfriend glow, it's been an interesting week for me. When investors and hedge funds started emailing me, at first I dismissed it. But it kept worming its way back into my brain, this idea that I could form my own company. I have the business plan in place, I have a lot of online experience now, and the odd but strangely gratifying vague Internet fame. I talked over the idea with Charlotte, and with Dr. Gardiner, and they were both supportive.

I was a little scared to talk it over with Darcy, though. Not because he'd disapprove. He wouldn't. Because he might have been disappointed. Especially when I had to turn down his offer of a job at Pemberley Digital.

Yes, he offered me a job upon graduation. And I know it wasn't just because we're dating, but that was exactly the reason I couldn't take it. I want to be with him, but I don't want to be the girl who dates the boss. It would undermine his credibility at Pemberley and start me off on the wrong foot with everyone there.

I'm much happier just being his girlfriend. And making plans to move to San Francisco when I get my master's is a big part of that happiness. I fell in love with the city at the same time I was falling for Darcy. And according to Dr. Gardiner, I might be able to apartment-sit for her friend again, whose South American sabbatical is being extended to next year.

I haven't told Charlotte about that part yet. She might self-implode in apartment jealousy.

"We were wondering," Lydia said, "if you needed any employees."

"Employees?" I asked, bewildered. "At my currently still fictitious company?"

"Yep," Lydia said, and Mary nodded in tandem.

"Like who?"

"Like me," Mary said. "I'm graduating in May, too, and I'll be getting my bachelor's in accounting . . ."

"Your major is accounting?" I cried. "Not bass guitar? Or, er . . . poetry?"

"No," Mary replied, her voice flat as ever. "It's accounting. I'm going to take a year to save money before I start applying to business schools—and I thought actual business experience might help me more than working at a pizza place. Plus, I'm hoping you'll pay better."

"Again—the company is still fictitious, Mary."

"Anyway, since I'm facing a difficult job market just like you, I thought it would be better to get in on the ground floor of something that grows. I can do all your budget work, spreadsheets, tax liability. And don't worry—I'd get my own place."

"Mary—San Francisco is expensive," I cautioned. "Can you afford—"

"I was planning on working remotely through the summer— and then when I do move up, I'll be bringing a roommate with me."

"Who?"

"Me," Lydia piped up.

"Lydia," I said, shaking my head. "If you want to move to San Francisco because of me . . . you have to know that I'm going to be coming home to visit a lot, right? And I'll just be a phone call away if you need—"

"Okay, that's adorable," Lydia snorted, "but this one's actually not about you."

"But you have school here—"

"If I take two make-up courses over the summer, I'll have enough credits for my associate's degree," she replied. "Which I can transfer to a four-year college. And there's a school in San Francisco that has a really good psychology program my counselor recommended."

My eyebrows were now permanently plastered to the ceiling. "Psychology?"

"I dunno." She concentrated on digging her toe into the carpet. "These past couple of months, I've really sort of enjoyed figuring out why people do stuff. You know, how the mind works. My mind in particular."

"Okay , , ," I ventured, "but how are you going to pay for it?"

"Student loans." She shrugged. "It's a Bennet family tradition."

"So?" Mary asked. "What do you think?"

What do I think?

I think everything is coming together. And it's kind of amazing

FRIDAY, MARCH 29TH

Wow. Has it really been a year? I remember sitting down with this book, frustrated at my mother and an idea forming in my head for a school project, and not really thinking beyond that.

And now, it feels like in the past two weeks my entire life has come together—but that's not really the case. Each step has led to this moment.

A year ago, I didn't even know Darcy. And then I hated him. But if I hadn't hated Darcy once, I couldn't love him so much now. And I do. I think I fell a long time ago, and only now am I allowed to feel it. I have a game plan for my career as well—something else I wouldn't have had without all the drama, hard work, and introspection over the past year.

A year ago, Charlotte was my partner in crime at school. Now she is large and in charge at Collins & Collins. Ricky has decided to move to Winnipeg, Manitoba, to be with his ladylove, and to become a connoisseur of Tim Hortons and poutine. Char is her own woman, head of a company—in name and reality—and working hard in her field. And even after a squabble, she's still my best friend. And always will be.

Jane is happy. It took her a long time to get there, but she is. Every time I talk to her on the phone she just sounds more confident, more radiant, more Jane. And regardless of how Caroline interfered in their lives, I have no doubt Bing and Jane will forgive his sister. That's just who they are.

Lydia is a different person than the one from last year. Not better, not worse. Just different. I mourn the fact that I never let myself know the girl from before but am thankful every day I get to know this Lydia. She's bright, and smart, and funny. And, yes, energetic. But energetic's okay, too.

As for me—I have a prospectus to create, my thesis conclusion to write, potential financiers to correspond with, and a boyfriend downstairs. He's making small talk with my dad, waiting to take me to dinner. He has to head back to San Francisco soon, and I'm already fighting my impulse to turn into that girl who gets all bemoan-y when separated from her boyfriend. But it won't be for long. I'm going up to the city next weekend, to meet with investors and let Gigi squeal her happiness at our relationship all over me. And of course, to spend time just walking around the city with Darcy.

Life . . . life is pretty fantastic right now.

I can't wait to see what happens next.

The End

ACKNOWLEDGMENTS

This book would not exist without the web series *The Lizzie Bennet Diaries*, and *The Lizzie Bennet Diaries* would not exist without the passions and talents of dozens. Many thanks go to Hank Green, for first approaching Bernie with the kernel of an idea for a way to tell Jane Austen on the web, then put up his own money to finance it in the beginning, and for bringing the awesome Nerdfighter community along for the ride. Then Michael Wayne and DECA took a chance on us, giving us the funds to keep going and the blessing of basic infrastructure (aka office space).

The series writing staff: Margaret Dunlap, Rachel Kiley, Jay Bushman, and Anne Toole all shaped the story and created quirks that made the show what it is. The actors: Ashley Clements, Laura Spencer, Mary Kate Wiles, Julia Cho, Daniel Vincent Gordh, Christopher Sean, Jessica Andres, Maxwell Glick, Allison Paige, Wes Aderhold, Craig Frank, Janice Lee, and Briana Cuoco brought their characters to life so much better than we could have ever imagined. Our production team: Jenni Powell, Stuart Davis, Adam Levermore, Katie Moest, and music and logo designer Michael Aranda made the show possible, gorgeous, and on budget (which, considering we had no budget, was a big plus!). And of course, our Emmy Award–winning interactive team of Jay Bushman and Alexandra Edwards brought Lizzie Bennet out from behind her camera and onto Twitter, Facebook, Tumblr, and into the world.

David Tochterman, Bradley Garrett, and Annelise Robey did the legalese that made this book a reality, and Lauren Spiegel at

Touchstone has been the best editor and cheerleader we could have hoped for. On a personal note, I (Kate) would like to thank my circle of writer friends, who sat across from me in coffee shops and made soothing sounds as I typed furiously, and my husband, Harrison, who happily played video games while I ignored him completely. That's love, people.

About the Authors

BERNIE SU is the Emmy Award–winning executive producer, co-creator, head writer, and director of the web series *The Lizzie Bennet Diaries*, for which he also won the Streamy Awards for Best Writing, Comedy, and Best Interactive Program. Su has written and produced several scripted web series, including *Emma Approved*, *Lookbook: The Series*, and *Compulsions*. Su is a graduate of the University of California, San Diego, and lives in Los Angeles.

KATE RORICK is a writer and producer for *The Lizzie Bennet Diaries*. She has written for a variety of television shows, including *Law & Order: Criminal Intent* and *Terra Nova*. In her spare time, she is the bestselling author of historical romance novels under the name Kate Noble. She lives in Los Angeles.

The Secret Diary of Lizzie Bennet

Bernie Su and Kate Rorick

By drawing on Jane Austen's timeless novel, Bernie Su and Kate Rorick created a modern-day *Pride and Prejudice* with *The Secret Diary of Lizzie Bennet*. In her diary, Lizzie writes about a year of her life and her experiences making video blogs (vlogs) for her graduate thesis. From Netherfield to Pemberley and back again, Lizzie navigates the dangerous waters of social propriety and relationships in the twenty-first century—both on and off the Internet. What starts as a simple thesis idea becomes a way for Lizzie to inform and reflect upon her life and her sisters' lives. With the unexpected success and popularity of her videos, Lizzie suddenly finds her vlogs and her life prominently displayed in the Internet's public eye. But as personal and revealing as the videos are, Lizzie's secret diary reveals her deepest anxieties and most private thoughts over the course of a dramatic year.

The book complements the popular website *The Lizzie Bennet Diaries* and its accompanying YouTube videos, which can be watched in tandem or enjoyed separately.

For Discussion

1. Jane Austen's *Pride and Prejudice* takes place in nineteenth-century English society, a world with strict and specific social parameters. How do the authors transfer the storyline to our modern world? Discuss how the authors make the Bennets' circumstances contemporary.

2. As the story progresses, we hear Darcy's description of his perfect woman: "Someone who is together" (p. 103). He then lists a set of ambitious qualities that are nearly impossible to locate all in one person. How does this list compare to Darcy's description in *Pride and Prejudice* (below)?

   > "A woman must have a thorough knowledge of music, singing, drawing, dancing, and the modern languages, to deserve the word; and besides all this, she must possess a certain something in her air and manner of walking, the tone of her voice, her address and expressions, or the word will be but half deserved. All this she must possess," added Darcy, "and to all this she must yet add something more substantial, in the improvement of her mind by extensive reading."

   Do the authors modernize the qualities that Darcy looks for in a woman? If so, what is different? Which qualities do you think are essential for a well-rounded woman today? Are they different for a well-rounded man?

3. Mrs. Bennet tells Lizzie she is too idealistic, expecting everything in the world "to be as exact as it is in your head" (p. 141), and Lizzie admits this may be true in her diary. Do you think

she grows into a more realistic adult by the end of the story? Why or why not?

4. Discuss Lizzie's relationship with her parents. How do Mrs. Bennet's priorities differ from Mr. Bennet's? Do you think the Bennet parents understand their daughters? Give an example from the book.

5. Why does Lizzie refuse to settle for the job proposal Ricky Collins offers her? How does this proposal vary from the one he offers Elizabeth in Austen's story?

6. Since many of the characters in the story also watch Lizzie's videos, they quickly find out about any recent drama as well as how Lizzie reacts to and feels about it. Charlotte reminds Lizzie that Caroline Lee "made sure she was seen as [Lizzie's] friend on the videos" (p. 235). Does the characters' information from the videos affect the plot? If so, discuss how the characters benefit from this information. Consider Caroline Lee, George Wickham, William Darcy, and Lydia Bennet.

7. In Victorian society, social status was based on family lineage and wealth; in this story, the elite may come from money, but they are also heavily involved in California's technology bubble. Darcy's Pemberley is a Google-like place rather than a large estate, and his aunt acts as a venture capitalist for Mr. Collins's company. Discuss the similarities between the Victorian upper class and our contemporary technology companies. Consider how well this analogy works in the story.

8. Do you think Darcy was right to warn Bing away from making a hasty decision about Jane? How would you react if put in a similar position?

9. Lizzie tries to look out for both of her sisters but realizes too late that she has failed Lydia. After learning of the sex tape and watching Lydia's videos, Lizzie realizes "that Lydia has never been told that she is loved exactly as she is" (p. 314). What lessons does Lizzie learn from this experience?

10. Like in Austen's original, both Lizzie and Darcy are too proud for most of the book and hide behind their prejudices. How does each overcome his or her bias to give the other a chance?

11. At the end of the story, Lizzie finds out that Caroline orchestrated an incident at Bing Lee's party so that Darcy would mistrust Jane's love for Bing. Lizzie emphasizes that this "could have been cleared up by PEOPLE TALKING TO OTHER PEOPLE" (p. 349). Why do so many of the characters (especially Lizzie, a communications major) have such trouble communicating face-to-face? What do you think Lizzie learned about communicating from working on her vlog project and thesis?

12. George Wickham uses both William and Gigi Darcy for their money, but knows the Bennets do not have any money to spare. What, then, is his motivation for manipulating Lydia and posting a sex tape of her? And why does he create the site with a countdown, rather than having the video immediately available?

13. Because of the communal nature of online video blogging, Lizzie has many followers and regularly gets comments on her video entries. Think about and share your thoughts on how the Internet (and the thousands of fans who give Lizzie feedback) plays an essential role in this story. Is there an equivalent to this communal network in Austen's story?

ENHANCE YOUR BOOK CLUB

1. Watch some YouTube videos of *The Lizzie Bennet Diaries* (or, if you already have, re-watch a few of your favorites), and discuss how well the book pairs with the videos. Did you picture the characters differently? Did you enjoy reading or watching the story more? How do the experiences differ?

2. Try making your own video, by yourself or with a friend. Share your experience with the group—talk about your favorite aspect of making a video blog or about any difficulties you had.

3. This novel places Jane Austen's famous characters in the modern world. Other adaptations incorporate zombies or envision the characters' futures. If you were going to write an adaptation of Jane Austen's *Pride and Prejudice*, how would you frame your story? Share, discuss, and try your hand at writing a chapter or two!

AUTHOR Q&A

Why did you decide to write a novel?

Kate: We knew fairly early on that our version of Lizzie Bennet was pretty special and had a really interesting worldview. While Elizabeth Bennet from *Pride and Prejudice* is a timeless character, she is reacting to circumstances very much from her own time period — marriage being the only option for women, entailed estates, etc. In modernizing Lizzie, we found that her story on the videos also translated well to book form — after all, we still read. Plus, there were so many things that we only talked about on the videos and didn't get to experience, due to the limitations of the video format. In a book, there are no such limitations. We could be with Lizzie at the Gibson wedding, walking around San Francisco, or simply enduring her mother's histrionics about her single daughters. The book let us fill out the world in a way that the web videos — and their meager budget — didn't allow us to do.

Because the storyline already existed, what was your writing process like? Was it difficult to coordinate the story with the videos? Were you surprised at any difficulties or opportunities along the way?

Kate: The first thing I did when figuring out how to write this book was to create a really big, really detailed calendar of events. Where Lizzie was, when her videos posted, the movements of all the other characters, what party fell on what date and what happened there, who tweeted what when . . . It's an enormous and scary-looking color-coded document. It was incredibly important that the book fit within everything we had already established. Even though I knew the story very well from having worked on the show, I found myself referring to the calendar time and again as I tried to navigate where character moments should go. On the one hand, it forced me to conform. On the other, it forced me to get creative.

This timeless story works well in our modern times, with a few minor adjustments. What from the original story was the most difficult to contemporize?

Bernie: We wanted to modernize the independent woman. Back in the 1800s there weren't a lot of options in careers, and it was important to us that career choices be an underlying current to every major decision that our characters make. We didn't want it to be about finding the guy/marrying the rich guy.
Kate: One specific stumbling block I remember coming across when we were writing the series was the time it takes for information to get from one place to another. In *Pride and Prejudice*, if you needed to tell someone something, you had to write a letter, and at least a week would pass before it reached its destination. Now, everything can be found out at once, thanks to smartphones.

***The Lizzie Bennet Diaries* uses social media to give all of the characters a voice. How do you think this adds to the viewer's experience of the story?**

Bernie: The social media expansions adds three unique experiences to our interpretation of this story:

1. When the show was running, you (as a viewer) could talk to the characters and they could talk back to you. You could be a part of their stories.

2. You could explore more about the characters through their social media destinations; for example, Jane's Pinterest gives you a lot of insight into what she's going through during her arc.

3. You could experience the story from another character's point of view. What was Lydia doing when Lizzie and Jane are at Netherfield? What was Georgiana Darcy going through before she finally meets Lizzie? We have that for you; it exists for you to discover and explore.

Discuss your decision to make the book analogous to the videos, rather than an omnisciently narrated book like *Pride and Prejudice*.

Kate: While *Pride and Prejudice* is in third person, it sticks pretty strongly to Elizabeth's POV. There are only a couple of scenes that aren't told from her perspective. As she discovers new information, the audience discovers it as well. If Jane Austen were writing today, I wouldn't be surprised if she tried a first-person narrative. Lizzie's voice is so strong in the videos, carrying it over to the book was simply common sense. This is her story. She has to be the one to tell it.

How is the process of writing a work like this, one integrated into so many platforms, different from the usual TV episode or novel?

Kate: From my perspective, it meant we had a lot more data to work with. (Hence, the big calendar.) Every tweet sent, every photo posted on Pinterest, every comment on the videos had to be treated like canon. It can be mind-boggling trying to keep everything straight and to navigate a story between it all.

Bernie: It definitely goes both ways. If you write that a character says they're going to have lunch with someone, there's an obligation to acknowledge and verify that event through social media. We have to be hyper-aware of everything the characters are doing at any given time.

What did you learn from this experience that may help you in similar endeavors in the future?

Kate: Personally, I learned that when you tell a good story, it can be told many different ways. And instead of competing, they can complement one another.
Bernie: I learned to embrace alternate points of view. It goes back to the adage that everyone is the hero of their own story, even the antagonists. Yes, characters need to serve plot points, but why are they there—what are they really like as people?

Do you have any plans to expand *The Lizzie Bennet Diaries* any further in other media? If not, would you like to?

Bernie: This story is timeless and has been told across so many platforms, but with all the multi-platform content that we do, I would love to try to make an app.

What's next for Lizzie, Lydia, Jane, Darcy, and Bing?

Kate: What's next in terms of their stories? Well, perhaps you'll get to find out in the near-ish future . . .
Bernie: #spoilers